THE
MEDUSA PSALMS

WELCOME TO
WALPURGIS COUNTY

KYLE TOUCHER

Follow us on Amazon:

WELCOME
TO ANOTHER

CRYSTAL LAKE PUBLISHING
CREATION

Join today at www.crystallakepub.com & www.patreon.com/CLP

TABLE OF CONTENTS

Superstitious century, didn't time go slow?

—Black Sabbath, *Spiral Architect*

FOREWORD

A LLOW ME TO buy you a drink for not only purchasing this book, but rolling the dice on an unknown author. The time you invest reading my work does not go unnoticed.

In my writing, I've focused primarily on a little universe I inadvertently created when I wrote "Strange Acres" for a Halloween anthology back in 2021. Walpurgis County, Walpurgis Peak, the compass trickery concerning the mountain, old hills with old rules—I conjured it all on the fly in an attempt to invoke the weighty weirdness of nightmares as things go sour for poor, self-absorbed Beeley Ballantine. But even she, as you will see, does not remain comatose forever.

More followed, several of which appeared in Crystal Lake Entertainment's online *Shallow Waters* series. The theme gathered steam as I found ways to reference previous stories or overlap events and characters—not the newest approach, but the *method* became quite fun—and the more time I spent in benighted Walpurgis County, the more comfortable I became. A handful of *Shallow Waters* stories appear in this collection in their revised and, in some cases, extended versions tailored for this collection.

That's great, good for you, Toucher. Why are we here?

We're here to establish the foundation of this universe/setting beyond the confines of a monthly short story contest. These stories are not chronological per se, yet they serve as both timeline and travel guide through Walpurgis County's history and lore. There are redundancies, but life is like that. Two stories, for example, take place during Winter Howl. Other stories do not occur in the Purg (as the locals refer to it), yet it figures nonetheless. More than one tale references Halloween, as they were written with Halloween-themed open calls in mind.

The title *The Medusa Psalms* has lived in my head for nearly

1

thirty years, and my original idea was a novel comprised of four interconnected novellas published as a single volume. Plans change, but I'll tell you several of those original story elements survived, some of which are in this book. Instead, *The Medusa Psalms* is now a moniker under which all Walpurgis County (and associated shadowless atrocities) shall be gathered. Some may be novels, others novellas, and certainly further collections. You get the idea.

I hope these little movies unspool in the theatre of your mind in vivid, sanguine detail, and for a while at least, you forget about your car payment or Wednesday's impending root canal. If you're absorbed, that's your willingness to be the omniscient camera. If you're bored, well . . . that's my fault.

Okay, I'll shut up now.

Meet me in the bar after the show.

II

STRANGE ACRES

"**A**N OLD SOUL guards these fields," Vendor said as he secured the wooden hatch in Copperhead Farms' produce stand, a souvenir left peeling on the doorstep of a century long gone. He turned to the young woman, a freshling unimpressed with the old ways. "And with each new moon, that forgotten hero stalks the road."

Beeley took little notice. Instagram followers required her attention.

"With buttons for eyes and a voice silenced by ashes, his blade cuts ragged as a deal with the devil."

"That's dumb," Beeley said without looking up. She'd grabbed a perfect selfie next to the old scarecrow and busied herself applying a filter that added a cute bunny nose and framed her face with floating hearts. Only eight hundred Insta followers so far, but those numbers were sure to rise after her Indiegogo raised enough cash for a set of saline implants. No way Daddy was paying for that, so until then, she focused on her flat belly, arranged her blonde haystack hair *just so*, and produced photos teasing enough to guarantee clicks.

Beeley typed the caption: *Chillin' with my Scare-bro.*

Vendor lifted his chin toward the effigy and said, "Legend suggests not only an ageless watch over these sprawling fields but a genesis both terrible and cruel. Some say he's from The Great Elsewhere. Others maintain he led a faction of the forbidden Medusa Cult, right here, in Walpurgis County. Whether history or just story, I leave that to you."

Beeley scoffed and continued her search for the right emoji.

"Songs, dirges mostly, were written in tribute to him," Vendor continued. "Sad requiems the women no longer sing, rotting on sheet music no one can read these days."

1

An annoyed Beeley Ballantine said, "That's a lot of nonsense."

Rusty Jack remained silent. Staked into the dirt through a bulbous tumor of gourds and corn, the scarecrow gazed past the little stand through moldy eyes. His clothes, from soiled dungarees to a shit-stained hat, flapped in the October breeze.

Vendor shrugged. "Many would agree, but the rabble witch-burners, the persecutors, and zealots came nonetheless, eager to incinerate the Medusa Cult and purge its highest priest from Walpurgis County, which left our friend here to mind these parcels. A sole survivor, abandoned and alone. You know what I think?"

"No," Beeley said. She had no idea what zealots were, but she knew that persecutors worked for the court, and of course, at Halloween, you had to mention witches.

"I think Rusty Jack is *always* on the move."

She turned and finally awarded Vendor her full attention.

Vendor wore his hair longer than Beeley was accustomed to on men, especially older men, but he didn't wear it like some boomer hippie; he kept the gray mane swept back like Loki in the Marvel movies. Vendor's eyes, cloudy glass handfuls of night set deep into his skull, reminded Beeley of an old dog in his last days. Maybe when the pumpkin-selling geezer was young, like, totally over a hundred years ago, he may not have been bad to look at, but now he stared at her like a hooked-nose Creepazoid, a Facebook stalker spruced up with a handful of Paul Mitchell and a black leather vest.

"I think *you* moved him here," Beeley said, posting the photo. Soon, she hoped, chimes of approval and adoring comments such as *Luv U, Hot AF,* and *Imma yr nu Bae* would flood her iPhone.

The important work done, Beeley looked around.

Upon arriving at Copperhead Farms, she'd heard the faraway chatter of families, and there had been other vehicles in the dirt lot, older ones for sure, big sick-hop-era brutes. *Probably poor people*, she thought at the time. *They drive old cars.* It struck her odd that the now barren parking lot contained nothing but her little white A3 Hatchback and its own tire tracks to keep it company.

She'd come to Copperhead on Route 54, the largest of Walpurgis County's two main arteries. Beeley's original destination had been Fullmont's Feed and Seed and their annual jack-o'-lantern display, where she hoped to snag a few Halloween-themed photos and call it a day. However, a giant hiding in the sycamores leaped into the corner of her eye, and her plan changed.

A peeling, wooden relic, this giant, a mammoth advertisement featuring an old-time cartoon cowboy riding a pumpkin like a bronco, one hand on the reins, the other clutching a windswept hat revealing hair like Vendor's unruly mane. In his holsters, ears of corn. In his gun belt, carrots standing in for spare ammo. The rowels of his spurs, glowing stars trailing dust like plummeting comets. An antique from a world that didn't exist anymore.

The sweeping, curved lettering read:

COPPERHEAD FARMS
SSSSSSENSATIONAL PRODUCE
NEXT RIGHT ►

About the height of a telephone pole and wide as a school bus, the sign offered enough kitsch to stir Beeley's interest. How many times had Beeley driven Route 54, oblivious to this weather-beaten fossil?

I'll bet there's stuff there I can use, she thought as she hit the turn indicator and pressed the brake. *Tractors and other farm junk, but, like, super old. I'll add a pumpkin or two, grab a couple of hot snaps, and my Insta will totally blow up.*

She followed a second sign, an urgent gloved hand pointing its index finger. She turned right onto a dirt road, a lumpy unkempt thing that wound through trees that blocked the sun. By the time she entered the Copperhead lot filled with old cars, the road had taken so many twists she wasn't sure how far away from Route 54 she'd traveled.

Now standing with her hands on her hips in front of the leaning pumpkin stand and the oddball scarecrow, she saw where the access road met the parking lot, yet the rear of the sign was clearly visible above the trees—which to Beeley was, like, totally weird because it had taken a good ten minutes of zigzagging to get to the Copperhead lot from Route 54.

To Beeley's left, dominating the field bordering Widow's Holler, an old Victorian farmhouse, its roofline a mountain range of gables and chimneys. A hexagonal turret brooded above the wrap-around porch. No detail had been spared.

I'll have to get a picture of that, she thought. *I'll tilt my camera and make the pic all Halloweenie.*

Corn, towering green stalks of it, separated the property from the drop-off into the cramped but steep valley of Widow's Holler. In the hazy distance Walpurgis Peak jutted from the earth like an abscessed tooth, clouds casting slender fingers of shadow over the mountain's stony hide. She sighed and spun to face Vendor, bouncing as bubbly-hot as possible without looking, all, like, totally on purpose and stuff. Vendor's expression, etched dauntless as the mountain, refused to budge.

"These fields have suffered fire and now produce only famine," Vendor said. "Yet more is harvested here than any other farm in Walpurgis. Why do you think that is?"

Beeley shrugged. If her phone didn't chime soon, she'd undo the top two buttons and up the ante with a bit of cleavage. "My Daddy owns the John Deere dealership in Jasper. I'm sure you could ask him. *All* his clients are farmers."

"It's never machines, dearie, never what people do. It's what's *inside* them."

Beeley rolled her eyes, remembering when her eighties-obsessed mom made her watch *The Karate Kid*. It tested the limit of Beeley's self-control to stay put, finish the lame movie, and not pull her hair out with pliers. The entire story was nonsense—no one *ever* got ahead by being the underdog. In the real world, you have to be *sassy*, you have to be *sexy*. If you're to take the big prize someday, you have to make people believe they want to *be* you.

The wind hissed, the corn suddenly a xylophone of hollow bones. Bright sunshine glowed in Widow's Holler, deep with October gold, but for some reason, it appeared slightly darker—no, Beeley corrected, *slightly later*—near the farmhouse, that time of day when the back of her mind never failed to warn that night is coming. In that odd patch of dim twilight, throwing long shadows on the pale grass, the house glared at her with its empty black windows, a mansion with a vampire asleep in its basement.

Vendor said, "When the moon refuses to show its face—no shadows, no crickets—Rusty Jack hits the road."

Beeley smirked and shook her head. She may have Ozark blood in her veins, but damned if she'd be chumped by some gourd-hawker or get sucked in by tall hillbilly tales.

Nineteen-year-old Beeley Ballantine was more sophisticated than that. She was Los Angeles-bound as soon as she had the dough, eager to elope to her new life in the Audi Daddy had leased for her. If she lifted her TikTok numbers enough to become an Influencer, that would land her on the L.A. Radar. Anything was preferable to working another summer with those goobers at Daddy's John Deere dealership, and if she had to wait tables, hopefully at Nobu in Malibu, whose website and Yelp page she visited often, that would do until the L.A. wheels turned, but with time and opportunity slipping through her fingers, Walpurgis County had to be rear-viewed—and fast.

She looked at her phone. No comments.

What's taking so long?

Vendor opened his arms wide, gesturing to Walpurgis Peak with the grace of a Broadway dancer. "These are old hills, dearie," he said.

"Everything here's old," Beeley said.

"Indeed. Look at each field. The barren patch over there, with the rusted thresher blade, the parcel still resides in 1908. Further south, where the road sent you to me, 1954. To your left a spell, in the house that borders Widow's Holler, it's perpetually 1924. Where those black, leafless sycamores stand, the clock tolls 2077— even *I* steer clear of that one. There are many more, but these pockets, these *Shimmers*, are unique to Walpurgis County. But here, at Copperhead Farms, they are numerous. And formidable."

"So. Not. True," Beeley said. "My brother is a serious gamer, and he knows the old Terminator movies inside and out. He knows you can't do that kind of stuff without a robot or a time machine, or whatever."

"Rusty Jack moves *within* the Shimmer," Vendor said. "Leave the Meridians and bulky handiwork to the amateurs. The Shimmer is the true test, the Avenue to The Great Elsewhere."

Beeley sighed and turned her attention to the combine blade, a twenty-foot-long knife designed to rotate at speeds rendering it little more than a blur. She figured it must have been left behind for decoration, like the antique tractors and windmills she hoped to see here. Weeds choked the silent field-thresher, poking between its teeth at crazy angles like a circus daredevil tempting a lion.

A Harvester, she knew. You couldn't be the daughter of a John Deere dealer and not know something about farm equipment. *But it's really, like, the olden days over there? How is that possible?*

Even at this distance, the thresher oozed danger with its

elongated octagon of razors. A spinning, ugly cutter. Sleeping, yet eyeing her. A predator in the tall grass.

She knew there were plenty of stories about men swept into ravenous combines, leaving them mauled and maimed. In fact, the story of Widow's Holler was about just such an event.

Greedle Olin, the grizzled, bearded hayseed who seemed to have nowhere to go but Daddy's shop, smoking a corn cob pipe and running his mouth all day and every day, had told Beeley some real whoppers over the years. Farmers spouted bloody disaster stories the way sailors spun tales of ghost ships.

Thresher machines are blood-crazed murderers, Greedle had said as his pipe bobbed between stubby teeth the color of dry firewood. *A serial killer on the loose, but without the mind to think like one.*

Beeley, resenting her summer vacation working in the parts department, eyed the red-nosed codger over the top of the cash register. Clearly enjoying the attention of the ears he'd caught, Greedle went on.

A true story goes one of the old-timers—Alek Weizeszky was his name—got himself shredded by a mule-powered combine in the early 1900s. Through some freak accident, the thresher grabbed his leg, drew him in and mangled it up to the kneecap, which miraculously stopped the blade—then something spooked the mules, and the blades turned again. Caught his arm at the shoulder, and in he went, screaming like a hyena, it's said, and all that came out was a lumpy red stew. His bloody shirt stuck to the blades and flopped around like a bear with meat in its teeth until a couple of farmhands were able to stop it. Horrible scene.

A few weeks later, distraught and hopeless, his wife Ewa leaped from the valley wall with their two sons in tow. But the creek was dry that year, and all that waited below was rocks. From then on, Beeley, that little valley was known as Widow's Holler. A Germanic family, Gennckes was their name, always had an eye for that property and took the entire six hundred acres for a song not long after the tragedy. Next thing you know, Walpurgis County is host to Copperhead Farms.

Beeley, usually eager to forget Greedle Olin's horror stories and now of a mind to dismiss Vendor's pumpkin stand performance, realized the shop pest's words had found their place—things Greedle said aligned with the old man's carnival tales.

After that, Beeley, Greedle told her as he pulled up a folding chair, *it all went sour in Walpurgis for more than a decade. No farms but Copperhead produced anything of value. Its competitor's livestock dropped dead, and prominent men committed suicide in dreadful ways. Rumor spread, associations with a snake cult were made, and the reverend at the time, Waushburne was his name, urged his flock to decapitate any copperhead snake in Walpurgis County. Townsfolk took to executing all manner of serpents, not just copperheads, as I guess you can imagine. Snake heads stacked as high as your ankles, buckets filled with them, their bodies left for the hawks and vultures. Still, the blight worsened. Close to broke and blind with resentment, the town took it upon themselves to end Johannes Gennckes and his family, foreigners whom Reverend Waushburne repeatedly accused of killing Alek Weizeszky through sinister means. Their retribution was not kind, Beeley, and they treated Gennckes according to the direction of the Reverend. They took care of business—but his family must have got wind of it and escaped because they were nowhere to be found.*

"Strange acres," Vendor said. "The old story of this place, yes?"

Vendor's voice pulled Beeley from her woolgathering.

What?

"Just ask Rusty Jack," Vendor added. He leaned over the wooden counter, palms down and elbows up. All he needed was a glistening scorpion's stinger looming overhead as he shifted his gaze to the scarecrow. "He was there at the bitter, fiery end."

He couldn't know what I was thinking, Beeley thought. Her eyelids fluttered as she followed Vendor's eyes to the old, worn-out scarecrow.

To Beeley, scarecrows resembled crude, homemade dolls, something a sad Mormon girl clung to during the pioneer days. Rusty Jack was no plaything, and even Beeley saw there was purpose here, buried beneath decades of weather and the glaring eye of Walpurgis Peak.

"His face looks like it's wrapped in a bag," Beeley said as she took a cautious step forward—Instagram, for the moment, forgotten. "Like it's wearing a hood or whatever."

"Typical for the condemned," Vendor murmured.

The breeze pressed against the fabric, hinting at the shape

beneath. Whatever the sack concealed was beyond human proportions.

Drowned Syndrome, she told herself. *That's what it is, like the kids with the big, goofy chins and weird eyes. Missy Baines says they call it that because at some point, they drowned in the womb, and then they're born all retarded.*

The sack, cinched with rope, bisected the upper skull from a mandible easily as long as Beeley's forearm. With its huge, exposed jawbone off-center and hooded face, it looked as if old Rusty Jack had been doomed to the gallows, then taken a mean right hook across the chops. A wooden button, host to a spreading colony of mold, had been sewn over each enormous eye socket. Perched atop the hood, a weather-beaten, wide-brimmed hat painted in crow shit. Beeley now recognized this misshapen head as an animal skull, not the newest idea in Walpurgis County scarecrow aesthetics, but nothing like this. Nothing so *mean.*

Rusty Jack's tattered sleeves had been stuffed into the mouth of cracked leather gloves, his fingers curled talons. His shirt had not been spared the decades, tufts of brittle leaves and dried corn husks peered through the gaps. Unruly straw poked from fissures in his trousers, and down below, the scarecrow possessed but one foot—a worn-out boot spattered with dark stains.

Slung over one shoulder, an Indian medicine bag adorned with beads and stones, complex figures Beeley had never seen before, not even close to the hex symbols painted on some of the older barns in Walpurgis County. These were *angular,* more tooth-like. The language of meat-eaters. Stuck into a decaying belt leaned a rusted hunting knife with a serrated blade the length of a beer bottle.

Arms spread wide and ankles loosely crossed, future Instagram Influencer Beeley Ballantine had been to church enough times to realize that Rusty Jack had been crucified, a condemned mannequin lashed to stakes with fence wire, a foreign skull and eyes buttoned against the world.

She reached for the knife, a nasty-looking one similar to Daddy's, the one he took along on deer hunts with his buddies.

It's for skinning and gutting, he'd told her once. *Makes a bloody job easy.*

"The knife is sharper than it looks," Vendor warned. "As I said, tread lightly."

Beeley rolled her eyes but reached for the deerskin medicine bag instead.

"That, dearie, is Rusty Jack's Deathbag. It's *every* year in there."

"I saw *Jeepers Creepers II*, buddy," Beeley said. "You can't scare me like that."

Yet, she reminded herself. *You can't scare me like that* yet.

"All of Walpurgis County knows that upon each new moon a light is kept aglow in a single window. Keeps Rusty Jack on the road. Away from their homes. You must have seen that by now, or heard about it, yes?"

Beeley recalled nights of stars and deep clouds, no moon eyeing her from above, and below, homes, lightless save for a lone candle placed in a window. But had that been only every now and then? Perhaps one or two nights per month?

"Once you see his shape in the starlight, it is, as they say, curtains."

All of that was bullshit, of course. The old guy enjoyed yanking her chain, sprinkling a little Halloween spirit with his woodsy pumpkin stand, spooky dummy on a stick, and creepy house in the background. He probably lived there with his mother and twenty cats.

Maybe snakes, Beeley's mind whispered. *Maybe copperhead snakes. Maybe the town didn't get them all.*

"That's not going to make me buy a pumpkin," Beeley said, arms crossed, phone refusing to chime.

"You are not here to buy," Vendor scoffed, pointing to Beeley's phone. "You're *selling*."

It took a couple of seconds, but Beeley caught Vendor's drift. Her cheeks flushed. She pursed her lips.

"My daddy's clients bring us all the pumpkins we need, so I don't need yours."

"Any of his clients lost in these fields, dearie?"

Beeley snorted, but the hair on her arms stood up like cactus thorns.

Vendor's brow crunched into a V-shape, eyes retreating into his skull like a wasp in a hole. His pupils stung her from the hollows of tiny, dark burrows.

"Anyone Daddy cares about send him desperate letters from the early 1950s? Does he get scratchy, noisy phones call from 1924? If not, *he will.*"

She wished she'd seized the opportunity to catch his witchy performance on video; it would have made an awesome TikTok. She had the perfect caption: *Roadside Creepazoid. Ewww.*

Vendor pointed to the scarecrow. His words smoldered, embers from a witch's fire. "Know this as I learned firsthand: it's knives that make the decisions of the world, but the Deathbag is eternal."

Beeley straightened her shoulders. "I don't believe a word of this."

The worming sensation beneath her hair and the sharp buzz spreading over the back of her neck like a stranger's hand broadcast a different message.

I should leave.

But what if my fans need a follow-up photo?

"Emptiness is the hunger that drives men to greed, and greed that keeps them subservient," Vendor said, its meaning completely lost on her. His lips turned upward into a disingenuous smile, and with his wasp eyes and witch-voice, it reminded Beeley of some horrible thing she'd seen in one of her brother's video games. "The soul is in the blood, dearie, and Rusty Jack knows that better than anyone."

Beeley's phone chimed. Eager to look anywhere other than the Creepazoid, she swiped the screen, and the first reaction to her post popped up like a reward.

OMG Rusty Jack.

Beeley frowned.

A second bell. *B-careful.*

Then a third. *Imma call U later Inside 2nite*

Beeley eyed her Instagram post. She beamed saucy and smiling with the cartoon bunny nose, but instead of the scarecrow's elongated head angled toward the pumpkin stand, it was turned toward camera, peering over her shoulder, mouth wide as a bear trap. The playful hearts, usually Valentine red, wheezed black with soot. Cracked in half. Leaning sideways.

"Hey, that's *not* what I posted!"

A fourth bell. *No Moon. Stay Safe.*

Fifth bell. *1 light in the window*

Beeley glared at Vendor like he'd cut in front of her at Starbucks.

"What the hell is *this* all about?" Her lips knotted into a little barnacle as she held the iPhone out for Vendor to see. "You were here, you saw. That is *not* the photo I took."

Vendor raised his single, V-shaped eyebrow. "Rusty Jack has his eye on you, dearie."

"I don't think it's funny, Mister. You've been trying to scare me since I got here, and this is some trick of yours, I'm not buying it. I'll tell my Dad what you did here. He's got a lot of friends in the county, you know. Cops, city council, mayors, *everyone*."

"Daddy will be of little help, dearie." He pointed at the horizon behind Beeley. "The sun sets quickly here, and this stand will close for the night, so either buy yourself a jack-o'-lantern or take your chances on the road. The moonless road. *His* road."

Beeley turned west and faced the throbbing sun, an inflamed pustule on a suicide mission behind the dreadful edges of Walpurgis Peak. The sun lit the clouds afire, and by the time the corona glowed at the horizon line, they'd be the color of blood. The shadow of the mountain crawled over the foothills.

"That's impossible," Beeley argued. "I just got here. It's only two in the afternoon."

Vendor examined the menu bar above her Instagram post. "Six thirty-six, it says on your toy. You know how it is on the back roads of Walpurgis County, dearie. Things *Shimmer*."

Beeley craned her neck past the stand where the antique blade rusted in the golden glow of magic hour. She thought of that poor woman, Ewa Weizeszky, who leaped to her death into the valley just beyond the house, holding her children's hands all the way to the bottom, her husband devoured by a murderous combine, their fortune dead on the vine.

It's closer now, she realized. The rusted thresher blade had moved yet persistent weeds strangled the machine tooth as if it hadn't budged in decades. *That's impossible.*

Vendor backed into the shadows, murmuring, "These are old hills, dearie, with old rules."

Beeley spun toward the farmhouse. Full evening there now, the brush of twilight painting the tall grass violet and the old Victorian the color of bruises. The porch swing surrendered to the push of the wind, and even from here, she heard the agony of its chains. The weathervane atop the turret pointed directly at the mountain.

Standing at the foot of the steps, a figure—male, tall, waif-thin. His shabby rags and the brim of his hat flapped in the night breeze.

Before she could look away, a solitary lamp in a first-floor window bloomed alight, shining like a jaundiced eye. The figure took a lopsided step backward, nearly losing balance.

Something moved in the corner of her eye, and she wheeled around to the abandoned thresher blade. There the gaunt figure was again, standing next to the giant harvesting knife, staring straight at her with his bleached button eyes, animal jaw agape.

Rusty Jack, relieved of crucifixion, had noticed Beeley Ballantine.

She looked for the decorative pile of gourds and corn, the base of Rusty Jack's stake. Scattered like petrified runes, their color gone, they lay amid a confusing network of single boot prints and a long, shallow drag mark.

He only has one foot. This isn't happening. This isn't real.

Crows called in their brittle, grating voice, an ugly denial of Beeley's hope, as if Vendor's words mocked her from the trees. *Oh, dearie, this* is *happening.*

Crumbling pumpkin vines, long dead yet bursting with fruit, pushed through the rough dirt. Though nearly mummified, the vines writhed with purpose, like tentacles seeking purchase with bright orange fruit for suction cups, untangling and separating from one another—a Celtic knot undone.

A path opened.

"A road," Beeley said. "His road."

Behind her, the stand's wooden hatch dropped shut with a hollow rattle.

Once charming as a movie set, the Copperhead Farms pumpkin stand leaned like an invalid. A relic from a ghost town with planks missing and support beams gone, the collapsed roof lay on the ground in a Jenga pile, entwined with weeds and neglect. At night's onset, with no chance of a moon, its doorway yawned like a malformed mouth, and should it cough cough, Beeley feared copperheads loosed upon her feet, wreathing her ankles like muscled, slithering ropes, their spade-shaped viper heads eager to bite and inject venom.

Realization struck.

Copperhead Farms had been dead a long time. The sign that led Beeley here, with its cartoon cowboy riding a bronco pumpkin, had been in a ruinous state for God only knew how long, or worse, had never really been there. Perhaps the locals had razed every inch of this place looking for the Medusa Cult like Greedle Olin said, fed up with bad crops, dead cattle and husbands, and one mysterious family prospering above all others. They killed the farm, but the farm refused to die.

And now, dead vines bore fruit in a field where it was a summer afternoon in 1908, a scarecrow free of its moorings standing abreast of the gargantuan knife that had shredded Alek Weizeszky, while a few hundred yards away, deep twilight surrounded a gloomy farmhouse two decades later. Impossible, absurd, ridiculous even, but Beeley Ballantine's eyes did not lie.

A thousand yards past the thresher, the wind wheezed through the skeletons of twin sycamores. Dark, ugly clouds prowled above, silhouetting the trees like frozen, black lightning. Walpurgis Peak, off-axis and leaning in the murk, had suffered a mortal wound as if a prowling colossus had sunk its teeth into the meat of the mountain and it bled a talus of debris. A far future, 2077, she was told, eyed her from the lightless side of the Shimmer.

Even I steer clear of that one, Vendor had told Beeley.

The stupid stories she'd dismissed from Greedle Olin and the Creepazoid were true: everything here was a ghost trapped in an immense time prison, the Shimmer was real, it brought only danger, and she was out here all alone.

I didn't imagine I heard those kids and their mothers in the field. All those cars, those old 1950s cars—that's exactly what they were—were still in that time, and so were they. Further south, he said, it's always 1954. I heard an afternoon from sixty years ago.

It was time to be anywhere but Walpurgis County, where the namesake mountain resembled the Devil's fang, and its legends eclipsed the darkest of campfire stories. Beeley turned tail and scooted toward where she remembered parking her little hatchback, the cute Audi set to whisk her away to the western shore, to sunshine and glory.

Her phone bristled with Instagram likes.

Looks good, Babe

Rusty Jack whoa

Get home safe

SOMETHING'S COMING

The last post, displayed in a font she'd never seen, from a user named *Elsewhere*, accelerated Beeley's agitated shuffle into a brisk walk.

Swiftly fell the guillotine of night, and the farmhouse, surrounded by the persistent, dense azure, watched her with its glowing, solitary eye. No crickets or shadows as the moonless black above offered only the infinity of stars, where, unknown to Beeley, nameless horrors waited to descend upon the world. Shadowless.

Instagram beckoned.

Call me soon

Babe Lookin' Hawt—Scarebro not

THERE'S A KILLER ON THE ROAD

She risked a glance over her shoulder. In his stiff-legged killer's stance, Rusty Jack gawked at the burgeoning trail, a path opening, *becoming*, as vines parted and the thresher blade slowly turned like a fan at low speed. He dragged his maimed leg, and the Deathbag bounced on his hip.

Beeley's phone chimed incessantly.

Meet up a Feelanders later?

Dollar beers

OLD HILLS WITH OLD RULES

Rusty Jack set his solitary foot on the road.

Beeley ransacked her purse for the key fob. Button pressed before she pulled it from the bag, she swooned with immediate relief at the sound of the familiar Audi chirp.

Farther away than she remembered. Head cocked to help her pinpoint the sound, she hit the button. again.

CHIRP.

There—but a different location than before. Off to the left. Further still.

Night came on so suddenly, so fast. So . . . so *totally.*

Instagram persisted.

BURNED TO DEATH AT COPPERHEAD

Love and miss that face XXO

IT'S KNIVES THAT MAKE THE DECISIONS OF THE WORLD

Surrounded by all that dark, Beeley picked up the pace, squeezing the fob like the switch to a morphine drip. The Audi cried out from yet another direction and farther away, but she was grateful to see the headlights flash.

"There you are," she said.

The car seemed endlessly away, the headlights no more than a bright pinprick in the nightvoid.

Ahead brooded the farmhouse with a powerful Autumn gust

curling beneath its eaves. The weathervane remained fixed upon its titanic master.

The car is too far, but maybe if I really haul ass in a straight line, I can reach the house. Bang on the door. Ask for help.

Beeley remembered the scarecrow, motionless at the foot of the steps, eyeing her through that warped, black hood. That knife, a *gutting* knife. Had he left bodies in the house? Was there blood in there?

No, there's a light in the window. Keeps him on the road.

But what year is it in there?

True dread took hold.

"I'm in deep shit," Beeley said, fumbling with her iPhone, the only link to the Now World. She pressed 1 on speed dial. Daddy's number came up.

The phone made a friendly little robot noise, and despite the flood of Instagram traffic, the screen displayed NO SIGNAL.

"No," she whined.

She redialed. Squeeble-Beep. NO SIGNAL.

"Fuck!"

Beeley bolted for the farmhouse. Within seconds—if time still functioned linearly within the Shimmer, that is—her breath grew hot, her armpits wet, and her clothes uncomfortable.

The solitary light, a beacon in an imperious house wreathed in moonlessness, beckoned. By now, she saw the ornate detail work carved into the pillars, shutters, and massive front doors. The place must have been a palace back in its day, but now it was a monster all its own, an ogre where time hadn't moved an inch, yet this light offered the lone hope of rescue.

Back in the 1920s, that's where I am. Back when they took care of business like Greedle said.

She stabbed at the key fob again, and this time, what should have been a comforting chirp cawed like a bird on the wing, the headlights a faint dollop on a horizon that never seemed to stay in the same place.

No, no, no, please.

The phone chimed.

LOOK BEHIND YOU

Though Beeley's mind insisted the opposite, she obeyed.

The thresher. So odd to see it drowned in that yellow-gold swath of setting sunlight though she stood in dreadful night, rolling on its own, the steel a blur. Rusting motionless in the field for over a hundred years, the ghost machine, now balefully alive, churned dust and debris, widening the road, chewing up brittle vines, and spewing pulverized fruit. The air bloomed rife with the unmistakable aroma of pumpkin, triggering for Beeley memories of long-forgotten Halloween parties where monsters were still make-believe.

And even worse, *somefuckinghow*, Rusty Jack led the way.

Her phone chimed so rapidly there was no way to keep up with it, but Beeley didn't care anymore. She wasn't anyone's Boo or Bae—only reaching the light that kept the limping scarecrow on the road mattered.

I'll bet old people live there, her mind babbled. *Old people have landlines. I'll call Dad.. He'll come get me. He knows the roads—*

His road, the Creepazoid had said.

The thresher blade raged in a chorus of hollow, popping noises, shredding hundreds of pumpkins to ribbons.

The bright, autumn scent hypnotized her, dragged her mind back to jack-o'-lantern carving parties in grade school, scooping out seeds and fibers while pretending to be grossed out, tossing the mess at her brother, then waking up in the middle of the night after she'd dreamed her family had been killed by a madman—a hooded figure with a knife and a bag slung over his shoulder. He opened his bag—his Deathbag—and inside swam the memories of those he'd slain, leaking from the heads of her parents and brother, floating in thick blood like carrots in a horrible, fetid soup. Nightmares oozed from their ears, trauma poured from slit nostrils and lies from mouths opened like gutted fish.

No, no, I never dreamed that. That's not true!

But God, the night pressed thick and oppressive here, a literal presence, something with *weight*, the weight only known in nightmares when dread holds dominion and absolutely everything in the dream is wrong. Time stumbles compressed, every action burns with urgency, and death will not be swift if the dream is not escaped. Old Scratch will prolong the suffering, feasting on your terror and smearing your disbelief upon his face like warpaint. He has power here. He takes your memories and warps them, finds what you love, and stabs you with their suffering.

The house. Now only yards away.

But her social media was, like, totally blowing up.

almost there, Boo.

EYE, KNIFE, RAVEN, DOLL, COFFIN

The house towered immense, far larger than she anticipated, a factory of shadows, but Beeley fearlessly leaped onto the first step, stumbled, and clambered up the remaining stairs. The porch swing's chains squealed, its frame rattling like dry bones. Through the lace curtains, she recognized the shape of an antique oil lamp, an oasis in the middle of the night's vast desert.

Her phone coughed one last chime.

"Shut the hell up," Beeley screeched.

BEHIND YOU, DEARIE, the message read.

Beeley turned. Standing at the foot of the steps, just as Insta had said, and exactly as she knew he'd be—Rusty Jack, defiant of crucifixion, a leaning amputee, animal mouth a cave beneath his filthy button-eye hood. He set one hand on his knife, the other on the Deathbag. A new road, *his* road, carved by the thresher blade and plowing through multiple decades, led from the summer of 1908 to the farmhouse.

In the glow of the oil lamp, Rusty Jack drew his knife in a graceless staccato, an old movie with missing frames. His shoulders spasmed, followed by the bird-like tilt of that horrendous head, the freakish animal jaw snapping shut with a chalky *thunk*. Behind him, the ravenous steel monster waited for permission. Past the hungry blade, in the gold of a forever sundown, Widow's Holler, gorgeous with green trees and floating butterflies; beyond, the Dragon—Walpurgis Peak, the Overfather of this terrible place.

Wherever—or more accurately, *whenever*—she looked, the brutal spike of Walpurgis Peak *always* loomed in the far away; north, south, east, west, it made zero difference. The mountain was the gnomon of a massive sundial, the axis of a clock that never told the truth. And there it was, splattered in the majesty of the setting sun, when the last time she saw it, it leaned bleeding and agonized in 2077.

Corn husks and dry leaves rustled beneath the scarecrow's shirt. Rusty Jack fumbled with the Deathbag. The inside *Shimmered*.

"You can't get me now," Beeley said. For a second there, she actually believed it. "They left the light on here because they knew about you."

It's every year in there. The Deathbag is eternal.

Vendor's smoky voice crawled into Beeley's mind. She imagined him in an old house, *this* house, scurrying across the floor in the same pose he'd struck at the stand—palms down, elbows up, a grotesque insect hunting in the dark.

Rusty Jack curled his fingers, and like a trained dog, the blade leaped forward and stopped the moment the scarecrow extended its palm. The thresher never ceased its mad spinning, gnawing dirt, weeds, and God knew what else. The scarecrow leaned forward, the infinity hole of the Deathbag palmed in a filthy leather glove. Through his freakish mandible, an ugly wind moaned.

But it wasn't the wind; it was a *voice*, a husky, stormy voice.

"Old rules," the scarecrow croaked, windswept and rustling with crumbling husks and brittle straw, stones rolling through ancient ashes.

That thing is fucking speaking to me?

The blade—a blur of ravenous teeth.

Retreat at an end, Beeley stood with her back to the door. Anyone inside must have heard the commotion because the blade roared loud as a fighter jet, and she harbored no intention of keeping her voice low.

Beeley wheeled around, banging the door until both glass and hardware rattled.

"Anyone home?" Beeley cried out, eyes tearing, snot draining onto her upper lip. Behind her, pure, pristine suffering—inanimate farm relics miraculously alive, and the madness of forever compressed into the Deathbag.

"I saw your light. Please, open this door!"

The doors parted, and she didn't hesitate.

Beeley Ballantine stumbled into the third decade of the twentieth century.

The oil lamp snuffed out.

Darryl Ballantine kept one eye on Greedle Olin, currently making a nuisance of himself in the parts department, and the other on Ned Dorry, who had spent the last half hour poring through tattered John Deere parts catalogs, looking for a water pump for his 1985 JD2550. Ned didn't believe in "goddamn computers," so

Darryl let him search the old way all he wanted. But Greedle's pipe smoke bothered Ned, and Darryl teetered on the verge of intervention when his iPhone rang. He pulled it from his vest pocket.

The screen read:

UNKNOWN—WALPURGIS COUNTY

Darryl put the call on speaker and headed to the parts counter, where Greedle leaned running his yap and puffing smoke like an old steel mill.

A scratchy female voice spoke.

"This is the Operator. I wish to speak to Darryl Ballantine." The operator pronounced his name *Ballan-teen*. The line burst with static, reminding Darryl of the old days when the national anthem played at midnight on the family television, followed by snow. "I have a collect, person-to-person call from Beatrice Ballan*teen*. Do you accept the charges?"

A garble of noise barked from the iPhone speaker, a flood of rushing static and intermittent knocking sounds.

Greedle snapped his mouth shut and looked quizzically at Darryl, pipe in one hand, a Welch's grape soda in the other. "Who the hell does *person-to-person* anymore?" he said.

Ned didn't bother looking up. "Who the hell uses an *operator* anymore?"

"Beeley, is this some type of prank?" Darryl said. "Are you streaming this to Facebook or something?"

The operator said through a field of grating interference, "Sir, I need to know if you'll accept the charges."

Greedle looked at Ned, his bloodless skin nearly the color of his beard. "Does that operator sound familiar to you, Ned?"

Ned said, "I was going to ask you if that sounded like Mathilda Greene. Remember her? Mathilda the Mouth, we called her back then, worked for Ma Bell since she was a teenager, but she retired in the sixties."

"And she died in the late seventies, way past the age of ninety," Greedle added.

Darryl's eyes bounced between the two men while the phone hissed and squawked. The operator, clearly annoyed, raised her voice.

"This is long distance, sir. *Very* long distance."

Beeley gripped the earpiece and peered around one of the columns. At first, she'd been flummoxed by the antique candlestick telephone and its dial, and even more so when she received something she had never heard before—a dial tone. Beeley, ever the student of television, emulated what people did in all that old shit her mother watched: she called the operator.

Despite staggering flat-footed into the house, she'd been quick and dragged a small table in front of the door. Darkness rendered the place nearly impossible to navigate, yet Beeley made out the faint outline of columns, and she stumbled between these touchstones until she landed in the tiny telephone alcove. It was miraculous the telephone worked at all.

Now, with one eye barely cresting the edge of the beveled column, Beeley watched Rusty Jack, leaning upon his lone foot, pounding the glass with knife in hand. The doorknob rattled, the pane shook, but for the moment, the little table held fast. The thresher blade buzzed behind him as it mangled the bottom step, wood separating in a series of hard cracks and ugly, violent knocks.

Will you accept the charges, crackled through the line, and then by the grace of some wonderful miracle she hoped to contemplate later, a broken version of her father's voice burst through the interference. He sounded like he was on Mars, but so what, it was Daddy—and Daddy fixed everything.

"Beeley, is this some type of prank?" Daddy's voice, buried under a century of static and noise, a ghostly blend of old-time radio and childhood memory. "Are you streaming this to Facebook or something?"

"Daddy, you have to come get me. I'm at Copperhead, but I'm lost. I'm lost in all this night."

The door broke open, the glass shattered, and the night Beeley dreaded poured inside. The thresher blade would not be hindered, and even in this crushing murk, she saw the blur of its fury, felt the vibrations through the floor, and heard the crash of chewed wood flying like shrapnel and slamming into everything.

"Wait. Did she say it's *night* there?" Greedle Olin's voice said from that other, far away planet. "Tell her to get the hell out of there right now, Darryl."

He must be on speaker, Beeley thought.

"Daddy, Greedle, I'm in the farmhouse," Beeley said. "Come to the big farmhouse. They're outside, Daddy. There's the scarecrow. I know it's crazy, but the scarecrow's *alive.*"

Greedle shrieked, "Get out of there, Beatrice, do *not* let it touch you, don't even *look* at Rusty Jack, *especially* his Deathbag!"

"Shit, Greedle," Daddy said, aggravated that he didn't—or couldn't—comprehend. "Are you part of her nonsense—"

"Darryl, good God, you don't get it. She's at Copperhead. She's stepped through the *Shimmer.*"

Beeley watched Rusty Jack limp into the foyer, leading the way with his shit-splattered hat, hooded skull turning side to side, button eyes searching. His boot scraped the hardwood floor, dry as lung cancer. Only a few seconds, Beeley feared, until that combine blade finished with the front steps and gnawed its way into the house.

"Daddy," Beeley whined. "Daddy, I'm really scared, *please . . .*"

"Jesus, Greedle," her father groaned. "Beeley, you and this fool stop this right now, you hear me?"

Greedle must have moved closer to the phone now because his voice was as loud as Daddy's. "Darryl, Copperhead is never in the same place, finding her on that property is next to impossible. Beeley, listen. *Listen.* Tell that goddamn scarecrow to lie down and die. Tell him the Architect, *The Architect of Zero* demands it. Tell that snake warlock Johannes Gennckes to obey the old rules, and lie down and die."

"They're here, they're in the house, this ugly ghosthouse. The man at the fruit stand said that it's knives that make the—"

Greedle interrupted, "Find the dirt road. It's real and that still exists no matter what or when. The dirt road that brought you there, you need to find—"

A terrible screeching noise flooded the earpiece, an ingot in Beeley's ear. She pulled away, Greedle Olin still shouting, but squelched by old wires and a hundred years of bad connection.

"Tell that Godless bastard Gennckes to lie down. Do *not* go near the bare black sycamores, Beeley—keep away. *The Shadowless Ones.*" Greedle's voice tumbled and sank into the eventide.

The connection to 2021 slammed shut, and she let the earpiece fall.

When the thresher devoured the foyer, the house began to die. Ceiling moldings shed nails and plaster, and wall panels peeled away like a snake shedding skin. Paintings and sconces slid to the floor. A chandelier snapped from its mooring and committed suicide on the dining room table.

A wheezing Rusty Jack dragged himself through the dust and debris, knife in hand.

Beeley's path, an obstacle course of overturned chairs and splintered house meat, narrowed as she fled further into darkness. A horrific snarl of death music resounded from the parlor as the blade pulverized several columns, the grand piano, then the fine china.

Beeley slid around the corner into the drawing room, her heart a jackhammer, yellow terror bursting pungent from every pore, dust in her nostrils, tongue dry as a bone. Her eyes landed on a portrait above the mantle, and though she knew better, she stopped.

In a moment of clarity, Beeley flipped on her iPhone's flashlight.

The portrait eyed her like an intruder.

Of course, she thought.

Long, curled nose. Hair pushed back from his face.

Who else could it be?

Johannes Venduur Gennckes, the brass tag read, *Oil on Canvas, 1913.* He stared down at her with those wasp-hole eyes. His black waistcoat, a masterwork of tailoring, barely concealed the hilt of a massive, sheathed knife. A fine leather medicine bag, painted and bejeweled with markings and shapes Beeley now knew all too well, hung at his shoulder. In the portrait's murky background, Greek columns like the ones she'd briefly glanced at in her history textbooks lay smashed to rubble. Beyond, an ancient city in flames, columns of smoke rising into the sky, mushrooming into gargantuan, black fists. Among these ruins and keeping to shadow, she saw it, albeit for only an instant—a Gorgon's hag face, eyes black with prehistoric hate, her crown alive with serpents, terrible vipers with spade-shaped heads. Copperheads.

Them. The Medusa Cult.

"Greedle was right," Beeley said. "He knew it was you."

Rusty Jack pushed into the drawing room, filthy and boneless, a ventriloquist's dummy covered in decades of dust and neglect. Behind him, the blade obliterated rugs, chairs, the banister, a furious mouth devouring one century at a time.

Beeley fled the parlor, her little iPhone a bobbing white firefly. She lost her footing and fell flat-faced into the kitchen. She scrambled to right herself, slipped on the tile, then slipped again. Tired, frustrated, and afraid, Beeley finally made it to her knees, filthy hair plastered to her sweaty forehead, cheeks streaked with smeared makeup. She looked up, and Rusty Jack stood amid tiled walls, fallen things, and hand-cranked meat grinders. Cast iron skillets hung from hooks like bested prey.

"This is it, the end of the line?"

In one glove, Rusty Jack offered the Deathbag; in the other, a corroded knife, its serrated edge a galaxy of teeth that, to paraphrase Darryl Ballantine, made a bloody job easy.

The scarecrow cocked its massive head, and from that mouth poured the dial tone from the candlestick phone, a brain-dead droning of another era, a single note of ugly music from Elsewhere.

She stood and leaned against a counter littered with severed snake heads. Dead black eyes stared into the plaster ceiling. Gaping mouths, fangs extended, threatened a terrible death delivered by ruthlessness and the primal will to survive.

Beeley's phone chimed.

No Instagram this time, only a black and white video, something from the olden days, like those sped-up, silent comedies projected at the old-school pizza joint Daddy liked, the movies filled with scratches and missing frames. Neglected history left to play out in obscurity.

An uncooperative Johannes Gennckes, face taut, skin browned by the sun, resisted mightily as a handful of grimacing men pulled him from the house. He bumped the porch swing, sending it into motion on creaking chains. Arms like tree branches and legs the length of shovel handles, the captured giant stumbled on the steps, the stairs devoured by a manic thresher blade as Beeley begged her father for rescue.

A solitary oil lamp shone in the window adjacent to the door, the commotion outside illuminated by the headlights of primitive cars and pickup trucks. Angry people wielded shotguns, while others stood armed with little more than lanterns and pickaxes; a small mob deep into years of poverty and fed up with ratty patchwork clothes, gaunt faces, and a world seen through dark, desperate eyes. Beeley felt the hundred-year-old urge for retribution push through the crowd.

Shrieking and bellowing, the mob bound Gennckes and pushed him into the tall grass. Beeley squinted and steadied the phone, not entirely surprised by now to find Walpurgis Peak sneering beneath a moonless 1924 sky because, at Copperhead Farms, that damned mountain was visible wherever you looked—even a memory streamed from nearly a hundred years past.

Rising from that grass stood a pair of crossed fence posts, a sample of Copperhead Farms' bounty at its base: gourds, corn, and grain, a bundle of prosperity denied a population that had reached its limit.

As if a poor editor had been at work, the scene jumped, and now Gennckes hung upon the cruciform like a common thief, wire binding each wrist and his crossed ankles. Vitriol and spit flew as Gennckes cursed the entirety of Walpurgis County in a language Beeley did not recognize.

Gennckes' voice burst from Beeley's iPhone like the bray of a gargantuan animal, a wounded giant bleeding in open country. But in the picture show, the call was a fast-moving shock wave, flattening the knee-high grass surrounding Gennckes in a fifty-yard radius. The cars, buffeted by the sound, trembled on their suspensions. Men fell. The farmhouse door slammed shut.

A man in black, facing Gennckes, his clerical vestments soiled and face eroded with disapproval, braced himself against the invisible force. He lowered his head, one hand holding his wide-brimmed hat in place, the other pressing a hymnal to his chest. As the wave passed, Reverend Waushburne straightened and pointed an accusatory finger at the man he'd sentenced to death.

Several men fired their shotguns into the air, while others cheered with farm tools raised. Rake, shovel, hoe, and scythe. Dust swirling in the anemic beams of headlights. The silhouette of a dark farmhouse against the distant tower of Walpurgis Peak.

A man brought a stool and set it in front of Gennckes. Waushburne climbed on top, and snatched the massive blade from his enemy's waist. He held it aloft to the moonless sky, hat tumbling from his head, eyes wide in rapture.

Bound and belligerent, Johannes Gennckes writhed on his crooked cruciform, each convulsion mightier than the last. "It's knives that make the decisions of the world." The words crackled from the speaker, spoken not by Gennckes, but Reverend Waushburne. The mob cheered.

To Beeley's horror, the Reverend ripped open Gennckes' throat in one swift swipe. He went to work like a butcher on a hog, sawing at the neck with hard, urgent strokes. The blade trailed blood in a slow-motion arc as Waushburne raised his arm in victory, and Gennckes' head, eyes hateful, mouth agape, tongue lolling like a serpent gone to sleep, fell. It landed face down, defiled and spurting, the body a dreadful snarl of joint-bending spasms. Rage unsated, Reverend Waushburne hacked off Gennckes' left foot with all the finesse of a man clearing jungle with a machete. Blood-soaked, he admired his work to the overwhelming approval of the mob.

The locals quickly fetched a ladder from a pickup truck and leaned it on the cruciform. A round man in overalls scrambled up and slammed an odd thing atop Gennckes' spurting neck: the head of a donkey. Washburne tossed the round man his blood-spattered outer vestment, and within seconds, a decapitated Johannes Gennckes hung hooded and humiliated.

"The last snake dies this night, defiled with the jawbone of an ass," Cried Waushburne, eyes to the sky, his enemy's bloody knife an emperor's scepter.

Someone snatched the Reverend's fallen hat, tossed it to the man on the ladder, and by the time he descended, the first torch had been lit, and Copperhead Farms was ablaze.

"Your story," Beeley said, holding the iPhone out, hoping in some way Rusty Jack saw what she saw. It was stupid, of course. Rusty Jack/Vendor/Gennckes knew the story all too well, the screen now displaying the opulent farmhouse engulfed in flames. Partially obscured by smoke, the Lord of Walpurgis County, that unholy, growling mountain, remained silent.

The low battery indicator flashed, and the image winked out. Time—for the phone at least—had come to an end.

She heard Greedle Olin's words: *They took care of business— but his family must have got wind of it and escaped because they were nowhere to be found.*

Beeley groaned, "Oh God, Daddy, why did you leave me here? Why won't you come get me?"

"*Old hills*," came a voice from beneath the hood. Ashes tumbled from the scarecrow's enormous mouth.

She tossed the dead phone into the shadows. Whether it shattered in 1924 or 2021, it really didn't matter anymore.

"It's like you said earlier. Once I see you in the starlight, it's curtains."

The scarecrow set one glove on the knife, the other on the dreaded Deathbag. It held the cursed purse open, the pocket a fractal maelstrom of infinity, something Beeley could never find words to describe.

"*Old rules.*"

"I can't remember exactly what Greedle wanted me to do," Beeley said, gutted now that she knew for certain there would be no California sun. No Nobu. No LA lifestyle. No one would ever want to *be* her. Walpurgis County never let you leave, and if you died in the shadow of the mountain, your soul remained in the Shimmer, where decades were stepping stones, and the centuries a crooked path that always led you back to where you were. "But Greedle says even *you* need to obey the rules, so lie down and die."

The burned-out house fell silent, the screeching violence of the thresher fading like a nightmare from childhood. The kitchen window's twin panes offered a bleak winter upon the foothills of Walpurgis Peak to the right and Widow's Holler bathed in summer's golden dawn to the left. Through a wound the combine blade bored into the parlor, a glimpse of the end times. 2077.

Beeley's eyes fell to the Deathbag, where it's every time, where it's every year. The *then* shimmers with the *yet*, and each century, saint and snake trod the rich soil that paves the roads—which keeps monsters at bay by the glow of a single burning lamp.

NOTE TO SANDERSON

SANDERSON:

A small cadre of scholars maintains a comet slammed into the earth in 12,000 B.C., hurling the planet into a devastating ice age. The engine of the world seized, and life all but stopped—global cardiac arrest. The survivors washed ashore on Mount Ararat, gasping with survivor's guilt.

Yet amid this turmoil and blight, something bored deep underground. It—*they*—brood there still, licking their wounds.

Nineteenth-century naturalist Henry Akeley postulated, through a combination of scientific deduction and the acceptance of shunned knowledge, a snarl of cosmic parasites, not a comet, plummeted Earthward from ancient night skies. Banished from one dimension, he insists, to another via an opening reality's complex weave referred to only as *The Gate,* downward these entities spiraled, vile things, tumorous with idiot rage, cursing their sentencing to the void.

Upon impact with our infant world, catastrophe.

But catastrophe's offspring is opportunity.

From one of Akeley's erratically scrawled notebooks:

My God, they're everywhere. They're all over the world. Their wounds bled legendary, near-fatal. If they were to survive the aeon on a world traumatised by their arrival, the solution must be congruent with the scale of circumstance. Though plunged into a terrible dark age of endless night, The Shadowless found solace in the Earth's global ruin.

I pored through the Akeley Archive, a collection of soliloquies spoken onto Edison wax cylinders and fastidious, hand-written journals, meticulously preserved in Georgetown University's underground class-1000 clean room vault. During this three-year project, I cross-referenced his findings (and yes, in some instances rantings) with passages in books Georgetown was not so boastful about possessing: feared tomes, alternate accounts of history rejected by scholars worldwide, broader in scope than the apocryphal gospels rejected by The Council of Nicaea, such as Hermund Kolbe's *Das Grauenhafte unter uns (The Horrible Among Us)*, the fourteenth-century occult opus *The Discoveries of Crosius*, and perhaps most blood-thickening, the collection of Vatican-confiscated Medusa Cult writings, *Deos Sine Umbra (Gods Without Shadow)*.

Henry Akeley, unprepared as I was to accept it, was right. Crippled but not incapacitated, bound but not incarcerated, an atrocity broods ageless, comatose beneath the great sentinel mountains of the globe.

Translated from Kolbe, chapter four:

Take heed. Below incalculable alpine weight, a loathsome devilry murmurs; an idiot darkness scheming since the primal days of the world.

Montana's Chief Mountain. The Eiger in Switzerland. Sagarmatha of the Himalayas. Tupangato in Argentina. America's dreaded ogre, Walpurgis Peak. Mexico's rumbling giant, Iztaccihuatl. Ygg'r'su, brooding beneath the Gulf of Aden. Kilimanjaro. Denali.

These and other mountains shield a secret kept on this planet since men cowered in caves. Fallen as one insane entity, but now split into many, The Shadowless dream in growling stasis in the belly of the earth—The Undervoid—kept alive by a bio-mechanical colossus—

Wait.

Sanderson, I must inform you of a great deception. What's presented as fact through academia and media, from *Smithsonian* to *National Geographic,* is simply theatre, theatre on a grand scale. Those who claim they know are clueless; either guessing or, to be blunt, indoctrinated by global deceit so pervasive and airtight no one questions it anymore. The definition of truth appears to be how vast the number to whom you can tell it.

Glaciers are widely believed to have carved the haggard face of the Northern Hemisphere. However, spurned by Akeley's hypothesis and now confirmed through painfully detailed inquiry—both manual and computer-aided—I can state unequivocally that glaciers did not scar the world; that honour belongs to a centuries-long global construction project.

Imagine monstrous excavations beneath these colossal fangs, tunneling and boring into their granite roots, hurling ore and slag recklessly into rivers, lakes, and oceans, choking canyons with debris, and burying forests beneath quadrillions of metric tonnes of detritus. Exterminating countless species. Asphyxiating the atmosphere, blotting out the sun. Muddy seas lazy with viscous waves rolling like tired dogs.

The result?

There is a network of machines. Great machines, Sanderson. Mechanisms that hiss and throb beneath the mighty peaks of our world. They are pumps, life support systems, if you will, mechanized, yet alive. They spider for miles—no—*thousands* of miles beneath the surface of Earth as we go about our trivialities, make our wars, bury our dead. They thrum united on one ugly, blasphemous mission.

To keep The Shadowless Ones alive.

Consider what we've been told about the nature of seismic activity, the Richter scale, aftershocks, liquefaction, undersea earthquakes, and tsunamis. Tectonic plates. Expanding Earth. *Sunspots*, for God's sake.

All bogus.

Earthquakes are connections made within the machine network.

Because these machines are living mechanisms, they function similarly to neurons, seek out like cells, and connect, fortifying the network and perpetuating survival. When connections are made, their *essence* merges. In old Internet parlance, we referred to this as a handshake. In seismic terms, it's a tectonic shift—a massive discharge of energy as physical and, God, how I wish this not to be so, telepathic connections are cemented. Colossal sections of the earth's crust shift to accommodate the neural link, splitting open, venting gasses, and redirecting geothermal pressure to volcanoes.

Humanity dies by the thousands. The sea takes its trophies. Illness and trauma spread as fissures open and their fetid machine waste vents into our atmosphere. Disease is their byproduct, their exhalation—as carbon dioxide is ours. Human beings exhale a life-giving fuel for the greenery of this world; the invaders vent the pestilences of cholera, malaria, and influenza, all unknown to this paradise before the Shadowless fall. Temblor and disease, eternally wed.

But like every machine, these monstrosities require fuel.

The ugliness that sustains these machines is incomprehensible in its wickedness. Incapable of ingesting our irradiated ores in their raw state, they extract sustenance only from poisoned organic matter. Too ghastly to contemplate, most will dismiss this information as fanciful at best, petulant science-denial at worst.

From *Deos Sine Umbra:*

> *Tumble both corpse and carrion into the Great Step Downward, flesh alight with the firestones of Vulcan's labour. They dream; sated bellies in the womb of the Earth.*

Firestones of Vulcan's Labour: Uranium, Radium. Tritium, Strontium. You understand, Sanderson? The machines are fueled by radioactive ores but must be delivered in a living host, a most wretched method of sustenance.

My God, it is not precisely clear in the texts whether or not what I say next is true, but passages point to something even more fantastic: evolution does not exist. It is physically impossible. But *De-Evolution*, the *regression* of a species, is. It is my hypothesis that what we know as the Australopithecines, Homo Habilus, Neanderthal, and other proto-human species were genetically manipulated *backward* from modern humans to create not only a slave race to excavate the haven for these giants but likewise serve as the living medium for these ores—Corpse and Carrion.

Also from Kolbe, chapter four:

> *The wildling offshoots of men, sired of marrow and seed, birthed motherless in discarnate wombs, toiled in the earth's deepest pits. Spent of strength, waterskins all, perished; gorged to capacity with firestones then sacrificed.*

NOTE TO SANDERSON

Dead on their feet, poisoned by the most lethal, toxic elements this planet harbors, these brutes were worked to death and used as fuel. As the Pleistocene raged, humans—the pitiful remnant of our ancestors that survived the cataclysm—fled south.

Upon uncovering this ghastly truth, there is little doubt I have stepped into a whirlwind of danger. It is in the Medusa Cult's interest that this global secret stays unknown, and they will spare no expense or resource to ensure it. The moment this message is sent, know I have steps in place to remove both my physical and digital footprints. My time, not only in Georgetown, is at an end, but I will not sit idly by and wait for my assassin. I am not suicidal, I will not hang myself in a hotel room or any such thing.

This research has been compiled onto several two-hundred-fifty-six-bit-encrypted hard drives, distributed to individuals known only to me but not one another—a security bulwark against Medusa Cult agents—to be made public should any tragedy befall me. Know that Medusa Cult operatives are not the black-suited agents of old. They are the grocery clerks, road workers, or the friendly police officer. *Eyes everywhere.* But as a gesture of good faith, I have prepared a small sample of the raw data for you to assess, accessible only via the decryption key sequestered in this message's metadata. Should you still possess the inclination to broker this to your contacts in Boston, your finder's fee, of course, will be generous.

But make no mistake, Sanderson, the information on these media drives contains conclusive evidence that they are *here*; they are *awakening*. According to both Akeley and the ancient volumes mentioned above, they squirm anxious for The Architect of Zero, the adjudicator of ultimate chaos and ruin. It will claw without mercy through The Gate, the repugnant slit from which their Nightrealm poisons the universe.

Humanity sleeps, unaware of its impending sacrifice upon the altar of disaster, as further cataclysm is in the offing. What we call The Ring of Fire gnaws at the edge of the continents. Fuji. Kamchatka. Pinatubo. Anak Krakatau. Tonga. All connected—the jugular vein that feeds a godless heart. Behold: Fukushima and the breadth of its horrors.

Look at the North American fault map and marvel at the enormity of the machine network. Conduits, massive faults such as Cascadia, San Andreas, and Appalachia approach completion, full connectivity. Soon, earthquakes powerful enough to slide entire mountain ranges into the sea will bully the continent, generating tidal waves so massive the Atlantic will push westward from Chesapeake Bay to the Ozark, the Pacific east from Los Angeles to Boise.

Science has lied to us about everything. The Vatican is not without guilt—they sequestered this information for centuries—but it is Medusa Cult loyalists who polish the apex of this pyramid. Brilliant operators have infiltrated every pillar of society, weaved a shroud that has kept humanity bound for several millennia, and they delight in calamity. I remind you of Akeley's words: *they're all over the world.*

Earth is truly a unique planet, an oasis of life and fertility. Conversely, the cosmos is little more than a swirling porridge of sinister intent, a malignant void steeped in blood and servitude, murder and totality.

When The Architect of Zero arrives, our end will not be swift. Despite the scale of these disasters, our extermination will take decades. By all accounts, The Shadowless Ones will breach the mountains and seas under which they languish, strapped to their bleeding life-support mechanisms, then prowl the world with their Master, dragging with them a miles-long spiderweb of abhorrent technology, a colossal yolk sac sputtering bile and pestilence. Billions will bear witness to the ultimate cataclysm, the end of all things.

The unimaginable inheritors of Earth, ruling over a global cemetery.

Akeley knew. But he went to Chief Mountain anyway:

Though my body trembles rife with disease, teeth lost, skin pallid, my mind reels, alight in revelations. I will accompany Mr. Coombs to the glacier north of Exeter, here in the divine beauty of the Montana Territory.

I hear rumblings in the ice, the rhythmic thrum of its pulse, and dare I speculate, its very breath in the frozen floe. Our world is not what it seems; our legends manufactured to secret the truth from the eyes of a population too docile to accept a mammoth nightmare of ugly proportions, eternal night and abandon.

Dear God, help us all.

NOTE TO SANDERSON

Sanderson, take my advice and find a place for your family that is green and lush, quiet and in tune. Whether this catastrophe arrives in three or fifty years, I cannot say. But watch for increased seismic events, each more devastating than the last. Let that be your timepiece, the grandfather clock ticking away the fleeting moments of a doomed world.

Again, if this information interests your client, contact me through our normal channels.

Sincerely,

Albert Wilmarth

BILLY BEAUCHAMP, DISCOUNT EXORCIST

WALPURGIS COUNTY. Whenever I think I'm done with this place, I find myself at Halligan's Hardware, replacing my claw hammer, buying fresh nylon cord and duct tape, and smiling as Freida Halligan eyes me over her bifocals as she rings up the items. I smell the Ben-Gay she put on before leaving the house that morning, and when she speaks, I know she had Cheerios for breakfast. Over the years, my vocation has sharpened my senses like a set of Japanese knives. But to be fair, anyone could have detected a pungent analgesic at the small of her back.

"Looks like you're planning another rough outing," Freida said. She brought the hammer about an inch from her eye. If she wanted to read the price tag, why not put on the bifocals? They were for show of course, surly pipsqueaks were less likely to shoplift from a grandmotherly figure. At least, that's what Freida said one night at Go Drunk Yourself, the liveliest dive bar in Walpurgis County, right smack dab in the middle of Bleary Street. Honestly, GDY is the only dive bar, as Walpurgis County—the Purg as locals call it—liked to keep things simple and old school. As far as the people here were concerned, technology apexed with TIVO, and the last good record to hit the stores was a toss-up between the *Nine To Five* soundtrack and *Honky Tonk Heroes* by Waylon Jennings.

"Hammer's ten bucks, Freida," I said.

"Just checking, smarty-pants. You back for long?"

Telling Freida my plans was like renting a billboard on Route 54. "No, not long. Just a quick dip and off I go."

"Must be nice to have such an interesting job that takes you to so many interesting places."

Last Thursday in Fever Bend, Kansas, I watched a twelve-year-old boy with his knees facing backward crab up the walls of a barn—his dripping tongue a good fourteen inches long—and in a

34

language thought to be dead for centuries curse the entirety of God's creation. Three horses dropped dead on the spot, the barn doors slapped back and forth as if caught in a hurricane, and by the time we shoved him into the grain silo and finished the job, the precocious little scamp had bitten me three times.

Interesting? Sure.

"Life on the road, you know," I said instead. "Summer's heating up, so things get busy out there."

"Don't I know it." She bagged the items, then reached under the counter and produced one of the store's color fliers, filled with sales and discounts. "You want this month's Deal Doubler?" She set her hand on a hip popped sideways like an old-time burlesque performer. Having never seen plaid so warped out of true, I silently grieved for her husband.

"Sure, Freida, toss it in."

"You be safe out there, Billy. The sun drops low and fast this time of year. Don't let the shadows get you."

I smiled and winked.

"*The* shadow," she corrected.

By the time I rolled up to the Collier place on Midsummer Road, just west of Widow's Holler, the temperature hung hideously in the hundreds, the humidity horrendous in the nineties, and my blood sugar brooded in the basement. I climbed the three steps to the house, a rickety joint with paint laid when *Gunsmoke* ruled CBS, now peeling like a skin disease. Old-style doorbell—you pulled a brass knob attached to a cable. *Dorrrrng.*

It had been a while since I'd had a look at the Collier property. God love them, they hadn't sold a single acre to developers and most of it was still in full production. Corn over here, alfalfa over there. Nice to see some traditions in place, except for one. Way in the haze, I spied that ugly incisor piercing the earth from below, Walpurgis Peak. Ugly son of a whore. Nothing good ever fell upon it, rolled off it, jumped from it, or grew upon its slopes. You'll forgive my brevity on my feelings toward that eyesore, but as I burn my memoir to paper, know that its history will be revealed.

Yvonne Collier opened the door before I could turn around, though it was impossible not to hear her unmistakable, thumping approach. Yvonne had been born with an outsized club foot, and some said it was because she had been conceived so close to Widow's Holler, or worse, the Shimmer-shifting spectre that is Copperhead Farms. Widow's Holler lay adjacent to that nexus of weird even by Purg standards, and everyone knew to steer clear of that six-hundred-acre shitshow whenever it showed itself. The Collier property was unfortunately nestled near the two, that is, when Copperhead Farms saw fit to appear.

"Billy, I'm so glad it's you," Yvonne said. She extended her hand, and I took it in both of mine. Her bones rode closer to the surface than they used to, but her skin radiated warmth, her spirit intact. The last time I saw Yvonne, a few strands of gray intruded at her temples; now it seemed to have set up shop. Her eyes remained Ireland green, her cheeks high and rosy, her smile a sunbeam. Still, a sadness resided in the sag of her shoulders and the slight stoop of her spine.

"Of course, Yvonne," I said. "It's good to see you."

And that was true. Yvonne and I had known one another since the late seventies. She was four years older than me, but as a teenager, she and I became fast friends after I drove a demon out of her father's International Harvester tractor, which had taken to carving pentagrams onto Barry Ellison's summer hay field. One extraordinary high school evening, I accosted Yvonne outside Chamber House Wine and Spirits, gave her a ten-dollar bill, and told her to keep the change. Five minutes later, Yvonne dropped a sixer of Mickey's Big Mouth onto my passenger seat. *Go easy,* she said. *Or you'll hork all over your prom date.*

She stepped aside, holding the door while leaning on one gargantuan shoe.

"Betsy's not *too* wild today," Yvonne said. She closed the door and gathered her hands in a knot in front of her apron. "I guess the Collier house has to deal with these intrusions from time to time."

I thought of her father's old sputtering tractor plowing demonic crop circles. A little holy water in the fuel tank and that scrappy scooter seized right up. The engine clanged to a halt, the exhaust pipe coughed a tumor of noxious smoke, and the gear shifter wiggled back and forth like a seismometer's needle. Yvonne watched me that day, saddled upon her mare, hips lopsided from that giant bulky shoe that wouldn't fit the stirrup, her wide-brimmed hat corralling a luxurious mane afire with the setting sun.

Despite her deformity, I always found her beautiful. I should have told her. She needed to know.

"There's always an uptick in the summer," I said.

From upstairs, *DHURRRUUUH.*

Yvonne rolled her eyes and shrugged. "Looks like Betsy knows you're here."

I sighed. "We know *that's* not Betsy. Other than this little hiccup, how's she been?"

"Not without problems. Her resurrection was unexpected, but you know how it is, we endure for a cure. She didn't take well to it, it's not like she can go out and get a job like some others can. Could you imagine her answering phones at the call center in Danielsburg?"

Thank you for calling. How may I help you? Have you heard The Shadowless Ones, writhing ageless in the fetid womb of the stars, fell blasphemous to Primal Earth? CLICK. *Hello? Hello?*

Walpurgis County could be tough on everyday people. But outsiders? *Normies?* Man, they were utterly ill-prepared for it. The local tourist trade suffered its death blow in 1988 when Hotel Jasper, a mid-nineteenth-century jewel located above Pop Sweeny's general store, slipped in and out of linear time; *Shimmered,* as we say around here. In one room, it was suddenly 1932, another 1947, in the lobby, 1887—you get the idea. When the pendulum swung back to 1988, twelve hours of actual *linear* time had passed, and several guests remained trapped in different decades or centuries. One guest staggered out of the lobby, a seven-year-old boy upon entering, and a ninety-three-year-old man upon exiting. He died in the parking lot, tapping the chorus to *Dream Warriors* by Dokken in Morse code upon the asphalt. Strange, but true.

The Purg had never been anything but fertile ground for the corruptors of men, who, mirroring the event at Mount Hermon aeons ago, dropped to Walpurgis Peak but never had the goddamn decency to leave the neighborhood. Demonic squatters—the laziest kind—causing nothing but trouble. As these writings are my testimony, my life largely in confrontation with them, believe me, you'll meet them en masse.

"I'm glad you thought to call me instead of Barley Hughes and his Exorcisto Cartel Action Vans or whatever the hell it is he calls them."

I knew Hughes' company's name was *EVAC: Exorcism Victory Anywhere Crew*, but despite that awful name his business flourished, and customers seemed thrilled when EVAC's black and purple vinyl-wrapped mini-vans, the color scheme obviously nicked from Black Sabbath's *Master of Reality,* pulled into the driveway.

I preferred my interpretation of the name, but whatever.

Yvonne smiled, but her gaze dropped. "Barley's very expensive. He breathes really heavy and sweats from his earlobes. Makes me nervous."

I nodded. He'll be selling franchises soon, and putting guys like me, *experienced* guys like me, out of business. The Walmart of Demonic Expulsion. Is nothing left to tradition anymore?

"Indeed, Yvonne, but I have a long history with this squatter trash. I've faced plenty of them. Some more than once." I opened my vest, lifting my shirt to remind her of the nasty scar Virazel had given me in 1999. We had some unfinished business, he and I.

"Nasty bugger," Yvonne said. "If Lena hadn't been on point that day and sewn you up, God knows how that would have played out. The whole of Danielsburg was pretty worried about you."

"I'm lucky she married me, despite my hurling Mickey's Big Mouth all over her on Prom night. She doesn't like to come along on the job these days, you know. Once the kids came on the scene, that was pretty much the end of it. She quit cold turkey and made me take out a life insurance policy. I lied like rug on the application. New York Mutual doesn't cover Exorcists, just so you know."

"Smart girl. Look, Billy, I don't know which one of that riffraff is using my big sister as an oven mitt, but you go up there and tell that little shit to knock it off." She stuffed her hands into her apron pockets and pursed her lips. "Kick his ass off our farm."

From upstairs rang the icy clang of a shattering window, then the thump as something clattered to the roof. Yvonne shook her fists and stomped off in her leaning way, taking a hard right at the kitchen.

"*Betsy!* Betsy, you get back here right now!"

I followed, and there, through the fan of windows around the breakfast nook, ran Betsy, fresh from the bedroom, half the footboard and one shattered bedpost still lashed to her leg with a length of rope. She stopped for a second and kicked off her remaining sandal, and it spiraled into the little yard fenced off for the chickens.

Betsy had not bothered with a shirt this afternoon. I couldn't blame her. It was piss-hot, and she weighed about two-twenty. Her sagging teal sweatpants looked to be the size of boat sails. Her hair was a greasy, gray mess.

"Game time," I said.

I reached into my leather bag, which I'd recently bought from a weird Bohemian girl on Etsy, who offered to run it through a Bedazzler for thirty bucks, and pulled out the nylon rope I'd just bought. I caught a whiff of Freida Halligan's Ben-Gay.

Betsy, dead for nineteen years, refused to lie down and pass on—as some do here in the Purg. Often, the dead congregated at bus stops, panhandled outside the CVS, or landed in manual labor jobs, like loading carts at the Home Depot in Franklin or sweeping the kitchen at Big Ben's Diner. They had their way, and the living had theirs, but Betsy was no marauding flesh-eater or any of that movie nonsense. She simply had no pulse, blood pressure, respiration, or eye dilation. Despite the heart attack that killed the funeral director deader than a hammer when Betsy rolled off the slab and rifled through his Arby's Beef N Cheddar combo, she hadn't hurt a soul. Still, she managed to put away the funyuns and snickerdoodles like a champ, and after a few years, Yvonne had her trained to perform basic housekeeping duties. For example, the last time I dropped by, Betsy mopped the mudroom, not far from where we now stood. Yvonne rewarded her with a pack of Twizzlers.

This type of possession shenanigans, occupying the dead and running them around the back forty like a wind-up toy, *had* to be Virazel. That prick is a third-tier fallen angel, a street sweeper, sub-literate by angelic standards, and about as ham-fisted as it gets. The only reason he *ever* got a piece of me was that I had the young man's temerity to show up to a job with three whiskey sours in me. Well, four. The last one was a double. My wife, Lena, doesn't tell that story anymore.

"I'm going to run a Feisty Foal on Betsy, so step back," I said. I'd never charge Yvonne full rate, but she deserved a little extra, so I tossed in a touch of theatre, and I had the lasso spinning over my head by the time I was down the back steps. Betsy made pretty good time, despite her bedroom furniture anchor and sweatpants congregating around her ass.

I whooped like a cowpoke and even clicked my tongue as if

summoning a horse. The rope generated a satisfying *whoosh* as I built momentum and aligned my eye. Just as Betsy was about to break right and disappear behind a neglected pyramid of milk cans, I let the lasso go.

Bullseye!

Betsy turned out pretty spry for a dead gal. The night she choked to death on a hushpuppy—although hospital records indicate popcorn chicken—she had won the Tri-County Women's Wrestling Championship. Those old skills don't perish with death as we'd like to believe, and all the lasso did was add me to the collection of detritus she dragged around the field.

She pulled that hard right after all, and I missed the milk cans by inches. Dirt tumbled into my mouth, eyes, and down my shirt.

Thirty minutes ago, I mused snide little comments about Frieda Halligan's Ben-Gay. Now, look at me, shamefaced and filthy by a low rent fallen angel's antics. All seen by Yvonne, I might add, a client to whom I owed professionalism and bang for the buck.

Grass and dirt pelting my face I trumpeted, *"In the name of the most High, He who commands you, the Creator of All things, God Almighty, I command you to leave his servant this instant!"*

Betsy stopped on a dime. I'll admit, I was relieved my opening salvo was enough to apply the brakes.

She turned, scowling in the tall grass and unbearable heat. Though dead, sweat poured from her like bacon grease. Betsy fumbled with my cheap nylon rope, a laughable twine pressed into her doughy skin, flabby breasts, and deep navel. The other rope, Yvonne's top-of-the-line Equestrian-grade jute, held fast, noose-like about her ankle.

"Beauchamp," Betsy said. I knew that voice. Old as the stars. Virazel.

Virazel pushed Betsy's mandible outward into a horrible steam shovel, shifting bone and sinew in an ugly demonstration of power. The son of a bitch didn't have to, he knew how human anatomy worked, and Betsy could have spoken his venom-hate without it. Virazel simply reveled in the dispersion of torment, especially upon this poor, reanimated soul.

"You carry scars," Virazel croaked. Betsy's bottom row of teeth extended six inches past her upper lip. A ghastly horseshoe. "I savor your wounds."

Not only had I accumulated dirt and grass stains, but my shirt and vest bunched up around my ribs, my old scar in full view of the demon who had given it to me. I freed my wrists and straightened my clothes.

Betsy's dead eyes stretched wide as the demon licked her lips. "I can reopen that for you. Feed this bitch-cow the tender meats you're keeping from me."

Virazel, of course, knew of Betsy's voracious appetite, and that she preferred Nabisco to Foie gras. Demons bathe in the reeking steam of corruption, the violation of morals and will, but a low-velocity cretin like Virazel couldn't force a hippie to buy a handgun, let alone make Betsy Collier eat my guts. Instead, Virazel shifted gears and went for the low-hanging fruit of insult, twirling Betsy around like a little girl in a princess outfit, dragging with her all that splintered debris. She curtsied afterward, index finger crammed into her nose to the third knuckle. It was humiliating, pathetic, and wrong.

"She belongs to us now," Virazel said. "Unspeakable torment until the pig dies."

Clearly this boob didn't bother to check Betsy's pulse, either.

"Not so fast, pal," I said, straightening my vest and hair. Pulled fifty yards downrange left me without my Bedazzled Battle Bag and my Exo-tools, so now came the time to improvise, adapt, and overcome.

I risked a glance over my shoulder and gave a little wave. At some point, Yvonne had grabbed binoculars and a lemonade, settling in for the show.

"Look at me, Beauchamp," Virazel said.

I turned back, and Betsy spat a creamy white, clam chowder glob the size of a Bic lighter at me. It was an easy dodge, but my gaze followed it to the grass. I'll confess both surprise and revulsion when it sprouted gooey legs and fled toward the milk cans, parting the grass as it scurried away.

"You've been practicing," I said. "Good to know you can hock a goober like an eight-year-old boy. I'd rather watch her phlegm than your amateur hour ass." Demons *hate it* when you make fun of them. They thrive on fear and surrender, very similar to playground bullies or government bureaucrats. Zero humility, and a red line on hubris.

"Her terrors gather in stinking pools, Beauchamp. I churn them to paste. She coughs them into your doomed world—"

"Be silent!"

The demon's voice shut off as if I'd thrown a switch. In his insolence, Betsy squatted like a gargoyle and stamped her foot, imitating a circus horse counting to ten. She flicked a reptilian tongue—an old staple, but popular—and rolled her eyes back until only the bloodshot sclera remained visible. From the direction of Widow's Holler, several crows burst from the trees.

I palmed Betsy's forehead. If you have ever wondered what it feels like to touch a corpse with a raging fever, ask me because now I know. Her sweat, a translucent, lumpy gravy, stank of the eldest of horrors, the fear of becoming prey. Her mouth dropped open, and with no respiration to sully the acoustics of her lifeless throat, I heard only Virazel's mewling as he cowered from the word of Almighty God. He was right to be afraid.

"You, demon Virazel, filth of the abyss, you stand in awe of His Kingdom. He *commands* you to release His servant."

Betsy reared back, nostrils opened like the nozzle of a garden hose. A vile lowing filled the sweltering afternoon. Deep in her spirit, Virazel writhed.

"I visit your mother in her dreams." Betsy's voice roiled like a nest of scorpions, an offensive choir of snapping claws and dense, dripping venom. Her Adam's apple swelled into a colossal toad's bloated croak-bag. "She knows where you go at night. She sees the blood on your sheets and how you hate what you see in the mirror. Such agony she endures, knowing you drove your father to suicide. Mother weeps over the scarlet abortions you forced upon your women. Their souls belong to me."

Again, further nonsense. My mother died in 2001 from a cerebral aneurysm. My father remarried in 2006 and owns a hardware store in Utah. I'm still married to my first girlfriend, Lena. We have two kids, and they have families of their own. Demons are liars, but because this clown is an *uninformed* liar, Virazel landed on Walpurgis Peak instead of Mount Hermon with the A-Listers.

Palm firmly upon Betsy's forehead, I pushed her to the grass.

"Jesus, Virazel," I said, "you're a clueless idiot."

"Nazarene!" the demon cried.

Betsy skittered backward. A rope of drool braided with her greasy death-sweat like an ugly, elastic band. The indignities had to end.

BILLY BEAUCHAMP, DISCOUNT EXORCIST

I recalled the words of a wise man I knew: *always try the inexpensive solution first*, and that's when the idea came to me. "Alright, dummy. Let's get this handled. You're looking to make a deal. What is it? What do you want?"

History proves every deal with the Devil results in the poor sap falling into the worst trap imaginable, and at the end of the contract awaited only Hell. But Virazel was no Devil in the proper-noun sense of the word, so this was like talking cryptocurrency futures with a coffee pot.

"Dominion," the demon said. Betsy snapped her teeth at a passing dragonfly. No dice.

"Okay, that's a start. And just where would you like that to be? The Purg is full, as you know."

"Away from this human cesspool."

"We'd have to put you in the Demon Relocation Program, then."

"You lie, Exorcist."

Well, yes. But he's an asshole, so fuck that guy, right?

"Not so. I am here solely for the benefit of the woman Betsy Collier. We strike a bargain, you're granted leave of Walpurgis County by the Demonic Reassignment Bureau."

"*Reassignment.*"

"You bet. You've worn this place out like an old boot. In fact, a few months ago, Đŭrrà The Incestuous attained his own fiefdom in California's Bay Area. Interesting homeless population, *lots* of opportunities. He jumped at the chance. I brokered the resettlement for UzŽ-Hɓ as well. You no doubt heard how *that* all played out—tentacles popping up through every manhole, the entire municipal bus apparatus in Estonia pulled down into the Undervoid. It was *all over* Twitter."

"*Twitter . . .*" the demon mused.

I allowed Virazel to bring Betsy back to her feet, and he responded with a slow, contemplative nod. Now that her eyes had rolled back into place like 7s on a slot machine, I saw bewilderment and, if I interpreted Virazel correctly, genuine interest.

"Excellent," I went on. "But we'll need to hammer out an agreement. There is, luckily, neutral ground at Hotel Jasper."

The shadow of Walpurgis Peak had grown long since I last dared glance its way, its leading edge near the Collier farm border. The very shadow of that monstrosity to demons was like spinach

43

to Popeye, so best to wrap this up before Virazel became emboldened, crammed a corn cob pipe in his mouth, and tooted Sarin gas from it like a steam locomotive. The murder of crows from Widow's Holler split apart, cawing and bristling, eager to be away from it. I was reminded of Frieda's parting words: *You be safe out there, Billy. The sun drops low and fast this time of year. Don't let the shadows get you. The shadow.*

"And what in return, Beauchamp?" Virazel said. He lifted Betsy's leg and produced a vile flatus. Demons. Insolent by nature.

"Betsy."

"Meat-pig is with us now."

"You release her and accompany me to Hotel Jasper *discorporated*. She's been through enough. It's the only way it works. Rumor has it Sanguina, Bleeder of Souls is bored and leaving Chicago for Johannesburg. Power hates a vacuum, old chum. Chi-Raq could be just the spot for you."

Virazel appeared to consider this, raising one of Betsy's eyebrows as a predator's smile cracked her face in half. She pulled my brand-new rope from her body and let it drop.

"Chicago," Virazel croaked. "The windy city." Betsy passed gas again, and he laughed like a matinee villain.

"A toddlin' town," I said. "The big league."

"I will bring them despair. Hopelessness. Lingering suicide."

"Well, that market's been cornered, but you'll manage. Release this innocent, Betsy Collier, Virazel. *He* commands you." I pointed at the sky. Betsy followed my finger to the clouds. When I snapped my fingers, her eyes locked to the silver cross around my neck, held out between thumb and forefinger. Virazel scowled.

"Every deal requires compromise," I said, "Or the hammer drops hard."

I looked around for a suitable container. The barn stood about fifty yards away, but the rusted milk cans were close by. One of them rattled. Betsy's little Boston chowder phlegm creature undoubtedly—speaking of Chicago—toddled around near there.

"I *lust* for your scars," Virazel said.

Virazel could not resist a final act of defilement, so he pulled Betsy's facial features to pieces. Her mouth stretched to vulgarity, teeth wiging in her soft gums like Chiclets. Uvula elongated into a terrible, wiggling worm; he commanded it to lie convulsing on her parched, lumpy tongue. Her skin blushed into lividity's dead-blood hue, swelling her spit-slick abdomen. Virazel frolicked. A gleeful child aroused by animal cruelty.

"I harvested your blood," Virazel said. He guided Betsy's hand to her rumpled sweatpants and feigned stroking an invisible member. No way this chump would ever make it as an A-Lister, let alone in Chicago where the gangs would eat his lunch. "I dipped my mighty cock in your wounds to sire a horde of creeping minions. Like the plague locust they swarmed, gnawing flesh, grinding bone, shitting poison. They stuffed the mouths of—

"*Into the metal prison, Demon!* By the will of God Almighty, *do it!*"

Leaning back like a guitar wizard in the throes or a blazing solo, I flung both arms toward the stack of rusted milk cans.

A touch of theatre for Yvonne? Well, maybe.

Just a little.

Betsy howled and dropped bonelessly to the ground. The bedpost splinters lashed to her ankles poked from the grass like tornado wreckage.

If you want to bag a demon, one surefire method is to strike while the pompous ass is distracted, usually, as in this case, with self-aggrandizing blather. Running his mouth—well, Betsy's mouth—and off mission, I seized the moment. To my right, the topmost milk can shuddered and banged.

From the porch steps, Yvonne burst into applause. I turned to wave (I may have winked, I'm not sure) and watched as her expression changed. She pointed toward me, *past me,* then crammed her fingers in her mouth and produced the loudest whistle I've ever heard.

I'd made a terrible error.

I'd chosen the wrong milk can.

Betsy's little phlegm gem, that multi-legged wiggler, crawled out of the topmost container with a loud clatter. Now grown to about the size of a kitten, it scurried over the lip and waited. Imagine a fat, green-gray beetle with all the despicable properties of snail skin. In place of a head was nothing but a slit of a mouth. It ogled me with eyes on stubby, gelatinous stalks.

Early in my career, I exorcised a lesser demon from a man named Rufus Brissel. At the start of the ritual, hairy spider legs burst from his nose and rectum with all the finesse of a Waffle House lunch special, and I puked. Hard. This may not have been as meaty, but certainly a contestant in the Exorcism Grotesquerie Semi-Finals. No time to blow groceries, though: Virazel had to be slammed back into that milk can, *pronto.*

"I will open your wounds, Beauchamp," the Virazel-phlegm-beast gurgled, his voice the size of a thimble. "Crawl inside. Shit cancer into your bones."

The stalked eyes twitched, that line of a mouth warped with every syllable. The critter reared up, presenting its slimy belly, the constellation of legs wiggling like terrible hairs at an insect's mouth.

I always keep a little silver, the great sterilizer, equalizer, and immobilizer of all things evil, on hand. In fact, the old-timers dropped a silver coin into milk cans just like these to keep the harmful bacteria at bay. And here I was, a hundred-and-fifty-some-odd years later, up to the same old trick. A Sunshine Mint .999 silver round, a little tarnished, but its chemistry true, lived in my vest pocket. As I rushed Virazel, I slid my fingers in and grabbed it.

A few hurried steps brought me face to face with that faceless thing, and as Virazel leaped, limbs out, mouth shrieking, I extended my left hand, just like Heisman immortalized on his eponymous trophy, and the pint-sized demon slammed into it. The inertia sent the critter tumbling back into the steel container. I dropped the coin into the can, reached down, grabbed a couple of bricks lying close by, and clamped its prison shut.

Jailed by silver, the demon raged.

"Bravo!" Yvonne cried.

As much as I would have loved to enjoy the moment, the priority was Betsy.

I slid to Betsy's side—what's a few more grass stains? She lay on her back, half nude and humiliated but at last free of Virazel.

I cupped my hands around my mouth and yelled, "Yvonne! You need to get down here!"

I laid Betsy's head into my lap. Her eyes fluttered, mouth moving. I'd never held a dead person as they were dying, but that's how things are in Walpurgis County.

Toward Widow's Holler, the shadow of Walpurgis Peak wormed over the terrain, edging toward the Collier farm. Virazel's milk can had to be moved before so much as an inch of gloom touched it. With only the slightest nudge from Walpurgis Peak,

Virazel would be free faster than a genie fleeing the lamp, silver or no silver.

Yvonne dropped to her knees, took her sister's hand, and pressed it to her cheek. Betsy smiled best she could and offered a weak groan.

"Virazel drained her," I said. "Awful as that was, here's a golden opportunity for Betsy to move on. Send her to Heaven."

"Arby's?" Betsy said. She smacked her lips and chewed.

"Yes, baby," Yvonne said, her voice daisy sweet. I now saw the years she'd carried and wondered how she'd put up with so much for so long. "Lunchtime is over. It's time to go to bed."

"Midnight snack," Betsy said, little more than a hum. She nodded as if this was a very good idea.

"That's right, honey. Soon it'll be snack time."

"I see White Castle. The drive-thru is open tonight. So. *Pretty.*"

Yvonne looked at me. I nodded and whispered, "The light."

Yvonne smiled, sighed, and sobbed at the same time. She smoothed her hand over Betsy's hair, then kissed her cheek. It was heartbreaking and beautiful, but no more than a hundred yards away, the ravenous shadow-fang of Walpurgis Peak loomed. I ached at its malevolence, and in the faraway, heard the thrum of the ghastly, subterranean monstrosity sleeping in its bowel.

"Go inside, see what the specials are," Yvonne whispered.

"*Sliders—*"

Betsy Collier, finally at rest.

I skipped steps fleeing Hotel Jasper. Yvonne sat double-parked in front, behind the wheel of her father's 1953 Oldsmobile 88, wearing cat's eye shades and a purple scarf. I hopped in the passenger seat, and she hit the gas with her enormous shoe.

I looked over my shoulder as we pulled away. The shadow of Walpurgis Peak stained the brickwork of Hotel Jasper now, wreathing the masonry in darkness. The windows glared back at me, soulless as you could imagine.

Two black and purple *EVAC* vans sped away in the opposite direction, off to wherever, eager to overcharge and no doubt offer extended warranty protection. I left them to their hustle. This poor lady had watched her sister die again, then, despite her grief, assisted me in the disposing of a very pissed demon whom I'd just double-crossed. I discarded the milk can in a dark hotel room closet where it's perpetually eighteen-something-or-other. The demon was less than pleased, and if he was a Cubs fan, doubly so. Real Chicago blues.

Enjoy your time in the Shimmer, pal.

That's a lot, even in the Purg, so for Yvonne, today's job was gratis. Discount Exorcist? It appears so.

"We need to get you in front of a sink, Billy. You're filthy as a kid that's been in a playground brawl."

"Drink first, if you don't mind," I said. "I mean, if you're up for it."

Yvonne nodded and tossed my phone to me. "It's not like Betsy's going anywhere. But first you call your prom date and let Lena know you're all right. No Mickey's Big Mouth. The whiskey's on me."

Yvonne straightened her back and smiled. We hooked a right onto Beltane Road, the setting sun pouring through the driver's side window. Still, after all these years, radiant fire bloomed in her wonderful mane.

This time I will not hesitate. She needs to know.

FLIGHT 2320

"**LADIES AND GENTLEMEN**, this is Captain Brisbane speaking—I have every intention of crashing this aircraft into Walpurgis Peak."

Julie Reese in 2A looked up from her copy of *I'm Okay, But You're A Goddamn Mess* and cocked an ear toward the overhead speaker as the first gasps of disbelief swept through the passenger cabin.

"Sounds like someone needs a Xanax," she said to her husband in the aisle seat, currently perplexed by Sudoku. "Did you hear what I just heard?"

One look at Dean told her he'd heard the announcement correctly. He may not have been the Marlboro Man, but Dean Reese was certainly no beta male rattling off a complex Starbucks order from the cabin of his Tesla. She'd never seen terror stretch his face, but now Dean looked as if he'd just witnessed a homicide in a church pew.

"That can't be right," Dean said.

"I would ordinarily ask you to secure loose items," Brisbane went on, "even pray for deliverance. Instead, I will allow you to determine our fate."

"Who does this asshole think he is?" Julie said, but her voice lost the three-way cage match against the screams of a flight attendant and the clatter of passengers swarming over the toppled beverage cart. Sunny Delight had never so gloriously flown the friendly skies.

Mimicking a game show announcer, Brisbane said, "Our co-pilot answered his question incorrectly and has been executed. Before we go to commercial, I call your attention to the fasten seat belt sign, as at Viceroy Air, safety comes first. However, I strongly encourage you to take the time to snag one last buzz before lights

49

out. So, I have decided, for the remainder of our flight, all refreshments are free of charge, and please—remain seated until impact."

The 767's wings dipped to starboard, then to port, resulting in an avalanche of bodies, pillows, and snacks. The locomotive beverage cart rolled toward the forward head, and some kid who looked like an MS-13 fanboy stopped it from slamming into the harried flight attendant. Nearly everyone screamed. Several retched. An infant howled.

"I said remain seated. Next time, up goes the nose, and the wings snap off. No fiery mountain spectacle, just a corkscrew of screaming all the way down. Do you understand the rules as I have explained them, contestants?"

Most of First Class, comfortable, obedient, and hopeful to stay that way, shut their traps. If they made it out of this alive, there were sure to be Facebook posts with praying hands emojis and fired-up threats of lawsuits. As for now, Instant Stockholm Syndrome, available in the new easy-pour bottle, flowed like box wine.

Except for Julie Reese.

"You cowards can all kiss my ass. We're not out eight grand for a vacation rental because Captain Shitstain has mommy problems. What happened to the whole 'Let's Roll' mentality?"

"Shhh!" hissed a fossil in 3B. She wore her new Adidas tracksuit, auburn wig, and a set of prosthetic teeth as fake as the Theranos business plan. Still, to ensure everyone in the servant caste knew she was not to be trifled with, a diamond the size of a chocolate truffle sat perched upon her finger. "Didn't you hear what the pilot said?"

"Shut up, you cow," Julie said. She tapped Dean, and they both stood. "Who wants to bust through the door with my husband and me, and snatch this asshat out of the pilot's seat? We can can all take turns beating the snot out of him. By the way, anyone onboard have flight experience? FedEx pilot, maybe? How about a Navy fighter jock toughened up by crazy shit?"

No one raised a hand.

"He said he killed the co-pilot!" Mewled Cassie, the Jurassic diamond truffle in 3B.

"Silence," Brisbane said. "The cabin is filled with cameras, and I hear everything. The transponder has been turned off, and F-16s have already scrambled from Whiteman Air Force Base. You'll do as instructed—with a chance to win fabulous prizes."

Julie, expecting to see one of the bulbous surveillance domes ubiquitous to bank lobbies, settled her eye on a small black button, just to the left of the seatbelt indicator light. She raised her middle finger.

"Win this, flyboy."

"Ah! The finger in 2A has volunteered to be our contestant. And now, *heeerrre's* the Flight 2320 Challenge!"

Herb Alpert's trumpet melody from *The Dating Game* warbled through the aircraft.

"Our first contestant is a potty-mouthed, entitled blowhard. She turned her nose up at the free Lexus as she held out for the Audi, attends Pilates three days a week, and pretends to help the local animal shelter by posting useless shit on social media. She pearly and surly, so give a Viceroy Air welcome to *Juuuuulie Rrrreeese!*"

Applause crackled from the speakers.

Julie's eyes narrowed into slits.

"Get on the P.A.," Brisbane said, "or it's nose-up, and down we go. Twisty-spiral-plungie-thingie."

Julie pushed Dean aside and grabbed the mic nestled into its little station next to the fire extinguisher. She pushed the button and feedback yarped.

"Ready?" Brisbane said.

"Let her rip, fuckface. No one else has the stones."

"That's why I like you, 2A. I knew it when you boarded. One-hundred-percent Calabasas sass."

"You have everyone clutching their pearls. You happy now, Brisbane?"

Most of First Class gasped. How dare their tormentor be challenged.

"Well, let's make it about *you*, Julie. Confess to your fellow passengers the worst thing you've ever done. Think you can do that and not rubber-stamp the death of two hundred strangers?"

Julie looked at her husband, who, though used to taking orders from Julie and willing to break the cockpit door down if she called for it, was clearly ready to shit a Buick. Sudoku was peanuts compared to this.

I'll just make up something, Julie thought. *The pilot is obviously batshit crazy. I robbed a Circle-K in Phoenix. I dug up Grant's tomb. I cooked Punxsutawney Phil on a spit. Anything but the truth.*

"I . . . when I . . . when I was in college I cheated on an English lit test. When I got busted, I panicked. I threatened the professor with a bogus rape charge. He backed down and gave me an A."

A buzzer resounded through the P.A, followed by a jeering round of boos.

"Sorry sweetie, no dice," Brisbane said. "Let's try again. I'll give you a hint: I killed my mother with a Garden Weasel."

The cabin gasped, and Julie's adrenal gland executed an emergency blow. As sweat beaded across her forehead, years of discipline took the reins. Detective Pomerantz, good as he was, couldn't break her, even her old boyfriend Louis, who certainly voiced his share of thinly veiled suspicions, failed to pry a single morsel of confession from her. Damned if she'd confess to anything in public, let alone in front of Dean, and certainly not for this crazy, suicidal bastard.

Will Brisbane follow through? Kill us all?

She pressed the talk button and said, "Your bluff suicide mission is alerting everyone on this airplane that you're a weakling bedwetter, Brisbane."

Someone from economy class hurled a can of Diet Coke at her. It fell short, tumbling near Cassie in 3B, foaming and spraying. Julie, stunned by the lack of survival instinct on this airplane, laughed.

"This comes from beyond me, dearie. A voice larger than the sky. You see, Walpurgis Peak *speaks* to me, Julie, its belly swollen with every dark secret of the world. And it tells me your mother begged you to stop. She raised both hands as you swept the blades across her palms like a thresher. She even reached for the Swiffer Wet-Jet to ward off the blows. Teenage angst gone too far, eh?"

Julie inhaled deeply, never breaking eye contact with Dean. She shook her head and twirled her index finger around her ear, then rolled her eyes. *Stay in the game. Dean's a sweet oaf, but he'll know if you break face, even for a second. Maintain.*

"You laughed when you opened her neck, giggled because the murder weapon had a silly name. *Garden Weasel.* I'll bet the infomercial plays a little differently for you these days, yeah? Ask your husband if he's rethinking that as a gag gift this Christmas. Might want to look into the Shake Weight instead."

Her blood sprayed over me like a broken water main. I tasted hot copper and salt, terror and acceptance. I waited a good thirty minutes before I washed it off. I felt her life drip down my clavicle, onto my breasts, over my belly, waning, fading, exiting. "Walpurgis Peak looms dead ahead, Julie of 2A. It glares at me, poking through the clouds with its black, dead eye of truth. Nothing good ever came off that unholy mountain, but I'm willing to cleanse this world of people like you and take a pile of others with us. Confess now. I pinky-swear I'll bank away, and we won't end up on its razor slopes. Ask your fellow passengers how they feel about your stonewalling. The mountain knows, and so do I. Bare your soul, speak your sins, and the weight is lifted. I remind you F-16s are inbound, and if I do not respond, they will shoot us down. Forty-five seconds to impact."

Julie felt every eye bore into her.

Dean looked like a guy in a movie deciding which bomb wire to cut.

Cassie the 3B sow sneered as if someone botched her Panera Bread order. "I knew you were a bad person," she spat. "Murdering your mother. And now you'll get us all killed."

I dug late into the night, sweating and laughing. After the pigs had their fill, I burned and buried . . .

" . . . burned and buried the bones," Brisbane finished.

Impossible. Did I say that out loud?

"Thirty-five seconds, ladies and gentlemen. If you want to get in that last cocktail, now's the time. Bonus points, Julie, if you look your husband in the eye. Do not hoard your guilt. Be kind. Share with others as we stare down death, stare down that vile mountain. I wish you could see through the cockpit. It's ravenous. Walpurgis Peak *wants* us, wants *you*. Put an end to it, Julie. Stop hiding. Stop pretending."

The adrenaline overdose and thirty years of secrets pushed up her esophagus in an ugly, serpentine twist. She wanted to puke the words out: *I did it, I killed my mother because I was angry, I killed her because I'm fucking crazy, I killed her because I'm evil and irredeemable, I'm a Godless taker of life, I deserve nothing but to burn on that mountain.*

She pressed the button and raised the mic to her lips.

"My name is Julia Reese, and I—"

Impact.

THIS IS A GREEDY, JEALOUS HOUSE

Walpurgis County Historical Society
3235 Beltane Road
Ian Emerson, Curator

The Vanderbaum Archive
Select Journal Entries and
Correspondence

August 18, 1874
This infernal heat harbors no intention of abandoning its onslaught. The carpenters, steadfast in duty, have made significant progress following the acquiescence of summer rain to merciless sun. These men of brief education and great technical ability never risk so much as a glance at the house where they've toiled in excess of a year. The masons and tile setters, who have completed their kitchen work and installations of the water closets Agnes so adamantly insisted upon, have but a few days work in residual. Still, they are eager to leave. Some cite contracts in Rhode Island as a reason for departure, as several families have broken ground on manor houses there. Others mutter and turn away. Ordinarily, I would never oblige such impertinence. However, this house grows in the shadow of a watchtower of a mountain, and to those weak of nerve or simple of mind, its majesty intimates and suffers no indifference.

Tomorrow the ironworkers arrive. At long last, the weathervane I commissioned from a master blacksmith in Guingol, Pennsylvania crests my masterpiece.

THIS IS A GREEDY, JEALOUS HOUSE

August 20, 1874
Yesterday, Agnes and I took tea and biscuits as the ironworkers manned the scaffolds, a scheme of rickety catwalks erected like a shield around the house's great, hexagonal turret. Within this turret resides the dressing room of my dear wife, who requested of the architect—a poor soul now deceased by his own hand not a month after delivering the final drawings to me—a view as wide as the sky, with tall, unashamed windows. What a jewel he set upon draft paper, realized by master craftsmen into breathtaking opulence. It shall be crowned by one of the finest pieces of ironwork forged upon these shores.

Their labor endured long and arduous; several hours spent with ropes and pulleys, heaving the mammoth sculpture, a splendid wrought-iron rendering of crows in flight, aloft. With the last nail driven and the final rivet hammered, it was set, and the ironworkers looked to Agnes and me. We stood and offered them forthright applause. On the heels of our celebration, the wind, an uncharacteristically virulent and frigid blast of winter in these searing August days, immediately seized control of the weathervane.

My illustrious murder of crows went awry. It swept the turret clear of workmen, the weathervane's enormous arrow a scythe wielded by a master harvester.

They fell like marionettes freed of their wires, colliding bonelessly with the scaffold and initiating the collapse. Four men died, one unfortunate soul a scarlet patchwork of dreadful head wounds.

Our land tasted blood.

Hence, the weathervane points *only* at the mountain in the distance, the vicious claw of Walpurgis Peak, the wind's direction inconsequential.

Part of me sees the truth of it.

December 19, 1874
Winter Howl, as the locals call it, is here. For three consecutive nights, a merciless, polar wind screams down the face of the mountain, not only turning the mirror surface of Dead Neck Lake into a cataract of ice but trumpeting the arrival of the dead season.

As we sat before the fireplace, Agnes, four months with child, rummaged through a crate of old books and discarded artifacts discovered during one of her shopping excursions to Danielsburg. An ardent collector of curios, her finds were always of peculiar interest.

"This is the Journal of Linus C. Tuttle," she said as she slipped on her reading spectacles. "Reformation Brotherhood Wagon Train, it says. Shall I read to you of the beginning of the frontier days? Perhaps it brags of Indian adventures and gold mines." She leafed through its pages, humming and smiling, content with her reading. Soon, I noticed her winter cheer had turned melancholy, her expression grave. She resembled a prophet in the firelight, sent here with urgent news.

The wind lowed like a bull sensing slaughter.

"We should be on our way from here," she said, then mounted the stairs to bed.

April 8, 1875

For two agonizing days, Agnes suffered the onset of childbirth.

And during these miserable, scream-filled hours, the sun, as seen through the grand turret windows, never left the horizon behind Walpurgis Peak. It lay mocking like a wincing, critical eye, ablaze with blood-hued reds and the yellow fires of Perdition. The clouds dripped with it, the surrounding forest appeared as if set on fire, smokeless and eternal, and my dear wife's bedchamber was thrown into a maze of scarlet shadows, a wind-driven ballet of shapes distorted enough to be unrecognizable, yet stir feelings of familiarity and dread.

At the final moment, when the harried midwife insisted I be ushered from the room, Agnes's gaze fell upon me with horrible resignation, a silent plea. *Release me*, that said. *Please, Frederick, the pain.*

A tide of blood followed, the floor dark and slick with it. Lord, how she screamed, and how powerless I was to soothe her.

An overwhelmed Doctor Belasco managed, however, to deliver the child.

Frederick Lucius Vanderbaum II. The first born unto this house.

Agnes held him and kissed him.

By morning, exsanguinated, she expired.

Doctor Belasco considered the floor, dry, yet stained as if Agnes' blood had been consumed by the woodwork, and simply remarked, "The soul is in the blood."

November 11, 1875
The wet nurse, Marguerite, has been invaluable. She claims to be of original Walpurgis stock and is dedicated to Frederick. They spent untold hours on the floor where Agnes bled out. "Otherwise, her death has no meaning," Marguerite said.

Frederick is aged but seven months. He walks regularly and possesses uncanny verbal skills.

The first word from his lips was, of course, *Mama*. But the second, dear God, the second.

Shadowless.

March 3, 1877
At less than two years of age, Frederick is reading, an unimaginable, astonishing accomplishment. On several occasions, I discovered him in the library, unaccompanied and unafraid, a book opened, his fingers caressing the pages, mouthing the words in his petite voice, yet his eyes are not upon the page; they stare wide at the monster in the haze, the mountain that—impossibly— shows itself no matter what direction of the compass the eye is cast.

I confess a father's pride eludes me as I find his ability an abhorrence. I loved Agnes with the totality of my heart. We wished only for an heir to carry our name, and now our heir sits spellbound by books years beyond his understanding. The sight of him in his rapture was a fright to both eye and spirit, and I resent his birth ending the life of my beloved.

As sleep eludes me each night, a memory of Winter Howl returns, and I relive my wife's words as the fire-lit prophet, a warning from a man thirty years dead.

We should be on our way from here.

She knew this entire county, not only the house, was damned, born with unslaked thirst; so much so it brought forth her hemorrhage, a devouring all its own, this benighted pile of brick and board, fed by the blood of her womb.

Had I listened, had I been less bullheaded and whisked her away from here, would she have survived childbirth? Would Frederick's development not have been so accelerated?

I brood over the days prior to the house's completion.

The Architect, self-slain upon delivery of his drawings. Had an unbearable knowledge—or worse—unwholesome hand, spurred such action?

The weathervane—a weapon. Had wrought iron been urged into action by that insatiable peak, sending men to their deaths and damning these acres with tragedy?

March 22, 1877
Neither servant nor Marguerite will attest to the origin of the books I discovered tucked away inside cabinets, beneath furniture, in Agnes' dressing room, which I had sealed not long after Frederick's birth.

Terrible volumes. *Deos Sine Umbra. Das Grauenhafte unter uns.*

Witch-books, banned and burned.

Here. In my house.

But is this my house?

I am both a prisoner and trespasser here; there is a purpose to the place I cannot determine. The house merely *tolerates* me.

September 11, 1880
Frederick, now five years of age, stands abnormally tall, yet I have not witnessed the boy take a single bite of food in a year. He sits cross-legged on the floor of the library at all hours of the night, adorned in the fine robes Agnes left behind. Incense, provided no doubt by Marguerite, wreathes him in the smoke of far away lands. Large, ancient books lie open before him. When he speaks, the gas lamps pulse in tandem with every syllable.

"I listen to the boards of this house," he said. "Sawn from trees harvested on *Walpurgisnacht*, they know the will of the stars, the tears in every drop of snow upon Walpurgis Peak. My dear mother suspected, but by then it was too late."

Did she know I would never escape the house I built?

"The house *is* Walpurgis County, Father. It is sinew and bone. Tendon and eye. Memory and future. But know this: the mountain and The House of Vanderbaum are now *one*."

I stared at my five-year-old son, a freak of abnormal growth and frightening intelligence. His voice is that of a sweet little boy, but his words are those of a sage, or worse—a magician.

"Father, there are rules, old rules, and they will be obeyed. You will see that a road is laid to serve this House, and you will name it *Beltane Road*. There will be no other dwelling upon this road, for this is a greedy, jealous house. If I am to be its master one day, then I must obey its king."

Frederick's brow furrowed. At that moment, I saw the man he would become. In that slipstream of time I realized I had not only sired a tyrant of a house but a warlord of a son. This accursed, ugly brute. I dread each brick, every pane of glass, that vile weathervane.

Doors slam with an impudence I thought not possible, a trap eager to spring should I dare breach this unspoken contract and seek a life elsewhere. This house requires a captive.

I have not left the walls of this place since the night Agnes died.

December 20, 1880
As I write, Winter Howl blows ferocious. Near the fireplace, Marguerite nurses Frederick. I find it profane and ugly at his age—not in the sense of Oedipus, but a wickedness all its own. She of Walpurgis blood, and through these years she has passed whatever that entails to him, all in the bosom of this monstrosity I built, a brooding servant to a Master that bellows at the onset of winter.

Frederic suckles at a Shadowless teat, staring at me with one predator eye.

April 19, 1882
I am allowed outside to watch night fall upon the newly laid Beltane Road. It winds across the terrain, a disheartening ribbon of servitude disappearing into the approaching murk.

I do not look at the weathervane.

I know the direction it points.

LIFE RETURNS

I

"**U**NCLE JOHN ISN'T in bed — he seems to have been moved."
I turned over, and there stood my sister Annie, flashlight in
one hand and a Scooter Pie in the other. She pulled me from a boy's
dream, a fantasy of heroism and valor. Suzanna Reed, my crush
since nursery school in San Diego, had found herself in an awful
playground predicament, and I, her champion, gifted with
superpowers and newfound fearlessness, swept down from the
schoolyard's highest eucalyptus and whisked her away from peril.

As Suzanna swooned, blue eyes sparkling, cheeks flushed with
gratitude, sure to reward me, Ian Emerson, an insignificant dweeb
with an overactive imagination, with my first kiss, I opened my
eyes to my redheaded, wide-eyed sister. Annie stomped her feet,
pivoting like someone with a terrible need to urinate, hurriedly
munching her Scooter Pie while waving my Six Million Dollar Man
flashlight like lighthouse suffering an aneurysm. When Annie
became agitated, she snacked, she wiggled, and tolerated nothing
less than my total attention.

"What do you mean, *moved*? And get that flashlight under
control."

"He's not there. Not in his *Sospice*, or whatever that nurse calls it."

I sat up.

"Show me."

Annie tugged me out of bed and onto the cold floor. Outside,
Winter Howl, three nights of frigid wind screaming down the
merciless slopes of Walpurgis Peak, announced the arrival of what
the locals called The Dead Season. It blew through Walpurgis
County singing the praises of the blight ahead—long nights, bare
trees, iron skies, and endless snow.

We crept to the first floor, conspiring agents in a late-night

60

subterfuge. Years ago, in our house in California, my sister and I had done this very thing to sate the burning curiosity brought by Christmas Eve, unable to wait until morning, eager to see what luxuries appeared before the tree between the hours of eight and midnight. Steve Austin's bionic eye was on the case, illuminating the living room and the empty hospital bed standing where the sofa used to be and where the Christmas tree should have stood.

In pale D-Cell light, Uncle John's deathbed looked like something salvaged from a haunted infirmary, a mangled pile of sheets in a corral where human livestock suffered and died. The bladder of his IV bag hung on its stand, and the tube, usually secured by tape to his left arm, lay in the bed like a sleeping snake with a solitary fang. The yellow stink of illness hung in the room like cigar smoke.

"You're right, he's gone," I said.

"How? He's been on *Dorphine*," Annie added.

I love Annie, but some words never clicked in her head, and after numerous scowls and pouting lips, my correcting her ceased quite some time ago.

"That's right. Dorphine keeps him quiet."

"The wind woke me, so I got up for water. When I saw Uncle John was gone, I grabbed a Scooter Pie and came to get you. We should look for him."

I thought, *Should we?*

She eyed me as she had our father when one of her toys broke or a doll lost an eye.

"*Right?*"

The wind coiled around the house. Windows rattled, nails creaked, and pipes groaned. On this, Winter Howl's third and final night, only God knew how many trees and chimneys had been marked for execution.

Annie and I arrived in Walpurgis County in 1976, and though technically home, we were a long way from home, never adjusting to three nights of shrieking banshee wind.

"Right," I said, voice swallowed by a house old as silent films, built when mahogany meant balustrades, brass hinges, and glass doorknobs. The kitchen stood off to the right, its begrudging acquiescence to modernity the Whirlpool fridge and dishwasher. The stove brooded enormous in its alcove, a hulking, cast-iron, match-lit relic, probably too heavy to replace and certainly sufficient for the forest witch to bake Hansel and Gretel. The light fixtures were as dated—*retro*, we'd say these days—as one may imagine, the floor a grid of black and white tiles.

 From the nook behind the pantry, where a dark cubbyhole sequestered the basement door, we heard a faint shuffling sound. Annie turned to me, slid the last of her Scooter Pie home, and swallowed hard.

"The basement," she said.

There was no place he'd rather be.

In southern California, cellars were few and far between, so to Annie and me, a basement represented wealth and success, a fabulous TV room bursting with fun things to do. Most basements are a house's cold, ugly underbelly, crammed with plumbing, spiders, and forgotten things. The cellar of 1864 Gethsemane Lane was no different, a brick vault with the immense weight of the old Craftsman upon it, a mausoleum for memories where its caretaker showed only on laundry day to use the Kenmores beneath the staircase. No warm family gathering spot or air hockey table in a room filled with neon beer signs and sports memorabilia.

I came to find it was something else entirely.

"Well, maybe he's in the bathroom," Annie said.

Bathroom? He shits in a bedpan, I thought, but before I offered my snarky comment, we heard a faint, muffled *thump*.

Best-case scenario—Uncle John crawled out of bed and ended up behind the pantry, propped up against the basement door, eager to return to his underground obsession. My mind's eye saw him in a puddle of pee with his pajamas askew, banging his head like a loose shutter.

Worst-case scenario—he'd made it to the cellar, morphine be damned.

Instead of doing the smart thing, the *sensible* thing—running upstairs, waking Aunt Mary, and telling her Uncle John had gone You Know Where—we crossed those old checkerboard kitchen tiles, nearly tiptoeing past the stove, a fiend forged in harder times. Its primitive robot jaw was shut for the moment, still hungry for the slightest morsel, eyeing us with ceramic handles canted at the angle of angry eyebrows, smelling our child meat through the gaping holes of its burners. I could only imagine the horrors confected in such a monstrosity, a Sears & Roebuck catalog relic from the age of steam engines and buttonhooks. Gas hissed in its cold, black bowel.

Eager to be past the thing, it was Annie who rounded the pantry corner first, hand clasped around my forearm. When the flashlight beam fell upon the basement door, she uttered a sharp little *yip* and squeezed.

"Are those *nails?*" she said.

"Keep the beam steady."

A nervous circle of light hovered over the scuffed doorknob and tarnished keyhole.

Nails the length of cigarettes had been driven sideways through the heavy wood and into the jamb, a bizarre array of thorns, heads flattened and bent, the door panels gouged as our mysterious carpenter worked.

Thump.

We flinched.

"He's in there," she whispered.

ThumpThump.

Confidence boosted by this improvised deadbolt, Annie and I stepped cautiously forward. Ahead, wounded door panels and bent nails. Behind, the hissing kitchen. Beyond *that,* Winter Howl prowled the streets.

Another antique—nothing as dreadful as the oven—presented an opportunity too ripe to resist. I'd seen it done in a hundred movies and a handful of *Scooby-Doo* episodes. Hell, my sister and I had even tried it when we first came to live in the old house.

I put my eye to the keyhole.

A pyramid of light shone at the foot of the stairs, a dusty beam cast by the solitary bulb above. Sick, yellow light, the color of urine and tooth decay. It had been nearly a year since I had set foot in the basement; it was *his* domain now, and Uncle John was welcome to it.

But you want to see. You want to know.

The doorknob rattled, twisting it from the other side. I stumbled into Annie, and down we went. The flashlight rolled away, the beam now a carpet of light shining on the opening between the door and the hardwood floor. The black gap breathed arctic air into the nook.

Through that dark slit, I saw it. An eye. A jaundiced, smoky eye, stained from disease, dilated from morphine and basement darkness. Bloodshot and bulging. Intoxicated, yet lucid. *His* eye. A gray-green dust, fine as baby powder, spilled from the tear duct, a miniature avalanche tumbling down the slope of his nose. Bulging veins. I imagined Uncle John lying on the other side of the door, curled up like a wretched seahorse, panting, crippled and crazy.

"Ian, we go now!"

The wind bellowed, a bully on a rampage. A massive cracking sound followed, no doubt one of Gethsemane Lane's mammoth sycamores crashing into the street. How could this house withstand a third night of abuse if this ferocious wind possessed the might to snap a sycamore like a twig?

A pasty finger wormed through the crack, supplanting the eye, tapping a madman's telegraph message with a long, filthy nail. It flipped over and curled in the beckoning gesture everyone knew.

Come here.

I recognized the split nail on his index finger—Annie too—but neither one of us wanted to say what we already knew. Uncle John had crept from his deathbed and either crawled or fallen down the stairs into that benighted basement, among the spiders and pipes, the nexus of his illness, the source of his fouled mind. The green, crumbling dust. The Shimmer.

Thump!

He was something else now. Something *other*.

Uncle John smashed the door with a firm, deliberate fist. Fury and anger, a man not to be ignored.

!!ThumpThump!!

Aunt Mary nailed the basement shut. How could we have slept through noise like that?

The finger corkscrewed; a prisoner shimmying beneath barbed wire, tapping and trembling, knuckles like pebbles beneath pale skin the color of Spackle.

Come here.

Annie scrambled to her feet, and even with her slippers caught in her nightie, she managed to pull me up. Eyes wide and breath hot as summer, she shuffled in place, crinkling her Scooter Pie wrapper.

"Ian, we need to go upstairs and wake Aunt Mary, right n—"

A flurry of impacts swallowed Annie's voice, followed by the hard crunch of pulverizing wood. Cracks appeared in the door's bottom panel. The crown of nails groaned, the door flexed, and the knob danced in its mooring. But that splintering, that *crushing*, was more frightening than the finger, more severe than the eye. It was a jailbreak, an escape. Uncle John wanted out, and a pair of shit-scared kids were in no position to stop him.

The first tooth appeared, sawing—no *gnawing*—through the door like a mountaineer's pickaxe. An incisor, of course, impaler and meat-ripper, blunt instrument, and delicate tool, seized a small section of the traumatized door panel and pulled it away.

More frozen air escaped through the frayed hole, our private Winter Howl. It snaked around our feet, found its way up my pajama legs and Annie's nightie. My teeth became chattering, clacking castanets. Annie shivered. We backed away, holding one another like a couple of trembling cowards in a misty graveyard because tonight, as far as Walpurgis County was concerned, that's precisely where we were.

More savage gnawing and the gash opened wider still. Steve Austin's fallen bionic eye brought it all into view.

Uncle John's final days had taken their toll. He'd succumbed to emaciation long before condemned to his deathbed, nails fungus-laden claws, hair an oily nest of neglect. But to see his face through that ragged hole, that bloodless, albino white, the color of the Meerschaum pipes my father used to smoke, turned my stomach. Broken blood vessels erupted all over his face and neck like rivers on a map.

He's frozen, like Winter Howl.

Then, crazier thoughts: *He* is *Winter Howl. He* is *Shadowless* ...

His entire mouth filled the space now, a wet, open cave lined with bleeding, receding gums. The insane array of slender shards jammed between his teeth made him look like a man who had eaten a porcupine. Another violent bite. Solid mahogany crumbled.

Uncle John's spidery fingers found their way to the edge of that wooden wound, pulling at the loose ends as his teeth worked the perimeter. It reminded me of the nature films from school, macro photography of caterpillars buzzing their way through leaves. It was worse than that: urgent and sloppy, furious and devil-driven.

His tongue flopped and lolled, eager to form a sentence too ugly to be spoken, a vocalization of those bizarre symbols scrawled on the books that lined his study.

He uttered a simple command instead, but his voice was *wrong*—a dead man's larceny, a robber of innocence.

"MARY. BRING HΣR TŌ mE."

Annie screamed.

65

2

W AIT.
I'm way ahead of myself.

I was eleven years old that terrible night in 1978, Annie nine. When fate uprooted us from sunny San Diego and hauled us across the country to Walpurgis County, I was her age, and she a delicate, wounded girl of seven.

How did the two of us end up in such an awful predicament, parentless and imperiled?

Since you asked . . .

Aunt Mary was our father's sister—*semi-estranged* sister, to be exact. In June of 1975, not long after school let out for summer, our parents, Clyde and Emily Emerson, booked a tenth-anniversary second honeymoon adventure to Hawaii. In a last-minute Hail Mary—no pun intended—after a couple of long-term babysitters had fallen through, Dad bit his bottom lip and called his only sister, prepared to beg if needed, and asked if she'd fly out to San Diego to keep an eye on the niece and nephew she barely knew.

He hung up, looked at our mother, and shrugged.

"Mary jumped at the chance to get away, and was glad to pay the airfare herself."

"You think she's moved past all that . . . " Mom said, wiggling her fingers as a stand-in for words that eluded her. She finally dropped them into her lap and sighed. "All that Witchiepoo idiocy?"

"Well, she's still with John if that's what you mean."

My parents reckoned Uncle John an unwholesome influence on my father's sister. Keep in mind these were the days of Transcendental Mediation and EST. Reverend Moon and Anton LaVey. Richard Nixon in deep shit with the deep state. My mother dismissed Aunt Mary as a crystal-rubbing hippie hanging on to the Summer of Love's frayed ends, led around by a leering conman. A concubine for a creep, a gullible mark, not the ideal candidate to watch the kids for ten days while they were off boozing on Waikiki Beach.

Dad saw her as a flouncy butterfly bohemian, the harmless black sheep sister. When her name came up, he never failed to mention, *You know, kids, your aunt was the Home Run Queen of the 1959 girls softball team. Ten touch-em-alls in thirteen games. A real slugger.*

"Married to that charlatan is bad enough, Clyde, but I don't like that we never know exactly *where* she lives. Remember when I tried, purely out of family courtesy, to send her a Christmas card? Did you know I couldn't find this Walpurgis County on any map, or locate its Zip Code in the directory? I mean *nada, bupkis*. Even Marty at the post office was dumbfounded when I asked him to use whatever resources he had to get that stupid card on its way, and he came up blank as a sheet of notebook paper. Finally he suggested Walpurgis County: General Delivery. It never came back, so for all I know it's in the incinerator with letters to Santa Claus, or it *was* delivered and she just doesn't give a damn. Mary doesn't call the kids, *ever*, not to mention utter indifference to their birthdays. What kind of an aunt does that? Stupid as I was to even *think* about sending her a card, you can honestly forget about her even *acknowledging* Christmas, with all her cosmic-commie-Godlessness. Last time we saw her, not long after Annie was born, she wore a pendant that looked . . . I don't know . . . blasphemous. She burned sage and spoke idiotic, hocus-pocus Age of Aquarius B.S. over both the kids. Remember *that*? *Jesus!*"

Dad rolled his eyes.

"It's that goddamn man she's with. Don't get me started on John Ingersoll. She worships that loser like a cult leader. You may not want to admit it because she's your sister and you love her, and I get that—but that man is cancer."

"I know, Emms, Mary's a little out there, but she's the only move we have left. It's that or cancel our trip."

"Leaving Ian and Annie with a wackadoodle is worse than missing a few days in Honolulu. I can watch Hawaii-Five-O and live vicariously through Jack Lord."

"Hey, come on," Dad said. "We've been planning this for a year. We have one small problem, and you're ready to toss it."

"Jesus, Clyde, it's *Mom-Radar*, and mine is *screeching*."

"Well," Dad said as he turned his pockets inside-out, which

meant *I've already laid out a bundle for airfare and hotels, and it's too late for a refund.* "What do you want to do?"

Two days later, Aunt Mary showed up in a Yellow Cab, dressed in bell-bottom jeans and a floral-print top with flowing wizard sleeves. She wore enormous, purple Elton John sunglasses and a floppy Janis Joplin hat, which barely corralled a sprawling mane streaked with gray. She made her way up the driveway with an overnight bag and a big leather purse. Behold, The Home Run Queen of 1959.

Annie and I were excited to see her, having met her only once when I was younger than Annie, and she was a newborn—so Annie didn't remember her at all.

Our mother watched from the kitchen window, arms folded, barely concealing a scowl with a smoldering Kent King bobbing in her lips as Aunt Mary stood outside the window and waved.

After an icy welcome from Mom and warm hugs from Dad, Aunt Mary took her shades off and looked at Annie and me.

"Ian, you're big as a horse. Annie, you're a beautiful redhead sure to break hearts. You two ready to have a little fun while your folks have theirs?"

The way Mom's face crumpled like a paper bag, I thought she was about to pass a kidney stone. Instead, she quipped, "Just make sure everyone stays alive," then left the room without so much as a glance at anyone.

Aunt Mary watched Mom stomp away, looked at us, sighed, wiggled her eyebrows, and smiled bigger than Dallas.

"We have ten days of fun to plan," she said. "Soon as I'm settled in, we'll make a list. Sea World, the Zoo, burger joints, and silly hats!"

We loved her immediately.

Six days after *that*, ecstatic in a whirlwind of activities and staying up late, popcorn and movies, ice cream at the beach, and take-out food for dinner, our parents were killed in a sight-seeing plane crash on Oahu. I, of course, was not given the details—it was Aunt Mary who took the phone call, and the sorrowful way she looked at me with the receiver to her ear froze my heart—but the nickel version, if there could be one for such things, is their twin-engine Beechcraft slammed right into Diamond Head in front of everyone and their dog, killing all on board instantly, then rolled down its slope in a trail of flames. I was told there had been television news coverage of the smoking aftermath, and to this day, I have never seen it, nor want to.

The big question after the funerals and wakes (as this story unfolds, I will talk about many horrific things, but I will never, *ever* speak of that) was, of course, what to do with us. Our paternal grandparents had been dead for years, and our mother's folks were so old that there was no way they could handle two traumatized grandchildren. Mom was an only child, and our godparents were never named. There was, as they now say in conference rooms nationwide, *a resource deficit*.

Enter Aunt Mary and Uncle John.

Our unimaginable shock was compounded by the months-long process of selling our home and all its contents. In the meantime, family court filings circulated through the system, and the custody forms were notarized, circumcised, canonized, or whatever-ized. By spring of 1976, Annie and I had become permanent residents of 1864 Gethsemane Lane under the guardianship of our father's next of kin: John and Mary Ingersoll of Danielsburg, Walpurgis County.

We cried nearly the entire way across the country.

Uncle John, a balding, six-foot-plus cornstalk of a man significantly older than Aunt Mary, drove the entire way and never once complained about fatigue, traffic, or weather. It was as if he was on a job more than a rescue mission, dedicated as a soldier, focused as a circus acrobat. Having never met the man until he arrived in California to sign the legal documents seven months after our parents died, I honestly did not know what to expect other than the opinions fed to me by our mother and Aunt Mary's half-hearted praises on the nights he'd call. I had spoken briefly to him on the phone, Annie even less, and his voice seemed neutral as beige paint. From where I stood, Uncle John was just a boring old man doing his wife one hell of a favor.

But there was an air about him, an indifference far beyond the aloofness of most middle-aged men. It's not that he seemed burdened by their guardianship, but that Annie and I were something to be studied. That look in his eye alone made me fear for my sister.

We'd never been this far east or more than two hours from the ocean, the road ahead a vast black stripe painted atop the desert. With our hearts broken and our friends left behind, it felt like we'd gone from paradise into peril, dependability into disaster.

When Aunt Mary occasionally twisted around to watch Annie and me, I saw that same heartsick expression when she took that call from the Honolulu Police on that horrible afternoon. The year previous had planted dark seeds, and cynicism had begun to take root, so off her look, I suspected a sympathetic facade, the kind of happy face Mom put on after she and Dad had a little tiff. I immediately chastised myself for thinking such a thing. Aunt Mary had wept deeply for her brother; she'd done her best to hold motherless children together as their world collapsed.

But when she looked at Uncle John, her demeanor changed to that of a dog in fear of its master. The compassion in her eyes extinguished as they turned round and sad, her rosy cheeks pale and hollow. Aunt Mary's shoulders fell—slight but noticeable—the happy-go-lucky aging hippie transformed into the bedeviled wife. How she looked at us had been genuine, and worse, I began to think Mom had been right about Uncle John.

I remembered what Dad said: *She jumped at the chance to get away.*

Our second day on the road found us on Route 60, headed east through New Mexico. Gargantuan high-tension towers lined the highway, colossal sentries disappearing into the big nowhere. An old-style gas station came and went.

Annie leaned into my ear and whispered, "Do you think Aunt Mary's afraid of Uncle John?"

Aunt Mary's nervous eyes appeared in her sun visor's little vanity mirror.

Hush now, you two. He hears everything.

Uncle John clearly possessed some type of bully radar because his barbecue smoke eyes immediately snapped to me in the rearview. The leading edge of a smirk pinched one cheek.

She's right, boy. I hear it all.

Annie stayed close to me from then on, so much so that we shared a bedroom for nearly six months after arriving at that brooding Craftsman on Gethsemane Lane. Despite our early introduction to tragedy, Aunt Mary wanted us to have an everyday life.

That proved wishful thinking on her part. Our arrival in Walpurgis County felt like something out of those Hammer horror films Dad and I used to watch, where the first sight of Dracula's castle drove a bolt of terror into anyone unlucky enough to set eyes upon it.

Walpurgis Peak was no different.

Upon exiting the interstate, we entered a confusing snarl of turns egged on by orange arrows: DETOUR, they read. Clearly familiar with this route, Uncle John steered the big Mercury onto a two-lane highway, Route 54. The road began its slow ascent, and before long, the hills bulged with boulders like giant tumors, trees sprouting between them at crazy angles, entwined into a nearly impenetrable canopy, splattering wild shadows upon the road.

At the end of a seemingly endless curve, we saw it: a mammoth fang, a sole ugly tooth. Walpurgis Peak pierced the tree line, casting a monstrous shadow over the forest below. Annie and I had never seen anything so colossal. So atrocious.

Annie gasped, not in wonder like when she first laid eyes upon Disneyland's Matterhorn, but as if she'd stumbled upon a car wreck, or the site of her parents' plane crash. Her mouth drooped into a dark 0, sneakers pressed against the back of the driver's seat. Her eyes bulged, trembling in their sockets, too overwhelmed to look away.

Paralysis surrendered to tears, and she crammed her little face into the crook of my neck and bawled.

Uncle John laughed under his breath, then celebrated Annie's anxious dread by humming an ominous tune. It was years later I recognized it as *Night On Bald Mountain*.

He straightened in the driver's seat like a tower guard. In fluent German he said, *"Sie blicken auf das majestätische, eines der Wachberge der Welt!"*

"John," Aunt Mary said. "You're making it worse." She turned and saw Annie crushed against me, face red, tears flowing. She glared back at her husband, and if looks could kill, he may not have dropped dead, but he would have been in ICU for a week.

"It's not okay here," Annie said through spit-bubbles and sobs. "I want to go home. I want to go to *our* house."

I wrapped Annie in both arms and said to Uncle John, perhaps more pointedly than he was used to hearing, "What did you just say to Annie?"

He gawked at that hideous mountain, marveling at its jagged hide and crooked granite spine. "I didn't say it to her. I said it to you: *You gaze at the majestic, one of the sentinel mountains of the world.*"

Our eyes met in the mirror, Uncle John's ill with smoke, a gray edging toward black, mine nervous and inexperienced. He cracked an arrogant smile, the grin of an old man who gloats because he'd outlived his friends.

"John, *honestly*," Aunt Mary said. She folded her arms and stared at her lap.

Uncle John didn't speak to either Annie or me for a couple of days after that.

The nexus of Walpurgis County is, without a doubt, that ugly eyesore of a mountain, the deliverer of the Winter Howl phenomena I mentioned earlier. Some say a second tier of fallen angels landed on the slopes of Walpurgis Peak not long after the first drop of traitors at Baalhermon, dragging with them the knowledge of metals and elixirs, the workings of the cosmos, and *phramakeia*—all forms of magic and sorcery. Whatever the legend's genesis, the mountain is a vile, blasphemous stack of blighted stone, crooked as every deal with Satan. It broods over its subjects, jealous and deranged. Insane.

I vividly remember my first day at Danielsburg Elementary, about a week after we arrived. I stood between the jungle gym and the carousel, unnerved by the sight of that monstrosity and the dreadful thought that it was *looking at me*. As a southern California transplant, I wasn't accustomed to large mountains, I'd seen them only in movies and books, and to be in the proximity of one that was certifiably mad brought such an overwhelming sense of dread that I still grope for the proper words to describe it.

Behind Danielsburg Elementary's central hub of brick buildings, Walpurgis Peak dominated the miles-away haze, appearing all the larger for it. I turned North toward the town center, where Route 54 snaked up a rise in the landscape to meet Beltane Road, and there it stood again in mocking arrogance, the light completely different—the *hour* of the light, I should say. Clouds shunned it, even crows wanted nothing to do with it. East toward the morning sun, its contemptuous silhouette an immense siege tower left behind by an invading race of giants.

Impossible? Absolutely—just not in Walpurgis County. Par for the course as we adjusted to life without our parents and the upheaval of culture shock, haunted by trauma's lingering spectre.

LIFE RETURNS

The house on Gethsemane Lane was part of it, a Craftsman built in the time of iceboxes and chain-pull toilets, gas lamps, and servant's quarters. As the months dragged on, we became not immune to the bizarre conditions in that house but certainly desensitized. The weird tales I heard of Dead Neck Lake and Copperhead Farms only added fuel to the fire. To a newbie, Walpurgis County felt like the night before Halloween and the day after an earthquake.

So, please bear with me; we must detour further. My memories of Uncle John's odd unraveling should be told in as much detail as I can recall, as his dark identity fed yet a darker obsession, culminating on the final night of Winter Howl, 1978.

And yes, it's all about the basement.

3

ANNIE HAD STOPPED blubbering by the time Uncle John took a right onto Beltane Road, but the sitting pee-pee dance persisted until we pulled onto Gethsemane Lane. The house was quite lovely from the outside with its dark green siding, white window frames, stained pillars, and generous porch. We'd been raised in a small tract home a few blocks from a Stop 'N' Go and a walk-up burger joint, so to us, this dual-chimney hulk nestled between massive sycamores was like moving into a mansion.

Uncle John pulled the Mercury into the garage, hauled the bags from the trunk, and disappeared without a glance. Aunt Mary showed us into the enormous old place, and once we'd had an eyeful of the grandfather clock, stained glass, and Persian rugs, she ushered us to the second floor on a staircase large enough to have its own area code.

After an hour or two of exploration, including the Jack and Jill bathroom just like *The Brady Bunch*, Aunt Mary brought dinner. Fried chicken and all the fixings. Despite the depressing cross-country drive and our horrendous first sighting of Walpurgis Peak, this first night, at least, was off to a pretty good start. She did her best to make us feel welcome, and we didn't have to eat with Uncle John.

Aunt Mary wore several necklaces adorned with crystals, hummingbird feathers, and tiny pewter doodads. All she needed was a silk scarf and jangling medallions to complete her transformation into the county fair fortune teller. However, this evening, Aunt Mary was chef and waitress, still a mixer of elixirs, and dinner smelled terrific.

"I'm sorry about this afternoon." She set the little table near a window partially obscured by one of the gigantic sycamores. Far away, the summit of the mountain glared at the house like a gouged, ugly eye. Despite a slight tug of dark fascination, I managed to pull *my* eyes away. "He's not used to having kids around. Actually, that applies to us both, I'm afraid."

"He was mean to me," Annie said without hesitation.

"I know, Annie-girl. I'm sorry about that. I'll talk to him tonight, tell him to cool that hot streak of his."

"I'm staying in here with Ian."

Aunt Mary stroked Annie's red mane as her eyes shifted to me. "That okay with you, big fella?"

Face-deep into my second drumstick, I nodded. There were two beds in the room anyway, and although at my age I should have preferred to be alone, this house was new, the trip terrible, the mountain an unforeseen scare, so I wanted Annie with me.

Months later, not long after Aunt Mary shuffled Annie off to her own room (and more than ready for solitude after many Scooter Pie episodes spawned by her bad dreams), I woke regularly around 3 AM, restless and anxious. I feared Annie's nightmares, a relentless replay of the death of our parents, were somehow contagious, so if I woke up in the middle of the night before dreams settled in, then so much the better. I preferred fatigue to nightmares.

I'll just stay up. I have books. I'll be tired at school but who cares.

After a few sleepless nights, I heard murmurings downstairs, quiet at first, muffled and indistinguishable, easy to dismiss as the TV or Uncle John and Aunt Mary talking. But at this hour? I knew the TV explanation was bogus the second night I heard Uncle John's unmistakably beige rasp, and Aunt Mary always hit the sack by nine.

Is he speaking to someone? On the phone?

Doubtful. The house was equipped with ornate, heavy phones, the stuff of old movies, barely a generation removed from the antique candlestick model used by Yvonne De Carlo in *The Munsters*. He was no fan of such things, so I dismissed it.

I got up and tiptoed barefoot to the top of the stairs. Nothing but shadows in the living room, a single lamp in the study cast a wedge of light onto the parquet floor.

By the time I reached the spot between the kitchen and the study, it was apparent the noise emanated from the basement, a *mechanical* sound, an undeniable rhythm, buried, it seemed, in the echo of distance, as if the sound emanated from miles away—but in the basement nonetheless.

Whurrrmp-Fwack—Whurrrmp-Fwack

I imagined rods on rails, pumps pushing fluids, the chug of a terminally ill locomotive. I'd been in the basement a handful of times, and other than a Stanley toolbox, garden tools, and an old wheelbarrow, I never took Uncle John for the handyman type. The study consumed his time, filled with books the size of a Rand-McNally atlas, bindings scrawled in languages I didn't recognize, plastered in designs that looked like a cross between cave paintings and astronomy diagrams. His time was spent with his mind, not his hands.

Uncle John's study radiated its own sense of warning, but if I wanted to know more about this odd machine noise, I'd have to traverse the kitchen's checkerboard tile, pass that hissing predator stove, and peer down those steep, dark stairs.

Cross the path of one ugly brute to perhaps lay eyes upon another?

Not tonight. No way, José.

A few weeks after my first night outing, Annie gave my shin a little kick beneath the dinner table. She flipped a nod toward Uncle John as he stared into his soup, one eye on the bowl, the other rudderless and floundering.

She mouthed the words, *Is he drunk?*

Muttering and grumbling, Uncle John's unshaven turkey-neck skin crawled over his Adam's apple, his razor sudden stranger. If there's one thing about Uncle John you could count on, he was neat as a pin. Now his hair clung unwashed to his scalp, forehead clammy and misted with sweat. Dirt under his nails. Grime on his fingers. He looked like a villain in a Clint Eastwood western. But drunk? Unlikely. I'd never seen him drink so much as a beer.

I shrugged and mouthed back, *Sick?*

"This house has been chosen, but nothing is free," Uncle John croaked, voice brittle as his cracked lips. "We pay for the privilege, one way or the other. Bags hiss. Mighty ingots slide inside the Great Machine—"

"John, the *kids*." Aunt Mary interrupted.

He leaned and examined Aunt Mary with his single, focused eye. Soup steam eddied around his nose and wide, convoluted ears. I noticed his gumline receded since the last time I'd been this close to him. Inflamed, fleshy pillows billowed from between teeth with their roots exposed, miniature piano keys carelessly stuffed into his skull, a few now leaning at lazy angles.

Uncle John smacked the table with his open palm. Everything shook.

"Not a word from you, barren Aphrodite," he said, pointing a filthy index finger at his wife. "A womb of old twigs and a snatch to match. A dime store witch harboring dreams of becoming a sorceress. No need to scour the Undervoid for a suitable dish to bake my seed, no need to sully my altar—"

"*Goddammit, John!*"

His mouth snapped shut, but not for long. He shifted his poisonous gaze to Annie and sneered.

"You may prove useful when you're old enough to bleed, Freshling. Only a few more summers need pass until we find out." With his swimming eye, he winked at her. "Don't be like that corn husk at the end of the table."

He reached out to touch Annie with his dirt-crusted fingers, but she sprang like a Jack-in-the-box, pushing her chair back until she was out of reach of his scarecrow's arm. Smart girl.

"Clyde and Emily. It took most everything I had to reach them from this distance. You know how hard these things are, Freshling? What it takes from a man to serve Those Others, let alone summon the guile to ask for a favor, access to their realm?"

"What do you mean *reach* Clyde and Emily?" I said.

"John," Aunt Mary said. "John, no. Just don't. Don't go there." She summoned Annie with a rapid beckoning gesture. Annie went to her.

Uncle John spread his arms wide, dipping his shoulders as his voice mimicked an airplane's struggling engine.

"*Neeeeeeeer!*"

Pitching side to side, his lazy eye rolled. He focused the good eye on me from beneath cinched eyebrows, chin nearly in his minestrone, arms straight as a board.

"It was mayday for less than a minute, but what a long minute it was. That poi-eater in the left seat never knew what hit him when the stick became dead weight. I'll bet he turned white as his Haolie payload."

Aunt Mary wrapped her arms around Annie. She glared at her husband with an ire that I, even then, suspected had brewed for quite a while.

And then I read it on her face.

You killed my brother.

Uncle John's entire demeanor changed on a dime. When he spoke again, it was in our father's voice, a perfect match of his cadence and timbre. He even mimicked Dad's facial mannerisms, down to his intermittently raised eyebrow when making a point. It froze me to my marrow.

"Guess we won't be needing the shuttle bus back to the Hilton, Emms, because *this* second honeymoon is *kaput.*" Arms imitating the wings of their doomed Beechcraft, he twirled his index finger as Dad was known to do when he conveyed a royal SNAFU. His face opened into our father's lovable grin, the one that had charmed our mother, his clients, and even my little league coaches. "Hope you paid the life insurance and fed the cat, because this is it, Emms. We're tits up and tootle-oo!"

Annie burst into tears. Aunt Mary was out of her chair and down on one knee before you could say Jack Robinson, shielding Annie.

"John, you monster!"

Uncle John's desiccated lips opened, every nightmare tooth a yellow gravestone. He summoned his rusted voice, still soaring on his makeshift wings, eyes never leaving mine.

"Everyone screamed when they saw the mountain come at them—don't think for a second they didn't know. They felt *everything.* And Diamond Head is a *pussy* hill, son—it's nothing compared to the *Master*, the Master outside these very windows, Sentinel to the Shadowless, a feeder of giants."

You bastard, I thought, but too stunned and intimated to speak it. He read my face, changing voices at will and speaking now with the exaggerated drawl of a tent revival preacher.

"Mayday! Mayday! Can I get an Amen? Oooo Lawdy, weez gwine up to hebbin! *Neeeeeeeerrrrr!*"

He dipped his arms again, enjoying his sick pantomime of that twin engine Beechcraft as it whined toward the volcano overlooking Waikiki Beach.

"Fadder, son and Holy Ghost, dat Heavenly Host done gots da most! Pass me dems grits and melba toast, cuz down we heads straight for da coast!"

When I looked for Annie, she'd been ushered out of the dining room. Aunt Mary wheeled around to Uncle John, her mouth pulled into a sneer, eyes narrow, focused slits of hate. She may have grown accustomed to years of abuse and suffering, but now that abuse had been turned toward an eight-year-old girl. John Ingersoll had finally crossed the line. She waved for me to join them.

But my God, had he really caused that plane to crash?

Uncle John moved with serpentine speed and seized my wrist, twisting so that I did not doubt his intent or willingness to follow through. *I will snap your bones, boy. Stay put.*

"Up to your room, Annie-girl," Aunt Mary said. "I'll be there in just a minute."

Annie bolted upstairs, sniffling, snuffling, and finally slamming the door.

"You hear things at night," Uncle John said, voice barely above a whisper. "A rhythmic sound?"

His smoke-colored eyes bored into me. No matter how innocuous, I felt every little secret was visible to him. Something had transformed him over the last three weeks, and if it was sickness, it gestated quietly until exploding in one ugly episode, moving now hell for leather.

"Answer me."

Thoughts jumbled, emotions frayed, I said, "Yeah, I do," my voice thin and girlish, the pressure behind my eyes near the breaking point. If I cracked and blubbered, things would only get worse. My God, how I wanted my parents here, Mom shaming him while Dad beat his ass with a 9 Iron.

"Your sister is closed off, but you're beginning to see. Do you want to see, Ian? Do you want to know what thrums beneath Walpurgis Peak? How it feeds?"

The very mention of that mountain made me squirm.

"There are doorways here in the Purg. *Shimmers*, we call them. And this house sits atop one that opens at will. It can stay closed for years, decades, even, but lately, ever since you arrived—" He looked over his shoulder to the nook behind the pantry. Although the basement door stood out of view, its presence was suddenly felt.

"Time is fluid. It moves, it *flows*. Come to the coal chamber. You'll see it. *Feel* it."

I tried to pull away. He squeezed. It hurt.

"There's a spark in you, Ian Emerson. Why else would I have gone so far out of my way to get you here? It took over a month's recovery time after reaching out six thousand miles to Hawaii. You think that was *easy*?"

My God, he's serious.

"Your stupid aunt put on a show for nearly a decade, had me fooled that there was nothing special about you. Why else do you think she ignored you and your sister for years?"

I didn't know what to say, gripped by my father's murderer as he scanned me with a liquid, sloppy eye, the sour stink of his breath blended into a noxious gas with the odor of his stale soup. I hoped for Aunt Mary to sweep in and break up this little heart-to-heart.

"But that Christmas card from your mother changed everything. Once I touched it, I knew. A mother's connection runs very deep, and hers was no exception. It was all over that stupid red envelope."

I recalled Mom's agitation at trying to get that card to Walpurgis County. That was in 1970. By the time Aunt Mary arrived at our house in the summer of 1975, Mom had written her off. But she was right about one thing: Uncle John had Aunt Mary in his grip.

"Your aunt was never *disinterested* in you. She thought she was *protecting* you from me. I have plans for your sister, yes." His eyes narrowed, even the goopy one, and he licked his lips. I'd broken my nose when I fell off my bike in second grade, and it bled like crazy. I wished that for him now. "But *your* talents need to be steered. Coached. You were born for Walpurgis County—*you just don't know it yet.*"

The table shook again, a greater violence than Uncle John's flattened palm.

Aunt Mary stood at the foot of the table, leaning onto an old, battered Louisville Slugger. She'd slammed its business-end smack-dab between the pork tenderloin and Corningware bowl of green beans. Her locomotive stare had all the steam of a woman who, at least this night, had had enough.

"Reliving your glory days again I see." Uncle John released my wrist. I was out of the chair so fast I think it surprised him. He looked at Mary with that smoky, disconnected sheen. When someone says glassy-eyed, they don't know what they're talking about, but one look at John Ingersoll is the definition of redefinition. He flicked his hand toward The Home Run Queen of 1959 as if shooing a pest.

"Get upstairs, Ian," Aunt Mary said, her breath deep and steady. Her chest and shoulders heaved, but her hands trembled. The butt of the Louisville Slugger tapped out a faint rhythm on the table.

"You leave those two kids out of all this, John. That's *not* why they're here."

I backed up against the sideboard and stood like one of those guards at Buckingham Palace, arrow straight with a PhD in Shut The Fuck Up.

Uncle John tilted his chair back, cool as a crime boss. "Heroine doesn't suit you. Stick to the tourism of crystals and tarot. Be the carnival spook you were meant to be and stay out of business beyond your scope and vision."

Aunt Mary's face flushed red, and Uncle John's lit up. He'd hit paydirt and meant to collect.

"You're more amateur than auteur. A bumbler in the shadow of greatness. Consider your fortune, allowed to stumble through a series of parlor tricks and the whims of lesser gods while in the presence of the Master."

For a moment, Aunt Mary appeared crestfallen. I thought about her talismans hanging on the windowsills and the sage burning on the mantle. The bathrooms displayed framed sketches of smiling, coy fairies and watercolors of butterflies leaving steams of brilliant light in their wake—all hippie-dippie stuff, a manifestation of too much Avalon and Middle Earth, Ren-Faires, and coffee houses.

In Uncle John's study, it was dusty books with unreadable nonsense on their spines, an odd device that looked like a cross between a telescope and a sextant near the window—always pointed toward Walpurgis Peak—and several taxidermy crows mounted in flight above the fireplace. If it was a pissing contest over who was more ooga-booga, well, Uncle John had that title in the bag.

Aunt Mary regained composure. His insults may have lodged under her skin, but they would travel no further.

"There's no excuse for this. You're saying terrible things to them, let alone *me*."

"I've seen *it*, Mary. Here, through the Shimmer. The boy should be privy to it. Open his mind's eye."

She jabbed the bat into the table. The silverware clanged.

"No."

"It has *needs*." He purred the words. "Sustenance. Continuance. Longevity."

She did it again, harder this time.

"*No.*"

"It's true, all of it. I was haunted by doubt, but no more. It's there, thrumming under Walpurgis Peak, keeping one of *Them* alive. I told the boy this and now I'll tell you. It never revealed itself to me until they came to live here." He held his hands up so Aunt Mary could see. "Look at my filthy hands. I labor because there's a treasure beneath this house that they want, and in that sweet Freshling upstairs."

She turned to me, but never let her grip on the bat falter.

"Ian, out. *Now.*"

I didn't waste any time and made for the stairs. Before distance muffled their conversation, I distinctly heard Uncle John say:

"They chose this house, Mary. They'll have their way."

Uncle John did something I'd never thought him capable: he laughed. It was the laugh of someone who has discovered gold on the family's back forty, a cry of glee and disbelief followed by the cackle of a man determined to keep the gold for himself.

When he'd finished, there was a moment of silence.

Aunt Mary said, "Not on my watch."

4

FOLLOWING HIS CRUEL performance at the dinner table, Annie and I gave Uncle John a wide berth. He spent his days in the study, his nights in the basement. Aunt Mary, on the other hand, had grown more doting and loving—especially to Annie. How my mother had ever misinterpreted her behavior will always be a mystery to me.

Weeks passed. Nights came and went, and I rarely slept them through. With greater frequency, I heard Uncle John leave the bedroom, wheezing in his stale bread walk down the staircase.

He'd become gaunt as a gravedigger. I couldn't remember the last time I saw him eat, and on several occasions, I heard him puking in the bathroom. Aunt Mary seemed immune to his retching; she never once raised a finger or inquired about his welfare. She'd made her point that night with the Louisville Slugger.

Uncle John couldn't care less, as his focus was clear. Every night it was up out of bed, followed by a brief struggle with the stairs. Not long after, I heard his sandpaper voice and the cadence of some kind of pump or lathe, but what did I know at eleven?

Of course, I knew. He'd looked me straight in the eye and said it at the dinner table over his soup and murder confession.

The Machine.

Most mornings found Uncle John at the dining room table, eyes rheumy and bloodshot, skin and lips cracked like a man who had crossed the Mojave on foot. Aunt Mary waltzed right past him without a word, although she never failed to fetch his coffee and, I think, gloated at his inability to consume it.

"Beneath every sentinel mountain of the world," the ashen man mumbled, hissing as he pulled back from his steaming cup. From underneath his deteriorating eyebrows, he shot a rueful look to

Aunt Mary, then focused on me as I ate my cereal. King Vitamin, if you must know.

"Follow me to my study."

I froze for a moment with my spoon halfway to my mouth, milk dripping. I glanced toward the kitchen, hoping to catch Aunt Mary's attention, but Uncle John's voice, now the timbre of a much older man, brought my gaze back to him.

"Do it."

He disappeared into the study. I'd only gawked at the room from the outside, wondered about its flock of stuffed crows, and the brass scope pointed at the mountain. I never dared enter, and not out of some sense of obedience. I *knew* the place was wrong. Still, at its threshold that morning, a rush of adrenaline tempted me otherwise.

I wanted to see. I wanted to know.

Plus, I'd been invited.

He leaned against a beast of a desk. Whatever he'd been up to in the basement was all over his rumpled shirt and khakis. He set the cup down and crossed his arms.

"You can stand out there if you like, Ian." He looked to the brass scope. The early morning light cast a soft beam through the window, painting the apparatus in fire. "Or come in here and hear the unspeakable secret of secrets."

How do I say no to that? I wondered.

Instead, "Are you feeling okay?" was all I could think to say.

"None of that matters."

I stepped inside. There was no rush of cold, no whispering voices from the Blank Dimension. Just a room filled with pursuits foreign to me, books, devices, and carvings that would have never been allowed in our house in San Diego.

Uncle John studied me. Not with his eyes—they were closed. He took a deep breath and exhaled an ultra-fine plume of dust from his nostrils.

"You fight curiosity," he said. "A barrier built in an old life."

Although I felt as if I'd been called on in class and hadn't been paying attention, his voice harbored no anger or discipline.

"You can't stay at the top of the stairs forever. One night you will come down there, *with us*. They're all over the world, young man."

"What's all over the world?"

LIFE RETURNS

Uncle John grinned a wide rictus of a smile, the eater of children in a fairy tale. He opened his eyes.

"Machines. Grand Machines. And one is here, the beating heart of Walpurgis Peak. Each one keeps one of *Them* alive in stasis, a dream-fugue state beyond our comprehension. Wonders. Terrors. *Magnificence.* The price we pay to fuel its might is high, the reward incalculable. When the day comes, the world will gawk like idiots, speechless in the presence of greatness."

He turned his head to the window, and I refused to follow his gaze. Uncle John couldn't help but adore his precious mountain, a mammoth cripple rife with dread and osteoporosis, snarling atop the wilderness. How many hours had he spent with his eye to that elaborate device of his, part mariner's sextant, part astronomer's lens?

Instead, I examined the bookshelves. Packed to the edges, several large volumes lay atop rows of books to accommodate the overflow. Lots of leather and gold leaf, but very few titles in English. Some bore no title, only weird, geometrical symbols, things I'd seen in old films, set dressing from a wizard's lair or perhaps the home of the witch from whom that oven was stolen.

"They'll emerge," he said, voice like gravel, eyes still on the window, one hand on his hip. All he needed was a skull in his palm to complete his Hamlet impression. "Tethered to their miles upon miles long apparatus. Imagine this."

He raised one hand toward the ceiling, craning his neck as if to glimpse the top of some enormous skyscraper. "Beings high as the sequoia, fierce as any war, roaming this world—*their* world— in anticipation of the Master's arrival." His hand dropped to the desk with a soft *thunk.*

"Master?" my voice barely above a whisper.

Uncle John leaned in. For the moment, I'd utterly forgotten he'd taken responsibility for my parents' murder, leered at my sister, and abused the aunt I'd come to love. He smiled like a harlequin on the verge of suicide, a skin mask of puffed gums and loose teeth, tongue white and dry as a bone. To his right, the murder of stationary crows cast deep shadows on the wood-paneled walls.

He breathed the words with a penitent's reverence.

"The Architect of Zero."

What happened to him in the basement? He's losing his mind.

"Not yet, Ian. The mind will go last. I know you yearn to come down the stairs. Cross the threshold."

He raised his palms, dust pattering the carpet as his fingers unfolded. His blistered fingers never had time to callous; he'd worked his skin raw.

"These hands maintain a small part of a grand design, aiding the Broken One in its convalescence, an old, hurting warhorse. And yet, my service, though small, does not go unnoticed. See how the sun burns through the window, how bright it is, how full of hope? Now, look at the desk, Ian. See my reward."

I looked at the desktop. To my amazement, Uncle John cast only a *partial* shadow, gray and sick, half the opacity as my own. The light passed through his body as if he'd been rendered translucent.

I looked at his hands and back to the desk, hands to the desk; a simpleton enthralled by a bouncing ball.

"Yes," he said. "*Becoming*. Becoming *Shadowless*."

Impossible.

"No, Ian, with The Shadowless Ones all things are possible. All things can be seen. When The Gate finally opens . . . " After a breath rattling with pebbles of phlegm, Uncle John ran the tip of his tongue underneath his upper teeth. A few surrendered to the pressure, moving like the piano keys I imagined them to be. "I said you were born with a gift. It needs to be developed. Down below, there, in the basement, *I* can teach you. Young hands mean faster work, but old hands show them how."

What adventurous boy would refuse such a thing, even if offered by a shadowless ghoul? In the days of Evel Knievel, decades before PlayStation, you found your fun at the risk of a broken arm or a twisted bicycle. But foolish childhood bravery notwithstanding, I *feared* that man. Maybe no longer physically— he was too weak—but he'd been inside my mind easy as pie, not to mention he claimed to have slaughtered our parents remotely, *supernaturally*, from thousands of miles away.

That scared me.

He eyed Walpurgis Peak with a cult member's reverence, Renfield groveling as his master defiled him.

"I am no more than soup for its belly."

More basement rumblings. As the grandfather clock turned over to yet another small hour after midnight, gurgling pumps passed fluid into the deepest regions of some awful, gibbering device.

And each night, as Uncle John said, I stood at the top of the basement stairs, staring in wonder at the wash of green light from below, eager to join him. Eager to know.

He knew I was there, absolutely.

Whurrrmp-Fwack—Whurrrmp-Fwack

5

CANCER, MARY, Dr. Friedman said. *Metastasized, spread to his organs and bones.*
I thought as much, Dr. Friedman.

I had an idea of what a woman sounded like when receiving bad news, but Aunt Mary was not it.

He's unreachable, he doesn't really speak to me anymore.

When Dr. Friedman pulled up in his blue Oldsmobile Delta 88, a few weeks had passed since Uncle John revealed his fading shadow. I'd seen Friedman a couple of weeks ago disappear into the study to talk to Uncle John. A half-hour later, the good doctor emerged wearing the grave expression of an undertaker. Upon seeing his Oldsmobile roll up a second time, and too curious for my own good, I ducked between a bookshelf and an end table, mouse-quiet, eavesdropping as Dr. Friedman broke patient confidentiality with Aunt Mary.

Annie made no secret of her enthusiasm for Uncle John's decline, smirking every time he limped past us with his bowed back, toothpick legs, and hollow cheeks. After he passed, she imitated his old crone gait and trembling jaw, then looked over at me and giggled.

"I can smell the sick on him," Annie said one Friday night as we endlessly switched between the four available channels. *The Incredible Hulk* was a rerun tonight, so we had a gap to fill.

"Well, he's not bathing," I said.

"*I know.* He's *covered* in dirt."

"I think he's going crazy while dogging or whatever it is he's up to in the basement. I hear crazy people stop taking care of themselves."

"He's worse than crazy, Ian."

There was a clatter as the antique telephone fell to the floor. The phone's interior bells dinged, and Uncle John hissed as he struggled with the cable coiled around his ankle. When it pulled taught, he stopped, sneered, and with great effort, untied his leg and moved on. The phone remained on the floor, dial tone blaring, collateral damage from a much larger war.

"I think he's *gutagious*," Annie whispered after he shuffled past, reeking of sour sweat and dirty clothes. "He'll give us crazy germs."

He stopped, and I mean *statue* stopped. The only thing that moved was the tunnel of his shirt sleeve. He kept his back to us. His bald spot was now the size of his fist.

"It's *Con*tagious, you shitwit."

"See what I mean?" she said into my ear. "Even *he* knows."

Oh, he knew. He knew just where he was headed.

That day, crammed between the bookshelf and the end table, I learned I had a knack for stealth, and learned a new word to boot: *Metastasized.* Aunt Mary listened to Dr. Friedman, a man so old school he still made house calls.

"But it's the speed, Mary, the velocity at which it spread, it's . . . it's *uncanny*, that's what it is. I ran a blood panel and a set of X-rays on John a year ago and he was clean as a whistle. A cancer that moves this fast is rare, and usually caused by either some sort of continued exposure to a localized toxic source—and I mean like Times Beach, that town killed by Dioxin—or another cause that's pretty unlikely."

"What's the other cause, the unlikely cause?"

"There's a congruence with what's happening to John and radiation sickness."

"*What?*"

"I know, I know. But there are similarities."

My eyes widened.

Just what was that dust all over Uncle John? Would she mention it? She had to have noticed his fading shadow. Dr. Friedman had to have seen it.

"So, I wouldn't be overly alarmed at that possibility," Dr. Friedman said through a sigh. "It's not like he works at a nuclear power station, but I would be remiss to not mention it. If he hadn't had his annual checkup a couple of weeks back, none of this would have come to light. It was like pulling teeth, but John eventually gave me a blood sample. Honestly, I think he did it just to get rid of me."

"That sounds like John. So, cancer it is."

Dr. Friedman stammered for a second or two. Perhaps her

candor caught him off guard—cancer was rare in those days. "Nevertheless, I took the liberty of inquiring about space at the Oncology Center in Kansas City, and they *definitely* want to see him. That's why I'm here. Do you think you could talk him into considering such a thing?"

Aunt Mary's barely-contained chortle said just about everything.

"John is very stubborn, Willie," she finally said. "Nearly unreachable."

"We're likely beating a dead horse trying to get that man into treatment, I agree, but with the rapidity of its advance, maybe not tomorrow but soon, he'll be immobilized." He paused for a moment, either waiting for that to sink in or looking for a way to phrase what came next. "You'll need to be prepared for the inevitable. Without sedatives, his pain will be excruciating."

"How long does he have?"

I think Willie Friedman heard only despair, but I heard hope and anticipation.

"There are hospice agencies I can point you toward, a medical service that allows you to take care of him at home and ease his suffering. He can face the end with his family, not in some hospital full of strangers."

"I never knew such a thing existed. Hospice, they call it?"

"It's new, and a case like John's is a perfect fit. A specialist will work with you."

"That's very compassionate, thank you."

Aunt Mary paused, waiting, I think, for the right amount of time to satisfy the doctor that the tragic news had struck home. The grandfather clock in the foyer ticked and ticked. Finally, she said:

"When did you tell him?"

"Last Friday. Early."

For the past week, Uncle John had spent nearly every waking hour in the basement. Over the last three months, it had only been at night. He'd pushed the pedal down.

"How he ended up with something tantamount to radiation sickness really chaps my ass, Mary. I can't figure it out."

Voice tiptoeing to the edge of laughter, Aunt Mary said, "Well, they say cancer runs in the family."

"Try not to let John's cancer run yours."

6

S0, THERE IT WAS, the ticking clock. Uncle John knew his time was short, and he'd thrown himself entirely into whatever he was up to in the basement. Occasionally, I saw him in the study, shadow no more than a gray ghost following him about the room, muttering, scrawling away with one hand as he leafed through his immense antique books with the other.

I recall when he looked up from his reading and, as the saying goes, *looked right through me.* When I turned, Annie stood near the grandfather clock, sneaking a peek at the cadaverous old man. He leered at her with the eyes of a decades-long castaway, a bizarre union of desperation and starvation. He had plans for her, and there was little doubt The Machine, which I now began to hear even during the daylight hours, was central to it.

Annie looked at me quizzingly every time I raised the issue of the noises from the basement. I could buy that she hadn't heard a thing in the middle of the night. But at two in the afternoon—*on a Saturday?* Impossible to not notice. But oblivious she was, and now when I saw that unholy thirst in Uncle John's eyes, I knew. Through some power in his possession or control, *he had made it so that she could not hear it.*

When Aunt Mary found him the morning before Thanksgiving, passed out, face down on the kitchen tile in front of the witch oven, blood leaking from his nose and ass, greenish dust all over the place, she made the call. By nightfall, the hospice service had the bed and other medical gear in the living room. They'd cleaned up Uncle John and given him his first dose of morphine.

I'd thought his study the best location for his deathbed, among his secret books and front-row seat to Walpurgis Peak, but Aunt Mary had made her decision, I think, as a final jab to keep him away from the things he really cared about.

In the living room, he lay shadowless, waiting to die.

Thanksgiving was, of course, ruined. Instead of the house filled with the aroma of roast turkey, we smelled Uncle John's sick room.

Aunt Mary was heartsick, not over Uncle John on his deathbed, but a wholly torpedoed holiday. After the nurse left instructions and a phone number, then exited appropriately somber, Aunt Mary spent an hour with her sage and bells, candles, and crystals. An hour later, she flounced into Annie's bedroom, all smiles and bright eyes.

"Get straightened up and grab your coats, loved ones," she said to Annie and me. "We're headed to the Golden Bear. Best damn Chinese food this side of the Ozarks, and we'll have our own Thanksgiving."

Annie sprang from the bed and clapped. I hadn't seen her smile like that in weeks. *Months.*

"Can we just leave *him* here like that?" I asked.

Annie blew me a virulent raspberry, then looked up at Aunt Mary.

Aunt Mary didn't so much as blink. "He's going nowhere but down."

We went about our lives as Uncle John steamrolled to the end of his. Without Uncle John's nocturnal outings to rouse me, I began to sleep the night through. Aunt Mary locked the basement, abandoning the Kenmores in favor of the Fluff-n-Fold laundry service downtown. Whatever had given Uncle John his fast-moving cancer had obviously come from the cellar, and I dared not go near the place, Machine or no Machine. The morphine—or *dorphine*, as Annie called it—kept him at bay most of the time.

But there were incidents, Annie at their epicenter.

After dinner one crisp Autumn evening, Annie fished around inside the refrigerator, bold as can be with her back to the hissing stove, when Uncle John, whose last known location was dead to the world in a dope haze, suddenly shouted at the top of his lungs in a language so fierce, so *brutal*, Annie shrieked and dropped her RC Cola.

Aunt Mary and I arrived at the same time, she with a handful of flowers and polished stones, and me from the foyer. We found Annie standing closer to the bed than she would ever dare, gawking at Uncle John, who was now upright, eyes bulging like ping pong balls, one tight, focused, and bloodshot as hell, the other a lazy, watery egg.

His jaw hinged open, wide and long, the yellow stubs of his molars a collection of ruined stones. Just looking at his inflamed gums made my mouth sore.

"*Vgŋɲr!* HĐŐr!" An awful sound, a snarl of dead voices from a dead time. Stainless steel cold wrapped my bones and wormed into my spine. My teeth chattered.

"*Release him,*" Uncle John croaked in that inhuman coiled rope of voices, an abominable choir trapped in a dissonant harmony, the warbling dissonance between notes. "*We taught him fire and spells, the ways of metals, and the angles betwixt the stars. When your breed shat in holes and fucked like brutes, it was We who lifted you from primal mud.*"

Annie looked to Aunt Mary, then to me. She'd never heard such hideousness.

"*Release him. Send him to Us, to The Machine.*"

"You shut your mouth," Aunt Mary said. She nudged Annie away with her broad hip, holding her fresh-picked morning glories above her head like a priest with a crucifix. "I cast you out of this house!"

Uncle John brayed with laughter as his arms sprang wide, nails the color of cheap plastic. Dust pittering from his nostrils, mouth twisted in a sneer that was all malevolence, he looked like a gargoyle telling a fishing story.

"*Bring Us the* FℛℲ$ℌℒÏⅯ$. *Our Breeder.*"

"I said *silence!*"

Aunt Mary waved her pitiful handful of stones over Uncle John like a Navajo Medicine Man. She muttered something that, for all I knew, could have been Greek, Gaelic, or Gibberish. His face opened into a terrible open-throated yawn as he imitated a hyena's feral, mocking whine. The tendons in his neck pressed against skin that looked the way stomachaches felt.

Annie stiffened, nearly tilting back on her heels.

"*Mary the bungler, the she-witch of the carnival midway. Your unworthiness of this conjurer and supplicant is an insult to the Shadowless Empire. Lowly, crippled by delusional frailties—*"

"God *damn* your mouth!"

Snakelike, he flicked his white, dry tongue at my little sister. Satisfied with this debasement, he glared at Aunt Mary. The inflamed troughs of his eye sockets throbbed in tandem with his bulging carotid artery.

"But this FRƎŞHLÏИḠ . . . she is of interest to Us."

Faster than Uncle John's ruined anatomy should have allowed, those gargoyle paws reached out toward Annie, a profane sculpture brought to life. He clawed at her hair, pulled a few strands free, and swiped a second time. Before a screaming Annie could retreat, he brushed her cheek like a tailor smoothing a garment. The lazy eye wandered, the good eye locked with hers. His throat purred until that ribbon of voices spoke again.

"Our hand tastes pure innocence. The Machine will see to you, keep you well until you are warm of womb." He set that eye on me. *"Brother will assist us."*

"Bastard!" Aunt Mary barked. She slapped Uncle John's arm away then balled her hand into a fist.

He pretended to sniff his wife with a Labrador's dopey urgency, limp tongue wagging, dust and saliva dangling in dark muddy strands. His face puckered in revulsion.

"We smell a failed witch. The sixty-year-old apprentice."

Instead of driving that fist into Uncle John's teeth, a red-faced Aunt Mary yanked the IV regulator. Grimacing, she fumbled with the apparatus until a massive dose of morphine plunged down the tube.

Annie and I looked at one another with our mouths wide open.

"Ahhh, the Nightwater . . . "

Uncle John's hands dropped into his lap, his neck suddenly limp as rope.

"Release him . . . "

And he was out like a light.

Aunt Mary opened Uncle John's hand, snatched Annie's stolen hairs, and stuffed them into her pocket. When her tears came, they were in great, hitching sobs. We rushed to her and for a short time, the three of us stood crying like lost children.

"Release *you?*" Aunt Mary whined. She looked and Annie and me. A moment later, she spoke exactly as she had to Dr. Friedman. "I'll release *us.*"

Annie gazed at her with her doe eyes. "I don't care what *he* says. I love you, Aunt Mary."

"I love you too, Annie-girl. Did he hurt you? Are you all right?" Aunt Mary snuffled back a wad of snot and wiped her eyes.

Annie shook her head. "I'm okay." She pointed at the bed. "*He's* not."

LIFE RETURNS

Shadowless and emaciated, every breath a wheezing bag of bronchitis, that mysterious dust fell from Uncle John's inflamed nostrils, even as he slept. For all I knew, cancer dried you out, and that's why people withered. Perhaps he'd spend his last bedridden days mummifying from the inside out.

"I'm sorry, you two, if this sounds cruel," Aunt Mary said, "but your uncle is not leaving this bed until he dies. But this isn't like your parents. This is not a tragedy. Your Uncle John has become something else. You have to believe me when I tell you it's for the best."

Uncle John, the discarded mannequin. For a second, I wondered if she had overdosed him. If she had, I swore myself to secrecy. I'd never tell another living soul.

Aunt Mary pulled us in as tight, and at that moment, in a sleeping demon's sick room, we became a family.

1

"*MARY. BRĮŊG HƆΣR TŌ mΞ.*"
Annie screamed.

Insatiable childhood curiosity had the better of us. We'd made the idiotic decision to approach that goddamn basement, knowing the awful thing on its deathbed had returned to the scene of his obsession, and were the worse off for it.

Uncle John gnawed through the mahogany door like a beaver out of some wretched cartoon, chomping and spitting, bellowing through that awful chorus of voices. Dust streamed from his eyes and nose.

We bolted, Annie leading past the sick room and onto the stairs. Still holding hands, we stumbled at the landing, regained our footing, and shot up the final flight. Down below resounded the relentless ticking of the clock and the stove's serpent hiss.

Annie was not to be slowed by protocol or manners. She burst into Aunt Mary's room like a one-girl SWAT team, all noise and clatter.

"Aunt Mary, please get up!"

I flicked on the light, and there lay my aunt sleeping peacefully—but the night had just begun. A purple scarf had been tossed over a tassel-shaded jade lamp, and a sprig of incense burned on the mantle above the glowing fireplace. Shadows crawled over her heavy, hand-carved furniture and a stone lion watching from the hearth. Had it not been for the red wine, Sominex, upended Stanley toolbox with nails spilled all over—not to mention the Louisville Slugger leaning on the nightstand—I would have likened her *boudoir* to a fortune teller's wagon in an old werewolf movie.

Annie climbed on the bed and shook her. Her breasts swayed, her eyes opened for a second and rolled shut. She murmured something unintelligible.

"Aunt Mary, get up now!" Annie screamed, shaking her again.

On the rug lay a hammer and nails—make that *big* goddamn

nails. Aunt Mary had been busy with a little home improvement as we slept.

She groaned and pushed Annie away. My sister slid off the bed and stamped her famous pee-pee dance, rumpling the Scooter Pie's little foil wrapper over and over, close enough to Aunt Mary's ear to rouse anyone.

I glanced at the dresser on which the jade lamp stood, and there, in a circle drawn from lipstick, lay a toothbrush I thought I'd misplaced a week ago and the stands of Annie's hair snatched from Uncle John's hand. Around it stood a constellation of votive candles, various feathers, glass beads, and even a cigar butt. Aunt Mary had placed our personal items inside a magic circle, an ugly, primitive, yet oddly intricate thing similar to the benighted shapes I'd seen in Uncle John's books. Given everything I'd seen over the last months, let alone at the basement door this evening, it didn't surprise me in the slightest.

Winter Howl, the call of a miles-wide, braying wolf, stalked the house.

The Scooter Pie wrapper worked its own magic, and Aunt Mary opened her eyes. One look at my sister stomping her feet was enough, and she sprang straight up, sweeping Annie to her bosom.

"What is it, sweetheart?"

Guilt and fatigue. Whatever she'd done to Uncle John, she wore it on her face. With the weather a monster and fleeing the house an invitation to greater risk, she'd made the decision that we were to stay within its walls. Winter Howl had its own opinion on the matter, lowing accusatory like an army of ghosts set loose to right things before dawn.

Words no longer mattered for Annie when sobs would do. Now safe in Aunt Mary's arms, she looked to me to speak for her.

"Talk to me, Ian," Aunt Mary said. She cast a wary glance to the open door, cocked her head for a second, listening, then returned her attention to me.

"It's Uncle John. He's . . . he's . . . " My eyes fell back to the scattered nails and a well-worn rubber mallet. Years of being around my father, the building contractor, spurred a thought: *she drove nails with that thing? Where's the carpenter's hammer? The* claw *hammer?*

"Oh, spill it, Ian. He's *what?*"

"Uncle John is eating his way through the basement door!"

A series of bangs boomed downstairs, followed by the unmistakable sound of splintering wood. Aunt Mary closed her eyes and squeezed Annie tight. When her eyes opened, guilt and fatigue took a back seat to Mary Hazel Emerson Ingersoll, present and accounted for.

"Bastard," she said, gently pushing Annie back to arm's length. "He didn't touch you, did he? Either of you?"

Annie and I both shook our heads.

"Speak to you?"

I nodded.

Outside, the weather raged.

Inside, Uncle John bellowed.

"*MARY!*"

Volume astonishing, tone horrendous, I wondered how anything dared rival the thunderous bale of Walpurgis Peak. Aunt Mary passed Annie to me.

"Watch your sister. Do *not* follow me, do *not* let her go. Do you understand, Ian? I stopped him once. I'll sure-as-shit do it again."

"What is he? What did you do?" It was all in front of me, of course; my missing toothbrush, Annie's hair, the magic circle, wine, even the Louisville Slugger at the ready. I picked up one of the nails and held it out.

"There's no way we slept through all that noise."

The lamp flickered. A stunning blast of wind carved its way down Gethsemane Lane.

"I cast a little sleeping spell." She cracked a half-smile.

"You *what?*"

Her crooked smile provided all the proof I needed. What had Mom said all those years ago? *You think she's moved past all that Witchiepoo idiocy?* Well, Mom, the answer was a hard no. The sage burning, the little talismans hanging in the windowsills—more Sedona hippie than a cauldron-stirring witch, true, but perhaps she had a trick or two up her sleeve after all, despite Uncle John's relentless disrespect concerning her abilities.

"I cast a harmless spell to keep you and your sister quiet while I worked downstairs. You're a smart kid, your Uncle John sees that, and if he's right about anything it's that you're eager to see. *You* didn't know what went on inside this house? My God, Ian, I went so far out of my way to shield you two from him for all those years, and now he wants you to follow in his footsteps. He has designs on

Annie, wants to turn your sister into some sort of horrible blood bag for that monstrosity he worships. God damn me to the darkest Hell if I allow that."

"*MĄRY!*"

Deeper, louder. Nearly out of the cellar. I saw it in my mind's eye—not an image conjured from my imagination, but here, present as any sight that had ever played out upon my retinas. Uncle John lay on his belly, shoulders finally through the hole he'd gnawed, writhing a worm's best effort, skin like old bread dough that had failed to rise, hand extended, that finger curling. Beckoning. *Demanding.*

"*ČŌMƷ HĘRË!*"

Winter Howl answered in its aching whistle. Walpurgis Peak threw its full fury at the house, shaking windowpanes and loosening shutters. The trees slapped the glass like a coachman's whip. A blast of cold air found its way inside through imperfections in those rickety windows.

Why do you think I went so far out of my way to shield you from him for all those years?

You were born for Walpurgis County, you just don't know it yet.

Uncle John served Walpurgis Peak, he'd said it many times, made every effort to let me know. It was no leap to assume the mountain *wanted* us awake, thwarting Aunt Mary's amateur spell. I asked again, "What *is* he? What did you *do*?"

Her tone was exasperation, but her body language was all business. She took a slug of wine from the bottle and thumped it to the nightstand.

"For Christ's sake, Ian. Do you just want me to say it?"

"*MĄRŘRƷĘƷƷ!*"

"Your Uncle John is a sorcerer, and I stopped him."

Apparently not, I thought.

Annie's hands dug into my shirt.

Bat in hand, Aunt Mary tested its weight. Her mouth curled into a sneer, neck tendons like bridge cables. She turned to Annie with one raised eyebrow, just like our father.

"Did you *kill* him?" I blurted.

She didn't say anything.

"He was nearly dead already."

"It might seem that way, but believe me, whatever's in him is very much alive. That night, that episode when he pulled out Annie's hair, I filled John with enough morphine to kill ten men. And still, that thing squats in that bed day in and day out, reviles us, threatens Annie, and refuses to take what's coming to him. But now that son of a whore is going to stay where I put him."

She stomped out of the room like Buford Pusser in those Walking Tall movies, shoulders wide, bat in one hand, the other balled into a fist. She hung a left at the doorway and was out of sight. Her voice carried from the top of the stairs.

"Don't follow me, I'm serious."

We stayed put.

For about ten seconds.

I'd come this far, endured Uncle John's cruelty, his confession for the murder of our parents, his ramblings about The Machine and the Shadowless Ones. Hell, my sister and I had tiptoed around the man as he lay dying in the living room, driven mad not only by that pitiless mountain but also by a stable of night-filled books in his study.

I'd paid my dues. I'd earned the right to see. To know.

Nevertheless, dragging Annie with me was selfish and reckless.

Q

"OH MY GOD, Ian, she *really* killed him!"
I pulled Annie toward the stairs as she repeated this over and over. After the fourth time it hit me: Annie wasn't horrorstruck, she was relieved. But that relief was short-lived, the enemy had escaped his prison. Below resounded the thump of Aunt Mary's heavy footsteps and the snarl Uncle John's ugly gibberish. All around us, Walpurgis Peak reveled in the longest night of the year.

"He's obviously not dead," I said.

"No. Not dead *anymore*."

I'd seen a lot of weird things in this old Craftsman, but even I threw up my shields at *that*.

Why? You've seen a corpse at a bus stop. A mountain that's visible wherever you turn. You live with a man who claims to have killed your parents through a type of black magic. That study. Those books. That eye.

We reached the bottom step just as Aunt Mary flipped the kitchen light switch.

Uncle John lay on his belly near that beastly antique stove, the exact spot where he'd collapsed the day before Thanksgiving, his pajamas a TV hobo's shredded rags. One misaligned shoulder blade moved beneath doughy, bleached skin, his spine an ugly, segmented centipede. Behind him, a smear of dark blood, lumpy with green dust.

Uncle John lay on the floor with a hammer through his lung. The handle pointed away from his smashed scapula at a steep angle, the STANLEY logo barely readable through a stripe of tacky blood. I now had my answer about the mallet in her bedroom— Aunt Mary used the claw hammer to drop Uncle John, and the mallet to drive the nails.

But the nails weren't enough.

Uncle John refused to stay locked away.

Stay dead.

"John, you're dead," Aunt Mary said, poking him with the end of the bat. "But if that's not enough for you, I'll drag your carcass back down there and nail you to a goddamn post."

The corpse set his palms on the floor and raised his head. His face widened into a jester's grin, splinters the size of cactus needles in his bloody gums. He laughed like an imp in a wizard's lair, dust falling from his mouth, clumping in the places where it encountered leaking blood. His eyes never left his wife.

"Death is its own Shimmer," he said. "The Blank Dimension."

Annie said, "*I told you.*"

Moving with the grace of a rolling cinder block, Uncle John swung one hand onto the lip of the stove and hauled himself up. The claw hammer smashed between two of his ribs protruded like a perverse dorsal fin.

It was a stupid thing—a dumb horror movie thing—but we left the stairs and crossed the kitchen threshold, roosting ten feet behind Aunt Mary.

Because you want to see, Uncle John's voice rang in my head. *Because you want to know. You were born for Walpurgis County, you just don't know it yet.*

Once upright, Uncle John leaned decrepit with his face over the cold burners, chest heaving like a man panting after exertion. He drew no breath, yet there was a hollow hissing: the stove sounding its warning like a snake in a hole, promising venom.

His jaw swayed like a porch swing, perhaps broken by Aunt Mary or as he chewed his way out of the basement. Gruesome to behold, his mouth's movements did not match his words, but for the moment, his voice was his own, not that ghost choir.

"Old hills, Witch Hazel," Uncle John said. Even postmortem, his barbarous sense of humor remained. "With even older rules. And I know them all."

"Get back in your hole," Aunt Mary said. "You love that basement so much you can stay there."

She raised the Slugger. Locked her right elbow.

"I'll kill you again, John, I mean it."

"In front of the kiddies?"

He twisted his neck and looked straight at Annie and me, the lifelessness in his eyes betrayed by the wisdom of the dead, veins vile beneath the skin of his cheeks and nose. He spat a wad of phlegmy ore clear across the room at Annie. It fell short.

"My *Freshling.*"

Aunt Mary wheeled around. She extended the bat straight at us.

"Don't you two so much as *look* at him. *Out.*"

Her urgency, her grimace, and that Louisville Slugger proved a powerful persuader. I took one step back, but as soon as she turned to face Uncle John, I held my ground—I stubbornly and selfishly held my ground, holding my frightened sister like a hostage.

"They want young hearts, young spirits, Mary. The fuel for The Machine. It's the *ore*, the one I found, the one I was led to beneath this house. It feeds on the fruit of these old hills, and the old rule is that the ore must be delivered in the flesh or The Machine rejects it. Tethered to its might, this Freshling will provide decades of . . . "

Uncle John, brutalized and beyond death, smiled at Annie. My God, those terrible eyes. That crooked, broken jaw.

"*Receptacles.*"

With the same reptilian speed he'd seized my wrist at the dinner table, Uncle John's arm snaked past Aunt Mary—way, *way* past Aunt Mary. For a moment, the sound of breaking bones eclipsed Winter Howl as his arm extended beyond the limits of human anatomy. Humerus freakishly elongated, radius and ulna pulled like taffy, inverted elbow an impossibility, his skin resembled a sick, rubbery putty as it conformed to his arm's new dimensions, suddenly tasked with keeping its innards contained. Still, even magic has limits, and lacerations appeared as the fabric of his body could no longer pay sorcery's price. The tatters of his sleeves sighed to the tile below.

Dirty warlock fingers seized Annie's neck, and for a brief instant, a tug-of-war raged between a man dead on his feet and me, but the sight of that ten-foot arm and the desperation of Annie's squeal made my vision swim and my bladder ache to let go. I looked to Aunt Mary, hoping for a heroine's bravery—a swing for the center field fence into Uncle John's temple, for starters—but even she temporarily froze in that shocking instant.

His tongue pushed those loose, long piano key teeth forward, spilling dirt as it unrolled like a sticky, matted carpet. Then, that *voice.*

"ȘÙŘŘĘИĐȝř ţĦłș ƀŖĘĔđƐR, ƀȯ/!"

The wind bawled . . . *Dhuruuuuuhh* . . . fervid applause from Walpurgis Peak. At that moment, I realized I had a piece of it: that rope of twisted voices, many in one, was the will of that cruel mountain, or more accurately, whatever *slept* beneath it tethered to the Great Machine and used Uncle John at will—*because Uncle John was willing.*

I clenched my teeth and summoned everything I had, hands slick with sweat and wrapped around Annie's tiny wrists with nothing more than a boy's hope and the love of his sister as a bulwark against the clutches of a monster.

That grotesque hose of an arm yanked Annie from me, retracting in a sloppy wave of flesh and soft bone. It dragged my sister across the kitchen floor in her little slippers, clutching her Scooter Pie wrapper, her terror-wide eyes on me. Finally, I screamed, partially out of fright but primarily, guilt. I'd done this to her. I'd put her in harm's way and look what happened. *Look what happened, you stupid, selfish kid.*

Winter Howl punched the house, a fist determined to smash walls and crush stone. The lights flickered. The stove hissed, *Raaaaahhhhh . . .*

Annie shouted, "Leave me alone! Let me go!"

Uncle John squeezed, and Annie choked on words turned to ash. Every inch the villain, he licked Annie's cheek through a crumbling waterfall of his rotten ore, followed by a deep, satisfied grunt. He retreated, crunching through wood splinters and that smear of filthy sorcerer's blood.

Annie's splayed hands, two little starfish, shot straight out toward me. *"Ian!"*

"I'm taking this one with me," Uncle John croaked, "a bubbling egg sac for the Broken One. She will beget a new bloodline in the Undervoid. She'll last a few good years, then—"

Aunt Mary spat on the floor. "The *fuck* you will."

Simultaneously, we launched at Uncle John. She thrust the bat forward like a fighting stick, landed a bullseye to his solar plexus, and drove the walking corpse—and Annie—around the pantry and into the nook. I followed up with a linebacker drive into his hip. There was a dry *crack!* as part of his pelvis gave way.

Annie yelped, Aunt Mary screamed, Uncle John bellowed, Winter howled, and the entire snarl of us crashed through the ruined basement door and down the stairs.

9

W HEN THE WORLD stopped spinning, I saw a lone bulb, its jaundiced glow painting the brick walls in heavy shadows. Shadowless Uncle John was first to his feet, rags hanging, hammer buried in his back, Annie prisoner in his fierce stranglehold. Her breath fogged like cigar smoke.

Aunt Mary made it only as far as her knees. Dazed and bruised, she fumbled for the Slugger.

The basement did not disappoint—fetid, cold, filthy, filled with abandoned things and work's manic clutter. A sheen of frost clung to the galvanized pipes and the narrow windows that peered to ground level. A wound the size of a Volkswagen had been excavated in the middle of the basement. Shadows filled the jagged hole, and no telling how deep it went. The creepy bastard had obviously dug by hand; shovels, pickaxes, and a wheelbarrow stuffed with his beloved ugly green dirt stood nearby. The basement reeked of sewer, and with a turn of the head, I had my explanation. Uncle John had used the far corner as his toilet. No bathroom breaks allowed.

In that myriad of voices, Uncle John croaked, "BềħǫĽD."

The wind punished 1864 Gethsemane Lane, and the coal chute's cast iron door, which likely hadn't been opened since the late forties, rumbled in its frame. Below, in the derelict coal chamber, a searing line formed, a slit of green, nauseous light. I can't state it any simpler than that; this glowing fissure merely appeared, and yes, it shimmered.

The light bloomed, slathering the basement in its bile-green hue, Annie's red hair now black in that seasick glow. Buried in the throbbing warble of the Shimmer, I recognized the rhythmic thrum, the sound from all those nights at the top of the stairs. My mind swelled alight with curiosity, teased by danger and the searing urge to *know*.

Whurrrmp-Fwack—Whurrrmp-Fwack.

The Machine.

Aunt Mary groaned to her feet, sweeping the Louisville Slugger from the concrete floor and assuming her batter's stance. Elbow cocked and locked, she didn't pay the Shimmer so much as a glance. She stared Uncle John down like Hank Aaron.

"Let Annie go. I don't want to hit her by mistake when I break your skull."

Uncle John's lifeless eyes, a pool of deadsmoke, narrowed into slits. His nostrils shed dust like a broken hourglass.

"ṬHĪƧ ɃRĘĚđƐR Ĩş ƬRƎΛƧɄRЄ ȺИԁ ƆŎMÏИÇ wįƬȟ–"

She leaned into the swing, and Annie, God bless her, dipped a fraction of an inch. It was enough. The Home Run Queen of 1959 caught Uncle John right across the chops.

His unhinged jaw split, half tumbling down his chest in a miniature rockslide. Teeth rolled to the floor like dice. The remainder of his mandible dangled by exposed tendons or ligaments–hell if I knew the difference–but miraculously, the full brunt of the Louisville Slugger had somehow spared his upper teeth.

Blood?

It sprayed: a great ugly jet of it. Dust followed in filthy plumes.

He did not howl. He did not scream. Uncle John, a stick man with half a head, pawed at the space where his jaw used to be.

Annie, however, screamed long and loud. Ear-piercing and heartbreaking.

The dead man pulled my sister to the ruined cave of his mouth, poised like a vampire eager to feed, tongue prairie-dogging from the open tunnel of his neck. Annie squirmed and screamed, tiny hands clawing. A rain of dirty blood and shredded skin fell into her hair.

As Aunt Mary reared back for a second blow, the Shimmer shrieked. Agony from Elsewhere.

A thousand emerald stars died at once, and the Shimmer *opened*. There was no way I could have known this, yet I simply and unequivocally knew: a window into the filthy workings beneath Walpurgis Peak had ripped into existence through that blinding overload.

Alarming cold, the *true* breath of Winter Howl forced its way into the basement. This tunnel connecting *here* with a distant *there* existed beyond the territory of dreams, and through that pulsing membrane, I saw a network of mammoth tunnels bored into ancient ice and even older rock.

LIFE RETURNS

In the coal chamber a pathway opened between the house and Walpurgis Peak at best—and a portal to Uncle John's Blank Dimension at worst. Maybe both; maybe they were the same damned thing. Although instinct demanded I tear my sister away from this dead man and run, my awful curiosity kept me in its grip. Machine noise roared everywhere. Loud, brutal, unrelenting. A deathstink a hundredfold of Uncle John's private toilet, soured by centuries in this tomb accompanied that terrible cacophony, undoubtedly the atmosphere of Uncle John's coveted Undervoid. Centuries of rot. Aeons of corruption.

I saw it. I saw The Machine, certainly not in its entirety, merely a portion of its workings. Gashes the size of railway cars had been gouged into the walls of those immense catacombs. Broken ice and rock lay on the tunnel floors.

Those are claw marks. A living thing made those.

Within these wounds, enormous bars reciprocated and cycled, similar to the coupling rods of a steam locomotive's driving wheels. Vile, angry things, covered in bloody grime, dripping ochrous gobs with every thrust. Behind these rods, throbbed bags, bellows, organs—nearly fifty years later, I still don't know what to call them—that hissed and breathed, expanding and contracting, pumping dense fluid into leaking pipes venting reeking steam.

The Shimmer, an umbilical connected to the rotten gut of Walpurgis Peak and its workings, flaunted its ugliness. The Machine itself was plain wrong, an abomination, a blaspheme of engineering, built by slaves. I assumed a far greater danger lay at the end of these ancient tunnels, merely the outskirts of a bedchamber harboring something incomprehensible. Something massive. Something Shadowless.

"*Thê mÅCH|Ñ€.*" Uncle John's ugly witchvoice. With his tongue a wagging worm and jaw gone, speech should have been impossible. In a night of terrible miracles, no one thought to be stunned by such a thing.

Winter Howl responded with a frigid blast, the whole of Antarctica crammed through the glowing green slit. If the Shimmer was a window through time and space, *when* did that polar air originate? An Ice Age rendered in silly drawings of cavemen and woolly mammoths? The raving days of primal earth cowering as madness fell from conquered stars? My mind roiled, ablaze with foreign ideas, revelations beyond my years or understanding. As the snot in my nostrils hardened into crystals, a sense of elasticity washed over me, deja vu and fear of the future in a confusing snarl. To much for a boy to endure, but not enough to slake his thirst to see. To Know.

"ΒΕΠÆИŦĤ ĘṼệŘY Sₑₙₜlĵ̃'EĻ МóỤПŁΔŀN óϟ ϟ'H3 ωOϟŁɖ."

Whurrrmp-Fwack—Whurrrmp-Fwack—

Time bent, rolled, and skewed like a funhouse mirror. I thought of our old black and white TV in San Diego, the picture lost in a maze of snow and a Venetian blind tumble of black lines. When this bizarre horizontal roll cleared, I saw Uncle John leaning against his desk the morning he'd summoned me to his study, bathed in the green Shimmer light. Behind him, where his massive brass device gawked at Walpurgis Peak, the mountain shuddered as gargantuan cracks spread over its ragged, granite face. Like a volcano's pyroclastic flow, a spew of dirt and debris spat from a ragged hole torn at the foot of the mountain. Colossal. Immense.

This fusion of *then* and *now* served as a glimpse into an awful *yet;* a dreadful, cataclysmic future. In my mind, I knew, I *saw.* This was the contents of his books, the focus of his studies, the obsessive drive to serve his Master in the mountain's wretched gut. The end of all things.

The crows, the taxidermy sculpture from the study, suddenly materialized in this collision of hallucination and time, a tremendous black tapestry exploding in flight. It corkscrewed past me in a flutter of beating wings and jagged bird calls. I felt their heat, smelled the intimacy of their nests, and sensed their blind obedience to man, mountain, and a sleeping, wounded giant. Once past my field of view, they simply ceased to be, reduced to an echo against the cinder block walls and concrete floor.

He pointed at me from the past and spoke.

"It will end me, use me for fuel, soup in the belly of the Broken One—but only after my burden is shed. It wants a Freshling, and you to replace me."

If I stepped through that throbbing light, into the stinking dungeon beneath the mountain, what knowledge would be imparted to me? What would I see, what would I know? Would I too become Shadowless, no longer a citizen of this world or any oth—

"Ian, stop!"

Aunt Mary. I snapped out of my trance, eyes wide and mouth

open, my right foot inches from that excavated hole—the source of the ore that had rendered a man insane and riddled him with cancer.

Uncle John brayed with laughter.

"Two *Freshlings if it can get it.*"

"John," Aunt Mary said. "You should have stayed in that shitty bed and died like God intended."

He turned his mangled face to his wife, tongue poised like an awful snake in a hole.

Terrified by the man with half his head gone, Annie looked to the unholy rip of the Shimmer instead, gawking like an ape mesmerized by fire. The mechanism bellowed, breathed and hissed.

"Don't *look* at it, Annie," I shouted. "He wants you hypnotized. Look at me instead."

Aunt Mary rushed the monster, closing the distance, hair wild, eyes feral, oblivious to The Machine, concerned only for Annie. She brought the Louisville Slugger down like a broadsword on that unholy ten-foot arm, repeatedly chopping the shoulder joint. Although Uncle John's black art allowed him to defy physics, Aunt Mary's maternal nature proved beyond sorcery's reach. After several blows, the rubbery skin gave way, the malleable bones beneath collapsed, and finally—*finally*—Uncle John howled.

"ĐŰ́ŇŘЦЦ UŅ!"

Walpurgis Peak launched an ingot of hate straight into the house. It shattered every basement window, knocked pipes loose, flipped the wheelbarrow, and sent the Kenmores beneath the stairs sliding from their moorings. The hanging bulb exploded, leaving us in the Shimmer's seasick green light and the wretched stink of the Undervoid.

Uncle John screamed, not from pain, but his lost grip on Annie. He failed his mission, failed The Machine. Failed The Shadowless Empire.

I believe Aunt Mary nailed the basement shut because she knew resurrection was a distinct possibility, servitude to The Shadowless Ones Uncle John's guarantor. In her mind, the only way to keep him away from us was to seal him below. Who knows what story she planned to make up the following morning, but I think she cast her sleeping spell on us and went downstairs intending to overdose Uncle John on anything and everything.

Perhaps she found him in the basement, staggering around in his Machine Fugue State, digging his hole, rolling around in the dirt, whatever. Harsh words and threats were spoken, the toolbox lay open, and she grabbed the first thing handy. Old rage and resentment took over. When one blow would have been enough, she landed several, and that frail old man dropped to the floor. Selling his death as an accidental OD was off the table now, and needing time to figure out what came next and fearing the inevitability of resurrection, Aunt Mary hauled the toolbox up the stairs. She nailed the door shut with the rubber mallet, then staggered off to chug wine and pop Sominex until lights out.

But what waits below Walpurgis Peak would not be insulted, let alone bested.

Annie ran to me, half laughing, half sobbing, all joy, and we wrapped our arms around one another. Her hot tears and breath steamed through my shirt, and my heart pounded to the cursed machine's insane rhythm. I had to get her out of here.

As Annie and I fumbled toward stairs rendered to little more than a stack of shadows, we witnessed Aunt Mary's retribution. If she could kill him once, she could kill him twice.

She'd pushed her husband's corpse against the cinder blocks Adam-12 style—*up against the wall, feet back and spread 'em!*—her foot at the small of his back as she smashed that Louisville Slugger into the dangling hammer, driving a nail home into a savage, gaping wound.

"Fucker," she screamed with every blow.

WHAM *You* WHAM *Will* WHAM *Not* WHAM *Take* WHAM *These* WHAM *Children!*

I dropped my hands over Annie's eyes, but she would have none of it.

"Get him, Aunt Mary!" Annie screamed. "*Kick his ass!*"

Winter Howl bellowed.

Below and within, The Machine roared.

I pushed Annie up the first few steps. I turned when Aunt Mary called.

"Topside, Ian," she said, winded from her caning session. "Stack anything heavy you can find against the door." She tipped the Louisville Slugger toward the monster at the foot of the stairs. "This rotten bastard's not leaving this basement, but still, get your sister far away from him."

"Where?"

Aunt Mary impatiently shook her head. "Winter Howl ends at sunrise. Go to Miss Geraldine's across the street, understand? She'll know what do to. Do *not* look at the mountain when you leave. Do *NOT* look at Walpurgis Peak *ever again.*"

Uncle John, an emaciated old man dressed only in his shredded castaway pants, turned around, his ruined head a bizarre blend of dangling teeth, poisoned ore, and pulped meat. Those eyes, pearls of smoked glass filled with nowhere, watched us. His snake-like arm was gone for good, fallen to Aunt Mary's ferocity. What remained of his upper lip curled into a sneer, puppeteered by some vile thing sleeping on the damned side of the Shimmer. Impossible to be standing, let alone speaking, but it was so, and in this moment of desperation, he attempted to bargain.

"The Machine wants her, Mary. Needs her. The Freshling will provide vessels for sustenance. Someone will take John's place, and the boy is of age. We will train his eye, slake his thirst. In return, we will grant you the powers you always coveted. John's powers. He will not be needing them."

"No dice," Aunt Mary panted. She jabbed a thumb over her shoulder. "You two, gone. *Now.*"

Annie flew up the stairs. I began my backward ascent, eyes on the sorcerer and the wannabe witch.

A winded Aunt Mary, bloodied, bruised, sweat pouring from her brow, followed me in uneven backward steps. That was when Uncle John came at her with a leopard's speed, hand reaching over his shoulder like a warrior retrieving an arrow from his quiver. He produced the hammer she'd buried in his back and held it over that mangled half-head, tongue waggling, spit, blood, and dust flying.

Whurrrmp-Fwack — Whurrrmp-Fwack —

"MARŘRƎ£Ǝ£!"

"Ian, go!"

She swung and missed.

III

10

DAWN FOUND US in Aunt Mary's room, two worn-out kids curled up in front of a fireplace guarded by a silent stone lion.

A finger of sunlight shone through the lace curtains, draping intricate shadows upon Annie as she slept. She'd been dragged through Hell by that thing Uncle John had become, far more than anyone her age should endure. She slept fitfully, bottom lip trembling, hands opening and closing. Her Scooter Pie wrapper lay nearby, certainly worse for wear. I noticed it then in dawn's golden glow; a streak of white had appeared in her luxurious red mane, streaming away from her forehead, just north of her right temple.

I parted the curtains to Winter Howl's handiwork. One of the sycamores stood leaning, split in half—we'd heard that calamity early on—and several other trees along our street suffered severe damage. Enormous sheared branches lay drunkenly against leaning telephone poles, the lines sagging or down. Limbs the size of eighteen-wheelers populated the street like colossal prisoners shot during an escape attempt. Every car stood covered in debris, windshields cracked or outright shattered. Roof shingles lay everywhere. A wooden doghouse sat atop a manhole cover, neat as you please. Despite its disarray, Gethsemane Lane was dead quiet, utterly at winter's command, yet not a single snowflake had fallen. The morning offered only clear, biting, cold—so much so that I winced when I touched the glass.

I tossed wood onto the coals and blew the flame to life. A trip downstairs was imperative—best to do that with Annie still conked out—but only a fool would leave that bedroom without a weapon. Like Aunt Mary, I made the obvious choice. I picked up the mallet.

At kitchen's threshold, I replayed what we'd heard from Aunt Mary's room. Uncle John's hideous multi-voice uttered the ugliest things, vile personal insults in tandem with repeated blows. We listened to the doomed clank of the Louisville Slugger falling to the concrete, her dreadful lanced cow scream, and it was then that

Annie and I abandoned hope for her and assumed the worst. Surrounding us, the awful, bloodthirsty bellow of Winter Howl, singling out this house with its ire.

In lockstep with Uncle John's assault had been The Machine's gibbering glee as it knocked, hissed, and spat. To Uncle John—or more accurately his Master—Annie was little more than a breeder, and by God, Aunt Mary risked it all to keep my sister and me out of the clutches of darkness. And I'd left her alone in the basement with that goddamn monster.

I flicked the switch. No lights. The fallen trees had seen to that. The grandfather clock chimed the hour loud as church bells. 6 AM. The stove hissed its snake warning as I crossed its path, green dust and smeared blood beneath my feet, the shreds of Uncle John's pajamas where they'd fallen.

The pile of dining room chairs we'd stacked against the basement door still stood, our work shoddy and rushed. A push and a harsh word could have toppled it, and it required less than that for me to wriggle my way through. I held my mallet tight as I approached the door we'd smashed as we tumbled into basement darkness.

Profane cold owned the basement. Winter Howl may have turned the place into a meat locker, but a fair amount of early morning light found its way in through the broken windows. A soft beam of winter dawn shone at the foot of the stairs, and in it, Uncle John's molars lay in pulverized bone and green, poisonous ore.

I stopped on the third step and allowed my eyes time to adjust—allowed *everything* to adjust. My heart was a swollen ball bearing, my lungs dry bags, my nerves hard, cold wire. The mallet shook in a hand unused to wielding anything more lethal than a water pistol.

No machine noise. No ugly deathstink. No cancerous glow.

"Ian? *Ian* . . . is that you?"

Aunt Mary's voice, haggard and spent.

Her hand emerged from frigid shadow, covered in grimy, tacky blood, three fingers smashed. Adrenaline and a sense of duty had kept me glued together during the night, but now, seeing my sweet aunt wounded and bloody, I finally gasped.

"Don't come down here, Ian. Where's Annie?" A crone's croak, the trailer park grandma with a two pack a day habit and serious emphysema. Dry as kindling.

"She's sleeping in your room. By the fireplace."

"Good boy, good man. My *brave* man."

"No. No, I left you, I *left* you—"

"I *told* you to leave. He'd have dragged your sister into the Shimmer. I thought after I severed his arm I'd have the advantage. But, you saw him."

The last I saw of Uncle John, he'd become an unstoppable, horrendous half-headed thing pulling a Stanley hammer from his back. Behind him, a nest of moving shapes, chaos skittering in the Shimmer's sickly green light. Under the influence of so much adrenaline and urgency, I failed to register something *exiting* the Shimmer as I backed away—an enormous thing pushing through the Undervoid.

Aunt Mary leaned into the light. Wrist crushed, her right hand at an impossible angle, the elbow a swollen eggplant of bruises. Finally, the crown of her head appeared, the remains of her generous hippie hair a bloody snarl peppered with poisoned ore. The rest had been torn out and strewn about the bottom landing, a sludge pile of torn skin and long gray locks.

My heart broke.

Uncle John, you animal. You shitty, black magic animal.

Her hands pushed through the muck, hauling herself over the first couple of steps, one leg so severely broken she dragged it along, calf split, shoe missing, foot bulbous and purple. She outweighed me by a hundred pounds, but I couldn't stand there. Not again, not anymore. Without thinking, I stumbled down a few steps.

"I said don't come down here." Every syllable rustled like dry paper. "It's over. There's nothing for you to do."

"What happened?" Tears came. The word *happened* sounded like a balloon squealing as the air escaped.

"He had me face down in that wheelbarrow, shoving that awful dirt in my mouth, into my wounds. I thought he meant to drown me. No. He wanted me to share the same fate."

Aunt Mary hissed through a series of brutal, painful spasms. Finally, she threw her head back and screamed. Nearly scalped. Crushed eye socket. Those hideous broken limbs. Catastrophic shock. Uncle John had beaten her to a pulp with the very hammer she'd used to strike him down. It was miraculous she was conscious, let alone alive.

LIFE RETURNS

"Something reached out of the Shimmer," she said, her voice filled with doubt as if she didn't believe her own words. "It was shadows at first, like a handful of spiders on a light bulb. Heh. Funny how your brain works. I'm in the middle of being beaten to death and I thought in stupid similes. Happened so fast. I was barely conscious—but I *saw* it."

"The Machine?" I whined. The urge to blubber pressed against every nerve.

"No, Ian. The thing that *feeds* The Machine. Looks after it. I don't know how I know, I just *do*. Oh, Ian, it looked like a stomach with legs." Aunt Mary sobbed, perhaps the image in her mind too hideous to reconcile, a sudden, hard emergence from shock. "He would have given your sister to that thing, I'm sure of it. Maybe fed her to it."

I took another couple of steps toward her. The stairs groaned.

"But it squeezed through and snatched *him*. I saw its body on the other side, Ian. Under Walpurgis Peak; a slimy, fat thing with too many legs. When it passed into the basement, crossed the threshold, the part here, in this room, its horrible big asshole mouth became invisible. It *Shimmered*."

Had not Uncle John said he would die as soup in the Master's belly? Aunt Mary had fought hard and done the right things, she'd taken the fight to the edge of the Shimmer, and this creature, undoubtedly the source of that skittering swarm of shadows I saw as I backed up the stairs, had done the rest.

"It took him like a bird takes a worm. Slurped your uncle into its hole. After it gorged its belly, it backed into the Shimmer, then stood there looking at *me*. Those eyes, like lobster eyes, on stalks. It saw me. *Marked me*."

She coughed. A red glob flew from her lips, trailing dust. She stared at me with sad, exhausted eyes. Uncle John's green deathdust crusted her ruined face, her swollen, beaten mouth. The Home Run Queen of 1959 had touched 'em all for the last time.

I ached inside. She didn't have to explain what came next. Dr. Friedman had been clear about that.

"I'll stay here. I'm what The Machine wants now. There's no going back once you're infected with this . . . I don't know. Uranium? Iridium? Strontium? Dr. Friedman was right. Whatever it is, *it's so fast*. I feel it burning from the inside out."

"I'll get an ambulance," I said, desperate for any solution. I dropped the mallet. It bounced down the stairs, lost to darkness.

"Oh, Ian. Ian, I'm so sorry I can't be here with you and Annie."

"We'll get you out of there, I swear." Blubbering imminent.

Aunt Mary, on the stairs in thick mats of blood and hair, offered a weak smile and shook her head.

"No, sweetheart."

The coal chute's cast iron door rattled.

She raised her one good hand and blew me a kiss.

"I love you, my brave man. And tell Annie her Aunt Mary loves her more every day. But hear me: You and Annie need to leave this house. Leave Walpurgis County. Forever. It's poisoned. Dangerous. This house should burn."

The Shimmer ripped open with that terrible, shrieking noise, flooding the basement with hideous green light and raucous machine clatter. I could not see the fissure from the stairs, but it was clear that something was coming, a bulbous, heaving thing, grunting like a foraging grizzly, its hiss the nauseating gurgle of digestion. Its black, frantic shadow splashed against the far wall.

And, as Aunt Mary had said, too many legs.

It wasted no time heading down those ancient catacombs of the Undervoid to the wounded belly of 1864 Gethsemane Lane.

II

T WASN'T UNTIL the late nineties when Annie and I finally made it to Oahu. We stood on Waikiki and stared at Diamond Head.

Annie had tried several times to dye or cut out her white streak, but, as the Purg would have it, no dye ever took, and that area grew back faster than any other. Scars are like that, you know. They never allow themselves to be forgotten, and you only pretend they don't hurt. Believe me, I have plenty of my own.

Annie's sons sprinted to the warm water. Her husband, Kevin, cracked a Primo lager and watched them from underneath a big red beach umbrella. It was good to see unbridled happiness like that, young boys with normal lives and parents who loved them.

Annie and I didn't speak for a few minutes, we buried our toes in the sand and stared at the slope of the long-dead volcanic cone. As Uncle John had said one night long ago: *Diamond Head is a pussy hill, son—it's nothing compared to the Master.*

I'd be lying if I said I hadn't imagined over and over Uncle John in his study, poring over his sorcery books, combing through conjuring incantations to crash our parents' Beechcraft into the mountainside. At the same time, Aunt Mary toiled away in her room, repeatedly failing to concoct a love potion from a grimoire she'd purchased at Waldenbooks. I wished those evil forces would have turned on him that night, but in the end, I suppose they had— it had just taken a few years and the lives of our parents. He's part of that ugly mountain now, as is our lovely Aunt Mary. The willing and the unwilling seem to be fed upon with identical fervor.

"For years I never wanted to come here," Annie finally said. She wore big Gucci shades and a floppy hat Aunt Mary would have envied.

"Because it's a crime scene," I said.

"Sure, that's part of it. But I hate that I always knew the day I finally stood on this beach and looked at Diamond Head, I wouldn't be able to think about Mom and Dad—all I'd think about is that asshole who took them from us. Here we are twenty years later, and I've never said a goddamn thing about it, Ian. I never let anyone know what I know, let alone what *you* know. Not my husband, not anyone."

"I understand."

"*Do you?*"

The little girl in the strange house full of shadows was long gone. She lowered her sunglasses and looked at me like an expensive attorney waiting for an answer.

I nodded. "I think so. You have good reason to live in the flat lands."

"I'll never live near a mountain ever again. How can you *stay* in that place?"

Annie. She was allowed to leave, despite whatever designs The Machine had upon her. I often wonder what her dreams are like, and what she thinks about when she is alone in her thoughts, waiting for sleep to come. Whether she has Scooter Pies in her refrigerator, I cannot say, but when I looked down, I saw the slightest pivot from foot to foot. The pee-pee dance was, though muted, still alive and well.

Annie and I are not estranged like our father and Aunt Mary, but we are nowhere near as close as we used to be.

And I know why.

You were born for Walpurgis County—you just don't know it yet.

Turns out he was right. I never left the Purg, though I'd repeatedly tried. Every time I packed my bags, navigated that snake pit of detours, and made it to the Interstate, an hour later I'd look at a road sign and find that I was on Route 54 or Beltane Road. I eventually figured out that I was free to *travel* but would not be allowed to *live* anywhere else. Just like the old Eagles song where you can check out but never leave.

Shimmers and the occasional resurrection are nothing new in Walpurgis County, and over the years I've assembled an encyclopedic history of the place: Copperhead Farms, Eldritch Wood, Dead Neck Lake, the Vanderbaum House, even Beltane Road itself. The list of haunted places and benighted things goes on and on. I am its curator.

I kept Uncle John's library and the brass device through which he'd gazed at Walpurgis Peak. To this day, it still points only at the mountain, even though it's in a crate nailed shut and stored in the attic of the house I could not burn. The unspeakable secret of secrets.

So best I leave you here, on the side of the road with your suitcase at your feet, before we come to the sweeping curve that affords you your first glance of Walpurgis Peak.

Best I leave you in a state of blissful naiveté.

Before superstition intervenes.

WITCHFYNDRE

M Y DEAREST ANGELICA, *I am not a killer.*
But I have rid the world of numerous malignancies.

There is a unique character reserved solely for smoke—its ability to float, its innate will to seek the path that leads it toward those that despise it most, and most of all, its gift of disclosure. And with this abettor, the ethereal agent of truth, I have unmasked nests of darkness, hives of sinister intent.

As death stalks my eightieth year, I reflect on the decades past. That mirror, though some may point to its emphysema hue, shows me not the regrets of a man who spurned the warmth of hearth and home, achievements of career, and the inner beauty of creativity, but a gathering of vignettes of a life of resolve, dedication, total commitment to the mission at hand—even if it demanded fluency in the language of knives and the street slang of fire.

A box arrived from a tiny law practice located in Danielsburg, a small municipality in a place heretofore unknown to me, an impossible-to-find speck on the map known as Walpurgis County. Immediately intrigued, I opened the package to find a purple velvet bag. Within this bag was a pipe—a smoking pipe—a hearty, exquisitely carved piece of artistry, long in years and well into its life as an antique. According to the enclosed letter from an attorney named Devereaux, this pipe had been left to me by my Uncle Thomas, a relative distant not through a rabbit warren of second cousins twice removed, but family estrangement. His name rarely came up in family discussions, and when it did, flustered relatives quickly changed the subject.

Included was a letter from this mysterious relative, most of which I quote from memory:

WITCHFYNDRE

I, Thomas Stearne, your great uncle by blood on your maternal side, bequeath to you *Witchfyndre*, a pipe of renown. Crafted in Constantinople in 1104, this final work of Turkish master carver Murat Aydem, long-rumored to have gained his unparalleled ability from the jinn Ibn-Saal-Zahad—the most cunning of apparitions and sworn enemy of the dark forces which damned him to the lamp—is not only priceless but authentic as its moniker suggests.

Despite its extreme age and ornate appearance, know that its legends are true; its abilities—in the hands of one predisposed to incur such responsibilities—are without equal. *The smoke knows the way, and the smoke knows the truth.*

Dear grand-nephew, from afar I have taken great interest in your studies outside the boundaries of bloated academia and your thirst for sequestered knowledge. In this manner, you and I are kindred. As I pored through the Walpurgis County Historical Society Records, it became clear that our particular talent, which this pipe will reveal to you in good time, skips a generation. Like those who came before us, our work can be brutal and isolating, but bear in mind that it is essential. The Old Conflict never ends—only its participants change.

It is, therefore, my solemn duty to pass this legendary weapon of light to you.

Use it wisely.

Use it often.

This day in 1970 marked the turning point in my life, and if you indulge me for just a while longer, grand-niece Angelica, I will tell of how I became bound to its enchantments, raptures that led to the end of countless witches, and why I now pass Witchfyndre on to you.

I frequented the bohemian district of Roderick in those days, quick to attend any gathering of musicians, actors, sculptors, and novelists. As providence would have it, these indulgences of youth paved the way for the burden shouldered upon me.

Halloween night in Roderick, legendary for its sprawling carnival by torchlight bursting with wandering Elizabethan minstrels, fortune tellers, games of chance, and roasting meat, proved a lure too powerful to resist. As I donned my Puritan costume's Capotain hat—what I thought a clever contrast to the rabble of goblins and ghosts, ghouls and gravediggers—my eye landed upon Uncle Thomas' Turkish pipe in its place on the mantle, nestled between the flagstone's natural crags, a perfect cradle for Murat Aydem's exquisite work.

The pipe measured nearly eleven inches in length, the enormous curved stem supporting a sloping, flared bowl. Upon its surface, the master had executed the finest details in sharp relief: the profiles of predatory birds, the fierce expressions of hungry cats, the curl of a scorpion's tail. These hunters lay in a bed of blooming wolf's bane winding up the length of the stem, the carpels of each flower rendered into an agonized human face. Eyes wide and mouths agape, the tormented suffered in eternity, their fates known only by a man who had mastered his skill from the jinn.

Ibn-Saal-Zahad, denizen of the lamp, proved not as obscure as one may suspect. The name rang a distant bell, and after a few trips to the Georgetown and Slater University libraries, studying arcane, forgotten books such as Octavius Cornelius's *Viae Damnatorum* (Ways of the Damned), Pope Urban VIII's nightmare-fueled *Armi Forgiate Dall'oscurità* (Weapons Forged by Darkness), and Portuguese scholar Affonso Nicollao's exhaustive 1708 tome *Segredos da Irmandade Mediterrânica* (Secrets of the Mediterranean Brotherhood), the fog lifted, and his legend came into focus.

Furious he fell for more powerful jinn's beguiling, cruelly deceived and condemned to eternity in the lamp, Zahad swore retaliation on the wicked, the charlatans of the spirit world. "Mad Arabs, these sailors of the sand, harbor in their trinkets vengeful ghosts at war with one another." (Cornelius, page 114). Zahad vowed when his time came again to meddle in human affairs, the fruit of that union would bear "swords of fire against the ancient enemy, any and all that twist beneath the hoof of evil." (Nicollao, page 387).

WITCHFYNDRE

For a century Zahad brooded, furious in his prison, eager to work his will through the hands of his liberator. In 1104, Murat Aydem purchased the lamp from a merchant in Üsküdar. Within a month, he carved his masterpiece. I assume the pipe earned the name Witchfyndre in the Middle Ages, undoubtedly changing hands several times until it ended up in Western Europe. That knowledge seemed inconsequential each time I smoked the pipe in the weeks since acquiring it, focusing instead on the ancient clay's mellowing even the most robust tobacco. What a pleasure to smoke this ancient artifact, a thousand years of history in my hands. Of additional interest was the onset of colorful dreams following each smoking session, and at the time, I did not associate these hallucinatory and occasionally violent dreams with the pipe's supernatural workings, only my low tolerance to nicotine. The dreams unfurled fantastic, populated with ancient landscapes, fire-lit corridors, and shadowy figures cowering in blood-smeared doorways as I passed. I was feared. Reviled. I wielded power there.

Pipe and pouch in pocket, I joined the Halloween carnival. I chatted with friends and mugged for the cameras, enjoyed food by firelight and ambient music—haunting melodies born of lyre and flute. Jack-o'-lanterns had been set into the trees, their root-bound snarls or knobby burl, and the tents of every vendor. A thousand flaming eyes watched the festival, Autumn's sounds and aromas welcome in the cool night.

The sudden, piercing clangs of a ship's bell hushed the crowd, a signal so clear even the music obeyed the call to order. I set my wine aside, slipped my hands into my cloak, and waited.

"Hear ye, revelers and ruffians," a man's voice cried out. "As the final hours of Samhain near, we celebrate in preparation for the Dead Season."

The crowd cheered with glasses raised. A few lit sparklers and waved them about. A rail-thin woman dressed as a witch set her broom to a sparkler and set it ablaze. A man in mummy garb backed away from her to a chorus of laughter.

"Trees show their bones, animals burrow to sleep, for they know the majestic occurrence in faraway Walpurgis County, Winter Howl, will trumpet its arrival in the frigid speech of the Shadowless Empire."

Walpurgis County? What were the chances that this portly

little man in a tricorne hat and buckled shoes, a person I'd never seen until this very evening, could know of such a place? Until the pipe arrived, *I* had known nothing of it. Without conscious intent, I pulled the pipe from my cloak, its carved surface cool to the touch. The pad of my thumb caressed the faces carved into the blooming wolf's bane; one lamented from a mouth pulled so far out of true it defied anatomy, another wept in desolate emptiness, and a third grimaced, consigned to its fate.

The speaker placed one hand behind his back and motioned with the other to four female effigies dangling from mock gallows, bound and bonneted, silent and swinging. "Pay your tributes as Autumn surrenders to Winter, much as these scapegoats, condemned of cat and cauldron, have paid theirs so the *true* Coven remains clandestine."

I packed the bowl and set the match to work. A tremendous volume of aromatic smoke poured from my mouth and nose like the first blast from a sleeping engine.

The smoke wreathed around the nine-foot-tall stilt-walkers in their skeleton suits, whispered past pirates and bar wenches, curved majestically toward the dwarf outside the palm reader's tent. *Seeking.* The ribbon of Latakia—Turkish tobacco, no less—drew my eye again to the town crier, an audacious perjurer in a red velvet waistcoat gloating at women hanged for his crimes. Effigies swaying, bell at his feet, he jabbed his thumbs into his vest.

"Glorious in their appetite, fiendish in their sleep beneath the great mountains of the world, they wait, driven insane by Death—"

Though slowed from drink, I did not fail to recognize the smoke's contempt. To say true, I reveled in its anger as Witchfyndre's bounty abandoned its leisurely stroll and stabbed toward the town crier with alarming speed. His eyes bulged as the floating dragon caught him between words, screwing between his yellow teeth, augering into the surprised o of his mouth, and plummeting down his gullet.

In the same unconscious manner I'd raised the pipe to my lips, I shouted, "Confess; the smoke knows the way, and the smoke knows the truth!"

Heads turned from the stage spectacle to me, the tall man in the black cloak with the antique pipe and pilgrim's hat. Surely, this was a set-up, a carnival gag.

Smoke, far more than I had exhaled, gushed from the man's

nose and wafted from his collar. A sheet of it escaped the inflamed rims of his eyes, which, now seized by terror and astonishment, immediately locked with mine.

I exposed him. This witch sees me.

The eerie familiarity of this scene did not chill my blood, but warmed it with righteous adrenaline. Upon my breath, I had set the resolute fist of Witchfyndre free.

I remember this from a pipe dream, colorful and ferocious, the extermination of Devilry in all its forms. The wicked choking on flames, puking smoke. They back into candlelit hovels as I pass, doors smeared red, a mockery of the Plagues of Egypt. But no doors can stop it; the smoke knows the way, and the smoke knows the truth.

What has Uncle Thomas bequeathed me? An adjudicator of a pipe, a bewitching all its own?

His first scream pierced the festival air, a terrible hybrid of shock and agony. Gagging on a thick rope of smoke, the town crier's tongue dangled from his mouth, shedding blood like a slashed goatskin. The crowd gasped and backed away from the gallows, their appetite for darkness suddenly, and unexpectedly, sated.

"Confess thoust witchery, heyre on the eve of All Hallow's, 'neath moon and eyes of God!"

"Dhuruuuuh!" he brayed in a twisted rope of voices, possessors struggling to flee a host doomed to burn as witches must. His nose split open, billowing smoke and pumping scarlet, painting his waistcoat and filling the air with the sanguine stink of the hunt.

The audience scattered; bottles dropped, dates forgotten, screams burying the rickety sound of carnival tents collapsing as the stampede gained momentum. Yet, I stood my ground, pointing Witchfyndre at that unholy vessel as he fell upon his back, buckled shoes kicking, a hot puddle of piss instantly turning to steam as he cooked from the inside. His tricorne hat tumbled away, trailing smoke as his hair was now on fire.

An ugly strap of bile, both acid and flame, burst from his ruined mouth. Like a failing dam, his teeth collapsed, followed by a flood of bubbling, boiling blood. His clothes, already yellowed from sizzling man-fat, burned away like flash paper, a magician's subterfuge scattering in the carnival air. Hideous smoke wormed from the dark hollow of his navel, the contents of his belly excommunicated by an internal pyre.

"*Burn, witch!*" I bellowed, the pipe was again at my lips, drawing another mouthful of judgment's cruel deliverer. I exhaled fragrant, billowing blue. Now that Witchfyndre had done its work, the smoke stayed with me, a welcome accomplice, whispering the noble details of my mission.

Our mission.

So, dearest Angelica, as my life on the run and as a persecutor of the Shadowless Empire comes to a close, it is you, and only you, that I entrust this weapon of light, the enchanted workings of a master carver which forever spearheads our pursuit of *Those Others*.

It is a solitary life, but we are not killers.

The jinn Ibn-Saal-Zahad—the apparition who turned the table on his tormentor through his creation of this eternal tool of ultimate persecution, is indeed the greatest Witch-finder of them all. His drive for recompense lives in the smoke. *The smoke which knows the way, the smoke which knows the truth.*

We can only follow in his footsteps.

Use it wisely.

Use it often.

"*Heareth tales penn'd in lofty epistles of witchfind'rs, solitary souls in likeness and mann'r, doom'd to the shadows and halls rife with whisp'rs and dour accusations.*

Beest fearful, lief ones, the architect of z'ro waits, scheming in dens of nimble-footed things hath built by hands yond fleer the l'rd from dark, dark skies."

THE HOUSE ON BELTANE ROAD

"**L**OOK, IT'S UP to you," Leila said, adjusting her Wonder Woman headband, using her selfie-cam as a mirror. "My little brother Paul tried the Vanderbaum house last year. He thought it was all Halloween hokum and whatnot. I don't want to sound cold, but he found out the hard way, I guess."

Benny looked at his cousin through a mask he'd made himself. Mom freaked when he'd hauled newspapers, her mixing bowls, a bag of flour, and various other staples from the kitchen to his upstairs lair, but it kept him off the X-Box and busy with something constructive.

In the right light, Mom said upon seeing it, *your mask looks like the flayed countenance of a long-dead ancestor.*

Benny didn't know the words flayed or countenance, but he knew ancestor, and that had a far more complimentary ring to it than *the mask you made looks like your old great-grandfather.*

In one hand he clutched a pillowcase he'd decorated with a screeching vampire bat. In the other, a plastic flashlight shaped like a Nantucket Lighthouse Mom had bought at Halligan's Hardware. Embossed on its side: *Lil' Beacon.*

"Found out what?" Benny said, turning away from Leila.

Even with Benny's vision impaired by the mask, there was no escaping the Vanderbaum house's glare. Twin chimneys punched from the gabled roof like the fists of some gargantuan, felled robot. The second-floor turret, and weathervane depicting crows in flight, reached skyward, silhouetted against the distant, hazy tower of Walpurgis Peak. A sprawling oak stood between Benny and the house, wind rustling the bare branches and unleashing a pack of feral shadows across winding Beltane Road.

"What we all know. Here in the Purg, little cuz, you need to stay on your toes. Full moons, solstices, hell, even *new* moons if you're out on Rusty Jack's road. This entire place isn't like the rest of the state. You'll see things; you'll *hear* things."

Leila sighed. Deborah and Sienna had promised to meet her and Benny on the corner of Sixth and Beltane, but as yet, no dice. After she fulfilled her obligation to watch Benny trick or treat and they dropped him back home, it was off to a total rager near Widow's Holler—two kegs, two bands. Rumor had it Gavin Haines copped a big score down on Bleary Street, and the party favor of the night was all the molly you could handle. Further rumor maintained a girl named Beeley Ballantine had disappeared near Widow's Holler the year before, at Copperhead Farms no less. Leila reminded herself to stay on *her* toes, molly notwithstanding.

In early summer, Benny's family moved cross-country from Phoenix, and he couldn't have been more relieved. Arizona blight brought him nothing but misery and friendlessness, and his family's awful financial situation made everything worse. When the invite came from his mother's side of the family, who had been in Walpurgis County for generations—the Purg, as he soon learned—to occupy a house on four acres willed to her from recently departed Uncle Sal, his parents jumped at the opportunity. Glorious green trees grew in abundance here, lakes glittered, streams bubbled, and in summer, thunderstorms—precisely what Benny longed for in the parched crust of southern Arizona.

Cousin Leila (*second* cousin, and whatever that meant he didn't know), seemed friendly enough and pretty to look at, although the brother Paul she talked about often was never anywhere to be seen. Whenever Benny asked, Leila said, "he's out, but he'll be back later."

Benny shifted his weight and turned back to Leila. His dad's black bathrobe, a stand-in for a druid's hooded vestment, hung massive on his little frame.

"They have jack-o'-lanterns," Benny said. "I guess that means candy, right?"

Leila looked up from her texting—Deborah and Sienna delayed. *Costume trubbl Luv U!*

"Like I said, it's up to you, little cuz."

"Is it dangerous?" Benny thought her eyes implied otherwise.

"Dangerous?" Leila shrugged. "It's just a house."

Benny stared at the Vanderbaum house, impressed and intimidated by its severe size and ghastly architecture. At its feet wound the black kingsnake of Beltane Road, a colossal serpent coiling across rolling hills and through tall, cockeyed trees. A handful of streetlamps glowed in the mist until darkness swallowed them.

"But the *only* house on Beltane Road," she added.

With a lungful of autumn night and without waiting for Leila, Benny summoned his courage and crossed Beltane Road. Leaves crunched beneath his Sketchers. Lil' Beacon cast a puddle of weak light on the cracked asphalt.

Several jack-o'-lanterns, aglow with harmless cretin smiles, sat on the steps leading to the wraparound porch. Above massive teak doors carved with ornate vines and leaves in sharp relief, shone an old-style carriage lamp suspended by chains. Dark windows stared at him from beneath gables tall as pine trees. Smoke crept from both chimneys in crooked, skyward rivers.

Before Benny stepped onto the curb, he turned to his cousin, who waved her glowing phone, motioning him forward. She nodded with overclocked enthusiasm.

When he looked back to the house, the doors had parted. His little bladder suddenly felt very full, a water balloon ready to burst. He couldn't turn chicken now, not in front of his cousin, not in front of a *girl*. Besides, Leila had said her brother had met this very dare just last year. Not her big brother, her *little* brother. Big difference.

It's an old house. It just looks *haunted.*

With doors that open by themselves.

Benny squinted. In the gloom beyond the foyer, a massive staircase stretched upward into darkness. A shadow, a serpentine centipede of night, seemed to move across the polished floor, urged on by the glow of a heavy stone fireplace. A sprawling gas-lit chandelier hung in the entryway, globes flickering in a slow, steady pulse. Red brocade wallpaper. Enormous portraits in opulent frames.

"Benny, sweetie, come inside. It's getting cold out." His mother's voice. Soft, lilting. A memory surfaced: Benny barely old enough to peer over the kitchen counter, watching Mom prepare a Duncan Hines cake. She handed him the dripping spatula. *Mmmm*, chocolate. Even here on the sidewalk, he sensed the promise of sweets, the scent of hot sugar. Home.

"Come give us a hand," she added. "We're making dessert."

Benny knew full well his mother was at their new place, minding his baby sister while handling the trick-or-treaters, and Dad was in his home office rushing to please a client in some other state. Still, her voice drifted from the parted doors, loaded with the soft, motherly authority he'd obeyed since birth. Impossible, her in this ogre of a house, yet it was so.

Standing now on Vanderbaum property, he set a foot on the first step, then the second. Old nails groaned.

Benny stopped, his foot inches from the third step, bladder aching, heart solid marble.

Turn and run or piss your pants—either way, you'll never hear the end of it. Leila's watching.

"Hurry up, Benny," Mom said, this time with a sprig of aggravation in her voice. "Before it gets cold."

Behind the Vanderbaum mansion, a hulking, wooden brute so vast Beltane Road had been laid around it, the colossal tooth of Walpurgis Peak devoured the night sky. No Lil' Beacon could light that granite monstrosity, and Benny knew, just *knew*, the wind that had brayed through the barren oak tree had blown from there, rushed down its jagged edge, and come for *him*.

Benny immediately wanted to be home—not here home, *Phoenix* home with its lonely ninety-degree summer nights, scorpions in his sneakers, and tarantulas in the garage. He suddenly didn't mind being friendless and forgotten as it wasn't his mother in that house; it was that mountain, that ugly, rugged hill in the murk, imitating the sound of home before it pounced—

"*The spatula is all ready for you,*" his mother cooed.

—and whipped his bones to batter.

In his mind's eye, he remembered an ingot of morning light stabbing through the kitchen window, how it set Mom's hair afire, the silly chicken holding a rolling pin embroidered onto her apron, the comforting heat of the oven, its hot mouth waiting for its chocolate treat, too. But that's not what coaxed him to the threshold. It was the voice of Walpurgis Peak, the first thing he laid eyes upon as their Toyota Sequoia rounded the turn on Route 54, poking above the tree canopy like some gargantuan fossil. Even the clouds seemed to keep their distance. The very sight of it spawned innocent terror in him, regressing to toddlerhood, longing for his onesie jammies and fuzzy nuzzle blankie. And now it loomed in the October night with this house to speak for it, an ugly ventriloquist act bound and determined to turn a Halloween dare into a child's recurring nightmare.

Benny looked for Leila, an ocean away on that corner, face in her phone. Behind her wandered ghosts and witches, superheroes and ballerinas, the night alive with giggles and bobbing flashlights, their attention focused on Sixth Street, not showing the slightest interest in the lone house on Beltane Road. Benny imagined shingles trembling atop every house unfortunate enough to lie in the Vanderbaum mansion's shadow. Rain shunned the ugly tyrant in summer, snow refused to fall upon it in winter.

"*Those Others*, Benny. Come see what they see, what they've shown me."

There was a *whoorrrf* sound from behind, coupled with the undeniable sensation of something sliding, turning, on the wooden steps. Benny wheeled around, clutching his pillowcase and pointing Lil' Beacon toward the sound. Hot wet breath and the stink of fear-sweat turned the inside of his mask into a choking, humid bag.

The jack-o'-lanterns had pivoted, abdicating their sentinel streetward stare in favor of the little boy frozen mid-step. No longer grinning goblins with triangle eyes, their faces had soured hideous; ugly stabs and a madman's hacks gouged in a fit of rage. Candlelight poured from angry eyes and slit mouths, offering only the scent of burnt pumpkin—lunatics gorged with the light of the moon that had driven them mad.

Whether tentacle or tail moved in the corner of his eye, Benny couldn't tell, but by the time he spun around from the impossible snarling jack-o'-lanterns, he caught only a glimpse of something huge crawling over the banister. Firelight gleamed as iridescent skin disappeared into the dark.

"*Leila!*"

A cold rush of air, born upon the forbidden slopes of Walpurgis Peak, belied the fire's cozy invitation. The carriage lamp suspended above the porch swayed, crazy shadows swimming everywhere. As if time had stuttered—*shimmered*—the way it only does in paralyzing nightmares, Benny now found himself at the threshold, eyes wide in disbelief, throat choked by a scream that wouldn't come. Winter poured from the house.

His mask, the flayed ancestor, looked down at him, bleached and skinless, haggard, and not only from Death—but *Infinity*. The tall figure, clad in a black flowing drapery of sleeves, the hood pulled up to mimic Benny's own slapped-together costume, but with all the dreadful details only something ancient, something eternal, could fathom, spoke.

"Behold, see me."

His mother's voice, hers but not hers, an imitation, the illusion of love and safety, eternally dangerous but impossible to resist; the serpent in the garden, the devil on one's shoulder.

He remembered how Mom had held him after he'd fallen from his bike and tumbled into rough desert dirt, crying like a baby, but now she had the teeth of a vampire, long and bloody, still hot from the human meat they'd fed upon. During a particularly frigid winter in Phoenix, Mom read *Charlie and the Chocolate Factory* to Benny as he languished with flu, but in this hideous version she made the Oompa Loompa songs about cannibalism and murder, and by the time the story ended, Charlie Bucket had gouged his eyes out with a candy cane. There was the time Mom bought him an orange pop at a roadside stand on the Navajo reservation, now eager to rattle off a list of terrible ingredients—his sister's tears, his father's failures, and his mother's infidelities. The mask smiled, but from its mouth leaked the frozen breath of the overwhelming eyesore of Walpurgis Peak and every deception played out upon its steep and treacherous face. An avalanche of empty promises.

It opened its robe. So many swarming, albino things teeming over the xylophone of its ribs. Wet mouths gnawing at the air, tails slapping exposed bone, clattering legs, and eyes on stalks. From the stairs, the steps leading into the black shadows of the second floor, the hissing of whatever had used the banister as its ladder.

This is a greedy, jealous house, and it will have its way.

A barefoot boy peered out from behind the robed figure, hair a mess, face ghost-white, dressed in a torn, filthy Batman outfit.

That's Paul, Benny realized. He didn't know how he knew, but it was true to the bone. *Cousin Paul.*

The boy rushed past Benny. The whoosh of his cape chilled the sweat at Benny's brow. Benny heard Cousin Paul sobbing as he clattered down the steps.

From the corner of Sixth and Beltane, Leila watched as Benny stood statue still before the Vanderbaum mansion's open doors, staring into the big black empty of an abandoned house that refused to grow old. A moment later, her hysterical brother bumbled into the glow of a streetlamp, and she waved her phone above her head so he could follow the light. A Lil' Beacon of his own. He'd lost a lot of weight over the last year, but it was good to see him and even better to have him home.

"I'm sorry, but you're taking Paul's place, little cuz. Welcome to Walpurgis County."

Benny lifted his gaze to the flayed ancestor. No eyes to speak of, yet he felt them upon him. He heard the maniac chirping of the albino horde as they fought and scraped against one another through this thing, this human-shaped prop, a dreadful mirror image of his Halloween costume.

Benny's teeth chattered in that glacial cold, that mountain cold, because when you died you went cold and stone cold meant stone cold dead and dead was dead and there's nothing to snatch you away from the mountain when it uses an old pervert of a house to call your name and make you remember the good things then make them terrible while it freezes you from the inside out and if Mom was here she'd know that dead means stone and mountains are stone the biggest stone is the meanest stone of all—

Lil' Beacon winked out.

The House on Beltane Road had what it wanted. For now.

THE NIGHTMAN'S LAST SHIFT

THE LAMPLIGHTER INN had seen better days. Situated on US Route 62, an insignificant capillary now that Interstate 40 drained the blood flow, the motel clung to life, beset by the anemia of neglect, the leukemia of dismissal.

Its sign, a massive replica of a Victorian-era gaslamp, was one of the few things that remained in any state of maintenance. It hovered over the parking lot, a Dickensian UFO, casting a jaundiced glow upon the dead dirt, deader stones, and wind-blown trash.

Lange sat behind the desk, scrawling in his notebook. Most of the drawings would land a schoolboy in the principal's office. The writings would interest even the most jaded Behavioral Science professor at Quantico.

A Frigidaire freezer hummed behind him, draped with a fancy paisley tablecloth Lange snatched in 2011 after a Georgia family's impromptu picnic near the empty swimming pool. Sandwiches and pop, chips and salsa. To spruce up the sad event, Mom brought desert flowers and purple paisley. After Dad popped his second Mountain Dew, Lange crushed his right temple with a sledgehammer. Right in front of the misses. Right in front of the kiddies. Dad crumpled like a switch had been thrown as an enormous jet of blood thrust from his left ear. After a few more bullseye hammer blows and a brief chase with the squirrely pre-teen son, the job was complete.

The best thing about a forgotten motel was that there was no one to spy on you, Lange wrote. *No one to tell you to stop.*

He may not have been spied upon, but Lange never escaped the sense of being *watched.*

As Lange cleaned up the picnic mess, he remembered a cold January night in 2000, naked below the towering gaslamp. The air was crisp and electric, icy, yet alive, as only the desert could conjure. In his hand, a Ginsu knife he'd owned since the eighties. Carved into his chest, the word FEED. From sternum to knees ran broad, bloody tiger stripes. Near the ice machine, a bludgeoned corpse known to him only as Davis.

He watched as fingers of cloud crept over the western hills, hypnotized as the mist irised open, an incredible eye, the vortex's center the pus-yellow of infection. In a stony baritone, Those Others—*The Shadowless Ones*—spoke from the Elsewhere between *then* and *yet*.

For two and twenty years you are bound to service, from here to the Great Step Downward.

Lange quickly bagged and tagged the Georgian family's soft parts with a wheezing Seal-A-Meal he'd bought from Craigslist. The hard tissues were disposed of in a moonscape of graves beside Firebrand Trail, a worm of a road so inhospitable even four-wheeled ATVs struggled to traverse it. Coyotes and buzzards unearthed them at leisure.

Their vehicles were sold to a disreputable scrapyard in Needles. On several occasions, Lange cheered the giant electromagnet as it dropped the car into the maw of the compactor. He wrote about what it would be like to die inside and drew several pictures.

Since that night in 2000, when that voice summoned him in that deep, dead tone, Lange dutifully opened the Frigidaire and retrieved as many bags as instructed.

They like it warm but not hot, he murmured, boiling water on the hotplate next to the Mr. Coffee. *Soft and buttery, it reminds them of when they were corporeal, when they could feast recklessly on worlds far away from here—*

Headlights spilled through the office window, pulling Lange out of his reverie.

From 2011 to 2000 and back again. A dream within a dream.

He snapped the notebook shut and scanned the office. Long shadows and no bloody Seal-A-Meal boiler bags. *Good.* The sledgehammer, Mrs. Justice, he called it, slept unseen beneath the desk, next to the Ginsu and an S&W 629. *Even better.*

The truck's brakes shrieked to a stop, headlights like giant, alien eyes unaccustomed to the California desert.

Lange watched the driver's silhouette. The woman bumped the heavy door shut with her hip, then reached into the pickup's bed.

She pulled out a long bag, slung it with little effort, and turned toward Lange.

Rifle. Lange thought. *Coyote or feral pig hunt. All alone, just her and her little Ruger.*

He ran his hand beneath his shirt, fingertips caressing the peaks and valleys of a servant's scar. FEED.

When they speak to me again, I'll provide a delicacy. I'll deliver sweet Mommymeat.

The woman sauntered toward the office. Jeans, boots, and a vest sheathed her body, and a cattleman-creased Stetson governed her mane. Behind her, the mother star's scarlet suicide mission into the western horizon.

She nudged the door open with the unburdened shoulder. The little bell up top jingled.

"You the Nightman?" she said from a pool of shadow, her voice lower than Lange expected—a pinch of Texas and a dash of Santa Monica.

I like that. Nightman.

She stepped into the shallow light, and Lange did his best not to squirm. Perfect. Maybe early thirties, fit, not a sliver above five-eight, dark eyes, and sandy-brown hair. Up top, a black Stetson with a snakeskin hatband adorned with teeth. Fangs. Needle-sharp viper fangs.

Lange smiled. His eyes scanned prey.

She wore a collared shirt beneath her vest, opened to the third button. Blooming colorful from the swell of her cleavage, the upper portion of what had to be an enormous tattoo. Serpents in rapture, intertwined on their journey up the stranger's neck, splitting off at her jawline to secret destinations behind the ear. A gorgon's mane by any other name.

"I am," Lange said. "Yes. The Nightman."

She nodded and pulled a mobile phone from her pocket. Her eyes went back and forth between the screen and Lange a couple of times before she nodded, satisfied.

"Lange," she said. She slipped the bag from her shoulder and dropped it upright to the floor with a heavy, no-nonsense thud.

Lange's balls and adrenal gland tightened.

"Your services to the Shadowless are no longer required," she said.

Lange pushed himself out of the chair, and it rolled back and struck the Frigidaire. With speed he thought not possible, he lunged for the revolver.

Enormous resistance, the pain instant and blunt. When he looked up, the tattooed woman leaned over the counter, eyes narrow, teeth showing. In her hands, a sledgehammer, far larger than Mrs. Justice, held out like a spear, the hammerhead smack-dab in the middle of his chest.

"No guns," she hissed.

Lange straightened, hands up, fingers splayed into starfish. The sun was almost gone now, but at the hills the mist returned, the ghost-hand of a mammoth witch. In unnamable fractals it churned, under-lit by the sun's surrender. The eye opened and spoke:

Lange-flesh. The gut-fruit of a Nightman's suffering. Two and twenty years gone.

"Outside," she said.

They faced off like gunfighters.

She charged like a lion.

The first sledgehammer blow destroyed Lange's clavicle and everything attached to it. He'd felt bones shatter, but never his own. The pain was unbelievable; dense, sluggish as pancake batter. He staggered backward in disbelief, jaw hinged open, throat silent.

Jesus, she's fast, he thought, *but you're sixty-three now. You're slow.*

She scooted forward, then slid to a stop. Flipping her weapon, she jabbed Lange's gut with the handle.

Those Others brayed: *Wound not his delicacies—preserve them unbruised, sweet as the night he carved himself in Service.*

Lange attempted to raise Mrs. Justice, but his crushed shoulder made that impossible. He choked-up on the handle, wielding it like a carpenter's apprentice. Useless against youth's superior speed, but if he could get inside her reach, Lange hoped to crush her windpipe, then break her skull.

She spun like a discus thrower and landed a powerful hammer-led roundhouse to Lange's mouth. A geyser of blood erupted black in the gaslamp's tetanus-colored light. His teeth scattered like popcorn, a Jiffypop tin left unattended.

Lange hit the ground howling, eyes bulging in different directions. Scarlet bubbled from both nose and mouth, thick with shock and snot.

"Old hills, Nightman," she said. "Old rules. Your service was temporary. Davis, back in 2000, that was you *replacing* him. See where we're headed?"

Gasping, Lange remembered Davis, palms forward in panic, forehead gushing, skull opened, the macaroni of his frontal lobe exposed and throbbing. One eye dangled from the snarl of his optic nerve.

Serve, the witch-mist purred through its haunted, yellow eye on that long-ago evening. *Take your knife and know Us.*

Now, leaning on the sledgehammer's handle, the stranger tilted her hat back and grinned.

"Shhhh," she said, index finger to her lips. She cocked her head cocked toward the hills. "Listen."

Their hills.

You shall be gutted, ground, and glorified. Forever feeding the workings of The Machine.

She ended Lange as if driving a railroad spike.

After closing the freezer and straightening the tablecloth, the Medusa Cult assassin sat in the Nightman's chair. A newer, more powerful sledgehammer slept beneath the desk.

She eyed the Ginsu.

Outside, the Vacancy light illuminated red.

Two and twenty years. FEED.

OUR LAST, RAVING DAYS

HE MEDUSA CULT.
Hayward said little else until he'd downed enough bourbon to settle his nerves. Slumped into the high-back leather chair, staring at the fireplace with one eye and the deadbolt with the other, his lips finally loosened.

"Most thought they'd moved on." He emptied the glass and set it on the end table. I filled it, careful not to touch his bloody sleeves or grimy fingers. "But that was all bullshit, of course."

Winter Howl, three nights of brutal, freezing wind roaring down the razor slopes of Walpurgis Peak, announced winter's arrival. On the first night of the mountain's frigid ire, Hayward's thunderous door-pounding pulled me from my evening work. With dawn several hours away, the annual Walpurgis County spectacle blew full throttle.

"Ask yourself, Darlo, why *wouldn't* the Medusa Cult remain in the Purg, the most bedeviled county in the United States? Consider the history. The Gennckes clan—a hundred years ago now—burned out of their home at Copperhead Farms, their patriarch Johannes crucified then beheaded at the hands of a vengeful reverend and starved, frenzied townsfolk. Think of the campfire stories, the old-time ballads of those six-hundred abandoned Copperhead acres, said to be stalked on moonless nights. Least of all the Shimmer, which split that farm's parcels into *decades*."

Hayward's manic delivery notwithstanding, he had a point. In the early days, before the towns of Jasper, Danielsburg, and Frederick had been unified under the Walpurgis County Protectorate, the area had been well-steeped in lore. Many a tinker and trader spread tales of the enormous cephalopods glimpsed breaching waters of Dead Neck Lake, tempting the early pioneers with offers of fortune-telling and incantation, spells to outfox time and heal the scars gouged by great aeons. Even then, the colossal sycamores of Eldritch Wood were rumored to hiss in the early evenings with *Arachnae*, a subspecies of human said to crawl supine, traversing the forest canopy upon enormous spider legs. Legend had it their web-ejaculate possessed aphrodisiac properties so effective it was often lethal to the recipient.

Most in the Purg knew these stories and made peace with them; those that did not suffered wretched misfortune when reality called. That unholy mountain, upon whose hide fires burned on every pagan holiday, was undoubtedly enough to cast an eerie discontent over the place, let alone the legend-weary foothills steeped in lore and monsters. It is important to note that Walpurgis County never appeared in the same place twice on a map. The lost stayed lost.

The Medusa Cult, however, proved another matter entirely, and to think they would abandon a place as fertile as this was indeed foolish—a point Hayward had always been eager to make. So much so, it cost him a decade. More on that in a minute.

"They're a predatory cult," Hayward said, "fueled by malevolence and hubris; but they're shrewd, and resourceful, Darlo, and now, on the move again. For centuries they've attempted to summon the great Adjudicator through The Gate. *Centuries.* They almost pulled it off in Rome in the 1860s, and had the Vatican catacombs not flooded, they might have succeeded. The cult retreats underground when any attention turns their way, yet brazen they remain.

"Their public front, Medusa Engineering, trades on NASDAQ, right in front of everyone and their dog. Deep in the inner sanctum of aerospace, warfare, bio-engineering, quantum computing, pharma—you name it. An enormous umbrella protecting an untold number of subsidiaries. They never relinquish an asset nor surrender the slightest granule of influence."

I leaned against my desk, eyeing my odd acquaintance, always remembering how out of place Hayward Decatur seemed in the Purg. Most who couldn't cope moved away and, to my knowledge, never spoke of Walpurgis County outside its borders. I believe this selective amnesia is an indigenous hex, bewitching residents since birth. Once gone, your memory of this place faded, like a dream you struggle to recall. A few belied that: the Exorcist Billy Beauchamp, LA Police Detective Elliot Pomerantz, and perhaps a few other Purg expats, but for the most part, our sequestered county remained as such. After you left—if you were allowed, that is—Walpurgis County simply slipped your mind.

Hayward never played the forgetting game. He'd stuck it out in the Purg and was even twice elected Mayor of Danielsburg, serving from 1994 to 2001. Those had been good days for him, but, as I discovered during private, inebriated conversations, Hayward harbored an agenda all along: the exposure and elimination of the Medusa Cult's enduring presence in Walpurgis County, no matter how sanguine or anemic. He often mentioned their intense interest in Walpurgis Peak, but these conspiratorial diatribes arose only after hours, with doors closed, bottles opened, and fires lit.

There's something beneath that goddamned mountain, Darlo, Hayward warned one autumn evening. *And they are determined to either retrieve it, or release it. I can't seem to put my finger on it.*

He trailed off, chasing his thoughts. I imagined his mind a jigsaw puzzle, and even though quite a few pieces had yet to be fit, he had a good grasp of the final image but was afraid of what it might be.

Tell no one, Darlo, he said just months before his arrest. *I have irrefutable evidence Medusa Cult operatives are here, in Danielsburg. These are not the black-suited agents of old. They are the mailman, the nice lady at the thrift store, a bum on Bleary Street. Deep cover.*

Given his history, I was shocked at *how* but not surprised *when* Hayward Decatur's mayoral duties came to a sudden, public end. Pulled over for speeding on Route 54 by Staties, Troopers Middleton and Blayne discovered a shower curtain-wrapped Marion Orr in Hayward's back seat. His obsession culminating in a meltdown was of little astonishment—but I didn't think he'd go full Chernobyl.

The Troopers cuffed Hayward and slammed him onto the hood of his Chrysler, sweating and manic, his suit spattered with mud and blood. Also in his possession were a shovel and a high-powered flashlight.

I did Walpurgis County a favor, the police report quoted him. *Even I don't know in what century she suffocates. But that witch . . . Never. Stopped. Screaming.*

Oddly, the case attracted little outside fanfare. Evidence, I think, of Walpurgis County's near-invisibility to outsiders. Any news agency would have been on the Decatur case like a free on lunch; the boundless potential for circus-like court proceedings an irresistible blue plate special. I've already mentioned how hard this place is to find on a map, but tar me for lying if it wasn't next to impossible to find any absolute references to Walpurgis County in news or history books—period. You may find one anecdote here or there, perhaps some odd tale about whispering cephalopods, but the next time you opened the book—*poof!*—gone. Walpurgis County preferred its secrets to remain secret, and the strange death of Marion Orr did not violate the old rules.

The courts processed Hayward fast—like shit through a goose, old-timer Greedle Olin told whoever would listen as he held court in his corner booth at Big Ben's Coffee Shop. *Judge Penniman is hiding something; more here than meets the eye. Hayward, I mean, Mayor Decatur, might end up hanging from a bedsheet before long. You trust ol' Greedle. Now pass me that sugar bowl, wontcha?*

Greedle might have been wrong about Hayward meeting his fate at the end of a sheet, but he was absolutely spot on about the court's eagerness to broom a sensational crime. How often does the mayor of a small town get busted with a corpse in his convertible Lebaron?

To much local amazement, Hayward beat the homicide rap on an insanity plea—but was sentenced to serve a dime-plus-five two counties over in Garland Grove Recovery Home. The story goes if his family hadn't ponied up a six-figure dowry, he'd done his stint at Bacchanale Psychiatric over in Frederick, and that would have been the end of him, bedsheets be damned.

Still, Hayward Decatur was not born of forgetful blood, and those souls always found their way home. News of his early release did not reach me until a hopped-up, bloodied, and apparently still-on-mission Hayward landed in my living room on the first night of Winter Howl. Nestled in his chair, he rubbed the back of his neck, sipped his bourbon, and pointed at my overstuffed bookshelves.

"Although it's well known the Medusa Cult possesses books such as *The Discoveries of Crosius* and *Deos Sine Umbra*, they fumble for the keys. There's speculation they've run into major stumbling blocks, one of which is conflicting interpretations of arcane symbology. More recently it's been speculated that translation isn't the issue—it's not a *language* barrier—it's that no human can fully comprehend the *equations*. Shadowless Mathematics most occult researchers call it, and there simply is no one in the Medusa Cult ranks powerful enough to ascend through whatever occult rituals or protocols required to make it all fall in line. *If you can't understand the question, you cannot provide the answer.*

"Enter Artificial Intelligence, with Medusa Engineering at the forefront. Not Boston Dynamics or D-Wave, not the Department of Defense or some spunky Silicon Valley startup—all of that is a con, a misdirect. A.I. is not some benign technological evolution conceived by brilliant nerds as the media would have you believe— A.I. serves *their* purpose. Put simply, it solves problems they cannot."

"Hayward," I said. "We've danced to this tune for a lot of years. This global plot, it's mammoth in scope, but for whatever reason, it always lands in Walpurgis County."

Hayward nodded. "There's a power here, and believe me, I wish I had a less ham-fisted way to say it. Artificial Intelligence takes them only so far; it addresses only the academic side of it. But the supernatural side, when they finally make their big move, will come from here." He tapped the end table with a knobby index finger. "This county." He tossed his thumb over his shoulder like an irate umpire. "That lunatic mountain."

"There's blood on your sleeve. I can't help but think of Marion Orr. What the hell happened tonight?"

"Oh, we'll get there. Just know I hear things, Darlo. I put the pieces together. I read between the lines. I'm called crazy since I dispatched that witch in 2001, but I'll tell you what I never told any of the doctors at Garland: I remain steadfast in my argument that she was—and remains—an agent sent by the Medusa Cult. Whether a reconnaissance agent to identify opposition leaders or she performed some other function, I never found out."

Even I don't know in what century she suffocates.

His quote haunted me. Marion Orr's body had been right there, in the back seat, wrapped and ready for disposal, clearly visible, plain as day. And now, ten years after the fact, those words rattled their chains surely as Winter Howl bellowed and moaned beneath the eaves.

But that witch . . . Never. Stopped. Screaming.

I do not think his statements that night were accidental or the product of a mind on the verge of collapse. Hayward retained possession of his faculties. He knew right from wrong—the main reason the insanity plea and the case's expedition through the court felt odd to me. Then and now.

An unmistakable air of danger surrounded him, of course. How can there not be after the shedding of blood? I'd met plenty of guys who shut off a lot of lights in Afghanistan and Iraq, even a few in Vietnam, and they never gave me the feeling I got from Hayward. I knew he'd never be violent toward me, but he'd killed for a different reason than a soldier, and there's a weight there that's hard to ignore. The stain of murder would never leave him, and a decade institutionalized, even if Garland Grove was, by comparison to Bacchanale, a luxury facility, didn't do Hayward any favors. Even with his sentence cut short, he was not released from duty. Hayward's mission remained.

He's spent ten years in a goddamn nuthouse, and his focus hasn't changed one iota. Aren't you the least bit curious why he hasn't been thorozined into coma?

"I know what everyone thinks," Hayward went on. "They think I'm an insane, certainly a convicted killer, or worse these days, a *conspiracy theorist*. But know this—the Medusa Cult plan has been in motion for centuries. Via Medusa Engineering's quantum computers and the plethora of psychoactive pharmaceuticals they've either developed, bought, or stolen, I believe they're finally ready. The marriage of Black Magic and High Technology is about the most dangerous union you can fathom. They're going to make their big move, Darlo. They'll attempt once again to open the Gate."

A lot to digest, yet Hayward's rants always drew seamless connections, and tonight, he was firing on all six. The elegance of paranoia shines in the effortless presentation offered by the afflicted, and in Hayward's case, I'd come to appreciate its unique beauty. Yet here in Walpurgis County, everything had to be taken at face value—monsters exist, the dead sometimes keep their day jobs, and sinister cults plot the end of all things. The moment you turned your head in disbelief, something horrendous moved at the corner of your eye, breaching the threshold of the shadow realm.

"Any truth to the rumor The Medusa gang was responsible for the CERN disaster in 2018?" I said. "I listened to a couple of fringe podcasts insane over it. If true, *that* sounded like a pretty big move."

"I'm glad *someone* is paying attention."

In 2018, the Large Hadron Collider at CERN, the enormous subterranean toroid on the France-Switzerland border, suffered a colossal malfunction. As of this writing, what we're told is the most complex and expensive machine ever built is still in pieces, and a great deal of the underground excavation is rumored to be slagged—though media would have the world believe it is closed for equipment upgrades.

"Not to your extent, but yes. A little. And I'll admit, when I heard about it, I thought of you. But is that legit? That true about CERN?"

Hayward nodded. "I'm sure it is. I can't imagine a better place than CERN for them to test the limits of their A.I. In the early nineties, Medusa Engineering attempted to open the Gate at the radio telescope complex near Socorro, New Mexico. It ended in disaster, and it took *years* to rebuild the VLA. The incident was sold to the public as a terrorist attack, which I'm sure you recall. I believe the wound in the world opened by the CERN bloodbath might never close. Billions in damage, scores dead, now only God knows what's creeping into our world from there. I know that sounds as if they met with success, but the Gate is far worse than that slit in reality, throbbing underground in the ruins of the CERN accelerator complex. Nevertheless, don't be shocked if something unholy rises from Lake Geneva.

"Which brings me to tonight, Darlo, *and* Marion Orr. The Medusa Cult is back in business in Walpurgis County. Right now, black Suburbans and a few long cars are parked at the Vanderbaum house."

Despite the global conspiracy to plunge the human race into darkness, his mention of the Vanderbaum house raised gooseflesh on my neck and forearms. The House on Beltane Road, as we called it back in the day. If you had the stones to approach it on Halloween, you risked disappearing into its maze of polished wood and whispering voices, lured by temptations known only to you.

Throughout the first half of the twentieth century, many a corpse had been carried from that house, a sprawling Victorian situated where the serpentine twists of Beltane Road began. Though abandoned since the Eisenhower era, the house had never shown the slightest sign of aging. Lights shone nightly. Smoke poured from the chimneys. The paint never peeled, the curtains never yellowed, and the garden remained immaculate. No maintenance crew tended the property, and no tax collector came calling. Only the massive oak tree marked the passing of years, a sentinel to the house's brooding hexagonal turret and monstrous weathervane. Behind it, sheathed in distant haze, the soulless carnivore that is Walpurgis Peak.

Hayward added, "These aren't low-level worker-bees, either—these are *players*."

"Davos at Dracula's."

"Good one," Hayward said into his glass. His knuckles, maimed by arthritis, looked as if ball bearings had been hidden beneath his skin. Hayward had to be in his late sixties now, a hard late sixties, and I only imagined how brutal incarceration had been on him. And here he sat in my living room, disheveled and running on about the Medusa Cult as he'd always done. The play never missed a performance.

"The Vanderbaum house is a serious place," he continued. "Even the crows know it's a dark nexus—probably explains that weathervane. Where else would one expect the Medusa Cult charity mixer to be?"

"How did you know they'd be here, tonight, during Winter Howl no less? The streets are impassable, there's shit all over the place, downed trees, you name it. I'm surprised you made it here, let alone a line of sleek cars in front of the house."

Hayward held his glass out, agitated and exhausted. As I pulled the cork, the wind brayed. Rogue branches, those I had been too lazy to trim last summer, slapped against the windows like bullwhips.

Hayward shrugged. "Garland Grove cut me loose last August, and I went right back to work. Things have changed in the last ten years; there's an active network now, a group who know just how evil and crazy these people are. Countermeasures, one might say. They maintain constant vigilance in information gathering and analysis. There is funding from places you wouldn't believe, and I am, in a way, a celebrity among them, so they've assisted me with living expenses and the like."

I poured him a drink and asked, "How could they have found out about you? There was a total press blackout on your case."

"Indeed. Back channels everywhere, my friend. Let's just say the real fighters don't watch TV."

I nodded. When evil makes its move, the resourceful gather to combat it. It's been that way since we first looked up to the night sky and heard the mad, hopeless snarl of the cosmos. For all I knew, maybe Hayward Decatur dispatched a Medusa Cult witch after all, and that type of grit attracts the brazen and ballsy.

"The Vanderbaum house. Did you see anyone in particular or just all the vehicles?"

"Both."

"You didn't *approach* them, did you?"

Hayward shook his head. "Not directly. I mean, I didn't burst through the door like the Terminator. I took the Encyclopedia Brown route, and spied through a window. It might sound *prima facie* gutless, but getting anywhere near the Medusa Cult, especially in that goddamned house, takes more guts than you think you have, let alone in sixty-mile-an-hour wind."

"Every Halloween I chickened out, plain and simple."

"Good call, Darlo, that's why you're still here. What's hideous, despite its reputation for devouring children, is the Vanderbaum house knows who you trust. The moment I crossed the property line, from the sidewalk to the walkway leading to the steps, it spoke to me in my sister's voice. My *sister*, dear God. Angela, w*ho's been dead for over thirty years,* insisted I confess my transgressions, make amends. 'Cut a switch from the oak,' she said, her voice utterly real, Angela's tone when she babysat me or the loving way she talked to her cats. 'It will know what to do. Use it to gouge out your eyes, then eat them. Blood for blood. Alone we atone, baby brother.'"

"I would have shit a Cadillac," I said.

"I thought I knew all of Walpurgis County's tricks; thought I had defenses against them. But I heard my sister's voice like breath in my ear, I smelled her soap and hairspray." Hayward shook his head and waved his hand as if shooing away a terrible waitress. He finally pointed at me with his glass. "It finds your intimate memories, the ones seared onto the motherboard, if you know what I mean. The House on Beltane Road is *rife* with the Shimmer, trapped in nowhere-time while in the grip of a dream paralysis."

Hayward downed his booze and winced. "Very few can bear it."

"They made you?" I said, reaching for the bottle. If the Mayor of Danielsburg was drinking on a Wednesday, then so was I.

Hayward raised his left hand. Grime and scratches, dirty nails, tattered scarlet sleeve. I noticed his collar, torn and similarly soiled, with a spattering of blood at the nape of his neck. I poured him another. 115 proof truth serum splashed into his glass.

"I don't *think* the albino saw me, or his acolytes, or whatever we should call them. He's definitely the big honcho, though. Easily six-four, ghost white. Remember the brothers in the seventies, musicians Johnny and Edgar Winter? Like that, but with an unmistakable beak of a nose, fingers like tree twigs, and a pair of blacked-out goggles. If any natural light had ever touched this creature, I'd be truly surprised. Everyone but him had their backs to me, but all of them were old. And I don't mean my age, I mean eighties and up, real fossils."

"No one you recognized?"

Hayward offered a shrug and a twisted cheek. He touched the back of his neck. "Maybe. My Medusa Cult trading cards were confiscated at the time of arrest."

"You can have mine, I'm not using them."

"Honestly, it was hard to tell. But what's important is this: the albino's bodyguard, *that* bitch, she sure got a good look at me. She's . . . something else."

The words *something else* left his lips cloaked in a deep sigh, the last syllable muttered into the glass. Garland Grove Recovery Home hitched an uncomfortable ride on Hayward Decatur, and every mile showed in his brittle white hair, craggy forehead, and liver-spotted skin. He fingered the back of his neck again, looked at his grimy fingers, and whispered, "*Goddammit.*"

"This bodyguard, she attacked you? The blood on your sleeve's a little hard to miss. Do I need to call Sheriff Gleason?"

He sprang from the chair like a man who discovered a spider in his lap.

"*Absolutely not!* No cops, ever again."

He stomped to the fireplace, set both hands on the mantle, and lowered his head. That's when I saw the spot on his neck, not a rash or a wound, but a blackish stain about the size of an old half dollar visible beneath the dermis. From its center spread a network of blood vessels and veins. I remembered my biology—it looked like a neuron.

"Hayward, what is that?" I said, leaning in for a closer look. Several scratch marks formed a clumsy ring around the neuron, the source of the blood at his nape. It looked as if Hayward had tried unsuccessfully to claw it loose. Several times. Honest to God, I'd never seen anything like it. To my shock, there was movement, a hard, sudden tremor in the affected area. Perhaps a blood vessel responding to his elevated heart rate lay trapped in that strange infection.

Or a growing parasite.

"I told you. She's something else."

The neuron expanded. The veins, fibers, whatever in hell they were, burrowed from its center, adhering to the curve of his neck, spreading toward the secret meat behind Hayward's ear.

He slapped at it, then quickly yanked his hand away with a sharp hiss.

"Did you hear that?" he whispered.

Before I could answer, he wheeled to me, expression a blanket of simultaneous disbelief and understanding, a bad boy discovered by an irate parent.

Winter Howl, the voice of Walpurgis Peak, trumpeting agonies and ire, prowled the streets of Danielsburg, filling the deep gully of Widow's Holler, and clawing the crooked spine of Beltane Road.

"My God, Darlo, *she's here.*"

From the door, a single, lock-rattling thud.

Like Wimbledon spectators, we snapped our heads to the sound.

Whunk.

Hayward grimaced and hunched his shoulders. His hands flipped palm-side-up, fingers gnarled into a pair of imperiled crabs. Whiskey glass abandoned, it fell to the rug.

"Darlo. I *feel* her."

Whunk.

"Open this door, Darius Lorren."

A woman's voice, void of rage or violence, yet all trouble. Professionals keep their cool, amateurs lose theirs.

"Do this now, Mr. Lorren, or I will execute alternate means."

"Darlo," Hayward said. The neuron-fibers sought his Adam's apple. His right ear darkened. "She isn't right. *She's half-human.*"

Whunk Whunk

"I need only to speak to Hayward Decatur, Mr. Lorren." The doorknob rattled.

I reached into my desk drawer and drew my pistol. I checked the mag and racked the slide. Good to go.

"I don't know if that will do any good," Hayward said, eyes on the pistol, his face a knot of tight, sudden misery. One of the black tendrils wormed over his jawline, reminding me of the veins I'd pulled from prawns and lobsters. "You don't want to end up like me, Darlo. For God's sake, don't kill one of these Medusa Cult witches and pay like I did."

A wave of unbelievable stink washed through my study. For the briefest moment, I thought Hayward, in his terror, had soiled himself. The sewer-reek hung dense and palpable, hot and putrid—the antithesis of the bone-numbing cold of Winter Howl. So sudden was its appearance, that my second thought was a pipe below the house had burst.

Hayward lurched forward in a bout of nauseous gagging. I followed his eyes back to the door.

I don't know how to state this in more simple—or polite—terms, but a black maggot the size of a dog swayed in the foyer. Behold, the source of the sewer stink.

A tendon of glistening dark muck tethered this abhorrence to the doorknob, another to the deadbolt latch. I imagined an oil or a polymer had been injected through the locks by our impatient visitor, seeped through the mechanism, coalesced into this repugnant, twisting worm, and, within seconds, assumed the stance of a serpent preparing to strike. It was idiotic to think such things. Movie hokum, yet here it stood.

Its blackish-green sheen held host to a network of throbbing veins, a stalk of sewer rot. It pulled the two support tendons taut against their anchors.

Hayward offered me his blackening neck. "She only *grazed* me with that thing, Darlo."

Sightless, for there was no indication of head, mouth, or eyes, the black maggot swayed like a charmed snake. Its apex bloomed, opening into a slimy imitation of a scallop shell. Minute capillaries, thin as spider legs, extended from this hood, swimming in the air, a mermaid's floating mane. Seeking.

"It's *listening*," I whispered.

Shock paralysis finally pushed side, I assumed the Weaver stance and raised the pistol into firing position.

Although I now stared only at the intruder through the front sight of my pistol, I needn't look at Hayward to know the neuron fibers had advanced further. "This parasite," Hayward groaned, "has to be how she found me. Sorry, Darlo—found *us*."

Done with probing, the maggot unexpectedly split into a ghastly Y-shape, one arm cocooning the deadbolt, the other the doorknob, shrink-wrapping to their contours. A fresh wave of hot summer stench poured from the foyer.

At speed, both locks exploded from their housings with a hard, splintering clatter, and whatever security the door provided dropped to the tile. I watched the reeking worm retract through the mechanisms, then the fist-sized wounds in the wood.

The door burst open.

Winter Howl's every ache slammed into the room.

Draped in Armani and the porch light's anemic glow, she stood with lipstick red as a firetruck with nails to match. She'd pushed her sleeves past her elbows and had her arms not covered in large open sores, I might have offered a snarky *Miami Vice* quip. But the sight of the black maggot racing into her opened flesh, like strands of black pasta retreating into those enormous, puckering pores on the underside of her forearms, made my skin crawl and my balls tighten into almonds.

Absorbed in this rapture, this reclamation, she closed her eyes. Her complexion, already olive, darkened once the totality of the muck entirely retreated to the safety of its host. As her sieve-like wounds sealed, the gale from Walpurgis Peak caressed her thick hair into an imitation of the tendrils that had spread so delicately from her maggot offspring. For a moment, she glowed radiant with malevolence, oddly beautiful in monstrosity.

The woman opened her eyes and glared at the former mayor of Danielsburg like a delinquent debtor.

"Decatur," she said.

Behind her approached a cornstalk of a man: black overcoat flapping, wind-defying black fedora, skin like polished alabaster, huge black goggles stolen from an arc welder's toolkit. He carried a black bag like a TV doctor making a house call.

"Well done, Jacqueline," the albino said. I could not identify the accent, a nether zone of Northeastern money, Southern influence, and European cabal.

Maggot business done, she crossed the threshold, moving aside enough to allow the towering albino through. She straightened her sleeves, eyes still on Hayward. That ungodly reek dissipated into the frigid air.

I should have double-tapped this scarecrow before he knew what hit him. By the look of Hayward's neck and the hideous thing that sought refuge through her pores, this Jacqueline, though, was sure to be a problem when her boss hit the deck.

I have more than enough grounds to shoot them dead, I thought. *But what of this creature? Demon? Witch? Monster Cartel?*

I've seen a lot in my years in Walpurgis County, but there is no shame in this admission. She scared me.

Still, I stood my ground. I'd been around firearms my entire life, but tonight marked the first time I'd ever pointed a gun at a human being. I fought to keep it steady, fought the anxiety and overwhelming cold of Winter Howl, but my shivering all but drained the Hollywood bravado from the moment.

"I like to know who's in my house, especially after a little B&E."

The tall man pressed a ghost-white hand to his chest. Offering a polite, but nearly imperceptible bow, he said, "Armand Jenks, Medusa Engineering."

Jenks gestured to the woman who harbored the black maggot. "My assistant, the inimitable Jacqueline Rawlings. You will forgive this trespass, Darius Lorren. Our business is with your associate Hayward Decatur—regarding *his* trespass."

"Everyone calls me Darlo," I said.

Armand Jenks dismissed me with a wave.

"Irrelevant. *Lower your weapon.*"

I hesitated.

"This instant."

Whether by magician's trick or psychology, I, through no will of my own, complied. Not only did the albino render me useless with a few words, but it was clear now whatever this Jenks character had on the agenda was about recompense. I was incidental. He shifted the goggle-gaze from me to Hayward.

"You carry a debt with us," Jenks said. He shifted the black bag so that both hands held it at his knees, like a man waiting for a train.

The neuron fibers tugged at the corner of Hayward's mouth. He looked the way Novocaine felt.

"I don't take orders, *Jenks,*" Hayward said, voice slurred, words bent. Despite the frigid gale, sweat erupted at his forehead and stained his armpits. "Or should I say *Gennckes.*"

Jenks. Gennckes. *That* Gennckes?

Jenks scoffed and said, "Ten years ago you decapitated one of our valuable assets, Marion Orr. Your release from custody was well-timed, fortuitous, one may argue."

Jacqueline moved toward Hayward.

Jenks continued, "You buried the head of Miss Orr somewhere on my family property, and the location has proven elusive. This evening, as then, driven by arrogant hubris, you interfered in matters beyond your comprehension. We will have Marion Orr's head returned and our retribution. There are rules, Mr. Decatur, and you *will* obey them."

I shot Hayward a look. I hadn't known that minor detail—Orr's decapitation. It was certainly kept out of the court records—I can confirm that because I read the transcripts. *The courts processed Hayward fast—like shit through a goose,* Greedle Olin had said. *Judge Penniman is hiding something; more here than meets the eye.*

That undisclosed fact now threw further shade on the legal apparatus of Walpurgis County, which, of course, also supported Hayward's argument: the Medusa Cult never left, and their talons pierced everything. In a way I could not comprehend, as Jenks confirmed, there appeared to be significant strategic value in the ten-years-dead head of Marion Orr, and the Medusa Cult was hell-bent on recovering it.

Even I don't know in what century she suffocates.

The Shimmer.

"While we reclaim what is ours and highly valued, know we immediately dispose of assets no longer useful to us," Jenks said. He pulled the bag open and dropped it at Hayward's feet.

Hayward screamed. I'm surprised I didn't.

Judge Penniman had been a lot of things—Medusa Cult lackey apparently one of them—but every side-hustle of his, as of tonight, had come to an end. His lifeless eyes retained the shock and surprise reserved only for the greatest of dullards, gawking from the black bag, past the stunned Hayward to the carved ceiling.

"The patron of your early release," Jenks said.

I harbored little doubt Judge Penniman had been at the Vanderbaum house. And if that was the case, and this beheading his fate, had the Medusa Cult laid a trap for Hayward with the Judge as bait? The final twist in Beltane Road for Penniman was not a meeting at the Vanderbaum house, but his head stuffed into Jenks' bag, up to his earlobes in his own blood.

Jacqueline pinched her middle finger and thumb together as if squashing a mosquito, then jabbed it toward Hayward. An enormous artery in her neck throbbed, and I wondered how much of the black maggot wormed through that artery, eager to escape or to squirm into her eyes and watch the show.

Hayward howled as tendons, tight as bridge cables, erupted from *his* neck. The neuron fibers yanked his lips like a man fishhooked, and to my eye, there would be no stopping its entry into his mouth.

"*Witches.*" Hayward panted. It sounded like *whiiddhez.* "My debt is paid." *mydeb ispai-uud.*

"Untrue," Jenks said as he slid the bag aside with his foot. "The Judge may have commuted your sentence at the price of his head, but that facilitated your return to Walpurgis County. There was debate, Decatur, as to whether you would make your way elsewhere, attempt to find a new life in hopes your trespass fades from memory as this place does with all the sleepers. But you are not a sleeper. You caught but a glimpse of the grand design; your curiosity will never be sated. I knew upon release you would return with the blind, ageless drive of a spawning salmon, and here you are. As for the accusation of *Witch*, it is beneath you, Decatur, but having never experienced death, you know not the true fragility of magic, the secrets kept from us by Those Others. Witchcraft is a triviality, the pursuit of amateurs. The Shadowless Ones are the Awakeners of Stars."

"Paid," Hayward slurred again.

Hayward was right. Despite Jenks' flowery words, these people were witches, practitioners of dark arts condemned by God, and the control they had excised over the both of us was nothing less than the grip of black magic.

"That said," Jenks went on, "all accounts are to be settled on this, the eve of the Summoning. Fortunate that you chose the season when Walpurgis Peak bellows its most dire warning. Though starved for centuries, she has never slept. The Machine in her belly keeps what waits in her womb very much alive, and you will assist in its fueling."

"Gate stays closed," Hayward barked, fog tumbling from his sad-clown mouth.

Jacqueline turned to her master and said, "After the Interrogator does its work, I'll remove this one's skin and drape it over the idiot with the gun. Anything they know, you'll know." For a moment a black liquid, surely the essence of the black maggot, pooled in the troughs of her eyes. I was right—it did want to watch. She blinked and it receded into her tear ducts. "As long as you don't mind the mess, that is."

Jenks almost smiled. "We will not be impeded, Mr. Decatur. Your immediate concern should be Jacqueline's Interrogator, which seeks your optic nerve. Jacqueline has, I hope to your satisfaction, demonstrated unique abilities."

"Part demon," Hayward slurred.

"Nothing as brutish. She is half *Sentinel*. The Interrogator is a fruit of their union, and if your knowledge is deep as your haughtiness suggests, then you know of what I speak. What sleeps below Walpurgis Peak is not unfamiliar with Harvesters and their living, loyal afterbirth. Sentinels are just that; afterbirth. Sentient, intelligent, a direct connection from womb to world. You will meet one firsthand when you are retched into The Machine's open hole."

"She's a Medusa Cult devil like you," his voice an out-of-tune piano, wires strained, tension in all the wrong places. If I figured out that he'd walked into a trap, then certainly he had, too.

"*Cult*, like *witch*, is an ugly word from an ignorant mouth," Jenks said. "Ignorance an unaffordable luxury. Sentinels bravely serve The Machine, and there are scores of them networked throughout Undervoid of this insignificant world. The greatest Machine of them all thrums beneath Walpurgis Peak, and its tethers span *thousands* of miles, seeking its kind beneath Chief Mountain, Denali, Kilimanjaro."

There's something beneath that goddamned mountain, Darlo.

The Interrogator's filaments snaked from Hayward's mouth and pooled in the deep gully at the side of his nose. He was in no position to doubt the albino's word, nor Jacqueline's parasite, now poised to avail itself the shortest route to his brain.

"If this world is so insignificant," I said. "Why does the Medusa Cult want it so badly?"

Jenks turned his attention to me, and I immediately regretted it. I'd never seen anyone so bloodlessly white, a living marble statue. This was the Purg at its worst, and my regret at summoning this man's attention turned to shame at my idiot, decades-long complacency, years spent in the vicinity if not the company of vileness, and my blasé attitude toward the supernatural and all its machinations. What a fool I'd been. Everyone is trapped in this fetid nest and refusing to do anything about it. That's how it prospered: forgetfulness and sloth. I should have shot the bastard on sight, then killed this Jacqueline woman, too.

"We will all be Shadowless in our last raving days," Jenks said, and he meant every word of it. "Does not the majesty of Walpurgis Peak speak volumes to that? Have you not trembled in its winter breath, pondered its forbidden slopes, seen what the spectre of that mighty fang can do when cast upon the angels who had crash-landed upon its hide? Indeed you have, Mr. Lorren. Like you, my lineage stretches to these fertile firesides, the black soil of bloody conflict, the broken bones of Widow's Holler. Every moonless night haunts our family's ancestral land. And here, all things end."

"So, your family *is* Copperhead Farms," I said. "Of course. It couldn't be anything else."

"Grandfather Johannes, The Elevated One." The albino was proud to declare it, and I wouldn't have been surprised if he slid one hand behind his back and clicked his heels. *Achtung, Walpurgisnacht!*

"Your clan never truly left Walpurgis County. You've been using the Shimmer there at Copperhead Farms to run in and out of this place, in and out of *time*. That place isn't abandoned at all. And for what it's worth, neither is the Vanderbaum house."

"Our holdings are vast. Know that what remains of Marion Orr is essential to locating what remains of Grandfather Johannes, both executed by zealots in similar fashion—but enough of history, you will learn it in time. Great changes are coming, Darius Lorren. Your associate," Jenks motioned to Hayward, captured and facing ruin, "like the judge, will not bear witness to them."

Scanning my desk, Jenks saw the scattered print-out of my current manuscript, rife with red-pen corrections, and a set of galleys from a book published in 2019. Face down near a desktop humidor, a paperback copy of my first novel, *November Cries Wolf*, with the author photo visible.

"But *you* will."

I saw only my reflection in his night-black goggles, where I appeared neutered as I felt. It wasn't that I was afraid; I was incapable of acting offensively against him, even with a loaded gun in my hand. Would I have put a bullet in his forehead had his grip not been upon me? I honestly like to think so, because when people of power and influence tell you their plans, you'd better believe they'll attempt to carry them out, and whatever this icy son of bitch had on his mind was nothing sort of The End of Days. All those years I stood by, dulled to the shadow of evil that darkened this county, and now that the moment had arrived for me to stand against it, I knew I was about to be puppeteered to do the opposite.

"And I expect you to document it."

Jenks added, almost as an afterthought, "Or you can put that gun in your mouth."

With that, Armand Jenks flicked his index finger and, Hayward's plight temporarily forgotten, I dutifully slid the CZ-75's barrel past my lips.

Here at winter's threshold, the mantle clock ticked away the final days of the world. Caught in a conflict between self-disgust and servitude, I tasted steel and oil, the darkest part of me wondering if I'd feel anything when the hollow point obliterated my skull.

"*Confess*," Jacqueline said, closing in, her scarlet nails an inch from Hayward's flesh, the Interrogator even less from the corner of his eye. Terror-stink emanated from the both of us, his the reek of resignation, mine a sour yellow teetering on the precipice of self-murder.

Jenks said, "The head of Marion Orr. Name the parcel."

Hayward's tongue lolled out on a carpet of spit. The spasms never stopped; his hands never straightened.

Hayward summoned the entirety of his will. "She suffocates," he said, his voice a cartoon distortion of paralyzed nerves, swollen tendons, and steadfast hate for the enemy. "*That witch . . . Never. Stopped. Screaming.*"

Jenks scoffed. "Mr. Lorren, I assure you, will suffer a tragic, bloody end."

He flicked his bone-white crab claw at me, and I pushed the barrel further into my mouth, moving my finger from the frame to the trigger. Another quarter of an inch, and I'd gag right before I blew the top of my head off.

"His death will be on you, Mr. Decatur. Prison this time, we will see to it."

"Marion Orr," Jacqueline demanded. "*Where* on Copperhead, and in what parcel, what *decade* is she buried?"

There was a small *pop!* as the Interrogator broke Hayward's skin, surfacing momentarily, rearing serpentine, mimicking its black maggot father's performance in the foyer. Jacqueline spread her fingers, talons pointed at Hayward, whose eyes spasmed as if current had been applied. I imagined the only thing visible to him was a blur of fingers and the encroaching darkness of the Interrogator.

It plunged into his right eye.

Hayward screamed, "*It was too dark to know!*"

Jacqueline closed the tips of her fingers as the Interrogator corkscrewed into the tender, wet meat. Blood spurted from the wound, splashing her face like warpaint. She didn't seem to notice, or if she did, she didn't mind.

The spasms ceased. His jaw dangled like a child's swing while his eye, blood-gorged and bulbous, revealed the last vestiges of the Interrogator finishing its journey beneath lens and cornea. Next stop, the optic nerve—and into his mind.

Jacqueline turned to Jenks. No one ever needs to see a woman smile like that.

"He's ready to talk," Jacqueline said. Then, for the first time, she looked directly at me, a slave sucking his suicide stick. "What would you like me to do with this one?"

Jenks raised his goggles and our eyes met.

He held me in a predator's glare, a temperament which didn't surprise me, but the color inversion in his eyes certainly did. His irises shone black as polished obsidian, rings of flawless night swimming in sharp contrast to the bloodless white of the sclera. To call his pupils arctic or azure would be a cretin's disservice to the color blue. I'd never seen anything close to a hue like that. *A color that has never existed before*, I thought.

Oddly enough, Armand Jenks did not appear to have eyelashes.

"The pistol or the pen, Darius Lorren," he said. "*Darlo.*"

Every word tumbled from his mouth in a wispy fog, but somehow, in the sector of my mind that he'd touched, I saw his words in their purest form; impossible geometry, *wrong geometry*, the product of accursed mathematics. Shadowless Mathematics—hadn't Hayward said so?—born of stars long snuffed out. They shifted and folded in methods surely unworkable here on earth, even in the nighted hills of Walpurgis County. There were but two possibilities—either this Jenks creature was not of this earth and operating on a level I could never comprehend, or he had sworn fealty to the worst darkness had to offer: nihilism and subjugation, a traitor to humanity and an enemy to life.

Jenks said, "One is a harder sword to fall upon than the other. But know this: there will be a Great Summoning. When this planet squealed in its infancy, the Nightworld had long since cast The Shadowless Ones out. Though slammed shut, but The Gate can be opened, and The Machine, the glorious global Machine, is in fine working order, connecting those survivors of ultimate cataclysm, convalescing beneath the vital mountains of the world."

Winter Howl agreed. *Dhuruuuuuhh* . . . a wretched foghorn from an unknown place on the map, a tone of warning and dread broadcast to the night watchmen upon mast and bow.

"There is an Architect, and its name is Zero."

Hayward, all those years ago, had done the right thing after all; he had dispensed a Medusa Cult witch, the conspiracy theorist vindicated—as they often are.

The smart money was on death, of course. Whatever secrets it held, even in death, the recovery of Marion Orr's head was sure to assist the Medusa Cult in unleashing something dreadful upon the world, and if I painted the walls with my brains, that would have been the end of it. The insufferable cosmic terror to come would never be known to me.

But I'm terribly curious.

I have a morbid desire to see how it all plays out.

Will there be a place for me in that New World Order, this planet ruled by ravenous insanities from some dimension I cannot comprehend? Surely not. There is no place for any of us there, but someone must remain behind with a focused, sane eye, behold the yawning Gate, and bear witness to whatever passes through.

I muttered something. Even Jenks could not understand me with my lips around the pistol.

Jenks, he of inverted iris and pupil, slid his goggles back into place. To be free of his gaze was like being relieved of long-standing pain, an emotional weight carried for years. I felt him release me, but somewhere in the hazy background, I heard not only the timber-crack of bone, but Hayward's defeated voice confess sin after sin against the Medusa Cult.

I used a shovel, I severed her head with a shovel. The mountain, in front of me, behind me, everywhere and wounded . . . covered in ash . . . dead trees . . . it was so dark . . . Angela, I miss you . . .

I pulled the weapon from my mouth and set it on the desk next to my book. How young and thrilled I was the day that author photo was taken. A life of creativity and a satisfying career lay ahead.

Now, none of it mattered.

"I expect only your best work," Jenks' voice, but far away, like an old radio transmission captured and hastily unscrambled. "Settle your affairs if that is important to you. The world is about to change."

When I looked up, Jacqueline, Hayward, and the black bag were gone. Splotches of scarlet muck led from the fireplace to the open doorway. One of Hayward's shoes had been left behind. I caught the last glimpse of the albino's coat as it cleared the doorjamb.

Spend enough time in the Purg, and you figure you've seen it all.

Not so.

In hissed the frigid breath of Walpurgis Peak.

Winter had arrived.

FLIGHT 2320: WIRE-WITCH

DAWN AND SMOKE. The reek of charred meat and smoldering plastic. 767 debris lay scattered like some angry giant's hideous dice throw, the tail barely holding on to the mountain's steep grade, its Viceroy Air logo a cruel joke. A hundred yards away, the upturned shark fin of the starboard wing towered above the opened fuselage, its human contents spilled upon sharp rocks and charred trees. A colossal engine leaned against a boulder the size of a school bus, papered with bits of clothing glued in place by burnt blood.

A barefoot Julie Reese sat up with the aircraft's PA handset fused to her hand. Her Lululemon outfit suffered a similar fate, melded into crispy, black tar with what used to be fair skin saturated with the finest moisturizers. Her husband, Dean, brutally slammed against the bulkhead at impact, was dead as Betamax. Dean's face made it through alright, but the rest of him had been dispatched elsewhere as the aircraft broke apart in a fury of jet fuel and primal terror.

Upon Walpurgis Peak's twelve-thousand-foot hide, where Captain Brisbane had deliberately crashed Flight 2320, Julie walked alone. She'd never witnessed such wholesale carnage, but as Brisbane had told everyone aboard in the minutes before impact, she wasn't exactly a rookie regarding the sanguine.

The clatter of tumbling debris startled her in the frigid pre-dawn murk, and she turned to see a hand tapping its way from a gash in the aircraft's nose, pushing aside a snaggle of smashed avionics. A thought flashed through her mind:

The cockpit voice recorder will have a complete record of Brisbane losing his shit, turning his murder/suicide into Let's Make a Deal. *Talking about me when I was seventeen. When I had less control. The world will know.*

Aggravated by that tidbit of news and unaccustomed to the

charred bulb her hand had become, Julie attempted to drop the handset—but dead nerves and fused bone require more than force of will. Exasperated, she looked to the golden gradient of the sky, host to a few clouds, not a single aircraft nor a curious news chopper. The F-16s Brisbane had claimed inbound from Whiteman Air Force base had been the first thing Julie saw upon opening her eyes, flat on her back, head ringing and fire everywhere, but they split like air show performers, peeling away from the mountain at full afterburner. There was no way they could have missed the crash site, and any military pilot would have performed multiple flyovers and radioed in reports, even she knew that. But not these guys. This goddamn snarl of a mountain was forbidden as meat on Friday, and the jets turned tail—

"I said, *HEY!*"

The voice snatched Julie from her woolgathering. The man hung halfway out of the crevice now, bloodied face to the sky, one epaulet dangling.

Those are Captain's bars.

"Oh, you shitstain!" Julie screeched.

She launched into a sprint, but the terrain was rough with debris, her feet bare, and her skin fused with super-heated nylon. Down went Julie Reese with an ankle twisted like an upturned root. Every part of her body bloomed with misery.

Julie hissed—not from pain, but aggravation.

"The grace of jungle cats," Captain Brisbane said as he clumsily rolled to the ground. "That's us."

No longer a disembodied voice from the cockpit, Jeff Brisbane stood and wiped the dirt from his shredded uniform. A large splatter of blood sprayed onto him when he'd jabbed a knife into the co-pilot's ear, staining both chest and face with a scarlet Rorschach test.

"God damn you, Brisbane," Julie said, propped up on her elbow. She stared at her ankle, now a swollen purple eggplant giving way to a foot turned in a way it should not be. Three of her toes pointed in different directions, like those signs indicating faraway cities. New Delhi: 8570; Edinburgh: 4580. She had no idea how she ended up barefoot when Brisbane slammed the plane into the mountain at 350 miles an hour and, more importantly, why people always lost their shoes in vehicular accidents and mass shootings. "Get over here so I can take a piece of your ass."

FLIGHT 2320: WIRE-WITCH

"Language, Grumpy Bear," said Brisbane, ever the game show host he'd mimicked as the mountain filled his windshield. "But rejoice, we are here . . . *here!* Marooned upon one of the sentinel mountains of the world. Do you feel what thrums beneath us? Our live studio audience sure does!"

"You killed two hundred people."

Brisbane looked at the crushed abdomens and flattened skulls, shattered laptops and fun-size booze. Face brightening, he bent and retrieved his hat. He put it on, adjusting it just *so.*

"No, Julie Reese of 2-A. *You* killed two hundred people, stubbornly resisting until it was too late. I offered you catharsis at least, redemption at best. Now look." Brisbane folded his right hand into a pistol shape and pointed it straight ahead as if looking straight into the lens of Camera One. "Pew! Pew! The Matricide Kid—alone among the dead!"

"And you," Julie added. "I might remind you it's all captured on the voice recorder."

Brisbane offered a curt nod, snapped to attention, then clicked his heels.

"*Zwei Mörder, Fräulein!*"

"Two killers. Cute."

"No one is coming to rescue us. We're on forbidden territory, salted land if you will. Dig this: Did you know that all air traffic is deliberately steered clear of Walpurgis Peak? What an error in FAA judgment *that* turned out to be; this place is like Disneyland in the middle of a black hole. I was drawn, summoned. The very sight of its wicked majesty poking through the moonlit clouds lit me up with understanding—revelation by any measure. I switched off the autopilot, and that jabroni in the right seat, Jimmy Whuzzisname, had a few things to say about *that.* Look at my shirt to see how it ended for him. Nevertheless, here we are."

"Just us two killers."

"*Zwei Mörder* indeed. Knee-deep in misanthropy. I noticed immediately at boarding. Hubris radiated from you like Chanel No. 5. This mountain did the rest."

A further hint of sunrise glowed at the horizon. Smoke billowed black, turning orange as it fled the mountain, eager to be away from it.

"You couldn't have known I killed my mother."

"With a Garden Weasel. Don't leave that bit out. I *love* that detail."

"Impossible."

"A dullard's word, *impossible*. The ultimate expression of a narrow mind and tunnel vision. In this place all things are revealed. I told you on board, Walpurgis Peak *speaks* to me. These are old hills with old rules, sugar beet, and one of the rules is you, as the unrepentant, must be provided an option. Think of it as a Best Buy extended warranty."

Julie scoffed, spitting ashes and loose fillings. She grimaced to her feet, quickly batting Brisbane's helping hand away. She hadn't seen the mountain in the moonlight as Brisbane had, but there was an undeniable electricity to the place— a *thrum*, he'd said—a murmur deep below. To be among such death and suffering would have unglued lesser women, but, for Julie, the subterranean rhythm seemed to soothe the insane situation: a lullaby from Nanna, a friendly, purring cat, an ancient, well-oiled machine.

"So, what of it, Brisbane?"

"*This.*"

Brisbane swept his arm wide to indicate a landfill of gnarled metal and burnt plastic, broken bodies and creeks of boiled fat, bloody clothes and deployed oxygen masks.

"Your refusal to accept terms, overridden by self-interest, resulted in the death of these people, not to mention the loss of a one-hundred-forty-million-dollar aircraft. I'll bet Lloyd's of London will think twice before renewing Viceroy Air's insurance policy."

Julie stared at him.

"In simple language, a recruitment," he said through a face opened into a carny's grin. "An *offer*."

With rescue choppers nowhere in sight and her skin a lava field of blisters and incinerated hair, Julie didn't know how long she had until the shock wore off and *real* pain set in. Dean was gone forever, and it was clear no one was coming to help, so with options in short supply, what did she have to lose?

"Let's hear it, Monty Hall."

"I've been instructed by Those Others to not only strike you down from the heavens like the second tier of fallen angels—those marooned on this stone knife thousands of years ago—but to make a one-time offer."

"Operators standing by, no doubt."

"They think you would make a fantastic Wire-Witch."

FLIGHT 2320: WIRE-WITCH

Julie frowned. Some part of her hoped for real estate or a barrel of Krugerrands, maybe a year of reconstructive surgery in the Bahamas. Hell, at this point, even a stiff drink and a couple Xanax would hit the spot. "Wire-Witch? What in shaved, hairless fuck is that?"

"The Voice of Nowhere. The Seducer. The Leader Astray."

She looked at her thighs. Burned black as beans. Blisters and gooey nylon-blood. Her brittle hair hung like abandoned rope.

"My temptress days are over."

Brisbane danced a Leprechaun's jig, never breaking eye contact as he spoke, festive just enough to make the sale in the epicenter of a smoldering necropolis.

"Door Number One: You are the loyal man's wandering eye, the self-inflicted wound. A suicidal thought as one of these dimbulbs stands at the edge of the Grand Canyon. The man at the pistol range taunted by homicidal urges. The woman with three screaming kids and a bathtub full of water. The seventeen-year-old girl with a Garden Weasel and a bruised ego. Those thoughts and actions will come from *you*; your most deviant lusts left to crossbreed and multiply, infecting sad sacks like the dead chumps of Flight 2320."

His dance stopped. Legs crossed, arms out, a smile wide as the prairie, Brisbane bowed.

"And there you have it."

Julie pursed her lips. Had she eyebrows, she would have raised them.

Brisbane righted a burned first-class seat, schlepped it next to Julie, then collapsed into it.

"Door Number Two: You lie among the dead, a nameless statistic, left to the eagles and coyotes . . . let alone what the Monster Cartel has living up here these days. Incidentally, Julie, it may interest you to know that as the entire complement of this aircraft died, their voices formed one unified, hollow bray of hopelessness. Oh, they saw it coming. They felt every flame. So be advised that time, reality—whatever *that* is—will snap backward, we'll crash again, and you will join them in that ugly final moment. I'd take a snapped ankle, and my cute little workout threads slagged to ruin over *that* any day."

"And what about you, Brisbane? What's your cut?"

Brisbane crossed his legs and shrugged. "Who gives a shit?

165

Damned is damned, girlie, whether atop this eyesore of a mountain or the sewer pits of Mephistopheles. I crashed a goddamn airliner on purpose, not a lot of wiggle room on that one come judgment time." He poked Julie in the ribs and grinned. "Am I right?"

His hat tumbled to the ground, the inside black with blood. Julie suddenly realized Brisbane had been mangled in the crash, dead as a hammer, and whatever his jaunty, animated manner conveyed was little more than a demon's trickery. In this bleak, cruel joke, the dead were not only the punchline but used like playthings.

"There has to be some sinister bastard more qualified than me. Go dig up a serial killer."

"I do not tell Those Others their business, I merely state it. But act before the sun reaches us, because that's when the offer—and we—expire."

"*Wire-Witch.*" Julie tried it on for size. Door Number One: how many could she push to the edge and over? Door Number Two: the obscurity of death.

"Walpurgis Peak is Door Number Three," Brisbane said, his voice filled with splinters, a ventriloquist's puppet struggling to speak independently after decades of words crammed into its mouth. "A prize you don't want."

The sun stung Julie's eyes. In a few seconds the first long shadows were due from the upturned 767 wing.

No matter what, this is the last sunrise I will ever see, here on the mountain that killed me.

Brisbane slouched in his seat, skin pallid, eyes glassy, the last moment before the master's hand slipped from the dummy's jacket. "Time's up. It either rewinds or moves ahead."

She pressed her ear to the ground, hearing only the ugly heartbeat of Elsewhere.

Speak to me . . .

BILLY BEAUCHAMP
AND THE MONSTER CARTEL

I
BIG BEN'S

THOUGHT I'D never work with the Monster Cartel until the apocalypse was nigh, but Walpurgis County has a way of surprising its most jaded natives. Here in the haunted-most county in the United States, a rabbit warren of hills and valleys presided over by the massive, saber-toothed Walpurgis Peak, the grotesque becomes the familiar, the obscene the everyday. One simply learns to nod and agree. The Purg is just that way.

In my travels as an earnest—albeit *discount*—exorcist, I've faced every manner of fallen angel, mouthy incubus, and petulant imp. I've never lost one soul to the abyss, but there have been casualties on other avenues. Trauma scars nearly all who have suffered possession, most permanently maimed from contortions brought by a demon's wrath. Families split from the strain, and suicides of loved ones unable to cope with the intrusion—and reality—of the supernatural are common. Every facet of exorcism is sadness, even in victory. They are all different, yet they are all the same.

Service to monsters would, at first glance, appear antithetical to my profession. Still, I go where I am called, so know that my experiences in Walpurgis County come to mind most often as I continue my memoir on this, the prolonged eve of my death.

So why don't I just get to it?

I saw Darryl Ballantine at Big Ben's, a diner seated at the nexus of Beltane Road and Midsummer Lane. The place hopped like a swarm of locusts between 5 and 8 AM every morning, and if you managed to grab one of the counter seats, it assured you first dibs on coffee and a sampling of delicious, crispy mysteries Persephone "Pipsy" Simms sprinkled on your pancakes, eggs, hash browns, you name it. They tasted great on everything, and if you asked Pipsy so much as the slightest question about their origin, she just winked and swayed in her tight uniform like a hypnotist's pendulum—and that was the end of your inquiry.

Darryl was a man hollowed since the disappearance of his youngest daughter Beatrice, or Beeley as she was called. Her last known location: the shunned six-hundred-acre spread of Copperhead Farms.

In earlier days, Copperhead Farms, adjacent to Widow's Holler, was known as the Gennckes Place, a Medusa Cult hotspot at the beginning of the twentieth century. Yet another reason this benighted county was forever snared in the Devil's grip, and perhaps, in some small way, a contribution to my calling, which summoned me at a very early age.

Damned is damned, my mother used to say when she acknowledged my penchant for driving evil spirits from the living and, in some instances, those who refused to admit they were dead. *But we do what we can here on earth so that we are ready when we're called to battle in eternity. You have the gift, Billy, and you are expected to use it.*

Thanks, Mom. No pressure.

I grabbed a coveted counter seat, and just as Pipsy set down my black coffee, Darryl groaned like a bull as he dropped into the seat beside me. He ran the local John Deere dealership that kept eighty percent of the county's farms running as modernly as possible, always in a faded JD cap and the same Levi jacket he'd sported since the eighties. Back then, his hair was dark brown and touching the tips of far smaller ears, and the thought of the scale approaching two hundred pounds was as foreign to him as Chinese New Year. But now, crescents held his eyes in shallow, bruised cups, face and body bloated, sleeves tattered, nails filthy. His skin looked like dry clay, his usually clean-shaven face a wiry yard of salt and pepper. When he set his iPhone on the counter, it popped awake, and a picture of his pretty daughter hugging a black Labrador had been set as his home screen. Poor bastard. I ached for him.

Small town rumor had it young Beeley had wandered off Route 54, likely lured in by the old Copperhead Farms sign, a mysterious spectre of an object if ever there was one. Every now and then, and no one had ever bothered to figure out a timetable, the sign—destroyed by fire a hundred years ago—became visible along Route 54 at random.

If you took the turn, the Shimmer grabbed you and twisted you around in a slipstream of non-linear time. Before long, local legend maintains, you found yourself in the grip of Johannes Vendurr Gennckes, executed as a warlock in the fire that consumed Copperhead's fields, the Victorian farmhouse, the whole damned thing. As to what truly occurred, as far as Beeley was concerned, we'll likely never know. Still, the story, gathered mainly from Greedle Olin, a frequent loiterer at Ballantine's John Deere shop, involved a scratchy, frighted phone call from Beeley to her father from the year 1924, facilitated, it's said, by a Ma Bell operator that had been dead nearly fifty years. Greedle claimed to have spoken to poor Beeley, urging her to find her way out before the Shimmer closed.

An insurmountable task, pulling a terrified girl back from nearly one hundred years in the past, so Beeley and her little Audi were never seen again—and it broke Darryl's heart.

Or so the story goes.

Life in Walpurgis County.

"Morning, Big D.," I said. "I'll get Pipsy to pour you some bean-squeezins." I held up my Big Ben's mug. The logo featured the famous London clock at the stroke of midnight, enduring a direct hit from a UFO—an homage to the Washington monument kill shot from *Earth Vs. The Flying Saucers*.

Darryl didn't so much as turn his head, but his worn-out right eye sloshed toward me like an egg at the bottom of a Dixie cup.

"Thanks, Billy," he said. "Coffee sounds great. I need it more than you know . . . I just can't get to sleep these days. I don't *want* to sleep."

I didn't doubt it. I could only imagine such devastating hurt, so I steered the conversation away from his trauma. "How're things at the shop? With winter close I'd guess it'll slow down a tad."

"That it will. The first wind always blows off Walpurgis Peak right around Halloween, you know. Starts the clock. I don't even want to talk about Winter-fuckin-Howl. The whole damned nightrope is unwinding."

As a kid, trick-or-treat in the Purg wasn't as festive as one might think in a county filled with spooks and steeped in ooga-booga. If you were smart enough to avoid the Vanderbaum house, where the Beltane Road began to twist and fold serpentine, you made it back to *your* house with a pail of Sweet Tarts and KitKats—but not before you felt that first slash of a polar cold knife its way down the granite blade of Walpurgis Peak. Six weeks later, Darryl's dreaded Winter Howl promised three nights of polar brutality hurled in feral anger. The Dead Season arrived on time, every time. Nightrope indeed; the noose strangling this place that never seems to finish the job.

"How's the demon relocation trade?"

"Funny way to put it. I used that exact term last summer when I did a *pro-bono* job at the Collier place. Not long after that, lots of work in the Midwest, a doozy in Winnipeg, then three glorious months at home. Just rolled into the Purg last night. Got a call from The Proprietor."

Darryl finally looked at me. His eyes lay nestled into a face gray as his hair. "Really? *The Proprietor.* Wow."

His cheek launched into a short burst of nervous twitches. His eye fluttered. Darryl rapped his open palm on the counter a couple of times, then drummed his fingertips. Knowing the Monster Cartel openly operated in these parts was enough to set anyone's nerves on edge, and a guy like Darryl would steer clear of trouble like that, even so, his nervous reaction seemed odd, but with Beeley gone, he had another darkness on his hands, and who was I to judge how he handed additional stress?

"Monsters," he said.

I nodded and sipped my coffee. Magnificent brew.

Without my knowledge, Pipsy had managed to drop Crispies into my cup. Man, are those things tasty.

While enjoying my Pipsy-enhanced coffee, an identical Big Ben's coffee mug appeared in front of Darryl. I watched as he moved his hand over the mug's maw just as Pipsy was about to sprinkle her fairy dust.

Persephone Simms may have worn enough foundation to

Bondo a Cadillac's rear quarter panel, but her powder blue uniform fit in all the right places. Darryl didn't seem to notice, another anomaly. Pipsy was a good-natured flirt, and he was always playful, and pleased to reciprocate. Today he was like a Mennonite in hostile territory.

"No, Persephone," Darryl said in a gruff, pitbull manner. I'd only heard a few people ever call her by her true name, and I had a feeling that was how he'd dished out the discipline at home.

Pipsy stopped, then slid her hand back into her apron pocket. She raised one eyebrow at Darryl, then smirked at me.

"He doesn't love me anymore," she said.

She reached out to pat Darryl's hand. He snatched it away.

"I guess that must be true. You found another waitress, boo-bear?"

Pipsy stared at him for a moment, reading his features. A moment later, she nodded with pursed lips and a short, light sigh.

Darryl's expression, save for the twitching left eye, remained neutral.

"Then I'll be back to take your orders shortly, gentlemen," she said.

"Just don't have a taste for them these days, I guess." He poured a generous sugar stream into his coffee and muttered, "Monsters calling on Billy Beauchamp."

"Indeed, Big D.," I said, "but The Proprietor doesn't use the phone; that would be *gauche* by Monster Cartel standards. The Cartel sends an Emissary, and his job was to make a show of it, a Royal Summoning in their eyes, I suppose. But it didn't go as planned."

"Only because he was in *your* house, Billy."

"No, it was *Lena* he had to worry about."

"Oh my."

I shrugged. "I was sawing logs at the time, but it was the Emissary's muffled pleas for mercy that woke me up. Well, that and Lena shouting *'Billy, wake the fuck up!'*"

Dreaming, down real deep, back at the house where I grew up in the Purg, stepping up to my Wham-O Slip 'N Slide, one eye always on that mountain smothered in haze. I hit the deck and corkscrewed down that yellow plastic sheet as cool garden water and the blazing summer sun played their tug-of-war on my bare skin. I recall the blades of grass at eye level and the unfortunate pile of dog doo adjacent to a sprinkler head as a voice reached through that swirling caul of ago-time to call me home.

Billy, wake the fuck up! Billy, goddammit, open your eyes!

In my line of work, you don't take chances at night, so at the sound of Lena's voice, I sprang awake and snatched my Sig-Sauer and flashlight from the bedside. I swung the thousand-lumen beam toward a pathetic mewling, which I initially thought was a possum or some sad critter crammed beneath the dresser. Lo and behold, there stood Lena in her slip, on the threshold of going full Sicilian, leaning on one foot with the mouth of my 870 shoved square into the kisser of a terrified monster.

"*Murrgo! Hgfbde?*" The monster gurgled. "*Jg'op?*"

No one speaks clearly with a shotgun in their mouth, so I spoke up.

"Lena, pull back, honey. I got him covered from here." I flicked on the laser, and the red dot danced between the monster's eyes. One off-color twitch of a tentacle—several had wormed out of his nose, likely a stress response—and he'd meet Mr. Hornady and the Double Tap Twins in .45ACP, my favorite caliber.

She chanced a look at me, all the while pressing the beast's back against the dresser, his mouth full of Remington. The monster's membranous bat-winged ears sagged yet beat a nervous rhythm on the face of my sock drawer.

"I'll kill this asshole, Billy," she snarled. "We pay ADT nearly seven hundred bucks a year for an alarm system, and this squid-nosed punk makes it into our bedroom? I'm *pissed*." She returned her attention to the monster and dropped the full weight of her forward foot on his ankle.

The creature howled.

"That's right, you little seaweed," Lena said. "You're in the wrong house, buddy."

We had our target in the killbox, Lena easily first on trigger if anything went skweenkie. This monster wasn't leaving this bedroom with so much as an earring as a trophy.

"Let him speak, Lena," I said.

She scoffed.

As a sweetener I added, "We may execute him still."

Lena slid the gun from the monster's lips and stepped back. She aimed the now-slimy barrel from the hip, however.

I sat at the foot of the bed. My hair looked stupid, my boxer briefs even worse. The monster, in his Capris pants and a forty-year-old Styx T-shirt, pulled his knobby knees to his chest. Patchy long hair spilled from his crown in greasy ropes. Toss in the tentacles receding into his nose and those freaky bat-ears and, I chose not to be too self-conscious about my appearance.

God only knows what he'd been in life. He squirmed like he was about to leave a pee stain on Lena's Home Depot rug.

"Let's have it," I said. "Who are you?"

The monster held his hands up, all twelve fingers splayed, veins and blood vessels visible in the translucent webbing between them. Whether it was gills or just horrible slits in his neck, I couldn't really tell, nor was I inclined to ask.

Anxiety pulled his face into a grimace, animal instinct kept his eyes narrow and his nostrils in constant motion. One of my favorite *Scarface* lines came to mind: *Look at you now, you stupid fuck.*

I glanced at the clock. 3:08. My *second* favorite caliber.

"Witching hour, Exorcist," the monster said.

"Adorable. Speak or I'll let Lena have you. She will turn you into Sicilian calamari. You'll be fed to the mountain lions."

"I am *Emissary*, I represent the Monster Cartel, Walpurgis County Chapter. I come to you on behalf of His Excellency, The Proprietor."

Lena and I exchanged a look. Exorcists and monsters weren't exactly enemies, but we weren't pals, either. A few years ago, I'd bought a round of drinks for some Cartel guys in a roadhouse outside a scab of a town called Olton, Texas. They seemed like nice enough chaps—until they had a bottle of Fireball whiskey in them. For some reason, they love the cheap stuff. By the end of the night, they'd dropped their human masks and convinced a waitress she was dying of lymphoma, and every song on the jukebox had its lyrics changed to such morose caterwauling I wished for some Norwegian Black Metal to lighten the mood.

"The Proprietor?" I said. "Well, it must be a big deal if he set you to Wyoming to fetch me."

"You are of *Walpurgis* blood," the monster hissed. His tongue flicked like a lizard's at the utterance of the word *blood*. "The bond is timeless, the dust that bore you is the ash spewed from Walpurgis Peak."

Ugh, even the mention of that mountain made me want to puke.

"What's the gig, Emissary?" Lena said. She maintained the 870 at his center of mass.

"Details," I added.

The monster shook his head, ears leaving a shiny slime trail on my sock drawer. If it was corrosive, that would be the end of that walnut veneer.

"I function as messenger only, Exorcist Beauchamp. I am authorized to tell you of payment for services, offer a good-will deposit. Call off your bitch-dog and we will talk." The Emissary opened his zipper and showed Lena his barbed worm of a sex organ. It slithered from his fly and tapped its bulbous head on the rug.

She pointed and laughed, then flicked off the safety. The monster's eyes widened.

"You may want to rephrase that," I said, sliding from the foot of the bed and crouching in front of the Emissary. He smelled like piss and fast food, window cleaner and a laundry hamper.

"I am authorized to tell of payment," he repeated, eyes never leaving Lena's. "Payment will be made in the Crypt."

"What? Payment in the Crypt? Stuff my coffin with Doubloons, Matey?"

I looked at Lena and grinned. She rolled her eyes.

"I think he means Crypto, Billy."

I tapped his knee with the barrel of my Sig—perhaps a little harder than required. "I may be able to live with that."

"*Crypto,*" the monster corrected. He reached into the pocket of his Capri pants and produced a tiny black device about the size of a USB charger. "Down payment for services on this Tary-Zor."

Lena curled her finger into a beckoning gesture, and the Emissary tossed it to her. She examined the slim, black device and said, "*Trezor.* I've read about these, Billy. He brought a down payment on a Trezor; a cold storage, offline Crypto wallet."

"You will have to go to your . . . *inner-net* . . . to verify the Tary-Zor works and your Crypt is waiting," the Emissary said.

"Grab your laptop and let me know what's on that device," I told Lena. "I'll keep squid-boy here on ice. We'll see if The Proprietor is worth my time."

The Slip 'N Slide would have to wait.

"So, how long did it take her to come back? I mean, squatting there in your Hanes with a monster leaning against your dresser had to be a little weird."

Darryl had a way of speaking with his mouth full that was effortless and clear. Perhaps years of experience, I don't know, but his voice pulled me right out of my story and back to Big Ben's. I wasn't aware I'd been running my mouth; I'd thought I was reliving the Emissary's visit in my mind, but, well, you get used to things like that in the Purg.

There was a short stack in front of me now, an over-medium egg on top with bacon on the side—and yes—Pipsy's Crispies. Now that's a breakfast fit for a king, or perhaps, even a Proprietor.

"Lena's smart, so only a few minutes," I said, pouring glorious Vermont tree sugar all over my breakfast. "And here I am at Big Ben's, so I guess you can say it all checked out."

"Nice to get work from high-end clients. Half of mine are behind on payments. I have two dead ones that pay regularly, though. The irony."

No argument there. Random resurrection was a phenomenon known only in the Purg. Sometimes, the risen retained their faculties, sometimes not, but it spoke to their character if the deceased could still make his farm equipment payments. Conversely, if a dead man sat at a bus stop all day humming Bon Jovi tunes or flashing strangers, most people ignored it and went about their business.

By the time Darryl wiped up the last of the eggs with a scrap of toast, I knew there was something on his mind. He sat while I finished, not speaking, watching the short-order cooks hustle behind hanging heat lamps. He attempted a smile, politely waving Pipsy away when she shimmied up offering more coffee, some part of him ashamed of his earlier, terse demeanor.

"Billy, can I ask you something?"

"You bet." I looked at my watch. "I still have a few minutes before the Rail shows up."

The Rail was a late sixties, jet-black Lincoln kept in pristine condition. I had a feeling someone in the Cartel may have been an old-school *Hawaii Five-O* fan. If it worked for Jack Lord back in the old days, it could certainly haul supernatural criminals around in retro style.

"The Cartel. The monsters, both human and inhuman, some of them have—*abilities*—right?"

"Enchantment. Raptures, even. Yeah, they can do some weird things. Some fly, others turn to liquids, piss fire, shape-shift of course, all kinds of crazy stuff."

Darryl leaned in. Those dark circles under his eyes were like rumpled, purple oil slicks. This man hadn't been right in over a year and certainly not stretching the truth about a couple of days of sleep deprivation. His breath smelled like a weird marriage of breakfast and kerosene. Whatever excreted from his pores made me think of embalming fluid.

Barely above a whisper, he said, "Old stories say some of them can open *Shimmers.*"

"That's an ancient rumor. Even so, who knows how hard those things are to control? Likely very dangerous. And God knows what that would be like in the hands of a monster."

"I'm wondering if they can do me a favor. It wouldn't be a *favor* exactly—I'd gladly pay them whatever they want, but I'm just about out of ideas. I can't find anyone to help me."

Darryl set his massive paw on my shoulder. His fingers trembled. Even his words ached.

"I want to look for Beeley. She has to be there, still at Copperhead, and I want to know if someone can . . . *send me through.* I've driven down Route 54 every day, every goddamned day, hoping that old sign would just appear, and I'd get lost too. Maybe I'd run into her, get her back to the road. I miss her so much, Billy. I miss my baby girl. Janet has been absolutely wooden since it happened. She never comes out of our bedroom unless it's to go into Beeley's room, rearrange the pillows, and cry until exhaustion. I can't concentrate at work; all I think about is Beeley, lost in all that night, between all those decades. I never believed the stories about Copperhead, but now I do."

Pipsy drifted past and dropped off our checks. She'd wedged mine between my plate and coffee mug. She gave me a quick over-the-shoulder glance, flicked her head toward Darryl, then slid her pen into a mane held at bay with Aqua Net and Hail Marys.

Darryl rubbed his face. It stretched like rubber, as if threatening to reveal the true face below. "She was terrified on the phone, *and I didn't believe her.* The only one who understood was Greedle, not only because he was there when she called but because he's old enough to remember all that creepy shit about Copperhead Farms. I want—I need—to try something other than hoping or wishing something *good* will happen. Understand?"

"Of course I do. I hear you, Darryl."

"You've saved a lot of people in this county, Billy." Darryl stood and dropped fifty bucks on the counter, more than enough for both our meals and a tip for Pipsy. "And I wouldn't have asked until you mentioned you're meeting with the Cartel—hell, The Proprietor himself. They'd never so much as acknowledge someone like me. I know you don't owe me squat, but I'm shredded, Billy. She's my youngest, and wherever she is, she's scared and needs her father."

I stood and took his hand in both of mine.

"You bet, Big D.," I said. "I'll see what I can do. Absolutely."

Darryl's sad, rheumy eyes welled up, and before the first sob could escape his lips and embarrass him, he broke my grip and headed outside. I watched him through the plate glass window, straightening his cap, eyes on the sidewalk.

I put the money where Pipsy could see it, then fished my check from its hiding place. A tiny plastic bag filled with Crispies had been taped to the bill. Under a little smiley face, Pipsy wrote: *For Darryl, who is far from home.*

Outside, a black 1966 Lincoln Continental, suicide doors, wheel skirts, curb feelers, the whole shebang, pulled up.

The Monster Cartel had arrived.

2
THE RAIL

STREETS STILL SLOPPY from the previous night's rain, the hissing traffic kicked up a dirty brown spray. A garbage truck rolled past, a brute of a thing with a brand-new vinyl wrap job proclaiming: *Keeping Walpurgis County Clean and Green!* as it puked black diesel smoke from its vertical exhaust pipe. Every car suffered mud except for the Rail, which gleamed as new as the day it rolled off the line in Detroit, Lansing, Cleveland, or wherever the hell these things were built back then.

When I stepped outside, every eyeball in Beg Ben's searing my back, the driver had already posted up at the rear passenger door. The Rail wasn't seen in town often, and if there hadn't been a sea of social media uploads happening at that moment, you could have colored me surprised.

"Mr. Beauchamp," the driver said with a small, polite bow. His eyes were far too big for his head, and his Ray-Bans offered little concealment. He stood about six-five, thin as a demon's promise, with hair that moved independent of the northern wind.

He pulled the door open.

I expected the pristine interior of the Lincoln, but the car was filled with *night. It* spilled from the cabin into the gutter, a flood of shadow, an oozing carpet of black vapor. I don't spook easily, but I'll admit, darkness tumbling from the threshold immediately gave this exorcist the heebie-jeebies, the electric adrenaline sting of a childhood nightmare.

"Do not be alarmed; that is only the *Nocturne*," a voice said, buried in that dense eventide. "Come inside, Mr. Beauchamp, as all is not as it appears."

I looked at the driver, who offered only the tight line of his mouth as encouragement. I stooped, expecting to be blinded by all that darkness, and yet, the moment my eyes crossed the threshold, I saw the warmly lit interior of the Lincoln: black leather, polished chrome, glowing opera lights mounted onto the C-pillars, everything save the seat behind the driver, which remained blanketed in darkness. I dropped into the enormous seat, and the suicide door immediately shut with a resounding *thunk*.

Dreams are reality and the surreal in mutual existence, and that's what it was like in the Rail. I felt as if dreaming yet fully aware, which led me to believe this entire vehicle may be a Shimmer of sorts, which explained the car's flawless appearance— it had never actually left 1966. If this was true, I'd have to speak to someone in the organization. I'd love a mint 1970 Dodge Challenger, just like the one from *Vanishing Point*.

A hand, human enough, reached out of the gloom. Protocol and instinct merge at these times, so I took it. His skin was cold, the hairs on his palms like tiny wires, or worse, the coarse feelers at the mouth of a crustacean. They squirmed as our palms pressed together. He pulled it back into the corner of darkness.

"I am The Proprietor."

"Billy Beauchamp."

"Your reputation, of course, precedes you, Mr. Beauchamp."

"As does yours."

I wasn't about to call The Proprietor *Your Excellency,* as the Emissary had referred to him. He's a monster after all—a blasphemy—but not irredeemably evil like that cadre of cut-rate demons that had, all those aeons ago, fallen from heaven to Walpurgis Peak. A strange line even for me to walk, but the Monster Cartel had paid up-front for a consultation, and I was obligated to hear The Proprietor out.

I also promised Darryl Ballantine I'd ask for that favor.

The Proprietor sighed and said, "Yes, my reputation, such as it is. But your success rate is impeccable. A natural. Gifted."

"It comes from God," I said. "I just wield the stick."

The Rail rolled smoothly down Beltane Road. The hum of the tires, the clockwork rhythm of the big V8, and its satisfying, confident growl vibrated my bones.

He leaned out of his night-corner. The Proprietor's long, gaunt face, a European aristocrat's countenance replete with a prominent nose, thin, colorless lips, and deep parentheses framing his mouth. His pinstriped suit boasted its bespoke lineage—no Men's Wearhouse for this cat—peak lapels, pocket square, amethyst cuff links. A tasteful blend of black and purple paisley was woven into his tie. Allow me to correct that—not paisley, a Mandelbrot, an endless fractal blooming with intricate detail the closer you looked. I chose not to stare at it for long, as it may very well have been a device to enter my subconscious via hypnosis, a power monsters were known to possess. Fashionable yet formidable, The Proprietor. A Boss.

"I thank you for the consultation, Mr. Beauchamp, and I must apologize for the bumbling manner in which the Emissary contacted you." His accent echoed pure East Coast blueblood, so much so that he could have played Mr. Howell in *The Addams Family Visits Gilligan's Island.*

"That little scamp was easy to handle," I said. "Well, my wife handled him."

"He is a relative, new to the machinations of Cartel matters. It appears he was promoted before his time. Even monsters must deal with bureaucracy and nepotism to a certain degree."

"I'm sure you can find a job in the mail room for him. Maybe answering phones or managing your Twitter feed."

The Proprietor laughed. That surprised me.

"Our problems within the organization far eclipse a bungling Emissary," he said.

The Proprietor reached into his interior pocket and produced a gold cigarette case. Etched in brilliant detail, it portrayed hopeless, distraught faces of agony; tormented men and women, some with eyes clenched shut against hideous sights, others wide in disbelief and horror, all rendered in sharp relief. If that was in this year's Fingerhut catalog, it'd be a hard pass from Lena.

"I don't smoke cigarettes anymore, but you go ahead," I said.

He opened the case. The inside exhibited pure black, utterly seamless where the fold had been. Once my eyes adjusted, I realized this was no screen, as one expected these days, but a flawless black mirror.

"I find this method easier than the paper dossiers of old," he said. "What I am about to show you is highly confidential. I trust you are a man of your word, a man of discretion. Exorcist and Monster operate in a world separate from the established, yet dwindling, rules of personal governorship. Still, as in any business transaction, the benefits are mutual when both parties remain true. These are old hills with old rules. Do you agree?"

"I could not have said better myself. You have my word."

"Very well. Behold."

The black mirror's interior swirled with light, recalling the purple hues of The Proprietor's tie and blood's scarlet hue. The Mandelbrot swelled toward me, endlessly birthing new details, fine lines, and curves like the unfurling stalks of budding ferns, erupting into a cloud bank of colors that—at least to my eye—had never existed before. I knew then I'd been bewitched, the very hypnosis I'd wished to avoid by staring too long at his silk tie.

I likened it to an ancient kinetoscope, a hand-cranked carnival attraction from the early twentieth century. As the grainy image moved in and out of focus, I recalled the old silent one-reel comedies playing at the Pizza Palace when I was a kid: Keystone Kops, Harold Lloyd, what have you. The playback speed sputtered unevenly, missing frames, yet bursting in vibrant Technicolor.

But this was no comedy. Outside a crooked length of ranch fencing, the monster stood lethal beneath a slit of moon. Overhead, the night spread vast and eternal, alight with the brilliant paintbrush swath of the Milky Way, God's handiwork profaned to silhouette such accursed ugliness. A glistening hide peppered with tight, wiry hair clumps reflected the moonlight as it lashed its great tail, a knobby rope of flesh and bone that terminated in a stinger the size of a beer bottle. The beast reared back, spreading its too-many limbs, their cloven pincers snapping like Venus flytraps. When it dropped back to the ground, its turgid belly-bag, swollen and greasy, dragged in the dirt.

There was no mistaking the humanity of its features warped with the tell-tale signs of possession. Cheekbones flattened, jaw elongated, lips pulled out of true, exposing the roots of long, blunt teeth. The monster snorted through a broad nose upturned like a sow's, warped by a demon's black loathing. Human eyes sought prey from dark hollows pulled toward the temple as though gaffed by invisible whaling hooks. Coarse hair dangled from a chin licked by a tongue far past human dimensions.

Into my ear The Proprietor whispered, "And Jesus asked the man who was possessed, '*What is your name?*'"

The Devil knows Scripture, my mother always said.

Should I know that? Should I know his name?

The Proprietor's voice might as well have been a hundred years away, an archaic recording rife with static and a tinny, grating resonance—entirely in line with the primitive moving images in the black mirror.

The beast closed its claws around the fence's upper rail and snapped it to splinters. It scurried forward, grotesque fat wobbling in waves, tail curled in a scorpion's arc. Directly in its path, and adjacent to an old pair of barn doors, stood a man, a ranch hand from the look of it, wearing jeans, boots, black hat, the works. The man spun at the sound, and just as the world of dreams demanded, he froze in terror.

The monster pounced with fantastic agility for such a bulbous brute, seizing the ranch hand like a cat on a rodent. The man's mouth popped open in a wide oval of panic and disbelief—death had set its will upon him, yet his mind told him it could not be happening. The beast delivered the stinger with all the compassion of a nurse dishing out flu shots, and the poor bastard's body went stiff as a flagpole. The stinger pumped its venom. The man's hat dropped to the ground and rolled away on its brim, and the scream that followed left his lips upon a waterfall of blood.

The monster's face split into the worst smile imaginable; the feral grin of satisfaction, the hot lust of blood-revelry. Other than the rat-like incisors, the teeth protruded in a jagged constellation of molars—big, hard, nasty grinders. That ugly mouth went for the newly paralyzed ranch hand, crushing bone, tearing cartilage . . . and, well, you can pretty much figure out the rest.

The black mirror fell quiet. My heart shuddered, my forehead broke out in sweat. I tasted Pipsy's Crispies and stale coffee as my breakfast threatened to reappear.

I've never, ever turned my back on a job, and for a moment, I considered asking The Proprietor to let me out, right here on Beltane Road, within sight of the Vanderbaum House. I also wondered if I puked in the Rail if I'd have to refund that generous crypto deposit and pay a cleaning fee.

"What in hell was *that*?"

"A monster, yet possessed," The Proprietor said. "You understand our problem?"

Shaking my head in contradiction, I said, "I do. A paradox."

"Indeed. However, even in this darkness, there is fortune—a window of opportunity."

"This, video capture, or whatever it is. How recent?"

"Time is relative to one's perspective, yes? Be content that this picture show is the only sample that I would ever show a human, and never anyone below your level of knowledge and training. Know now, Mr. Beauchamp, that certain individuals can capture incidents from within the Shimmer."

"This is information gathered via the Shimmer?"

"Correct. Purely random, but, alas, a *beneficial* find. Exorcist, I am confident you agree."

"Monsters are *never* possessed, to become a monster is a voluntary act."

"Exactly why you are here. Monsters have a long history, Mr. Beauchamp. Not damned, yet not welcomed into His kingdom. Imagine inhabiting the permanent Elsewhere within that hierarchy: human but not human, demon-scarred but not possessed. In a way, monsters are akin to Mary Shelly's brazen scientist—we deliberately chose to tamper with the forbidden without permission, without instruction, and certainly without humility. A man far wiser than me once said *it is only hubris if I fail*, and there lies the conundrum of the monster. We toyed with Devil-books, wove spells and mysteries with the aid of benighted mathematics, wormed our way in that invisible yet tangible night between the stars. Space, as you meatwalkers know it, is planets, nebulae, and comets. In reality, it is a limitless churning maelstrom of unspeakable banality, corrupted experiences left adrift, and furious, abandoned experiments wrought by beings so vile the True Death is preferable to suffering their gaze. Believe me, Exorcist, as unlikely as it seems, there are worse things than separation from God and Light; there is the knowledge you will evaporate into all that madness. And this is what it is to be a Monster."

I watched the Proprietor as he spoke, turning his golden Shimmer case with fingers elongated far past their normal length. Spider's legs, each tipped with a heavy, jaundiced nail, fondled the Shimmer-viewing device. The fine hairs on his palms swam in that familiar fractal, offering hypnosis for those too fragile to look away. When he looked back at me, his pupils had become slits, cat's eyes set deep into the long face of a man—or former man, I suppose—who now realized the bloom had been rubbed off the rose long before he'd first spotted it in the garden.

"So, you want me to perform an exorcism on a monster? I'll be damned."

The Proprietor blinked, and his eyes snapped back to normal.

He tapped his golden case on fingers that had also resumed their human form and slid the device back into his pocket.

"Damned would be a luxury for us."

3
THE SPEAKEASY

THE BLACK LINCOLN navigated the twists and hairpin turns of Beltane Road. Some years back I'd done this drive on a Harley, and there were times my knuckles went white, and my balls shrank to pebbles. Our intrepid driver seemed unfazed by all this, and he never slowed once through the turns, nor did we as passengers ever lean as the suspension flexed. Now I understood why it was called The Rail.

As morning sunbeams burned the fog away, trees whooshed past in a green blur. Ahead lay the intersection of Route 54, a meridian of sorts, where I shuddered at the presence of Walpurgis Peak and sensed the meat of the Ancients rotting on a titanic, snarling fang. We blew past the intersection, and to my right, I caught a glimpse of the magic-hour light bathing Copperhead Farms—where, in one of the parcels, perpetually a tragic afternoon in 1908; in another, an endless night in 1924.

"Part of Copperhead Farms is visible today," I said.

The Proprietor said, "The Shimmer stirs whenever the mood strikes it."

"Yet you've found a way to gather images from it."

"There are, in Walpurgis County, avenues."

The Proprietor's posture told me that was all he was about to say on the subject for now. He leaned back into his patch of night, with only his Monk-strap shoes visible.

The Rail stopped. I recognized the place immediately.

Penny Brynnwick stood on a flat parcel of land bursting with trees. She watched her daughters, three sets of conjoined twins ranging in age from early adolescence to late teens, frolicking upon the most bizarre, complex swing set I'd ever laid eyes upon.

Her sprawling house, broadly known as the Speakeasy, leaned among the sycamores, a tilted testament to storybook architecture. Smoke wafted from the precarious chimney, a brick companion a roofline that had seen better days. On a slanted gable populated by cawing crows, a weathervane pointed as all weathervanes in the Purg do. The haze-obscured mountain glared at the house. I turned away.

When I looked back to Penny, The Proprietor stood at her side. I'd never heard him exit the Rail, never so much as noticed the cool morning air enter the cabin. The driver stood outside my door, motionless except for his perpetually moving hair.

Though only four feet tall and about as pretty a redhead as any Irishman would ever hope to meet, I never grew accustomed to Penny Brynnwick strapped into her elaborate leg extension apparatus. This marvel of engineering, something out of a Jules Verne-inspired prosthetic catalog, enabled her to stand shoulder-to-shoulder with people of average height. She was not a dwarf; she was not a freak. Penny was simply *small*. But her daughters, despite the staggering odds of Penny giving birth to three conjoined pairs, truly defied logic; each set of conjoined twins comprised of mismatched ages—one pair aged nine and fourteen, another six and nine, and the third six and fourteen.

Impossible? Not here.

"Nice to see you, Billy," Penny said as I stepped out of the night carriage, grateful to be in sunlight again. "Give a nice Walpurgis expat hello to the girls on your way in. We'll meet you in the lounge."

You paid a premium to have the Brynnwick girls read your palm, your tarot, or, in some cases, your blood. If you were brazen enough to walk through that door and accept their offer of a triple reading, you were expected to possess the grit to endure the result. If weak in the knees, regret came far faster than it did to The Proprietor as he waxed philosophic in the Rail. Future and fate have been kept secret for a reason, another of the old rules.

I've seen a lot—and I mean *a lot*—of odd things, but the Brynnwicks played in a league of their own. The same engineer that built their mother's leg extensions must have designed the swing set, and the level of care and detail required to accommodate a fourteen-year-old girl joined to a six-year-old at the tailbone could only have been an act of love.

Their father built this, I thought. *Whoever that may be.*

"Good morning, lovelies," I said.

The two older ones barley acknowledged me, the other four giggled. All redheads like their mother, with sycamore green eyes.

Scarlet and Fate, aged nine and six respectively, hobbled out of their swing. Joined at the sternum and hip, Scarlet walked with a stoop to accommodate her younger sister, but her eyes never left me while Fate navigated the stepping stones.

"Good morning, mister," Scarlet said, her voice as fluffy as the cuddly raccoon printed on the shirt they shared.

"You might not remember me," I said. "I'm Billy. Believe it or not, I've known your mother since grade school."

"You're the Evictor."

I'd never thought of it that way. In fact, now that I had heard it, I kind of preferred it to the label I'd been given all those years ago: *Discount Exorcist.*

"You're older now. Your little beard is gray."

Kids never pull punches. True, my years-long experiment in a goatee-nurturing had borne white fruit.

"I'd say you're right about all those things, young lady."

"I hope you evict the Monster in the black car. They never bring anything good here—just more spiders and scorpions. But I like your vest and your boots. Don't they look nice, Fate?"

Fate looked up, smiling like a girl who had just discovered an all-puppy channel on YouTube.

What a cruelty, I thought. Delightful *souls in fouled bodies, conducting the Devil's business in a haunted place.*

"My sisters can read your tarot," Fate said, "but it's a hundred dollars. Scarlet and I read your blood, but it costs *a lot* more." She rolled her eyes. "*Mom* rules."

"I may not have time for that today, girls."

Fate considered this. "Maybe another time—we have lots of that. But Scarlet is right. I like your outfit. I wish we could wear a vest, but I'm not tall enough yet."

"Give it another two years or so," Scarlet said.

"I still want to go to the swimming hole later."

"Winter Howl's just around the corner. The cicadas say it's true."

Fate corkscrewed her lips.

"Sorry, sweetie, your sister's right," I said to Fate. "The water's way too cold right now."

"Not if we go when it's summer, *silly*," Fate said. She fluttered her lips, then tapped her foot like an impatient schoolmarm. "We slip in and out all summer long. Plus, the mountain is quiet then."

My expression must have changed because Fate obviously thought I required clarification.

"*Whenever* we want."

The Speakeasy Lounge leaned cockeyed as its exterior, the nexus of its unique charm. The bar appeared to have been carved from a single slab of wood, and in my opinion, the work executed by impatient cave trolls with blunt tools. Behind it hung an enormous mirror shattered into a permanent spider-web crack. A more cynical man might assume it paid tribute to the complex web the Speakeasy's clients willingly entered, but I deferred to what I knew of Penny's tastes and thought the choice had been purely artistic. Booze with no name lined the shelves, most local and far outside ATF control, some enchanted, some not. Certain bottles brought terrible dreams, prophecies, or the location of lost loves. Others purged your soul of guilt or grief—but most put the pedal down and got you plenty shitfaced.

Booths, upholstered in red vinyl, lined the walls. Large velvet oil paintings of the tarot, illuminated by soft pyramids of light, brooded above each table. The Tower, The Hanged Man, Judgment, The Magician. Death.

The Proprietor leaned his back against the bar. Penny watched the show on the golden Shimmer case.

"Drink, Billy?" Penny said, looking up. "I'd tell you to just pick whatever, but we can't have you incapacitated or experiencing a life-altering event before noon. I have some normie bourbon Riley Bevans aged in his basement. True, the barrel was made from his mother's coffin, but *whatever*."

Penny winked.

"Cute. No thanks, but I appreciate the offer."

Penny closed the case and handed it back to The Proprietor. She took a few steps toward the bar, a rusted mantis in that contraption of brass, wire, and well-worn wood. "After we lay this on you, you may change your mind."

"I encountered Orphas the Disruptor in a sweat lodge on the Crow rez," I said with a shrug. "Six went blind before I shoved it back into its hole. I can handle it."

My indifference—or at least my top layer of tolerance—to the diabolical, at times, bothered me. I had a feeling that very attitude, likely shared by so many of Walpurgis County, the primary reason darkness proliferated here. Familiarity may breed contempt, but it is likewise one hell of a growth medium for detachment.

"Last week, a client came in for a full workup. Mimsy and Faith read his palm, Candi and Destiny read his tarot, Scarlet and Fate his blood. He claimed he'd been tempted by the demon Izuriel. Met him in the men's room at Go Drunk Yourself, of all places."

"Izuriel," I said.

"Word is he's a real piece of work, Billy."

"Indeed. I know of him solely by reputation, but Izuriel's the only demon I've heard of with a drug problem. A low-rent con artist, the bait-and-switch king of the meth set. That shithole dive bar is the perfect hunting ground for him. The bar does, to their credit, make an excellent Old Fashioned. Regarding my knowledge of Izuriel's power, if you're susceptible and distraught, he can get into your head. He at least can do *that* right—if he isn't looking to cop an eight-ball on Bleary Street, that is."

As told in the Book of Enoch, the original fallen angels descended upon Mount Hermon, also known as *Baal-gad*—a wretched hive of Baal worship. In the days of Noah, their mission was simple: violate and corrupt the human race, teaching man the workings of spells, roots, and metals, the ways of the stars, and other obfuscated—or *occult*—knowledge. The curse of Eden all over again. *He wants you ignorant and compliant, but learn from us, and ye shall be as God.*

They ceaselessly abused the daughters of men, and these blasphemous pairings spawned detestable hybrids. These brutes, the *Nephilim*, some as tall as thirteen feet, not only devoured every living thing unfortunate enough to be within range of their cavernous mouths—including people—but, disastrously, polluted human genetics with their vulgar DNA. God sent the flood and put a stop to that shit, wiping out all life the Nephilim had contaminated. But pockets of the fallen remained, formless and without body, but still very much alive and capable of inflicting catastrophic psychological, physical, and spiritual damage.

The second tier, the incompetent bunglers of the fallen angelic host, plummeted gracelessly to what we know as Walpurgis Peak. These were the incompetents, the servant class, the slope-headed morons. Though beneficial to some degree in the overall mission of darkness, they performed the menial tasks, the grunt work. Imagine rodeo clowns in an area filled with the most dangerous predators imaginable, and you have Izuriel, a lowlife grifter, merely one among many. If there's any doubt about why Lena and I left Walpurgis County, reread this paragraph.

Penny said, "Billy, you're aware there was an incident, that Beeley Ballantine disappeared at Copperhead Farms?"

"Of course, everyone knows," I said. I thought of that eternal beam of hazy gold magic hour I saw as we passed the Route 54 junction. "Last year around Halloween. What does that have to do with this?"

The Proprietor and Penny exchanged a look.

I thought of Darryl's phone, popping awake with an image of his daughter and her big, goofy black dog, Darryl's rheumy eyes, the chemical stink on his breath, and the little plastic bag Pipsy had taped to my receipt. *For Darryl, who is far from home.*

"All right, what's going on?" I said.

The Proprietor said, "A father's carelessness."

"What's that mean?" I asked Penny.

"In short, Darryl Ballantine is desperate to rescue his daughter," Penny said. "He expects Izuriel to facilitate in some way. A bargain, of course, poised for disaster."

That fool, I thought. *That poor, reckless fool.*

"I talked to him at breakfast this morning. In fact, he wanted me to ask the Monster Cartel if one of them would, for a price, agree to send him through a Shimmer, presumably to Copperhead. A big ask, maybe an impossible one, but I agreed nonetheless."

"Yes, we saw that last Friday, in the blood-read."

"Today is Tuesday, it happened this morning."

"For *you,* it happened this morning," The Proprietor said, holding the golden case. "Which is why we elected to pick you up at the restaurant instead of your hotel."

However, even in this darkness, there is fortune—a window of opportunity, The Proprietor had said as we cruised down Beltane Road.

Of course.

"So, the Cartel *can* access the Shimmer at will—the stories are true. You knew I'd be at Big Ben's talking to Darryl just before seven."

"In a word, yes."

"Clever. Darryl's wrecked, Penny. If he drove out here and dropped that kind of dough on a full-spectrum read, while making noise about a run in with a demon, he's being pulled in all kinds of directions. He's clearly at the end of his rope."

The whole damned nightrope is unwinding, Darryl had said.

"He wasn't lying about Izuriel," Penny said. "Hell, Billy, you saw The Proprietor's evidence, and someone like Darryl would never make up a story like that. He's a John Deere dealer, the darkest thing he's touched is a copy of *Penthouse*."

I turned to The Proprietor, who set down a glass filled with a green liquid I didn't want to know about. An insect about the size of a golf ball crawled out and gasped to death on the cocktail napkin.

"Well, there we have it," I said. "A deal with a demon. That's *Darryl* in the video."

"Correct," The Proprietor said with a nod. "But Izuriel lacks discipline. He disrespects an arrangement set in stone over a thousand years ago between Monster and Demon."

"Color me surprised. He *is* a drug addict."

"Precisely, Mr. Beauchamp, Izuriel's urges often get the best of him. Mr. Ballantine, in his grief, presented a fruit too sweet for a demon to resist, and Izuriel has possessed Mr. Ballantine intermittently since Thursday of last week, the day before his reading. I am not excusing this demon's behavior, but *monstrosity is voluntary*. Mr. Ballantine, we feel, was reluctant at best."

Izuriel's been known to inhabit homeless people to feed his methamphetamine habit, so there was one reason Darryl appeared gray and drained—he'd been awake for days smoking speed.

I imagined Darryl in that little dive bar, sloppy and stumbling to the men's room, accosted at the urinal by the smooth talker from Walpurgis Peak, wearing a hobo's body like a cheap suit. Glamoured by the demon's eyes and swayed by his words, Darryl stood wide open in his heartache. Izuriel, a predator opportunist, immediately possessed Darryl, and off they went to Bleary Street to cop dope. The demon tempted him with false hope, leading him to the empty fate of all monsters. No wonder Darryl's eyes were set into deep channels of bruises—his skull had been repeatedly re-arranged while his heart broke into a thousand pieces.

"A doubling-dipping hustler," I said. "He has no intention of assisting Darryl, of course. No demon ever would. Still, what a shit he is. He needs to be spanked."

The Proprietor's face pinched into an expression of loathing. "This monster's behavior is unacceptable. Izuriel dragged Mr. Ballantine into the foothills and violated our interests there. It was a direct attack upon us, by using one of our own, such as it is."

Shit. There it is.

"So that wasn't Texas or some random farm in the Purg in the video, or Shimmer-vision, whatever you call it. That was Bleeder's Dairy. Darryl killed and devoured one of the Cartel's cephalopod wranglers. Direct interference with your . . . *livestock.*"

Bleeder's Dairy, for those that don't know, is very much as it sounds.

The Monster Cartel took control of the place (originally named Weider's Dairy but unceremoniously renamed by wise-cracking high schoolers) back in the early nineteen-twenties, right after executing their first big political move in Walpurgis County, alerting every major town—Danielsburg, Jasper, and Frederick—that the infestation of Elk-sized cephalopods in Dead Neck Lake had been "handled," which implied the entire population of tentacled giants had been yanked from the water and hauled to the foothills of Walpurgis Peak, where they were ultimately bred and juiced for the Cartel's benefit. This Public Service, as The Monster Cartel labeled it, opened the door for them to direct the trafficking of all contraband in the county.

Turf wars with old-school moonshiners followed, which did not end well for them. Before being fed to the first crop of cephalopods, most had their property stolen or pulverized, other resistors drawn and quartered in horrible tug-of-war matches, the betting, of course, controlled by the Monster Cartel as well. Monsters. They *will* find a way to make you suffer. By the time Clark Gable was a movie star, the Cartel ran it all: enchanted booze, drugs, guns, witch bones, underground casinos where the stakes were life and death, and, if the Rail was any measure, a cool Shimmer-based vintage car racket.

Bleeder's Dairy bordered Eldritch Wood, widely known for its winter cicadas and Arachnae, among other unsightly inhabitants. It was the perfect place to set up shop, a benighted corner of the foothills in the mountain's lethal shadow, surrounded by a dark forest filled with crawling things.

"Darryl killed *all* the ranch hands," Penny said. "And he's not aware of it."

"That's a lightning fast transition to monster. From what I know it takes months, sometimes yea—"

"Again, further violation of protocol," The Proprietor interrupted. "The reasons to expel Izuriel mount."

"How do you know for sure that Darryl is unaware of any of this?"

You saw him. You talked to him. His agony as a father was true, yet you never suspected possession. You missed all of it.

Penny said, "Would he have asked you for help, Billy, if he knew he had access to both demonic *and* monster resources?"

As I chewed on this, I glanced to the bar in search of the drowned insect recent of the Proprietor's cocktail. It was gone, but I noticed The Proprietor's jaw grinding a bit. Apparently, he liked his bugs to marinade a little.

"Penny, you have a point," I said. "Down in their core people know that no demon ever keeps his word. However, he may have hedged his bets, so desperate to have a Shimmer opened for him that its means were of little concern. But The Proprietor's right that at minimum this clearly violates the long-standing charter between monsters and demons, such as they are."

"Unprecedented," The Proprietor said. "A disruption to the order of things."

"You brought me to the Speakeasy so I can go all the way back to town and strap Darryl Ballantine to one of his tractors and exorcise Izuriel—so the Monster Cartel doesn't suffer a black eye. That about it?"

Monsters—another batch of twats wrapped in their own self-interests, I thought. *We can't have our little apple cart overturned. As Scarlet said, they never bring anything good here.*

If anyone needed my help it was Darryl, whether it was beneficial to the Monster Cartel or not. The tricky part was not only exorcising him of the demon but simultaneously fulfilling my promise. The poor sad sack got himself tangled in a seemingly irreversible deal with the worst cosmic scumbags in a shitty neighborhood. If I was his older brother, I'd slap some sense into him.

"Not exactly," Penny said. She spidered behind the bar, grinding the wire-driven gears of her leg extensions. Oil seeped from creaking joints and gaps.

"And I don't get your angle, Penny. Sure, Darryl had his

reading here with your daughters, which provided the Cartel with intel, but come on, this is basically a Cartel cover-up. The Speakeasy doesn't figure."

She smiled. "I'll pour you that bourbon now."

I lifted my chin to The Proprietor. Earlier this morning I sort of respected him. Now I thought he was just another douchebag in a nice suit looking to cover his ass.

"Any other details?" I said.

"There are three eviscerated wranglers at the border of Eldritch Wood. This is a cicada year, Mr. Beauchamp. That brings the Arachnae, who by now have descended from the trees and harvested the remains."

I watched Penny fill my glass. Her reflection split into an array of possibilities in the spider-crack mirror, a single moment of a thousand perspectives.

An array of possibilities.

It clicked.

The Shimmer.

"Someone *here* can access the Shimmer," I said to Penny.

She set the bottle down and leaned across the bar. She nodded and shrugged.

"My daughters, Billy."

I thought of Fate and the swimming hole.

Whenever we want.

"This is where we open the Shimmer, and this is the point to which you will return," Penny said.

"Wait. What—"

The Proprietor raised his hand to silence me and said, "You're to be transported via Shimmer to Thursday last. Your goal—your *gig*, as you say—is to exorcise Izuriel from Mr. Ballantine before any of these terrible events occur. If you are successful—*when* you are successful—Izuriel will have *never* possessed Mr. Ballantine, the deal will have *never* been struck, and no one will have died. A terrible tragedy, negated."

My eyes went from The Proprietor to Penny.

"This is rarely attempted, you know," she said, "deliberately sending outsiders through and back again. There's an old story about an 1880s Montana girl who supposedly conjured the Shimmer with the help of people like my daughters. She stepped through to rescue her father, interestingly enough, the inverse of what Mr. Ballantine asks of you. There's also plenty of speculation concerning the gold heist the night before the 2001 World Trade Center demolition, which may have employed the Shimmer as well. Most suspect the Medusa Cult for the New York job—which, I might add, is, I suppose, a tangential reason Ballantine made a deal with Izuriel in the first place."

To this day, the Medusa Cult maintained long tentacles into every facet of civilization and have rebranded themselves several times. Currently, their public front was the mega-corporation Medusa Engineering, which had its claws in everything from A.I. research to shadow government Pentagon contracts. Most normies perceived them as just another Google, Pfizer, or General Dynamics, which, if you ask me, is precisely how Medusa Engineering liked it.

"During Darryl's reading, he confided that he'd been told by Izuriel that he could be Shimmered back to 1908 and prevent the Gennckes family, who owned Copperhead, and by extension, the Medusa Cult, from ever achieving a beachhead in Walpurgis County. In his mind, if that never happened, his daughter would never have disappeared, let alone even ventured out that way."

"I thought he wanted only passage to Copperhead, find his daughter, and get the hell out of there. But he's thinking big—the old *go-back-in-time-and-kill-Hitler* chestnut."

"Effectively, yes. Which, in its own way, is *your* job now. But we want you to go only as far back as last Thursday."

"I would have brought my toothbrush this morning had I known I would be losing four days."

"You may, as it turns, gain them," The Proprietor said.

"And how do I get back? If it's all negated, the payment magically disappears too, I gather."

"We considered that. The device The Emissary brought is, from your perspective, from one day hence. Given the volatility of the cryptocurrency market, you may profit quite handsomely, especially after the balance is paid. Who knows?"

I snorted, "Tomorrow money."

The Proprietor took a single step toward me. His eyes had reverted to those awful slits I saw in the Rail. I elected not to look at his hands. "So. You accept the assignment, Exorcist?"

What the hell else was I going to do? Honestly, I couldn't care less about the Monster Cartel, they could go up in flames for all I cared, but that puke Izuriel could stand to be driven into a herd of swine and tossed off a cliff, just like Jesus handled Legion two thousand years ago. Broken Darryl Ballantine was up to his tits in a lopsided deal, and if I could do anything to help that man, even if not in the exact way he'd asked, I was all in.

"I think I'll take that bourbon now, Penny."

Penny pushed the glass of home-distilled bourbon, aged, so she said, in barrel staves made from Riley Bevan's mother's coffin, to me. Available only, don't you know, in the Purg.

"Your daughter referred to me as The Evictor."

"That sounds like my Scarlet."

I tossed back the booze. Smooth as silk-wrapped fire.

"So," I set the glass on the bar and looked at the Proprietor. He smoothed his tie and laced his fingers together. "Let's deliver Izuriel's eviction notice."

I'd never been invited to the Speakeasy's basement, and now it was easy to see why. The Monster Cartel had taken roost here.

The Grand Room, as the Proprietor called it, resembled a luxurious, wood-paneled Gentleman's club, a far cry from the slanted carnival attraction above. This space was certainly not without a bar, an elegant art-deco masterpiece reminiscent of the grand hotels of the prohibition period, the shelves stocked with formaldehyde-filled mason jars. In these jars struggled ghastly critters, wrapped in the snarl of their own broken appendages, mouths gawking in urgent, drowning gasps. Eyes, some with odd, W-shaped pupils, sat stacked in bowls like pickled eggs. Windchime arrays of bones dangled like the mysterious wares of an Asian street market, ripe with clinging meat that I could not identify. A host of cephalopod parts: severed tentacles, suction cups on Popsicle sticks, disembodied beaks, ink glands, all manner of repugnance—the bounty of Bleeder's Dairy—were displayed in lighted coolers.

A massive stone fireplace consumed an entire wall, its mantle carved into exquisite, intertwining snakes. Mahogany columns, likely harvested from some convicted manor house, supported a ceiling festooned with dazzling, geometric copper etchings. Pristine high-backed leather chairs had been arranged in little seating areas with teak side tables and ashtrays on polished brass stands. Tiffany lamps. Impeccable crystal glassware. An array of enormous Meerschaum pipes carved by masters.

This room isn't intended for your average beast, I thought. *This is for the elite, ruling class Monsters, and just like the Rail—not of this time. At the very least, the elements of this room never left their respective eras.*

I wondered what business The Proprietor and his predecessors had conducted here—and not only the petty crimes they oversaw. Clearly, it was a place of strategy and secrets, tie-loosening and debauchery.

When my gaze fell to the floor, I had my answer.

An octagonal rug lay like a supplicant before the stone hearth. Given a wide margin by the seating areas, it was easy to see why. An elaborate magic circle had been woven into the pile, an arcane symbol that could have only come from the rarest of grimoires. Not a pentagram as one might expect; more boastful of its lineage in dark art, the traditional pentagram foolish and childlike by comparison. An ancient design, a relic of the old ways.

Some maintain The Shadowless Ones stalked the soul-space between fallen stars throughout the blank aeons, before the goat heads, the inverted crosses, and all other manners of demonic imagery desperate metal bands currently feature on T-shirts, a severe caste of executioners far beyond the bumbling cretins expunged from Heaven to Walpurgis Peak, and this was their summoner. So vile is their legend, Bible scholars have said in jest that Satan distanced himself from them. *My dominion is Earth and the ruination of Men. What loathsomeness prowls the dark corners of the cosmos is not of my doing.*

Had not The Proprietor said, *These are old hills, Mr. Beauchamp, with old rules?*

As an interloper, I could only suspect what terrors had manifested in the sanctum of Monsters, beneath this den of fortune-tellers and blood-readers. They tolerated me because they needed me, I provided a service they could not, and, I might add, in a mercenary fashion to solve an uncomfortable problem.

And what I was about to do was not for the Monster Cartel, nor Penny with whom throughout the late seventies I'd shared many a high school class. This was about doing the right thing for a long-suffering soul.

I, Billy Beauchamp, the Discount Exorcist and newly-crowned Evictor, am no stranger to the weird, the dark, the impossible. I'm nothing more than a pure-blood human, I possess no supernatural powers but those that God allows to work through me. But evil is evil. You can sense it. You can feel it. Our innate survival mechanism demands flight or fight; it pounds the walls of your psyche like a dangerous neighbor on a midnight bender, and whatever decision you make, you are forced to live with its consequences.

The atmosphere in the Grand Room hosted a presence similar to the weird feeling in dreams, that odd feeling of *weight* in the mind, the surreal clarity of existing outside time. As that conjuring rug sucked every measure of warmth from the room, my breath fogged in serpentine ribbons, the sweat in my armpits crystallized. I clutched the cross beneath my shirt, then stuck my fingers into my vest pocket to make sure my emergency one-ounce silver coin was still there.

This is where they'll do it, this is where they'll open the Shimmer.

The bewitched room worked its influences upon me—that I could withstand—but the moment I returned my gaze to the complex weave, things changed. That conjuring rug, repugnant to my eye with its corrupt geometry and demonic symbology, pulsed with a subconscious, electric thrum of warning. Black magic had occurred here. Blood had been spilled. Sacrifices made.

I squeezed my eyes shut and prayed for protection and vigilance.

From somewhere behind me, Penny said, "Girls, it's time."

"It's easier if you relax, Mr. Beauchamp."

What a lovely voice, from everywhere and nowhere, tingling the tiny bones inside my ears, transmitting through every drop of water in my body. Part of me knew it was young Scarlet, and another part of me sensed the call came from Elsewhere.

Whatever to come, I had faith in one hand, and decades of experience in the other. When put together it formed one hell of a blunt instrument. *Do not be fascinated, do not be swayed. These are the machinations of evil, the sweets laid upon the table by the devil's minions.*

Or in this case, Shadowless minions.

"Eyes open or closed, it makes no difference. But see me, Mr. Beauchamp. See *us*."

Scarlet, leaning to accommodate Fate, gazed up at me. The twins wore a plain white dress of mismatched sizes, no shoes, and a garland of flowers arranged in each mane. Scarlet, the pagan maiden eager to plunge into the volcano. The look in her eye told me she had resigned herself to that day and had not that sacrifice spelled doom for her younger sister, I felt she would have acted on it there and then.

I felt sorrow for her. Though so pure and unafraid, I saw a future in service to monsters as they feasted on tentacles, traumatized children, and walked the endless line between desolation and damnation.

The conjoined sisters turned away and joined hands with the others. Six girls formed a perimeter around the magic weave. A freakish sight by any measure, but it would be a crude disservice to refer to these young ladies as freaks. In the Purg, bones fused in ways not seen, bloodlines ran long and true. Haunted and hunted had found refuge here, despite the bloody knife of Walpurgis Peak and the terrible events shat upon its slopes.

"*Pneuma*," said the tallest of them, Destiny I believe. Her twin, Candi, half her size and nearly half her age, repeated the word in a whisper.

"*Haima*," said another.

"*Mystiko*," said a third.

The last time I heard Greek, Lena and I were in a restaurant in Studio City, and she had to order for us because I was about four Ouzos into a future DUI. But in the presence of Penny Brynnwick's daughters, their words were clearly understood: *Breath. Blood. Secret.*

One second the magic circle was an ugly nightmare of lines and symbols—the next, an icy extrusion of light burst from those same lines. Shadows splashed throughout the Grand Room, and somewhere in the hollows of my heart, I knew if I stared at this shadow theatre long enough, I'd catch a glimpse of what waited out there, in the Elsewhere, that place of abandonment The Proprietor lamented over, the place where the monsters were left behind.

The temperature dropped. Serpents of frigid air slithered through the Grand Room. In their linen dresses and bare shoulders, these barefoot girls made me feel like a coward for shivering in my long sleeves, jeans, boots, and leather vest. Their hair, caught in the gale, sought the center of the conjuring rug.

Light everywhere. A gash of bleak winter hovered above the conjuring rug in a vertical, warbling line, the hum almost electric; deep and resonant. A slit opened in the world, and it was about to bleed.

The smallest of them, dear Fate, the sweet one who couldn't wait to be tall enough to wear a vest, touched the light ribbon and pulled. For the briefest instant, her skin became translucent. I saw her bones.

In her tiny voice, she said, "*Epochí.*"

The Shimmer opened.

In here, the immediate, the Grand Room. Through the slit of the Shimmer, parked in a pool of light beneath a streetlamp, idled Darryl Ballantine's Dodge Ram. He must have had his foot on the brake because the taillights shone bright, bright red. He leaned back in the driver's seat, cap askew, window cracked, smoke pouring from the opening. Heavy, severe music rumbled into the night—entirely out of character for Darryl. To look at the guy you know it's Skynyrd or Randy Travis, full stop.

"This is Thursday last."

The Proprietor's voice, probably an inch from my ear, yet sounding as if shouted from across a ravine. "Late of his meeting with Izuriel in the roadhouse, and the—"

I flipped my hand up to silence him. Unaccustomed to such dismissive treatment, the Proprietor shut his mouth like a bear trap.

"Scarlet, Fate," I said. "What can you tell me?"

For a moment, I wondered if I'd made a grievous error. Intruding on a trance often bore bitter fruit. Terrible stories have circulated about mediums dying while in that state, and what happened to them afterward was not pleasant. Most were weighed down in their graves, coffins nailed shut, tombs filled with concrete, the earth above sowed with salt and garlic.

Without opening her eyes Scarlet said, "The Shimmer will hold." Her face bloomed in the arctic glow. "Time may move in *fits*, though."

"It jumps around a little," Fate said with a nod.

"What about my life here, in this time?"

Scarlet said, "It's a tunnel or a highway exit. As long as the Shimmer is open, you can always make it back to the road."

"Like hide and seek," Fate said. "The game isn't over until you're found."

"May I pass?"

The room pulsed with vibrant light, my eyes inexorably drawn to that hideous magic circle. Every part of me knew it should be burned, any portal into that realm was an abomination.

"Try not to look at the rug, Billy," Penny said. "Focus on the past opened to you. Look at the road and step through."

Darryl smoked methamphetamine with greedy fervor, and that was no way for a man to rescue his missing daughter. I learned a long time ago that one must use the enemy's weapons against them to assure victory, and if this was my sole avenue to exorcise Izuriel, then that was precisely what I'd do.

"You may pass," said all six in unison.

4
THE SHIMMER

STEPPED INTO a November evening that no longer existed. In my timeline, I'd spent it with Lena in Sheridan, Wyoming. We'd gone to dinner at Deadwood's, danced a bit afterward, and even had a nightie-night Facetime with our son and granddaughters. But now I stood on the shoulder of Route 54, winter cicadas chirping in the deep faraway, as a possessed Darryl Ballantine smoked meth in his Dodge Ram, blaring Watain or Gorgoroth. Hard to tell. I'm not as up on my black metal as I used to be.

I crossed the road.

The music served as an unnecessary beacon. No mistaking demonic presence, as the area around Darryl's truck reeked of greenery gone to putrification, feces stewing in a microwave oven. Demons are vile, insolent creatures by nature, reveling in stink and corruption, the steam of decay, and the tearing apart of anything built by man. Izuriel, no exception.

I stood at the driver's window for a moment and watched Darryl, deep in his cups, blubbering like a schoolgirl while that shit Izuriel forced him to consume speed. Darryl gagged with every hit, face flushed, saliva spilling from his bottom lip. He spat smoke onto the steering wheel, then reared back, clutching his chest. For an instant he appeared on the verge of cardiac arrest, knuckles bone-white, neck a blanket of stiff, strained tendons. The next moment, he surrendered again to sobs while banging his head to the music.

I pounded on the glass.

Darryl didn't swivel to look at me—Izuriel did. Demon eyes rage swollen with belligerent, black hate, and after forty years in this trade, that's the one thing I'll never get used to.

He flicked Darryl's tongue like a monitor lizard. Atomized spit sprayed the window.

I bellowed, *"By the will of God Almighty, I command you, Demon Izuriel, to release His servant this instant!"*

The demon's response? The rearranging of Darryl's face. The man howled, eye sockets widening, bones shifting, skin straining. His jaw inched outward in a hideous, leaning J-shape, where three-day stubble wormed outward into a nest of angry wires, bleaching white as their length increased five-fold. Darryl's lips cracked like dry desert mud, blood bubbling over his chin as his incisors elongated into enormous rat teeth. His neck erupted into a lumpy terrain of swollen glands, inflamed tendons, and throbbing, speed-fueled arteries. He sat in that pain stupor, covered in scarlet warpaint, yet lifted the glass pipe to his lips.

"Fuck your mother, Exorcist," Izuriel said as he flicked his Bic.

Darryl's cheeks bloated with smoke. He exhaled a big fat hit of mind poison.

"Who are you? Which meatbag challenges me with petty God-talk?"

"Deliver us, O Lord, from the snares of the devil, and your servant Darryl Ballantine once and for all from that fallen and apostate tyrant and the flames of hell. *Be gone, demon!*"

Darryl turned the volume down. The night thrummed with millions of cicadas. I realized two things—the cicadas reminded me of sleigh bells, and we were closer to Eldritch Wood than I originally thought.

"You're late to a sinking ship," Izuriel croaked. He licked Darryl's bloody chin, ran his tongue over those enormous teeth, then cocked his head as if considering its subtleties upon his palate. "I taste grief and gullibility. Cheap hope and cheaper food. Your pet is in for a journey of *Becoming.*"

I punched the glass. "Don't you *dare.*"

"Behold—the Monstrous."

Darryl's palms flipped upward, and he pounded an ancient, tribal rhythm on the headliner.

"The old music," Izuriel said, swaying to the voodoo drumbeat. Darryl Ballantine danced humiliated in his Dodge, gibbering and drumming like a mental patient off his meds.

Izuriel stopped on a dime then raised one eyebrow far higher than Darryl's anatomy—even his augmented anatomy—allowed. Blood leaked as the skin broke over his eye socket. "Savor this, the music played in celebration when we took your filthy world into permanent night."

I grabbed the door handle and pulled.

The stink-heat rolling out of the cab was like a shithouse in August; a literal hell-bake, a chemical stench comprised of Darryl's shameful terror-piss and the unmistakable ruin of Hell's influence. Gagging, I laid my palm upon Darryl's forehead. *"Unburden this child of the Lord God. By the power of Christ, I command you!"*

Izuriel howled, mouth wide as a canyon, back arched and neck wire-tight. In a rapid, acrobatic move, he twisted Darryl until he lay on his belly, boots kicking the passenger side window. In an instant, this poor man's limbs elongated to ghastly proportions—forearms twice normal length, elbows sprouting cowlicks of rough, filthy fur, knees folding backward. Tangled now in a snarl of seat belts as he thrashed about the bench seat, every move snared him further. There was an ugly popping noise as two brilliant bloodstains, exploding like movie squibs, soaked his shirt.

New limbs, human yet not human, erupted from the wounds. They tore through his shirt with a hideous, bone-break brightness. Joints snapped into place, sinew pulled and strained beneath flesh eager to surrender to these new, horrid dimensions.

Darryl screamed.

Izuriel laughed.

"Both of you will die tonight," the demon croaked. A third limb burst forth, splashing a bolt of scarlet against the passenger window. All of Darryl's hands, old and new, now resembled gargantuan insect mandibles, clacking like castanets as they opened and closed. One took a wild swipe at me and missed.

The remainder of Darryl's shirt blew away from his torso, leaving only the collar and necktie like a clown's getup. He pushed himself up on his new appendages, mouth agape, rat incisors dripping. The monster's ugly belly bag rolled onto the driver's seat, heaving with Darryl's panting breath. Ripe armpit hair sprouted, squirming feral in long, glistening waves. In one swift motion, he severed the snarl of seat belts.

There was a tearing sound as his trousers gave way, and from the base of Darryl's spine, a knobby snake, that ungodly tail I'd seen in The Proprietor's cigarette case, unfurled into being. Runny fat poured down its length, pooling in the hollows of new vertebrae. A stinger, the color of filthy toenails, corkscrewed out of the heavy grapefruit-sized nub at tail's end, dense honey-bile poison oozing from its tip. In the Proprietor's back mirror I'd seen that tail do its worst, and I had zero doubt that Izuriel had every intention of using it on me. It stabbed the air between us and pulled back.

"You'll die where it's *haunted*, where it's *sour*, your gut filled with this filthy rat's drug venom," Izuriel threatened. "You'll scream, opened like a butchered sow on Walpurgis Peak. I'll bleed you on the very spot I fell to your beshitted world. Hear me, Exorcist. *Hear me.*"

Just like that—*whooom!*—time became elastic, exactly as Scarlet and Fate had promised. Imagine being inside an old VHS tape as someone pushed fast forward; Darryl's truck, the trees beyond, the pyramid of light from the streetlamp, even the monster itself, jittered, warped, and *separated*. It was as if the world had turned static, skewed crooked, then re-assembled. *Time may move in fits,* Scarlet had said, whether seconds or minutes, it was impossible to tell inside the Shimmer, as timelessness is fluid.

And now, in the world rebuilt, the monster Darryl was upright again, poised in the driver's seat, wearing his absurd Yogi Bear collar. At some point he'd drawn a smiley face into the bloody swath on the passenger window. He grabbed the shifter and knocked the truck into gear. Lurching forward, his fat-sac wobbled like silicone gel.

"Dodge trucks are built Ram tough," Izuriel said, but in my mother's voice. "But so was I. Heartless and indifferent, my boy. When you were born, I thought about crushing you beneath the wheels of our pickup or perhaps broiling you in mustard for your father. I also drowned your puppy."

The fearsome part about facing demons is that they get inside your head, rummage around in your past, and raise old terrors. Harvesting secrets and shame was the most formidable weapon in their arsenal, and *every* demon used it. The danger of their supernatural ability to look inside someone and simply *know* cannot be understated, and that powerful psychological attack had derailed many before me, even causing a few old-school Vatican Exos to off themselves. I endured one hell of an assault in Aberdeen, Mississippi that reduced me to hours on my knees in tearful confession. I'd never been laid so threadbare, wide open, and vulnerable to attack. In short: it's warfare.

But these benchwarmers, these second-tier fallen angels, just made shit up and hoped it stuck.

For the record, my mother drove a Plymouth Fury, Dad is an

if it ain't fried I ain't eatin' it kind of guy, and my childhood dog, Kernel Kane, died in his sleep at the age of sixteen. Izuriel may have been able to pluck my mother's voice from my mind, but that was pretty much the zenith of his psychic ability. Drug addicts. Whatcha gonna do?

"Close your ignorant devil hole," I said. "*He* commands it."

"Let's ride, Exorcist."

That broken face, that inhuman, ruined body. There was no bloody way I was about to get into the cab with that thing, but as the truck began to roll, I executed my best T.J. Hooker move and vaulted into the bed. I landed on something awful, a tractor part most likely, and bright, hot pain stabbed the small of my back.

We hit Route 54 like, well, a bat out of hell, fishtailing and sliding. He guided the truck into a smooth correction, and I'll admit Darryl impressed me with his driving skills now that he had three additional limbs and mandibles for hands. Add to that an eight-ball of meth stewing around in his brain while demon-possessed, and if it was up to me, he'd never have to pass a DMV qualification ever again. He stomped on the pedal. The big Hemi V8 growled at the night.

Route 54 ran bereft of streetlamps about a half mile past the Gethsemane Lane exit, and now nothing but dark autumn owned the road. I wondered if the Shimmer would allow me a glimpse of Copperhead Farms as it had this morning, four days from now, while I was on the other end of this intersection. No luck there, as Izuriel was on a mission: Watain was out, and Slayer was in.

I'll admit that riff in the bridge section in *Angel of Death,* coupled with those half-time drums, is a hard hook to ignore. When that band is in the pocket, you feel like a badass just for listening to it. For a moment, I grooved right along with him.

The truck tore down the highway, both Exorcist and demon banging their heads. I wrapped my fingers around anything I could find, and for all I knew, my life was in the hands of a fuel pump or a manure sifter. I'd either have to wait until Izuriel commanded Darryl to stop or find a way to get inside that crew cab and take care of business. I lucked out—the cab's rear window was a slider— and I wrangled my way to my knees and opened it.

Slayer and an enormous meth cloud poured from the cab, which turned out to be a blessing, as Izuriel's drug haze and the punishing music completely obfuscated my incursion. I collapsed

into the roomy rear seat—amateurish compared to my previous
Bill Shatner move—then set to immediate action.

I plucked the silver coin from my vest pocket and crammed it
into Darryl's monster ear.

"Fucking Exorcist!" Izuriel howled. Smoke poured from the
hole and his flat, wide nose. He dropped the glass pipe and it
vanished into the passenger side footwell.

I reached into my shirt and grabbed the cross Lena had given
me. In movies, necklaces pull free with a good, firm tug.
Unfortunately, I found out the hard way that Lena buys nothing
but quality. I pulled hard, the chain held fast, and I slammed my
forehead onto the rear of Darryl's monster skull, and holy *shit*, that
hurt. My vision went white.

Izuriel glared at me in the rearview mirror, smoke venting from
Darryl's ear and nose. A second later, the stinger whipped past, but
I managed to drop back into the seat—then lift the cross over my
head. This time, chain and all.

Izuriel yee-hawed like a hillbilly. He whooped like a Comanche.
He trilled ululation like women at a Muslim wedding.

"Smoke hubbas with me, my little errand boy," Izuriel cooed,
but in Darryl's voice. "Remember when you were young and you
could get away with anything? Tonight will be like that, a trip to
the old days, a night of dope and knives. We'll get *real fuckin' high*,
head down to Bleary Street, bag a couple of whores, cut 'em into
small digestible pieces—I have special blades for that. I know a
place where we can party all night. Talk it out. Sweat it out. I'll fuck
your ass."

Izuriel made a fellatio suggestion with one mandible-hand and
Darryl's tongue pressing against the inside of his cheek. Slayer, by
this time, had moved on to *Altar of Sacrifice*.

Oddly emboldened by metal, I grabbed the snarl of Darryl's
hair, jerking his head back and effectively taking his eyes off the
road. His Adam's apple, now swollen to the size of a peach, bulged
toward the cab's headliner.

A young Tom Araya and a furious Izuriel screamed in unison:
Enter to the realm of Satan!

"Yeah?" I said. "Enter this realm!"

With the other hand, I pressed the cross over Darryl's right eye.
Guitars roared, whammy bars dive-bombed, kick drums
pounded—and Izuriel coughed a rope of black muck onto the

windshield. Every drop of moisture in Darryl Ballantine's eye boiled away as fetid steam.

"This sagging shit-man is mine," the demon gurgled.

I managed to glance at the speedometer. Eighty-three.

"I wear the cloak of his misery, I gnaw red his broken, hopeless soul, I—"

"Be silent!" I screamed. "In the Holy Name of Jesus Christ, the only son of God, you are *commanded* to leave His servant, Darryl Ballantine!"

In a move that shocked even me, Darryl spat a centipede with a human face onto the dashboard. It squirmed, newborn and frail, on the Naugahyde and black ooze that preceded it, eyelids fluttering, the flopping jowls sagging beneath the wires of its antennae. Even over the driving music it mewled like an infant, a squeal of hunger and confusion. It reared and faced me, squawking and chattering, those minute humanoid eyes studying me. The black segmented body glistened in the dashboard light, the panels of its armor moving independently. Galaxy of legs skittering, it twisted into the defroster vent and disappeared.

Illusion? Likely. Freaky? Oh, you bet.

"He'll never find his little hoochie-mama daughter," Izuriel snarled, pushing Darryl's Midwest accent into full hillbilly twang. "He says that dumb fuckin' cooze stumbled onto Copperhead Farms. Said she was obsessed with selling her little titties on Instagram—whatever *that* is."

Darryl winked at me with his good eye. His mouth rose in a snide, arrogant smirk.

"But we've done her one better. Right now, she's being soul-fucked, *Shimmer-screwed*, over and over—ya'll better believe it, Exo-Hoss. She'll bear freaks, giants—*Nephilim* by any other name."

I pressed harder. I felt the rim of Darryl's eye socket shift as the cross penetrated flesh and bone. "Unclean spirit, robber of life, merchant of pain—"

"Her spawn will ruin her womb on its way into your world," the demon hissed. "Then we'll dump her split-open carcass."

Again, these clueless Walpurgis Peak rejects knew zip about anyone unless specifically told. As far as Izuriel knew, Beeley Ballantine could be holed up in a barn on Copperhead Farms in 1970 with *Knock Three Times* by Tony Orlando and Dawn in heavy top-forty rotation or sitting in a cornfield beneath the predator eye of Rusty Jack.

"Silence!"

Izuriel scoffed like a petulant child.

"Return this demon to the fires of Hell, the eternal prison of damnation, forever severed from the supreme hand of God Almighty." I yanked Darryl's mane harder still. By now the cross had branded his face like the hind quarter of a calf.

"No, no—that's where *you're* going, suck-boy. *The Great Elsewhere.* I'll have this monster seize your heart with his venom, then shit in the hole he chews into your belly. Get used to unhallowed ground because that's where you'll be scattered for the buzzards."

"You rotten begetter of death, you scrofulous weakling—in the name of Jesus Christ, *be gone!"*

The flesh hissed, boiling smoke as more black tar bubbled from Darryl's mouth. One of his new hybrid limbs flailed backward and caught me on the temple. It rang my bell, and I should have collapsed, but adrenaline kept me in the game.

Izuriel whipped around, wringing Darryl's neck into a barber pole of flesh and sinew. Demon eyes locked with mine, not even remotely watching the road. The black slime on the windshield shone iridescent in the dashboard light.

"I found him in a bar. Weak and blubbering. Fat and drunk. Desperate and faithless."

The entire cab rocked. At first, I thought we'd driven into a ditch, but we'd careened off Route 54 at close to ninety miles per hour, swerving onto a dirt road in a filthy cloud of night dust. Some part of Darryl's survival instinct punched through Izuriel's control, and he managed to right the big Ram with a skillful blend of steering and pedal work.

But I knew. The road took to an incline, and a steep one at that. We'd careened onto one of the tributary roads into the foothills cradling Walpurgis Peak. By the look of it with its well-worn wheel ruts and ranch-style fencing, this was Weider Road, the sole artery into Bleeder's Dairy.

"Giddy-up that mountain, boy!" Izuriel screamed. Darryl smacked himself upside the head with one of his new appendages. "Gonna find us one of them squid farms and slice this holy roller open. You like your exorcist guts hot, ain't that right, Darryl? Serve 'em up on a platter, sop 'em up with a biscuit. I'll feed you his cock and balls, Darryl my man. *Woooooah, Nelly! Whip. That. Ass!"*

Up we went, dirt and stone pulverized beneath the heavy tires. The trees up this way had long lost their fall leaves, arthritic branches stretching overhead. The winter cicadas sang loud and clear, a sure sign of Eldritch Wood, the last place anyone wanted to be when the Arachnae leaped hissing from tree to tree, feasting upon insects numbering in untold millions.

Darryl Ballantine wept. Even inside that stoned monster, he wrestled with failure and heartbreak. His dehydrated, branded eye managed a tear. I remembered his trembling bottom lip and his aching words this morning—now four days in the future.

I've driven down Route 54 every day, every goddamned day, hoping that old sign would just appear, you know, and I'd get lost too. Maybe I'd run into her, get her back to the road. I miss her so much, Billy. I miss my baby girl.

Cross still hot in my hands, when Izuriel opened Darryl's mouth to chide him again, in it went, Savior and all, to his uvula.

"The Power of Christ *commands* you to vacate this—"

Darryl lost control of the Dodge. We slid, and as the anti-lock brakes turned an already frightening curve into a thumping, shuddering chaos, I saw the wooden gate of Bleeder's Dairy, the leaning barn beyond, and as we spun right, the gnarled border of Eldritch Wood.

Time, that toy of the Shimmer, wrapped its cord around us and yanked. Bending metal and breaking glass. Slayer cut off like a switch had been thrown, Izuriel's mocking hillbilly nonsense suddenly silenced. Again, that sensation of being caught in video noise. Everything froze, fractured, and fell.

Ejected from the vehicle and within a fleeting, floating forever, I found myself in mid-air with millions of cicadas. They'd bloomed from Eldritch Wood in a ringing, black ribbon, the thrum of their wings generating turbulence around me, perhaps the very thing keeping me aloft. Their aroma hung heavy with moss, old leaves, and years of forest decay. That rhythm was everywhere, its cadence everything.

Below, in slow motion, the nose of Darryl's Dodge spat glass and steam. I watched the metal panels buckle and fold, paint cracking and bursting into minute flakes. The possessed monster rolled in the gravel, clawed hands digging for purchase, dust billowing, knobby tail elegantly serpentine through the fray. It was surreal to be here in the ghost grip of the Shimmer, weightless, unbound, yet unafraid, as tranquility, on occasion, steals terror's thunder.

Above, I was in the night shadow of Walpurgis Peak, destined to taste pain upon impact with its haunted foothills, the first in a series of steps that lead to where good men never dare. In this wretched mountain's umbrella of protection Izuriel was sure to attempt his worst.

I hit the ground hard, yet I could feel time snap like a cracking whip, washing through my nerves in a tremendous rush of *now*, then stretching as the whip recoiled away in a whoosh of *then*. For a moment, my point of view from the grime and gravel was little more than noise and warped lines. The sound of the truck crash reverberated in my head as if experiencing it at that moment—yet as I lay there *after* the crash, I saw it *happen;* I watched Darryl grapple with the steering wheel as the truck plowed straight into a forklift. The front end collapsed, the headlights exploded, the force of impact pitching the bed into the air. The driver's door yawned open like the entrance to a funhouse. Out rolled Darryl the monster in a tangle of limbs, tail, and jiggling fat. The momentum must not have been significant enough to complete the flip because the Dodge came down hard on its suspension and out flew my body through Darryl's open door. I watched with a dirt-filled mouth as a seconds-earlier version of myself twisted in the air, a silly ragdoll in a white shirt and black vest, tumbling boneless in the night gloom of Bleeder's Dairy.

Time caught up with me. I slammed into myself.

My entire left side felt like I'd been beaten with a baseball bat. Shock and adrenaline did their best to numb the agony—but pain is pain, and it will be heard.

"Jesus! Did you see that?"

A voice from somewhere. I heard the shuffle of boots, the crunch of gravel. Footsteps bumbling toward me.

"That Dodge just creamed Jessie's forklift. Big Boss is going to be pissed, man, real fuckin' pissed it was left out tonight."

I rolled onto my back. The stars, the heavenly blur of the Milky Way, shone through the swarming cloud of cicadas and the ragged canopy of trees. Steam billowed from the ruined front end of Darryl's truck. Shattered glass strewn everywhere, but no Darryl.

Until he roared, that is.

The men behind me, obviously Cartel employees, undoubtedly

dreaded the wrath of whoever—or whatever—they worked for. Bleeder's Dairy, far from the mom-and-pop operation of the 1930s which tended to a herd of lovely Holsteins, now carved giant, sentient cephalopods into edible delicacies for Monsters. There was very little doubt in my mind that they had seen their bosses at their worst. Feasting. Slurping. Snarling.

But when Darryl roared, these men screamed like schoolgirls.

And there, outside the crooked fence, stood Darryl Ballantine just as in the Shimmer video. Tail lashing, chest heaving, his wiry fur shone silver in the floodlights perched atop thirty-foot poles. His mandible hands snapped, and his gelatinous belly dragged in the dirt as he shifted his weight. Emboldened by the shadow of Walpurgis Peak, Izuriel made a show of it, eager to make an example of someone or everyone. When their blood reached maximum adrenaline, maximum terror, Darryl would attack—and that was the moment captured inside the Proprietor's cigarette case: when the demon crossed the line and violated the interests of the Monster Cartel.

I forced myself to my feet, my left side a sheet of misery, and when my weight came down on my boot, it felt as if my femur was made of ice and my pelvis fire. One of the ranch hands, a brick wall of a man who looked like he could be in a ZZ Top tribute band, froze mid-step, his gaze darting from the beast at the fence and the screaming man whose leg pointed in the wrong direction.

"Goddammit man, get the hell out of here," ZZ said. He held a shovel the way cavemen brandished clubs. "That thing has meat on its mind, son!"

A few feet in front of him was the guy I'd seen in the Proprietor's golden case, much smaller than ZZ, with a black hat, bootcut jeans, and a Levi jacket. In the video, he'd been surprised by the monster Darryl and suffered terribly for it. Now, that situation had never existed—a truck crash and a wounded exorcist had been thrown into the mix—and the time I honored my contract had arrived.

But the pain was unimaginable. Something had separated in my hip, parts swimming around in a Bolognese of loose nerve wiring and fried tendons. I'd fractured my elbow as a young man, and the agony of this eclipsed that by a mile.

"Keep it out of the barn," Black Hat said. "Big Boss will have all of us killed if a wild one gets in there. Tell Jesse to get the shotgun."

"No guns!" I shouted.

Ordinarily, I'd be all for stopping some Monster dead in its tracks, but this was Darryl Ballantine. I'd not only made a promise to a man, but I'd also entered into a contract with The Proprietor. The ranch hands were thinking only of the bounty in the barn—giant squid-things hooked up to the Cartel's juicing machines, a sight I could do without—but if someone unloaded a couple cartridges of double-ought on Darryl, it would only aggravate Izuriel, and the situation would bloom from bad to Apocalypse Now.

"Up yours, buddy," ZZ said. "We're smoking that thing. Order from Big Boss. *No unauthorized access to the barn.*"

I took a nerve-shredding step toward him. I'd broken a piggy bank with a hammer when I was seven, and that's what my pelvis felt like. "He's not here for the squid meat," I said. "He's *possessed.* He's looking at *you.*"

"All the more goddamn reason to kill the bastard," ZZ said. "Jesse, bring that scattergun now!"

Darryl threw his head back and wailed. The floodlights dazzled off the smoking silver cross still jammed in his throat. His tail slapped the ground in ire. The stinger gleamed.

My armpits and neck broke out in freezing sweat. Words clung to the dry rope of my tongue. "Look, you dumb bastards," I said through a mouthful of sand, "The Proprietor himself sent me here to deal with this. Now stand down and let me do my—"

Cicadas swooped into the barnyard, their sleigh bell warbling a weird Christmas carol fouled by Darryl's alligator hiss. But it was Izuriel who watched them, his right eye a cross-shaped husk. Smoke drained from the savage hole of his mouth. He slobbered more black bile into his wiry beard.

"Don't even look at it," I said, raising my voice over the cicadas. "Don't engage it. He's not like the Monsters you're used to. Get inside, I'll handle this."

ZZ, watching only Darryl, said, "And who the hell are you, you sorry-assed broken scarecrow?"

He had a point.

"Evictor," I said. Well, I *think* I said—the pain was excruciating.

"What?"

"He's an exorcist," Black Hat said over his shoulder, "Is that right, fella, you an exorcist? You telling the truth? This *Monster* is *possessed?*"

Before I could speak, Darryl plowed through the fence, lumbering toward us in an insectoid knuckle-walk. His three dorsal limbs flailed, mandible hands working themselves open and closed while that gigantic stinger loomed above in a scorpion's arc. Darryl's ridiculous collar and tie didn't seem so absurd now on this death locomotive, the shredded Incredible Hulk shorts were no longer a humorous contrast to his defiled physique.

Here I was in the exact moment portrayed in The Proprietor's black mirror. Four days ago was now, and the future was a memory of this event. If I allowed myself to drown in that paradox stew, I'd end up like Dwight Frye, grinning on the stairs in the hold of the *Demeter*.

The cicadas scattered. They corkscrewed away from Darryl, whining their holiday cheer, then twisted around the steaming wreck of his Dodge in a dense black vortex.

ZZ dropped his shovel and high-tailed it to the barn. Black Hat followed.

Izuriel, still choking on my cross, barreled toward me. His belly moved like a surgeon's glove filled with bacon grease.

I stumbled over to ZZ's shovel, picked it up, and crammed it under my arm as a makeshift crutch.

Darryl launched into a T-Rex sprint, legs pumping, shoulders rounded, and mouth snapping. From the ungodly mess of his spine, hairy limbs clawed at the air. He closed the distance so quickly that for a second, I truly wondered if I would die here in the Shimmer, shredded to death in nowhere time.

That's when the Arachnae dropped from Eldritch Wood.

5
BLEEDER'S DAIRY

GUSTAVE DORE WAS widely known for his etchings of biblical scenes, Homer's *Odyssey*, the Crusades, and his most famous works, the fully illustrated version of Dante Alighieri's *Divina Commedia*. *Inferno*, published in 1861, followed by *Purgatorio* and *Paradiso* in 1868, secured their place in the global imagination as the ultimate vision of Heaven and Hell.

Spend some time in Bleeder's Dairy and you'll notice two things: Hell is closer than you think, and Gustave Dore's take on Arachnae was absolutely accurate—to a point.

They descended upon us like Delta Force repelling from a helicopter, tethered to the canopy of Eldritch Wood by fine silver lengths of web. The web glands had, by and large, replaced their human genitalia, and they slid to the ground head-down, backs arched, mouths wide. Their torsos retained their human appearance, but similarly to Darryl's monstrous transformation, additional limbs—and there was absolutely no doubt that these were immense tarantula legs—sprawled from the dorsal curve of their spines. Nude and shameless they crabbed supine in the open barnyard, the breasts of the females exposed, testes of the males swollen, sagging like spoiled fruit.

The Arachnae were said to leap from tree to tree as they feasted on the winter cicadas, but legend had it their web, harvested and cooked into a paste, was sold by witches as the ultimate aphrodisiac. If I were a betting man, I'd lay odds that the trade in that particular commodity may be the one vice the Monster Cartel did not control. To me, they were equally vile as any unholiness familiar to the Purg, and here, on the slopes shedding the breath of that hideous mountain, to finally set eye on them confirmed my suspicions—they too were monsters, just not Monsters, members of The Proprietor's club.

Izuriel stopped in his tracks.

My instinct was flight, even with my crushed hip and shattered femur, but this might quickly become a bloodbath, and if I didn't find a way to remove Darryl from the equation, he'd wind up dead, and the mission would fail. For all I knew, the Monster Cartel was not above cutting their losses, leaving me floundering in the Shimmer forever. Moreover, who's to say the Arachnae, after a rich feast of bugs, didn't cap the evening off with a hearty slurp of exorcist blood?

The Arachnae surrounded Darryl, a pack of coyotes lusting for meat. Their eyes, black like polished marble, reflected the glare of the floodlights. Segmented limbs pattered the dirt. My God, to walk on their backs, vision permanently inverted. Tongues hanging. A horror.

"*Izuuuurielll.*"

The spider-hag crept into the center of the circle. White hair, hanging from an upside-down, wrinkled face, dragged in the dirt, the ladder of her ribs heaving with short, quick breaths. A matriarch ancient as these hills, this one. The others dipped their heads in reverence.

"*Izuuurielll,*" the horde repeated.

"Harvestmen, the lot of you," Izuriel said, swapping his hillbilly twang and slang for his true voice, the meat-eater from Walpurgis Peak. "Squirming until the swamp heat of your mother's womb cooked you tender. Never forget the might of whom you address, for you are the lowest—mites with the faces of men."

The demon narrowed Darryl's surviving eye and moved his tail in a slow, wary S-curve. He pointed the stinger at the one who had broken from the pack.

"Tarantos the crawling hag, still the same greedy whore I knew on these slopes. I told you the centuries would be cruel, but you were eager for my bed and fortune. Now look at you, Arachnae, dangling by your cunt from haunted trees, only to gorge on vermin. I *evolved* you. I made you what you are today. Where is your gratitude?"

Tarantos hissed. To see a human jaw open upward was ghastly, let alone the vision of her trunk bobbing as the spider legs shifted her weight. Her human arms, lean and muscular, supported wiry, grimy fingers kneading the air between her and the demon.

"We *are* these old hills," she croaked. "Unlike you, we obey the old rules."

"*My* hills, pest. *My* rules."

"There are no secrets at the foot of Walpurgis Peak. Izuriel the fiend, who cannot help but trumpet his weakness, his loud, belligerent hubris—we smell your lust for the human's drugs, the bowel-reek of your self-hate. Your mortified shame."

The Arachnae murmured in agreement.

I stood still. In the far dark, the cicadas thrummed.

Izuriel sneered and said, "Taste my shame."

Darryl squatted and shat right there in the dirt. My God, what an obnoxious, horrible creature. Although his scat slinked away from the drop site like a sea slug, the spider-people backed off at the sight of it.

"Petulant demon," Tarantos growled.

"Oh, mad Tarantos, I saw you already as half-spider, wretched with greed. How you must long for the days of flowing gowns and marble floors. Like every other empty soul spawned on this shit-covered world, you deserve your loss. Avarice made you a monster, and my seed spawned more. Now, back your litter away, or I'll have this reeking meatbag sting all of you to death."

Definitely some bad blood here. Tarantos had obviously entered into a bargain with Izuriel—likely centuries ago—and she'd allowed him to bed her as part of the deal. He betrayed her as demons always do, rendering Tarantos monstrous. Her posse was of his loin, the fruit of their lust, but she harbored zero affinity for the absentee father. What were the odds that my trip through the Shimmer and Darryl's terrible ordeal would converge on an old grudge between these two?

Well, too bad for Tarantos. She and her brood had dropped into the middle of *my* exorcism, and that's all there was to it.

I whistled. The complement of Arachnae skittered as their attention drew to me. All those ugly, upturned faces stared at the man with the twisted leg, filthy clothes, and shovel for a crutch. Izuriel simply spat at me.

"My apologies, Madame Tarantos," I said. "If you have a problem with this asshole, take a number."

Tarantos examined me with her repulsive upside-down face and said, "You too pursue this demon? He has cheated you?"

Izuriel laughed. Darryl's Yogi Bear tie danced on his chest. "*This* worm? He's my concubine. A place to rest cock and fist."

Through a shrink-wrap of agony, I offered Tarantos a short, curt bow. "Madame, I am Billy Beauchamp. Exorcist."

"*Evictor*," Tarantos corrected. She licked her lips with a tongue covered in coarse, slimy hairs.

"Evictor," the congregation repeated.

"*Beauchamp?*" Izuriel actually sounded impressed. "Beauchamp! At last, the famed tent-show revival huckster. A dime for a sideshow trick, then quick to finger retarded girls in the back of an old pickup. No wonder you're so ineffective. Best left aborted in a bucket, it's said about you. Spat upon by a mother's shame."

Okay. Maybe not *that* impressed.

Izuriel had no problem imitating my mother's voice, but couldn't so much as guess my name. See what I mean about benchwarmer class demons? What a chooch.

My left hand catapulted toward Darryl. I squeezed my fist until my knuckles hurt. Though grabbing nothing but open air, Izuriel felt every ounce of fury.

"By the will of *God*, muzzle it, demon."

Izuriel produced a harsh gurgling noise. One of his nostrils bled.

"You will release Darryl Ballantine before this night is through."

One of his mandible-hands clawed at his throat. He thumped his knobby scorpion tail. His good eye bulged.

Izuriel temporarily at bay, I turned to Tarantos and said, "This demon inhabits an innocent soul, who—"

The first shotgun blast caught one of the Arachnae in the belly. His guts blew out as his silk gland simultaneously discharged an enormous white rope, and for an odd second, I was crazily reminded of the old Silly String commercials from my youth. The poor bastard shrieked. He knew it was over.

"Right on, Jesse!" ZZ cried from behind. "Let 'em have it!"

The shotgun's slide racked behind me, but before I could duck, another blast resounded. This time, the slug whizzed past my head, and if this Jesse had been shooting double-ought, I would have lost an ear or worse.

The gored spider was struck this time in the neck. When his head separated from his body, blood geysered into the night. The rudderless torso sped away at a fantastic speed, dragging entrails, both ends spraying web and scarlet, then slammed against the leaning forklift. He danced an awful death jig, its hideousness compounded by not only the wounds but the sheer, twitching mindlessness of his limbs.

"Holy shitting *fuck*," ZZ said with great, heartfelt amazement.

Spinning in circles, Tarantos howled.

Jesse moved past me, racking another cartridge into the pipe. She was bound to clean house.

"*Cease fire!*" I screamed.

Jesse stopped and lifted the brim of her hat with the barrel of her Mossberg. Mid-thirties, I'd guess, sandy blonde hair, pretty features, but eyes dark as a strangler's. She had a tattoo on her forearm that read *Adios, Motherfuckers!*

She lifted her chin toward Darryl, who, even in his meth throes and possession, stood statue still, curious to see how this new situation would play out.

"This fat ass belong to you?" she said in an accent that was all Texas. She brought her eyes to mine. "You bring an unauthorized Monster to Cartel property, old man? Now I have spiders up the ass. You have *no* manners, buddy. Unannounced, rude, boisterous, and disruptive." She shook her head.

"Wait, you have it all backward," I said.

Jesse spat into the dirt. "My job is to protect the livestock."

Yeah? Well, in a different timeline all of you were eaten. Just by being here, I saved all your asses. Who's the livestock in that scenario?

"I am under the direction of The Proprietor. Let me do my job, and we'll be out of your hair."

"Big Boss?"

I couldn't tell if she was impressed or thought I was lying.

I nodded. "The same."

Jesse mulled this over, rolling her tongue over her upper teeth, beneath the lip. "First I've heard of it. Sounds hard to believe, the Cartel working with an Exo."

"He even sent the Emissary."

"The Emissary. *Raymond*? That nephew of his is dumb as a chicken."

"That's the one. Bat winged ears and capri pants. Apparently a Styx fan, too. The Proprietor *personally* hired me at the Speakeasy."

"Where those creepy kids live? Those blood-readers?"

Scarlet and Fate. Sweet girls.

"The Proprietor's a very serious cat," I said. "And this is a serious job."

"Shoot another one of them lowlife spiders, girlie," Izuriel said in Darryl's hillbilly voice. "They blow apart *reeeeal* good."

"Careful," I said to Jesse. "That one's possessed."

"You know, pops, I was once conned into a demon's bed." She smiled with only half her mouth and shifted her eyes back to Darryl. "But when I got wise to him, I cut his balls off with a straight razor. He bled then fled. This flabby idiot in a necktie is the same ilk. Looks like he could use a slug in the middle of that big, watery gut. I'll take his ass out for you right now; problem solved. Hell, I'll do it just for the bar story to tell. Now, there's no *way* he's Cartel, so I can't see how the Big Boss would be interested in him."

She raised the shotgun to her eye. "But he's right, these spider-fucks splatter pretty nice."

I may hire you one day, I thought.

Then it all went from bad to worse.

Several Arachnae flipped direction, warped genitals pointed directly at us. Web leaped from their bodies in a firehose stream, wet and sticky, shining in the floodlights.

A gooey rope seized the barrel of Jesse's Mossberg, pulling it downward, and she fired a slug into the ground. Who knows where it ricocheted, but the upturned dirt and gravel stung my face. Spared contact with the web, I stumbled on my shovel-crutch. My hip collapsed into rubble, and down I went into the worst possible position—on my back at eye level with angry Arachnae.

A male clambered across the barnyard, those inhuman eyes now focused on me. As he scrambled free of the little dust cloud stirred by his skittering legs, my attention, for some reason, focused on how his mutant tongue flapped and slapped.

Until he landed on top of me.

Pummeled by colossal spider legs is like being gang-jumped in a nightmare, pinned beneath the stink of a predator's breath and the ugly, innate revulsion we harbor toward creeping things. His face drew close as a lover's, mouth hole populated with unkempt teeth crammed with chewed cicada meat, reeking gums, and strands of mucousy saliva. Those black eyes, though, were not compound eyes as one imagines on an insect—spiders are arachnids, after all—but a black, polished marble. I saw my grimacing, bloodied face reflected back, shattering that detestable fear-paralysis.

I chopped at its side with the spade. The skin tore like paper, and bloodmuck bubbled from the wound in a thick, pungent custard. The monster shrieked, and though its voice was that of a man, the body tremors were all spider. There may be clinical terms for convulsions like that—your local entomologist may be able to help you—but the nerve damage I'd undoubtedly caused appeared unrecoverable. I imagined a terrible series of neuron misfires charging through its body as its bladder and silk gland let go. Hideous indeed, but better than chewed alive in its rotten mouth, the death hole for cicadas by the hundreds.

My hip screamed as I twisted my body in preparation for a second strike. What was left of his human hair wicked my face.

Chaos everywhere. I heard ZZ and Black Hat jabbering, then Jesse bellow, *"Heads down, you stupid hillbillies!"* right before she fired another round. Off to my side a horrible screech resounded, followed by atomized spider blood and a hairy leg segment tumbling past my eyes. Izuriel laughed. The cicadas screeched.

My assailant, leaking and wracked with tremors, struggled to remain upright. This was no time to go soft and allow it to live—it was him or me, and there was no way I would die trapped in the past.

That upside-down mouth snapped at me, and I jabbed the shovel's handle right in that tender spot between his nose and upper lip. There was a satisfying *crack!*, then the thing's head lolled bonelessly to the side. I'd rung its bell like Quasimodo, but as soon as I regained my footing, I had every intention of wielding the spade like a cleaver and finishing this wretch off for good.

Jesse reached in and snared the spider by its throat. His eyes bulged, glistening and afraid. My eyes bulged, surprised and relieved. She lifted the thing off me.

A discus thrower with inimitable Texas style, Jesse spun a three-sixty then let go. The spider tumbled across the barnyard in a bramble of flailing legs and dust. Upended, it lay on its human chest, gasping as bloody dirt bubbled around its broken nose, appendages flailing, the spade wound gushing. The creature was sure to bleed out—no two ways about it—and it showed on his face.

Next to the smashed hulk of Darryl's truck, Tarantos grappled with Izuriel. Two of Darryl's new limbs held Tarantos inverted, her legs pummeling his shoulders, mouth snapping. Izuriel shook her, the cartoon bully emptying the dregs of his victim's pockets. Web sprayed from her vulva in a broad, glorious umbrella.

"*Muuuutherrrr,*" moaned the Arachnae I'd wounded.

Tarantos turned her head to the sound.

Jesse squatted and pressed the barrel to the mewling spider's head. His expression turned pathetic.

"*Mother, please,*" he lowed.

Jesse locked eyes with Tarantos.

"*Daniel!*" Tarantos cried.

Jesse squeezed the trigger and ended it.

Tarantos screamed, and a second explosion of Eldritch Wood's winter cicadas burst from the trees. As her grief echoed across the barnyard, Izuriel grinned, lapping her anguish up like a dog.

"Suffer, hag," Izuriel sneered. He slid his tail between his legs and brought the stinger up so Tarantos could see it. "Another of your children dies weeping, crying for his mother. The she-pig with the gun did my work for me, so all this venom is for you."

Jesse had fired five rounds to my count, so if her Mossberg 500 was loaded to capacity, meaning a full magazine and one in the pipe, a single cartridge remained. Jesse stepped over the corpse and headed toward Darryl. Web muck stuck to her jeans and hat. A length of it hung sizzling from the hot shotgun barrel.

"Who are you calling *she-pig*, you *fat fuck*?"

Oh, here we go.

I howled to my feet and limped toward Jesse, who racked the final round into the chamber. Izuriel may not have realized it, but she had every intention of blowing Darryl Ballantine's head from his shoulders.

With a commotion brewing behind me, I wheeled around and saw ZZ and Black Hat on the run with the remaining Arachnae in pursuit. Once back at the barn, both men turned and looked at me. I saw it on their faces: full knowledge that they were about to leave Jesse and me out here among monsters, immediately guilty yet void of contrition. After those two fools slid the barn doors shut, the spiders clambered over one another in a blood-frenzy, beating wooden door planks and rattling the hardware. Why they didn't attack Jesse or, more importantly, rush to the aid of their mother was beyond me. Perhaps the Arachnae were just like ZZ and Black

Hat, suddenly selfish when survival was on the line, safe to pursue the unarmed.

No time to worry about those two; full-grown men in service to monsters should have learned to deal with terror by now. Although Jesse was only doing her job and defending the dairy, I had to stop her. If Darryl died possessed, he would go to Hell, and I mean *straight* to Hell.

And just like that, the Shimmer again made time its plaything. Jesse's finger squeezed the trigger. The internals of the mechanism became audible in stunning detail; the minute ping of the carrier and sear springs, the sear's turning, the hammer's first tremor. Its scale had been amplified in that temporal distortion, and what would have been nearly imperceptible clicks was now the enormous chorus of hydraulics, the whine of servos.

Tarantos' spraying web rained down in a strobe-light staccato, the smoke gushing from Darryl's mouth cascading with oozing fluidity. Slow-motion cicadas roared like wounded steers.

The spider leaped onto Jesse's back just as the hammer fell. Her hat spun in mid-air as the shotgun barrel swept upward and the concussion ring bloomed, trailed by a glowing fist of super-heated gas. The slug twisted from the barrel, trailing delicate tendrils of smoke. Jesse's face morphed into an expression of surprise and anger, eyes hot, teeth bared. I watched her pupils dilate, the vibrations in her cheeks and neck as she screamed, spat, and swore.

Time convulsed again, and Jesse was now on her back, snared in a hairy cage of spider legs. She gripped a serrated hunting knife, the blade slick with monster blood. Sound became a warbling collision of events; the shotgun blast, the shriek of the Arachnae, the scuffling of boots—seconds apart in real-time, yet overlapping in an unholy clatter. Before I could blink in that elastic reality, Jesse rolled to her knees, goring the she-spider between the breasts, penetrating the sternum, both hands on the pommel. Her face, covered in a warpaint of spider blood, had split open into a madman's grin.

"Exorcist, breathe deep. Taste her pure bloodlust. A woman after my own heart."

Izuriel. His real voice, in real-time.

"She'll bear my brood just like this Spider-hag, Tarantos the dangling Princess. The fat man Ballantine is mine. At my

*command he will murder everything on this farm, then split you
open with their bones."*

I looked away from Jesse's carnage, and the mewling,
distraught Tarantos in the grip of the monster Darryl.

Izuriel, still rag-dolling Tarantos, licked his lips at the sight of
a blood-smeared Jesse. The overkill she wrought upon the
Arachnae, the lone daughter brave enough to protect its mother,
was appalling—but, glorious or ghastly, that's the way of the
world—something will kill all of us, and rule number one is to stave
that off for as long as possible.

*"Make your move, Beauchamp. Walpurgis Peak never ceases
to speak to me, and it intends that we abandon this circus. Duel
as these old hills demand. Obey the old rules."*

A Dodge Ram approached from Weider Road.

Hemi growling, Slayer roaring from the speakers, monster at
the wheel, and a passenger performing the Rite of Exorcism from
the rear seat, the truck smashed through the wooden gates and
headed straight for a bright yellow Caterpillar forklift.

6
RESET

"THE POWER OF CHRIST *commands* you to vacate this—"

The glass smashed, and the airbag deployed. An awful seasick moment of near-weightlessness followed as the ass-end of the truck left the ground. Diamonds flew everywhere, slashing my skin, piercing my clothing, sputtering over the metal surfaces in the odd sizzle of tambourines.

The fat hairy thing rolled out of the driver's seat. A second later, I followed airborne, the impact upon the ground devastating. Three times I had experienced this, and in each instance, the pain was more concrete, more *here*—which meant I was in real-time, not a *perhaps*, not a *maybe*, but a *now*. Still within the Shimmer, but I'd been removed from one timeline long enough to allow any unforeseen possibilities to negate themselves—then dropped back in at the worst possible moment. A fresh start at the mouth of a predator if you will.

It had all gone sideways, and I had no one to blame but myself. Over the years, I had softened to all the evil and corruption on rampant display. Calloused by experience, I had, by and large, allowed it to roll off my back. The more tolerant of darkness I became, or at the very least unfazed by it, the more demanding— and more frequent—my jobs.

I imagined the Brynnwick girls standing around that horrendous conjuring rug, amid searing light and freezing gale. Somehow, they had rolled everything back ten or twelve minutes. Even though Scarlet and Fate had said that time in the Shimmer moves in fits, they also mentioned it's a highway with many exits.

If you can veer off the road, why not loop back?

Entirely possible.

Thanks to three sets of Brynnwick twins (whether at the behest of The Proprietor, it was impossible to know for sure), the game had been reset. I harbored every intention of executing this job with extreme prejudice, cicadas, ranch hands, and spider-people be damned.

I pushed through crumbling agony and stood. My hip joint bellowed. Again, that seasick feeling of cracked bones swimming in thick soup.

Darryl the monster had been ejected from the truck as before, but now he sat upright with his back against one of the light poles, his gaping mouth offering me a view of those rat incisors and more molars than a human should have. In addition to his cartoon necktie and castaway shorts, one square-toed boot remained, flayed in a banana peel burst. His extra limbs, all broken, lay in the dirt like cut wires. His right eye, branded, blistered, and bloody from the crucifix, opened—and that one, miraculously, looked human. Darryl was still in there, clawing to get out, but it was Izuriel who spat my cross out in a ribbon of smoke.

"You have friends in the Shimmer," Izuriel said, unable to disguise bewilderment and disbelief. "Walpurgis Peak *lied to me.*"

I leaned over him. "Tastes like shit, doesn't it?"

The monster raised its tail. The stinger slid from its fleshy caul like a rattler's fang, poised about six inches from Darryl's carotid. Demon-stink everywhere.

"Move not, Exorcist," Izuriel said, his voice hate and blasphemy, old world ignorance saturated in new world inebriation. "This blood bag will sting himself to death right here, he'll shit his lifeblood on the Nazarene stick I just spat onto unhallowed ground."

"Enough of your profanations, demon. I should have cleaned this night-hole of a county up years ago. Smile, you're the first turd I'm flushing *all the way down.*"

"*Meat-pig here weeps for a daughter stuffed with demon cocks on Copperhead Farms. I filled him with dope; ate him from the inside out. Another bite or two and his soul grinds to a halt in my belly.*"

I flashed on a memory of my mother, kneading bread dough on Thanksgiving morning: *Be sober-minded, Billy; be watchful. Your adversary, the devil, prowls around like a roaring lion, seeking someone to devour.*

The right side of Darryl's mouth trembled. The damaged eye excised a tear. I remembered him again at Big Ben's four days from now, so close to breaking down. He'd been devoured and hadn't known it.

Did Jesus not send the disciples out two by two? He gave them power over unclean spirits, and they cast out many demons.

It hit me: Darryl had invited Izuriel in, but he and I would have to be *in agreement* to push Izuriel out. He'd made a deal with him and suffered the intrusion of possession—he would have to *rescind* that offer, and when two or more are in agreement, so shall it be. Strength in numbers. Sometimes it really is that simple.

I grabbed Darryl's monster throat and squeezed. Rancid breath and all imaginable corruptions boiled from his maw in an awful, hot gale, every molar a headstone in a very old graveyard.

I said, "For Beeley, for your soul—work with me."

Darryl looked at me with one eye, mad Izuriel with the other.

"Darryl Ballantine," I said. "Hear me and answer. Do you reject Satan, his minions, and all his works?"

Izuriel voided Darryl's bowel at my feet and pressed the stinger against his prisoner's throat. That left eye bore every malignancy, nurtured every cancer you could imagine.

"Good to my word, Beauchamp," the demon croaked. Only the left side of his mouth moved, the schism in full swing. "Meat-pig will die in spasms, and you will fail."

I held fast, holding their gaze as Darryl struggled to speak.

"Darryl Ballantine," I repeated. "*Do you reject Satan?*"

Darryl's voice—thin as cellophane—but it was *there*, it was *him*. "I do, I do . . . reject . . . him . . . please, *God, please help me.*"

Now we were in agreement.

"*Save your servant who trusts in you, my God. Let him find in you, Lord, a fortified tower in the face of the enemy.*"

Darryl wept.

Izuriel laughed.

I placed my boot on that grisly monster chest. I'm not sure if Izuriel knew it, but I had him pinned in more ways than one.

The demon cackled, "When you were a child, I pissed all over you while your father watched. Let's get back to those days, Beauchamp. Sour sheets and shame, a drunkard's plaything in the middle of those long Walpurgis nights."

Izuriel was out of tricks, out of insults. Either kill Darryl in his monster state and risk being snuffed out with him—or bargain with me. That's how it goes nearly every time. Demons are grifters, con men with one foot in the other world. With their back against the wall, out come the offers—worldly offers—money, skirt, and power. The Big Three.

"I'll make you rich, Exorcist. You'll feast on a whore's red meat and rule this shitstain county with an iron fist and balls shooting molten steel. We'll tear up Bleary Street, cop that eight-ball, murder at random. Bend the Old Rules. This Proprietor you speak of, you'll wear his skin like a suit, drink from his pool of unearthly pleasures. Sound good?"

"I'm so sad," Darryl whimpered. His voice rang tiny, defeated—but human. His Missouri twang swelled with regret. "I miss her so much."

The stinger pressed in, forming a divot in his neck.

"It is *not* hopeless, Darryl," I said. "This demon is a falsehood, mixing lies with the truth to confuse you, to keep you separated and alone. Look at your hands. See the monstrous. Forced upon you."

Darryl raised his right hand. His expression morphed from grief to revulsion. The stinger, however, under demon control, did not budge an inch. He looked at me, tongue lolling about the left side of his mouth, looking to form words of his own, overriding not only the demon, but the horrendous amount of meth he'd ingested.

"Beeley," Darryl managed.

"*Refuse* him. *Reject* him. Lean on your faith and love for your daughter and join me."

"Bite the meat of your tongue, Exorcist," Izuriel hissed. Darryl's monster organ erupted with a steaming piss-geyser. It sprayed my jeans and sizzled on the fallen pine needles. "Urina tepeat Deo tuo, tremit mundus sub pedibus nostris."

Let your urine be pitched to your God, the world trembles under our feet.

"Your wife sleeps, but I will awaken her with cancer. A real nasty one. Womb and tit, brain and bowel. Blood in your home, death on your doorstep. All because you would not relent."

My wife? Oh, you fallen angel asshole; you obnoxious, junkie punk.

"Hear me, demon: The men William Beauchamp and Darryl Ballantine stand in agreement and will in the name of the Lord God of Hosts. Obey these ancient rites, tremble at the Holy name of Jesus Christ, and flee in the presence of those unified before God Almighty."

Darryl's face opened in wide terror; the look of a man fallen on the tracks who sees the train coming, the gazelle faced with a pack of hyenas, a child on the business end of an angry parent. His tail stiffened, and the stinger pointed skyward.

"Look above to Walpurgis Peak," Izuriel growled. "In its mighty shadow you stand. Though shat to your earth in the last war, we always survive, Exorcist, and I will live through this. Then come for your blood. Time is short, but we are eternal. Know what I say true, bound by the Old Rules."

"I command you, unclean spirit, obey me to the letter. I, who am a minister of God despite my unworthiness, cast you out, along with every Satanic power of the enemy, every spectre from Hell. In the name of our Lord Jesus Christ, begone and stay far from this creature of God. For it is *He* who commands you, *He* who flung you headlong from the heights of heaven into the sewer of Hell."

Darryl and I said in unison, *"DO IT! OBEY!"*

There was a flash, a dull, yellow infection of light. Darryl coughed it up as a luminous gel, a glowing phlegm. It slid down his chest and onto my boot.

Izuriel lay in the open now, corporeal, and best of all, vulnerable.

From the hissing front end of Darryl's ruined truck, movement caught my attention. A flashing headlight dangled from wires like a gouged eye, but from that open sore, a familiar shape wormed its way through, now plump and ripe since I last saw it fleeing into the defroster vent.

That fucker, I thought. *That junkie puke* did *have an escape plan.*

Remember the centipede with the human face, the one spat out by Izuriel on top of the Ram's dashboard—the one I thought was an illusion? Well, not so much. Now the length of a cat, it S-curved through the gravel and into the glare of the floodlights.

That obscenity, that bald, old-man face with sagging jowls and wet, drunkard's eyes, stared up at me, wiggling antennae sprouting from where a man's eyebrows should be. Below, it worked its shiny black mandibles. Hard call, but this creature was more repugnant than Tarantos by a nose.

I remembered my high school biology—*centipedes are venomous.*

But tonight, so was Darryl Ballantine.

The choir of winter cicadas burst into their warbling sleigh-bell whine.

The sentient phlegm crept from my boot. It oozed toward the centipede, then stopped—just for a second—and part of it, I swear to you, rose from the mass and twisted. I'm convinced Izuriel turned back and looked at me.

We always survive . . . I will live through this . . .

The centipede pounced on the demon snot in an instant, mandibles shoving in the goo, smacking noises and minute hungry grunts bubbling from that nightmare face. Glistening antennae beat a tribal rhythm on the gravel as it fed on its Master.

"Darryl, use the stinger! *Paralyze that Goddamned demon!*"

Darryl's lips opened into that rat-toothed smile I'd first seen in the Shimmer video, and he let Izuriel have it. When the stinger impaled the gob of demon muck, the centipede didn't miss a beat, continuing its feast.

Darryl's great tail spasmed. Venom flowed. The centipede squealed as the taste of its prize soured, but Darryl offered no quarter. I saw a mass move through that bonesnake of his tail, a mega-dose of poison rushing to the stinger. The centipede attempted retreat, fishtailing as dozens of legs pushed through the gravel.

"Venom, buddy, that's it. Give it to him, Darryl!"

Laughing best he could, Darryl corkscrewed the stinger into the slop, and by now, it was clear the centipede was also poisoned. Its armor-plating bulged, then separated. Liquid seeped from the fissures. Trouble for Izuriel.

A rustle resounded in the branches above, and down dropped Tarantos, web-tethered to the canopy of Eldritch Wood. Mouth hinged open, eyes pure slate, she stalked the centipede in slow, deliberate steps. Darryl did not relent—the spike remained in his prey, and the neurotoxin flowed.

She stopped short of the centipede. It would be of enormous benefit if Tarantos did not remember us and, more importantly, the violent death of her four children at Jesse's hand, which made sense in the light of the reset—but this is the Purg, where anything goes.

Darryl removed the stinger so fast, all I saw was a blur.

Everyone stared at one another until Tarantos spoke, and when she did, she looked directly at me.

"The Shimmer favors you, Evictor." Izuriel the Belligerent, imperiled. My children, though murdered, *now live.*"

The centipede whined as poison ransacked its body. The exoskeleton peeled off like flower petals. Its eyes rolled back. Antennae twitched.

"I want him."

The demon cleared of Darryl Ballantine, and my contract with The Monster Cartel fulfilled, I nodded.

"Madame, he is yours," I said.

Supine in her humanity and ferocious in her spiderhood, Tarantos seized the centipede with both hands. It screeched a grotesque imitation of a human infant, bawling a terror known only to prey. She may have danced a little jig at that moment, and I hope that banal description does not cheapen her glee, but there was little doubt Tarantos celebrated turning the table on the one who had cheated and then condemned her.

It was difficult to pay attention through such cataclysmic pain. I wanted to vomit—and not just from the stink of Izuriel's urine and feces and the sight of all the creeping things of Bleeder's Dairy—but from the overpowering presence of Walpurgis Peak. Izuriel's words of warning stayed with me: *In its mighty shadow you stand.*

I'd had enough of Walpurgis Peak in my youth and tried my damnedest every time back in the Purg to avoid the sight of it. But here, at the hills that suffered its avalanches and tantrums, to gaze upon its contemptuous slopes, its razor hide, thrust toward the sky like an obscene, granite needle, one had to, at the very least, respect its unabashed monstrosity. There was an excellent reason the Monster Cartel had chosen Bleeder's Dairy, as it stood nestled in the shadow of one of the great sentinel mountains of the world, and beneath it, a sleeping atrocity, a machine, it was said, that maintains a hideousness too foul to contemplate.

This vile ogre of a mountain, the feudal lord that broods over Walpurgis County; how many have been driven to blood or madness at its behest, thrown to the fires of abandon by the corrupted that fell here aeons ago? How long until it falls to me to end this reign of ruin?

"Beeley," Darryl sobbed.

Watching his sad, tired monster face with one eye and that granite colossus with the other, I smoothed my hands over my vest, and that's when I remembered Pipsy. Darryl had blocked Pipsy from adding her famous Crispies to his coffee. Why had he done that? He loved those things.

Because Izuriel had done that, right under your nose. You're slipping, old man.

Right before the Rail rolled to a stop outside Big Ben's, Pipsy Simms attached a small bag of Crispies to the bill. I fished the diner ticket out of the interior pocket and read the little note she'd scrawled on the back, beneath a hopeful smiley face.

For Darryl, who is far from home.

She knew. Dammit, Pipsy knew. Crispies were made with love, of course. Again, sometimes it really is that simple, and that's why Izuriel, whether he was in total control of Darryl at that moment or only partially so, denied her.

"I failed, Billy, I failed . . . I miss her so much. She's lost and it's all my fault. The demon lied to me."

The poor bastard. His body had been worked over more than anyone should endure. He'd shift back to human, but Vegas odds had it the pain would be insurmountable. And speaking of pain, I had about twenty seconds before the shock of everything caught up with me and shut my brain off for a while.

I collapsed next to Darryl. Misery moved through my pelvis in a sick, undulating wave.

His cross-branded eye watched as I tore the little bag open.

"Open your mouth, Darryl," I gasped. "I have medicine."

"No more drugs, no more. Ever."

"No, no, *life medicine*. Trust me. A gift from Pipsy Simms."

I thought he'd protest further, but Darryl complied. His jaw fell open, and I reached in past those enormous incisors and dropped the full load of the bag, perhaps a tablespoon, onto his tongue.

There was a crunching noise I never wanted to hear again—but not from Darryl. Not far away, Tarantos worked her way up the silver strand of web. The centipede, face wide open in terror, dangled from her mouth. Soon she was a rustle of branches in the shadows.

"*Sssssshhhhhimmerrrr,*" Tarantos whispered, her voice disappearing onto the trees.

The cicadas stopped.

In the distance, the barn doors creaked apart, and a rush of boots bumbled toward me. No doubt ZZ, Black Hat, and Jesse on their way to investigate a smashed Ram and a loud argument at the base of a light pole.

"Jesus! Did you see that?"

Was that ZZ? Black Hat? I couldn't care less. Fading fast.

"*Billy,*" Darryl said. "Billy, are *you* okay?"

I heard the first crack of Darryl's bones shifting back to their rightful position.

A searing white line, bright as the sun, as the Shimmer opened . . .

Lights out.

7
KANSAS CITY

LENA SAT BESIDE the bed, glasses on and a book in her hand. Behind her, the bane of decorators worldwide: mini-blinds. To my left, an IV stand and the usual gang of vital-sign monitoring gear.

Uh-oh. Not good.

"Hi there, tough guy," Lena said. She slid her glasses down and peered at me over the lenses. "I'm told an emergency hip replacement is a one in a million situation." She stroked my hair and smiled, but I could see the worry. It's good to have someone worry about you.

My tongue felt like it had been wrapped in a tube sock, but oddly enough, the intense pain seemed AWOL.

Wait. What? I have an artificial hip?

"Where are we? Don't say *hospital*."

"You're not in the Purg if that's what you're worried about. You were airlifted to the University of Kansas Hospital. Cartel chopper, no less. Who knew?"

My brain throbbed, clearly a Shimmer hangover and exhaustion. I'd been slingshot through time several . . . well, times, if you will, and my mind clattered like a bowl of marbles. I remembered Darryl in the truck smoking meth, blasting Slayer, his hillbilly insults, and our high-speed exorcism. Smoke boiled out of his ear. *Exo-Hoss.*

Lena said, "That call in the middle of the night scared the shit straight out of me. A few minutes later a black Escalade pulled up, and within a half hour I was on the Sheridan tarmac, boarding a Gulfstream. They say your hip was smashed like a potato chip when you were tossed from Ballantine's truck. Lucky to be alive after a wreck like that."

Lena looked toward the silent, blank television. Her face tightened. "God keeps looking out for you, Billy Beauchamp."

Because the training days are over, I thought. *Now the real work begins.*

"I'm sorry, honey, really."

Even through the curtain of painkillers the images came back to me: The Brynnwick girls around the summoning rug, Darryl's awful transformation inside the Dodge's cab, Jesse, the bad ass with her Mossberg, me floating outside of time with millions of winter cicadas, the Shimmer rewinding when things went bad . . .

Intervention. *Reset.*

"A Cartel rep met me at the KC airport, Billy. Big shot from what I can tell. He gave me an envelope and this case, this wretched cigarette case, and said you'd know what to do with it. 'It'll fill in the gaps,' he said."

She held up the golden Shimmer-viewer and expensive stationery sealed in wax.

"Tall, great suit, Prince Charles horse-face?" I asked.

She put a straw to my lips, and I drank.

"The same. I don't want you working with the Monster Cartel *ever* again. That little shit in the bedroom I could handle, but this Bilderberg undertaker I could do without. He's bad news, a real killer."

He definitely liked his cocktails to squirm, I remembered that.

"I agree."

Wait.

If I'd Shimmered back four days and set things straight, then the Emissary would never have appeared in the bedroom that night, three days from now.

For a second there I must have looked like a fish gasping in a trout basket.

"Don't get that Shyamalan twist-ending look on your face, sweetie. Your Cartel pal laid it all out. I have no memory of putting a shotgun in the mouth of a monster, but I certainly believe that it happened. Might have happened. Will happen. Whatever. Time fuckery, babe. Nothing bourbon and an eight-hour snooze in front of the bedroom fireplace won't cure."

"Darryl," I said. "Where's Darryl Ballantine?"

She tossed the envelope on the roll-away table and handed me The Proprietor's cigarette case. The deep etchings of faces in agony, consigned to flames of woe, ignored me in favor of their own torments.

Lena shrugged. "Mr. Creepshow obviously made his explanations, but they're for you alone. Now, let's talk about your Terminator hip."

"I figured I'd smashed it, but I was able to stand and finish the job. What's more, that shithead demon met the ass end of an old grudge. A woman scorned, as they say."

"Adrenaline and God, Billy. The ultimate pick-me-up. Listen, as soon as I leave, Nurse Ratchet and Igor the humpbacked orderly will be in to haul you out of bed. They want you walking. *Today.*"

"Think it'll hurt?"

"God, I hope so. It's what you get for scaring the hell out of me. We're not in our thirties anymore. Things break. It's hard to get vintage parts."

We looked at one another for a while. Lena never lost that little kitty-corner grin that first caught my eye in Mr. Kenway's fourth-period English lit class. She'd corrected him on the pronunciation of aluminum. 'Only English guys that smoke Dunhills say *aluminium*,' she'd said. I knew I had to meet her. The following Friday, we sneaked into the Danielsburg Cinema Twin to see *The Empire Strikes Back* because we'd spent our money at Big Ben's—and we've been together ever since.

"The Cartel was good to their word then," I said. "You have the crypto device?"

"I do. It was the second thing handed to me after your little care package. At today's rate, though, you were paid well over a hundred grand. That'll keep us in puffy socks and firewood all winter long, right?"

"Now we can get our *own* Bedazzler and I won't have to buy from that weird girl on Etsy."

"Like me, she has a crush on you."

Lena kissed me.

"Your work is important, but the danger petrifies me, and it should be a warning to you. One of these days . . . "

I squeezed Lena's hand.

"I can't retire. I've been too tolerant, lacking vigilance, almost *tolerating* evil, and that attitude keeps everyone in the Purg complacent. They acclimate; become blase. If you're born knowing there are fallen angels and monsters in your backyard, you learn to accept them. We should never be all right with that. It all goes back to that ugly mountain."

"Unfortunately, Walpurgis Peak isn't going anywhere, Billy."

"Well, true. The mountain cannot come to me."

"So you'll go to the mountain."

I nodded. "One of these days."

Look above to Walpurgis Peak. In its mighty shadow you stand.

Lena patted my chest, then pulled a Samsung from her jacket. "I'm going into the hall to call the kids, tell them what's what. You look at your Monster Cartel parting gifts. I don't want anything to do with that golden case, unless it's to toss it under a bus or dump it in a river. *Capisce?*"

I nodded. "Okay. Will do."

"Love you, Billy Beauchamp."

"Love *you*, Lena Beauchamp."

Once Lena was clear of the room, I opened the envelope.

Mr Beauchamp:

The success of our partnership pleases the Cartel to no end. Travel through the Shimmer invariably leaves gaps, blank spaces in the fine gridwork of human memory, and although this is accepted as normal in most cases, I believe your contribution to Cartel interests to be unique, and therefore, worthy of explanation.

Only the maimed of this word have free access to the Shimmer, and it is to them to whom you owe gratitude. Scarlet and Fate Brynnwick lobbied for a reconstruction of events, a rollback as you might say, affording you a second opportunity once it became apparent that the situation with Izuriel had spiraled beyond your control. It was not an indictment of your skills as an Exorcist (or Evictor, as Scarlet seems to find preferable), merely an intervention on behalf of Cartel interests. Random events and the decisions of men leave the door wide open to chance. These two gifted young ladies recognized the probability of mission failure and rightfully intervened on your behalf.

Your injuries were not anticipated in the scope of our mission plan. When they became manifest, I extended the full scope of Cartel services; no resource withheld. We have fingers beneath every door in society, Mr. Beauchamp and we can open them all. You will receive the best medical attention until you are fully healed, including any and all care when you return to Sheridan, and at zero cost to you. Consider this not only our obligation as professionals, but a bonus for a job well done.

As for the golden case, I am confident you will figure a means to operate the device. Your promise has been fulfilled.

Respectfully,

His Excellency Proprietor VXI
Monster Cartel,
Walpurgis County

Scarlet and Fate. I owe those girls a visit and something unique by way of thanks. I'll bet Fate would love a custom vest she and her sister could share, so maybe the weird girl on Etsy would receive one last job from me after all.

I fumbled with the case—about as gracelessly as you could imagine in a hospital bed while hopped up on Norco—but eventually, it snapped open. The black mirror, a sheet of night seamless as ever. Soon, the purple and scarlet Mandelbrot filled the space, hypnotizing me all over again.

There, in the golden light of a late afternoon, I saw a rusted combine blade overgrown with weeds. Pumpkins, bright orange and by the hundreds, lay scattered in the field. Close by stood a scarecrow as old as those witch-trodden hills, with its giant misshapen head and floppy shit-streaked hat. In the distance, hard to tell how many yards away, stood a farmhouse. Victorian job, a huge fiend of a building jutting with gables and chimneys dwarfed by a massive turret. Up top, a weathervane, as usual, pointing You Know Where.

"Copperhead. He made it. I'll bet I have the Brynnwick girls to thank for this, too."

And Pipsy Simms, of course. She had known how to bring Darryl home.

Out of a habit borne from too many years with mobile phones, I pinched the image to zoom in.

And it *did* zoom in.

The old farmhouse stood silent in the tall grass, wreathed in purple twilight. A lone oil lamp shone in a first-floor window. Before long, the enormous doors parted. Out into that deep eventide stepped Darryl, worn hard and put away wet.

Human, I thought with great relief. Barefoot and wearing nothing but the ridiculous Yogi Bear shirt collar and the tattered remains of his trousers, he stopped and turned back to the house, waving his hand in an exaggerated beckoning gesture. Covered with cuts and abrasions, face brutalized yet filled with a father's love, he stood tall and waited as a young woman crossed the threshold. Well, not *that* young. She looked to be in her forties now, hair graying and past her waist. She had been nineteen or twenty when Copperhead Farms tossed her into an unsolvable maze. Time lost to the Shimmer had done the rest.

Darryl Ballantine walked his daughter Beatrice down the stairs.

"Beeley," I said, and closed the case.

Then, my eyes.

AFTERWORD

Okay, show's over. Have time for that drink I promised? Good. Plant it here and our bartender will be along shortly.

In the meantime, here's a little background on each of the stories in this book.

STRANGE ACRES

The first story I ever sold, published—typos and all—in a small anthology called *Halloween Horror, Volume 3*. Unlike Back Sabbath, I do not think there has been a Volume 4. In the anthology's table of contents the story is listed dead last, and I still don't know if that's supposed to be a place of honor like a headlining band, or a down-and-out ventriloquist act who takes the stage during last call. Nevertheless, it was a huge thrill for me to not only have the story accepted, but to see it in paperback. Since we need to start at the beginning, "Strange Acres" leads this collection. It's been significantly tuned-up since the *Halloween Horror* version, but the story has not changed—it's just wearing nicer pants.

NOTE TO SANDERSON

This is, in many ways, a direct tie-in to an unpublished 2020 novel of mine entitled *Exeter*. However, while typing away, I realized that *Exeter* and Walpurgis County exist in the same universe, and this story morphed into a pile of needed exposition. If the stories in this book are read in order, the information here should make what follows easier to understand, so I dropped it in the hopper. And for my money, who doesn't like a little jog through alternative history and conspiracy?

241

Tip of the hat to Papa Lovecraft with Albert Wilmarth and Henry Akeley.

BILLY BEAUCHAMP, DISCOUNT EXORCIST

A rare case of a story written from the title down. When the term Discount Exorcist popped into my head, the original plan was lighter fare, perhaps a little irreverence in the face of bizarre, hideous things, and before I knew it, I'd written the opening paragraph and set it in Walpurgis County.

It's a short tale, but I like the character. Evil exasperates Billy Beauchamp, and he's had an assful. Nevertheless, he hasn't lost his compassion or sense of mission. Billy takes good care of his friends.

FLIGHT 2320

Snarky and dangerous Captain Brisbane is a real handful, but Julie Reese has her demons too, eh?

Originally a Shallow Waters piece. The month's theme was either dark humor or black humor. Whatever. Anyway, the opening line tucked it in the mythos, and off I went. If you think diversity hires in the cockpit are a dice roll, step aboard Viceroy Air.

Next time you set foot on one of those flying Greyhounds, imagine if the pilot was an all-out nutter. Or worse, overcome by supernatural forces.

Walpurgis Peak speaks to me, Julie.

THIS IS A GREEDY, JEALOUS HOUSE

I have fun with the Epistolary format. The diary entry method is tried and true, so when I use it, I like to set it in the nineteenth century and have a little fun with the language. Modern Epistolaries make imaginative use of email, Twitter, texts, post-it notes—goddamn smoke signals if you can pull it off—but the old way, at least to me, oozes Hammer Horror films, and I dig that approach.

A small origin story for the Vanderbaum House was in order, as it pops up here and there. Also, this is a tangential piece to "A Testament of Wanderers," which appears in the *Dead Letters: Episodes of Epistolary Horror* anthology.

AFTERWORD

You know what else? Weathervanes freak me out a little. I immediately associate them with creepy old houses; they give me the heebie-jeebies just enough to sound the alarm. There's a shot of one spinning in the rain in the 1972 film *The Other*. Funny, the stuff that sticks with you.

LIFE RETURNS

A family tragedy complicated by occult interference. That's one way to look at it. The other is I wrote it as a bridge between my previous life as a musician and the writer I hope to become. Fans of my old band will immediately recognize the title, and snippets of lyrics woven into the story are for them. However, for those unfamiliar with the music, believe me, it's fine—you don't have to be.

I think the story stands on its own, Easter eggs notwithstanding. Revised and cleaned up from the freebie novella released prior to my novel *Live Wire,* and this is the definitive version. Again, same events, now with a spit-shine.

WITCHFYNDRE

I like this one. So much so that I rewrote it for this collection. I was fairly new to tobacco pipes when I wrote the original, moving away from a long relationship with expensive cigars. I thought a vengeful Jinn, using his supernatural powers of wish fulfillment against the cadre of beings that he had become, conveyed its own sense of weird justice. Hey, both Aydem and Zahad got what they wanted out of the relationship, right? Sounds like a win.

Witchfyndre may pop up again, perhaps wielded by Angelica, recipient of Judgment's Cruel Deliverer . . . so stay on your toes, evildoers, as the smoke knowest the truth—but one day, it may meet its match.

THE HOUSE ON BELTANE ROAD

My second actual sale, even if it was run on Patreon. But goddammit, I was given money for it, and that's all that counts. Revised from that version for clarity and rhythm. Built in 1874, the

Vanderbaum house remains the sole dwelling on Beltane Road—there are other *structures*, but it is the only *house*. Even I don't know what's in there these days, as I only witnessed the seating of its weathervane and terrible events of Frederick Lucius Vanderbaum II's genesis. By the way, I just thought of this while typing: is the house on Copperhead Farms perhaps a mirror image of The House on Beltane Road? If that's the case, remember it's been thrashed by a combine blade.

Sorry, realtors.

THE NIGHTMAN'S LAST SHIFT

Just plain nasty, and Lange is a real piece of work. To be honest, I did have an old film poster from 1902 in mind when I began the tale. The film, titled *A Fight With Sledgehammers*, pitched as "the most thrilling film ever taken, full of startling situations from beginning to finish," ran about four minutes in length—now if that ain't flash fiction I don't know what is. And I thought: *who doesn't want to write a sledgehammer fight?*

This tale was written for *Shallow Waters* as well. Aside from a nudge or fix here or there, this is pretty much how it ran. I've never won the competition, but I think this came in third. The theme that month was *MOTEL HELL*.

I have memories of shitty desert motels, and I never felt at ease in them.

Neither should you.

OUR LAST, RAVING DAYS

It's a club . . . and you ain't in it.

Hayward Decatur, who copped a plea on a murder rap resulting in a ten-year stretch in a psychiatric prison, finds out the hard way that the dreaded Medusa Cult—and, by extension, Medusa Engineering—carries a grudge like a caveman with a stick.

This story features an appearance from Armand Jenks, the heavy from *Live Wire*. Those who have read that novel may notice Mr. Jenks has a slightly different appearance in 2022 than in 1993. I have a gruesome idea to explain that, and it's imperative I write it. When *Exeter* makes it out of my office and into print (which I plan to do next), you will also meet Jacqueline Rawlings' *seriously*

AFTERWORD

fucked- up progenitor and the unrelenting, God-awful Sentinel. Sometimes, not knowing is part of the fun, but stick with me, and you'll see.

FLIGHT 2320: WIRE-WITCH

I wrestled with adding this, fearing a sequel or epilogue to Flight 2320 may appear gimmicky instead of bolting them together as one story. I spent some time polishing it, adding a bit here or there, and found I really liked the idea of a callback before we head into the book's big finish, kind of like a short running before a feature. Jeff Brisbane, dead on his feet, still playing game show host, marooned on Walpurgis Peak with no hope of rescue.

Really, Julie, what do you have to lose at this point?

BILLY BEAUCHAMP AND THE MONSTER CARTEL

A lot of Walpurgis County history, a broken-hearted father, our intrepid, ragged Exorcist, methamphetamine, guns, spiders, and Slayer. Sounds like a solid weekend in 1980s Oxnard, California.

I had a great time writing this, especially the scene at Bleeder's Dairy. Dore's *Arachnae* is a powerful image (it's no weathervane, mind you), and I found a way to incorporate that hideous creature into the mythos. Truth be told, the Ballantine angle was not even a consideration as a plot device. The intent was to send Mr. Beauchamp through some sort of underworld, crime-ridden, diabolical monster rally, but after Billy's breakfast conversation with Darryl and the scene with The Proprietor in the Rail, it struck me that the mission *was* Darryl, and we were off.

As for the Monster Cartel in its entirety, we have yet to meet them. They'll crawl out of the woodwork, I'm sure of it. We'll take a peek inside that barn, too.

So there it is, "Billy Beauchamp and the Monster Cartel" brings us full circle with "Strange Acres," and I thought that was just the place to leave it.

So, order up, our bartender's here. After we sink this drink I have to split, though. Heavy slate ahead, stories to tell and endings to find.

If you had fun with this book, tell a friend, and leave a review.

KYLE TOUCHER

It's a jungle out there, and we authors truly appreciate your eyes on our pages. I know I do.

Oh, and Welcome to Walpurgis County.

Now you're a local.

Kyle Toucher
Winter 2024

ACKNOWLEDGMENTS

Aside from the hours of isolation in front of a laptop, no one writes a book alone. After my first draft of typo-filled contradictions, story holes and origami dialogue, I move on to frustrating evenings agonizing over commas and adjectives. When that's done, and the manuscript (buried four directories down with a title like *The_Medusa_Psalms_Third_Draft_V009*) looks like nothing more than a blur of nonsense, the time has come to fling the work to an editor.

Enter Monique Snyman. She stepped up on this project, and carried the flag above and beyond the call of duty. She went through this MS three times before acquiescing to my refusal to spell theatre as *theater*—even though I'm about as American as it comes—and the ugly truth that I often use semicolons incorrectly. We've had several therapy sessions at the clinic; I endeavor to improve.

Joana Halerz knocked the cover art out of the park based on a very clunky previz I had done. The first version met with immediate approval save for me changing the title from "Tales Of" to "Welcome To", and a nitpick about the weathervane. She enjoys her fabulous work, and it shows. Walpurgis Peak, now realized.

Naching Kassa has been *very* patient with me in gathering the things she needs to do her job as head of Crystal Lake's Talent Relations. I know the publishing business the way a meerkat knows how to make bowler hats, so I end up saying a lot of stupid shit. Turns out there's a whole other side to this gig. Who knew?

I'd be a jabroni for not mentioning Jaco Nieuwoudt, who slugged this manuscript into some voodoo program which formats it for publishing. I put the poor guy through hell on *Live Wire* with all the zany Dragonfire VLA Code, Medusa Engineering Documents, and that goddamn hard to work with Aramaic font.

Looks cool on the page though! On this one, I noodled a few paragraphs I couldn't stand a few days before the ARCS went out, and he was good as gold about accommodating that. He's on the short list of people I'd ask to help me bury a body—should I commit a crime on the other side of the world.

And Joe Myhardt, the intrepid Captain of the *Crystal Lake*, who said "that could work" when I pitched him this book. Hell, he published *Live Wire* (read it next, trust me), and even though this book isn't as batshit as that one, I think it's still a little hard to define—but that didn't stop Joe from dropping it into the publishing que. Next time, I'll do something more easy to classify. *A thrilling space opera set against the rickets outbreak of 2058,* or *A charming coming of age story about a boy and his clairvoyant wiener dog hustling their way through devastating potato famine.*

Nothing happens in a vacuum. You can write the greatest book in the world, but if there is no one to champion it, it'll brood there, four directories down, on a dark, silent hard drive.

Unread is unknown.

Thank you all.

AN EXCERPT FROM
LIVE WIRE
BY KYLE TOUCHER

ĮNTERVĮEW Į

DEFENSE INTELLIGENCE AGENCY
CASE No. NB-18266-00
October 16, 1993 08:06 HRS

D.I.A. INVESTIGATOR: Agent Julia C. Oberon
LOCAL INVESTIGATOR: Detective Sergeant
Hector L. Castillo

Subject Interviewed at Albuquerque, NM
Police Department Medical Detention
Facility.

SUBJECT: Barlowe, Nicole Lynn.
FEMALE CAUCASIAN, AGE 34.
SYSTEMS ANALYST, MEDUSA ENGINEERING
CORPORATION
ADVANCED PROGRAMS AND DEVELOPMENT
BOSTON, MA.

CLASSIFIED.
PRESS BLACKOUT.

BEGIN TRANSCRIPTION

Oberon: Before we start, Miss Barlowe, I want you to be aware that you are under no legal obligation to speak to us. Do you understand that?

Barlowe: Yes, I do.

Oberon: This is merely informal questioning, and if you do wish to have legal counsel present, we can stop until that is made so. I am not law enforcement; I am with the Defense Intelligence Agency. Do you follow?

Barlowe: Yes, absolutely.

Castillo: There is an entire herd of corporate lawyers downstairs, flown in from Boston and New York, I'm told. You have not been charged with anything, nor at this time do I have any intention to do so. Merely asking questions here, Miss Barlowe. A lot happened on the night of October 14th. Would you like any of these lawyers present?

Barlowe: Lawyers? Already? Makes sense, I guess.

Castillo: Do you consent to questions?

Barlowe: You bet.

Castillo: You are an employee of Medusa Engineering Corporation?

Barlowe: I was . . . well, I doubt I am anymore.

Castillo: For how long, may I ask?

Barlowe: Coming up on eight years. I was part of the '80s hiring blitz. Pentagon money arrived in Hefty bags, it seemed. Most anyone that rolled out of MIT with a GPA above 3.8 and solid credentials was snatched up by Medusa Engineering. I thought I'd arrived, you dig?

Castillo: And what are those credentials?

Barlowe: Computer Science my parents are in debt to the ceiling for that and the company paid for Applied Physics. I also dabbled in Cryptology because I love a puzzle.

Oberon: Let's talk about what happened the other night the fourteenth.

Barlowe: You'd never believe it.

Oberon: There's a stack of law degrees in the lobby that want to know.

Castillo: Whatever you remember, Miss Barlowe.

Barlowe: Dragonfire started out fine, then it all went sideways. How's that?

Castillo: A great start. Your work was conducted at the Very Large Array, the radio telescope observatory outside of Socorro, just south of here. Medusa Engineering has a partnership with them?

Barlowe: They leased us star time, and we, in turn, solved some computer problems for them. We did not use the radio telescopes *as* telescopes in the traditional sense at least that's what I was told. Inter-departmental chatter was *verboten*, you know.

Castillo: Compartmentalization.

Barlowe: It's how anything nefarious is run. Keep everyone on a need-to-know basis until it all goes to hell. Compartmentalization equals Plausible Deniability. What follows is an entire legion of employees acting like that fat Sergeant Schultz from *Hogan's Heroes*. [IMITATES GERMAN ACCENT] I know *noth-ing!*

Oberon: Somebody knows something, and today you're it. The VLA disaster is all over the news. NASA and DOD are making statements, but The Defense Intelligence Agency is making the inquiries. *Several* dishes are offline, and—

Barlowe: Offline? That's a nice way to put it.

Oberon: You're certainly lucky to be alive, Miss Barlowe.

Barlowe: A cop told me that just yesterday. You can't see it because of the bandages, but I'm rolling my eyes.

Castillo: Consider yourself in Federal protective custody. Doesn't get more secure than that. Guaranteed.

Barlowe: The *Titanic* had guarantees.

Castillo: Can you tell us what happened at the VLA?

Barlowe: Dragonfire was so utterly far out, no one sane would buy the conference room pitch. But Medusa Engineering has their reasons and I've come to realize those reasons are very, *very* old.

Oberon: That's the second time you used that term *Dragonfire*.

Barlowe: Just like in the military, each project has an internal code name. I honestly don't know its real designation. That said, even if I were to disclose what I know about it, I was fed so much bullshit I may be lying to you and not know it.

Oberon: Try me.

Barlowe: We'd be here until doomsday, and my face hurts.

Oberon: We have painkillers.

Barlowe: Let's say it had to do with capturing CME particles, isolating certain elements, then, via some technobabble no one would fully explain to me, relay it back to Earth via the DragSat II satellite. Back to Earth for well, for whatever it was they were up to in that black tent. And that goddamn tent operation is responsible for all the blood and fire, I guarantee it.

Castillo: CME?

Barlowe: Coronal Mass Ejection, a sun burp if you want to be cute. An explosion occurs on the surface of the sun, an ungodly spew of plasma escapes through a hole in its magnetic field the corona and it blows out into space at *crazy* speed. This was a particularly fast one, and we had thirty hours to scramble our pocket protectors to New Mexico and get the gear calibrated before the wave got here.

Castillo: That's some *Star Trek* stuff.

Barlowe: Aye, Captain.

Oberon: What were they looking for?

Barlowe: I'm at the kids' table, lady. Even with my highbrow degrees, I just wrangle data and look for patterns. You may have to go all the way up the rope if you want real answers but you'll reach senior players like Blasko Thorpe and chances are you'll hang from that rope. Your best bet is their barking Doberman, Armand Jenks. If Jenks made it out alive it was likely at the expense of everyone else.

Castillo: You work for the Science Mafia? That's a little much.

Barlowe: Let's just say I didn't know then what I know now. *La Coven Nostra* may be a better term.

Oberon: I'm no astronomer, but it seems unlikely something requiring the use of radio telescopes would take place during such a huge weather event.

Barlowe: Well, it didn't start out that way.

Castillo: Yes, the electrical storm. Less than an hour ago, the National Weather

Service sent us some pretty wild satellite photos of the Socorro and outlying area, all snapped on the night of October 14 into 15, between the hours of 6 PM and 6 AM. "Never has the formation of a cyclonic depression over a continuous landmass been reported, captured, or documented," they said. I had to ask what the hell *that* meant, and some egghead there told me cyclones, hurricanes, whatever you want to call them, only form over water.

Barlowe: And he's correct. An artificial event, Detective Castillo. I didn't go to cop school, and even *I* figured that out

Oberon: Moving up the timeline, you still maintain that later that night you were at Thompson's Kwik Gas on Route 60?

Barlowe: I do. All of this began at the Socorro VLA but it sure as shit ended at the Kwik Gas. When the kid and I ended up [GASPS] Wait. [SHOUTS] *The kid . . . is he okay?*

Oberon: Kid? What *kid* are you referring to?

Castillo: You were brought in alone, Miss Barlowe.

Barlowe: Yes, *the kid.* A boy twelve maybe? A real trooper, that kid. Marooned at that gas station with his old man. The cop *must* have picked up both of us. Honestly, after all that chaos, all that fire, the wound in my neck, all of it, there's blank spots small ones but I did *not* walk out of there alone. No way. Where is he? [RAISES VOICE] *My God, where is he?*

Oberon: Miss Barlowe, Deputy Youngblood's statement made clear that your state of mind when he picked you up approximately eight miles from the filling station was one of and I am quoting here " incoherent, near catatonic, suffering from severe burns."

Barlowe: My eyelids were burned off. So if you want to talk about the deputy's assessment of my behavior, I'd start there. Your Deputy *had* to have been the last to see him.

Castillo: Deputy Youngblood's write-up mentions only you, Miss Barlowe. No young boy.

Barlowe: I'm *not* imagining that kid.

Oberon: The burns; you were injured at the filling station?

Barlowe: I was injured all bloody night long, lady. The gas station was just the end of the line.

Oberon: This young boy you mentioned, is there a chance you became separated *before* Deputy Youngblood spotted you? Trauma is a twitchy thing, Miss Barlowe, *Doctor Barlowe*. Events get shuffled, memories scrambled.

Barlowe: It was all pretty insane at the time, I'll admit. My current trauma is *you* creating doubt. I know what happened. I was there. *That Deputy is lying.*

Castillo: You said just a minute ago that you experienced memory loss. *'There's blank spots, small ones'.* Seems, well, contradictory to what you're saying now.

Barlowe: It was me and that boy. *That* I recall.

Castillo: We have Deputy Youngblood's report.

Barlowe: Yeah? Well, do better, TJ Hooker.

Oberon: Anything else we're missing?

Barlowe: Just the giants.

-7-

STORM SIGNAL

LIGHTNING, DAD — DEAD AHEAD," Caleb said.

Caleb's eyes never left the windshield as he wrapped the headset's cable around his Walkman. He rarely saw towering thunderheads in his native southern California, and upon witnessing this searing bolt of plasma, New Mexico had his full attention.

Behind the wheel, Pale Brody kept an eye on the fine line of the eastern horizon. An endless procession of high-tension towers guarded Route 60, while above, distant, bruised, and bloodied, the clouds shed a curtain of rain, which set to work in smearing that perfect boundary between earth and sky. The lightning flashed again, enormous and impressive. He silently congratulated himself for changing the wiper blades on his '68 Fleetwood before leaving Los Angeles.

"That was just *huge*," Caleb said. "I can't wait to pass through it. I guarantee the day will not be able to get any cooler than *that*." He jabbed his index finger toward the sky show.

"You're right, Playboy," Pale said. "From here all the way to the Atlantic, the thunderstorms are really something else. We used to drive right through some certifiable whoppers back in the day. Did I ever tell you that in Nebraska we almost got caught in a twister?"

Caleb turned away so his father would not see him roll his eyes. "I've heard that story a couple times."

"That's why I change it every time I tell it, buddy."

Back in the day for Pale meant when he anchored the lead guitar position in a band called Mac Daddy. Mac Daddy was a mid-level hard rock outfit out of Pasadena, signed to a major label

262

subsidiary. Pale likely would never have joined a band like Mac Daddy—his guitar pastor preached Hendrix over Page—but the club scene in LA had only one lane in those days, and if you wanted to play pro, you drove in it.

Fun days nonetheless, those road trips, as Mac Daddy roamed North America, played loud, played hard, drank absolutely *everything*, and met absolutely *everybody*.

Caleb was just past the toddler stage when it all became airborne, and Valerie remained at home base with one eye on their son and the other scrutinizing the label's A&R guy. On a few occasions, Pale flew Valerie and Caleb out for shows in New York, Denver, and Miami. Those times had been good. Never rock star spectacular, but good.

Four years into the band's slow but steady climb up the ladder, they suffered a self-inflicted, humiliating blow. In 1988, Mac Daddy released a highly mocked, syrupy MTV power ballad called "I Wish You Missed Me," right as tastes began to change. Their upcoming album, *Relentless Boulevard*, absolutely died in the stores because of it, and the label tossed Mac Daddy like incriminating evidence.

The second whack in the balls came a month later, right in the middle of rescue negotiations with Capitol Records. Because of *Relentless Boulevard*'s dismal performance, Mac Daddy was replaced in the direct support slot for a major act's European tour; not bumped down a peg to opening band, just *gone*. Upon *that* news, Capitol stopped returning their manager's phone calls, then canceled future meetings. Within four months, the wounds proved fatal. The band split up.

Five years later, with the Nineties pendulum firmly set toward grunge and his marriage in the rear-view mirror, Pale hit the road for Austin, son in tow, eager to enter the world of record producing. Pale's old pal Billy Gaines and his crazy talented batch of post-punk-chicken-pickers were set to record a follow-up to their debut record, *The Tornado Alley Cats,* which had made some real noise on the alternative charts. It was not only gracious of Billy to ask Pale to produce their sophomore effort, but it couldn't have come at a better time, as Los Angeles was filled with ghosts; the house he was forced to sell, the shuttered clubs on Sunset, the handful of friends who had lost it all to drugs. If The Tornado Alley Cats' second record made waves, it could really kick-start a new career. *Produced By Pale Brody*—a future he could get behind.

"I'm glad we didn't fly—we'd have missed all of this," Caleb said. He squirmed as he did when his dad took him to see *The Empire Strikes Back* re-release on the Fox lot. The Imperial Walkers on the big screen blew his mind. "Just *look* at that."

Here on Route 60, part of Pale's slow road to Texas—when they could have just powered through on Interstate 10 and hooked a left at San Antonio—the scenic route revealed its treasures as God took X-Rays of the world. A purple river delta of lightning flooded the sky.

"Behold!" Pale said. He turned to his son and wiggled his eyebrows. "There's going to be a hammer—"

The hammer whacked the Cadillac square across the nose. Caleb had heard thunder a few times at home, rumbling far away in the San Gabriel mountains, but he'd never experienced such deliberate, solid brutality—and his dad was friends with the guys in Slayer.

"That's just crazy loud!" Caleb said, eyes wide as pancakes.

"Really is," Pale said. "Pretty deafening for a storm so far away. Maybe it's closer than we think."

Caleb leaned toward the windshield. The sun was nearly finished for the day, and soon it would light the underside of the storm, a promise of magnificent color.

"Sound at sea level travels at seven hundred sixty miles per hour," Caleb said. "We're about . . . what in New Mexico? Sixty-five hundred feet, maybe? So, it's a tad slower, seven-fifty, I'd guess, but that's still pretty fast. So maybe you're right about it being closer than we think. I love it, though."

"How the hell do you know all that?"

"I actually pay attention in school, Dad. That and, well, The Learning Channel is more awesome than you think it is. There's physics, biology, astronomy, all kinds of great stuff."

Pale shook his head and thought, *did he grow up when I wasn't looking?* "How come I never knew you were so smart?"

"Lots going on, I guess."

Pale sighed. Caleb had endured a lot of bad news since his mother's abrupt departure and had witnessed both parents at their worst. Still, the kid brought home A's and B's, had more than a passing interest in Yolanda Rivas two blocks over and had never kept a library book past its due date. His stomach wormed at the thought of uprooting his son, but the compass pointed to opportunity, and it had to be followed. Best of all, Caleb seemed to understand.

"By the way, I took one of your Marshall amps apart last year." Caleb tried to keep one eye on his father and the other on Route 60's descent into heavy weather. He wasn't sure how the old man would take the news his son had been screwing around inside a vintage1972 Super Lead, but currently emboldened by the compliment, if he was going to brag a little, now was the time.

Pale frowned, but his eyes smiled. "No, you didn't. How the hell could you do that? You were *eleven*. I never even saw a screwdriver until I was twenty-seven."

Caleb nodded. "I did. I mean, not all the way like unsoldering everything, but I took out all the power tubes, cleaned the contacts, all that. I removed the whole thing from the chassis and fixed a speaker output connection that was close to failing. I figured out how the effects loop you had installed works by reading one of the amp-nerd books you bought—but never opened—and also became fascinated with re-biasing. I didn't have the gear for that or the desire to electrocute myself, so I scrapped *that* idea."

"Dismantling that amp would have bought you a one-way ticket to military school, but amazing work nonetheless. Your mother always said you were born with special skills. When I was your age, I was into T. Rex and Little League."

"Most kids my age are into weed, Soundgarden, and *Penthouse.*" Caleb watched another jab of God-fire plunge into the desert.

Voice drained of boyishness, Caleb said, "And, well, Mom never really . . . got it."

"She had a hard time of it, you know," Pale said.

Caleb scoffed. "Sure."

"What's *that* supposed to mean?"

Please, not now. The ride's been great, the storm is awesome. Not now, Caleb, please.

"Nothing."

Pale felt compelled to plead his case, a man in a traffic stop.

"Your mom, and hell, me too, I suppose, expected the good times to keep rolling. I think she was holding out for the beach house and the Benz. We never made it past Tarzana and Hondas."

Pale thought: *But it was far more than homes and cars or the rock star wife-life. It sidewinded beyond depression or anxiety.*

After a while, she turned her back on her maternal instinct and had the audacity to blame her son.

Caleb shrugged. "She was weird. When she came home with those fortune-teller cards and mint cigarettes, I knew something was way wrong."

Tarot cards and Kools, Pale remembered. Valerie sulked in the guest bedroom for hours, greasy-haired and cross-legged on the bed like some strung-out Yogi, sheets twisted into a battlefield. Many times he'd walked in to find her with her face buried in her hands, muttering cosmic hippie nonsense. She obsessed over cards such as The Hanged Man, The Magician, The Tower, and The Fool. *The soul is in the blood, Pale,* she'd said while laying the cards out in a carnival huckster's version of solitaire, fingers yellowed, eyes exhausted and rheumy, the room hazy with smoke. *And that's why Caleb marked mine.*

A crack of thunder snapped Pale out of his unpleasant daydream. "Caleb, seriously. She loves you."

Caleb bent his face into a smirk.

"She had a strange way of showing it," he finally said. "I was there when you weren't, and Mom was . . . preoccupied."

"Playboy, let's not wade into the 'you weren't here' swamp."

Caleb remained unmoved when his mother finally packed her bags and split. On several occasions, prior to her withdrawal into the guest bedroom, he'd witnessed parents sloppy drunk, a pair of arguing idiots on public display while the valet at El Cholo or Musso and Frank brought the car around, followed by the silent, tension-filled ride home. By the time Mom stopped coming home on weekends, followed by lame excuses about "losing track of time with the girls," Caleb knew the writing was on the wall. He never suspected that she had another man, although he couldn't say the same for any suspicions his father may have had. Caleb's instinct was pure and unfiltered: she simply didn't want anything to do with *him,* and Dad was part of the package. Not long after, Tarot and menthol. She never ate. She stopped doing laundry—and you could forget about cooking.

The old man smartened up, cut off half his hair, put the brakes on the booze, and resumed running sprints at the park. With Mac Daddy cold in its tomb—with only a failed power ballad to keep it company—Dad began to receive road job offers from bands that had steady work. *Jimmy's in rehab, can't tour. Mark's wife is nine months pregnant; he won't travel.* Caleb finally figured out his father truly believed he'd be able to salvage the marriage if he stayed put and figured that later he'd be able to put his own band together if things turned around at home—so he passed on the gigs.

Caleb knew his father made a point to sound as hopeful as possible around the house. He never complained about the situation or the loss of income and dutifully manned the bilge pumps in an attempt to keep the SS Brody afloat. But when he was alone in his little home studio, Caleb could see the truth on his face as he sat behind the console, staring into nowhere with the guitar in his lap, amp buzzing, expended reel spinning, the tape leader slapping.

Despite Dad's efforts, it wasn't enough to stem the tide of Mom's detachment and isolation. She'd punched her time card a while ago, ate pills like tic-tacs, and once the Ooga-Booga Express arrived at the guest bedroom station, she covered the mirror in bizarre cutouts she'd harvested from various magazines, installed blackout curtains, hung weird little talismans, burned sage, the works. She smoked Kools as if they'd fallen under threat of a moratorium and flipped Tarot Cards like a dealer at the Bellagio. She only looked at Caleb if she absolutely *had* to speak to him.

Caleb had never told his father, but when he watched Mom back her car out of the driveway for the last time, he was relieved to see her go. Even before the meltdown, she'd always been on the icy side, kept him at arm's length. What loss was it to have her gone?

He'd always known he didn't belong to her.

Within a year of her departure, Dad had done several sessions around town (from prog-rock to pop, it all paid nicely), word got around, the phone rang more often, and things looked like they'd smooth out. When the discussions for Austin began, Caleb hoped it would pan out for the old man because neither one of them genuinely minded leaving LA. Caleb knew he would miss the ocean, but the world was covered with water. He'd find another sea.

"Yeah," Caleb said. "Let's talk about something else."

Pale nodded and smiled. "Next time, try the Fender Champ for your science projects. I can afford to lose that to experimentation."

"Give me a little time, and I'll turn that runt into a growler."

Caleb turned his eye to the electrical towers, which in his

imagination resembled colossal prisoners, *a Louisiana chain gang of captured robots*, he mumbled to his father. New Mexico lay bleak and unhurried beneath those giants, resigned to whatever punishment the sky saw fit to dole out.

Caleb said, "I can't wait, this is going to be intense." He whipped his hand around and snapped his fingers, a trick he'd learned from his father's guitar tech. "Showtime," he added.

Just as the words left the boy's lips, the leading edge of the storm flashed alive with forks of feral energy.

"This is the coolest thing I've ever seen, Dad. Seriously."

"Cooler than rummaging through your old man's Super Lead?"

Caleb shrugged. "Once you've looked inside the magic Marshall box, the mystery is gone. So don't make me choose."

"Listen up, Playboy," Pale said. He fished around for his nicotine gum. One left. Once Valerie had begun smoking like the 1950s Pittsburgh skyline, he'd become less enamored with his fealty to Camel filters. But a monkey on your back always dug in its claws, and after several setbacks, he had finally left that gibbering little imp at the side of the road. He glanced at the fuel gauge. "The old gal's tank is getting low, and unlike hers, mine is full. I'm also out of this shitty Nicorette gum, so keep your eyes peeled for an exit."

"Roger that."

"The weather guy said it would be high eighties and clear today, but what do you think, Mr. Speed of Sound?"

"I think we hit the weather jackpot, so who cares?"

When Caleb saw one of the electrical towers take a direct hit, the flare so dazzled his eyes it was like paparazzi inside the Cadillac.

"Wow!" Caleb said. "Did you see that? *Did you see that tower get hit?*"

Pale had seen it, and for a moment, his balls tightened. A half-mile away or so, one of the hundred-foot giants had been jabbed by a spear from heaven. Sparks blew from the impact, but the tower stood fast. Wires swayed; dust blew. Soon the rain would find them.

"No, I missed it," Pale said. He knew Caleb wanted to file a report. "Tell me about it."

"The lightning just came down like . . . like *a missile*. It hit the tower like Ba-*Boom!*" He flipped his fingers out and raised his hands to simulate an explosion. "Millions of sparks—and that glow!"

Caleb tossed the Walkman into the back seat like a toy outgrown. He pressed his hand to the passenger window, a starfish in an aquarium. In a minute or so, the stricken tower would be at their side, and there was no way he was missing that.

"These desert thunderstorms can get pretty wild, but in my experience, they pass quickly," Pale said. "Enjoy it while it lasts. But we need fuel, and my whiz reactor is about to go super-critical."

"Maybe we could just find a bridge, like in that awesome tornado footage you see on the news. People park under bridges, and the sound gets all crazy. You can pee in the bushes."

"Keep your eyes out for an exit, buddy. Bridge will be the last resort."

Caleb shrugged. "Might be more fun under the bridge."

Pale grinned. *More fun? This kid is fearless.*

"This is it!" Caleb said.

As Pale slowed the Caddy, Caleb rolled down his window. The injured tower stood in dim silhouette, a mighty steel lattice. At the crown, where the impact had occurred, the tower sustained an enormous black scar. The raw power coursing through that lightning strike had been tremendous, but the tower endured.

The wires hummed. At their connection point, a faint glow was still visible.

"What's that ray-gun-looking thing between the wire and the tower?" Caleb said, marveling at the giant.

Now that Pale thought about it, the dual rows of glass discs *did* kind of resemble a ray gun from an old science fiction movie.

"Insulator," Pale said, "Supposed to keep the power from running into the tower instead of flowing through the line. That would break the circuit, I guess. We have similar ones on the telephone pole behind our house, well, the *old* house, but these insulators are just gigantic."

"They're still glowing. Man, they must have taken a real beating."

The air felt alive, crisp, prickling with tension—everything to Caleb seemed to be on the precipice, like the apex of a roller coaster. He turned to his father.

"Smells like . . . like electricity? Is that possible?"

"Ozone," Pale said. "The smell of a thunderstorm."

"What happens if lightning hits the car, Dad? We're metal too."
Pale snorted. He threw up the index and pinky devil horns.

They both laughed, partly because it was mildly funny but mainly because the storm showed it could become a close, dangerous reality. Caleb put his window up, and Pale put the pedal down.

A quarter mile later, Caleb spotted a rusted sign that read:

THOMPSON'S KWIK-GAS
3 MILES
NEXT RIGHT

Caleb pointed. "*There's* our exit plan."

"Right on time," Pale said, but his voice was drowned out by rapid bashes of thunder, artillery fire from a sky-borne adversary.

CONTINUE READING LIVE WIRE!
HTTP://GETBOOK.AT/LIVE_WIRE

THE END?

Not if you want to dive into more of Crystal Lake Publishing's Tales from the Darkest Depths!

Check out our amazing website and online store or download our latest catalog here.
https://geni.us/CLPCatalog

We always have great new projects and content on the website to dive into, as well as a newsletter, behind the scenes options, social media platforms, our own dark fiction shared-world series and our very own webstore. Our webstore even has categories specifically for KU books, non-fiction, anthologies, and of course more novels and novellas.

ABOUT THE AUTHOR

Kyle Toucher (rhymes with *voucher*) is the author of the novel *Live Wire*, from Crystal Lake Publishing, the novella *Life Returns,* and the Black Hare Press Short Read, *Southpaw.*

He recently appeared in the anthologies *Dead Letters: Episodes of Epistolary Horror* and *To Hell and Back,* from Crystal Lake and Hellbound Books respectively.

Through his twenties, he fronted the influential Nardcore crossover band Dr. Know, made records, hit the road, and ignored college. Later, he moved into the Visual Effects field, where he bagged eight Emmy nominations and two awards for *Firefly* and *Battlestar: Galactica.*

He lives with a lovely woman, five cats, two dogs, and several guitars in house built when *Nosferatu* first ran in theatres.

medusapsalms.com

X: @kyletoucher
Instagram: @kyletoucher

Readers . . .

Thank you for reading *The Medusa Psalms*. We hope you enjoyed this collection.

If you have a moment, please review *The Medusa Psalms* at the store where you bought it.

Help other readers by telling them why you enjoyed this book. No need to write an in-depth discussion. Even a single sentence will be greatly appreciated. Reviews go a long way to helping a book sell, and is great for an author's career. It'll also help us to continue publishing quality books.

Thank you again for taking the time to journey with Crystal Lake Publishing.

Visit our Linktree page for a list of our social media platforms. https://linktr.ee/CrystalLakePublishing

Follow us on Amazon:

Our Mission Statement:

Since its founding in August 2012, Crystal Lake Publishing has quickly become one of the world's leading publishers of Dark Fiction and Horror books. In 2023, Crystal Lake Publishing formed a part of Crystal Lake Entertainment, joining several other divisions, including Torrid Waters, Crystal Lake Comics, Crystal Lake Kids, and many more.

While we strive to present only the highest quality fiction and entertainment, we also endeavour to support authors along their writing journey. We offer our time and experience in non-fiction projects, as well as author mentoring and services, at competitive prices.

With several Bram Stoker Award wins and many other wins and nominations (including the HWA's Specialty Press Award), Crystal Lake Publishing puts integrity, honor, and respect at the forefront of our publishing operations.

We strive for each book and outreach program we spearhead to not only entertain and touch or comment on issues that affect our readers, but also to strengthen and support the Dark Fiction field and its authors.

Not only do we find and publish authors we believe are destined for greatness, but we strive to work with men and women who endeavour to be decent human beings who care more for others than themselves, while still being hard working, driven, and passionate artists and storytellers.

Crystal Lake Publishing is and will always be a beacon of what passion and dedication, combined with overwhelming teamwork and respect, can accomplish. We endeavour to know each and every one of our readers, while building personal relationships with our authors, reviewers, bloggers, podcasters, bookstores, and libraries.

We will be as trustworthy, forthright, and transparent as any business can be, while also keeping most of the headaches away from our authors, since it's our job to solve the problems so they can stay in a creative mind. Which of course also means paying our authors.

We do not just publish books, we present to you worlds within your world, doors within your mind, from talented authors who sacrifice so much for a moment of your time.

There are some amazing small presses out there, and through collaboration and open forums we will continue to support other presses in the goal of helping authors and showing the world what quality small presses are capable of accomplishing. No one wins when a small press goes down, so we will always be there to support hardworking, legitimate presses and their authors. We don't see Crystal Lake as the best press out there, but we will always strive to be the best, strive to be the most interactive and grateful, and even blessed press around. No matter what happens over time, we will also take our mission very seriously while appreciating where we are and enjoying the journey.

What do we offer our authors that they can't do for themselves through self-publishing?

We are big supporters of self-publishing (especially hybrid publishing), if done with care, patience, and planning. However, not every author has the time or inclination to do market research, advertise, and set up book launch strategies. Although a lot of authors are successful in doing it all, strong small presses will always be there for the authors who just want to do what they do best: write.

What we offer is experience, industry knowledge, contacts and trust built up over years. And due to our strong brand and trusting fanbase, every Crystal Lake Publishing book comes with weight of respect. In time our fans begin to trust our judgment and will try a new author purely based on our support of said author.

With each launch we strive to fine-tune our approach, learn from our mistakes, and increase our reach. We continue to assure our authors that we're here for them and that we'll carry the weight of the launch and dealing with third parties while they focus on their strengths—be it writing, interviews, blogs, signings, etc.

We also offer several mentoring packages to authors that include knowledge and skills they can use in both traditional and self-publishing endeavours.

We look forward to launching many new careers.

This is what we believe in. What we stand for. This will be our legacy.

Welcome to Crystal Lake Publishing— Tales from the Darkest Depths.